The SOURCE of the SPRING

The SOURCE of the SPRING

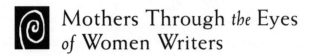

Mothers Through *the* Eyes
of Women Writers

Compiled *by Judith Shapiro, President*

Foreword *by E.M. Broner*

A Barnard College Collection

CONARI PRESS
Berkeley California

Conari Press books are distributed by Publishers Group West

Cover illustration: Diana Ong. Courtesy of SuperStock
Book design: Suzanne Albertson

ISBN: 1-57324-041-9

Library of Congress Cataloging-in-Publication Data
The source of the spring : mothers through the eyes of women writers :
a Barnard College collection / compiled by Judith Shapiro.
p.   cm.
Includes index.
ISBN 1-57324-041-9 (hardcover)
1. Women authors, American—20th century—Family relationships.
2. Mothers and daughters—United States.
3. Mothers—United States—Biography.
4. Women—United States—Biography.
5. American essays—Women authors.
I. Shapiro, Judith R. (Judith Rae), 1942–   .

PS151.S68   1998   97-52804
810.9'9287'0904—dc21   CIP
[B]

Printed in the United States of America on recycled paper.
1   3   5   7   9   10   8   6   4   2

isi umili
the source of the spring — the mother

—Ibo saying

The Source of the Spring

YOUNG VOICES
Winners of the Barnard College Essay Contest

Foreword

This is a rare compilation. Beginning with the introduction by
Judith Shapiro—"In some societies, women believe that heaven
is a place where they will be reunited with their mothers.... In some
societies, women are accorded great respect for being mothers,"—the
book warns that "Today ... we are living in a social world that is hostile to all enduring social bonds."

The book is a combination of essays by New York City high-
school students and Barnard alumnae, equally deeply felt.

One writer, Anne Bernays, remembers her mother, Doris E.
Fleischman, who graduated from Barnard in 1913, captain of the softball
team. Aside from her college-acquired skills, the mother was a curious
combination of Victorian housewife and twentieth-century professional
woman. Her message to her novelist daughter is a mixed one.

Joyce Johnson, in an exquisite memory, remembers her mother
and aunts, all of them, "the Girls," with mysterious artifacts in their
lives.

The emotional states of the essays vary—high and low. June
Jordan's memories are outraged. Erica Jong's are of her mother in her
quilted bed jacket or rushing off to her ballet lesson, though now they
have reached a truce, she and her elderly mother, like "glass unicorns
who might break each other's horns by kissing too passionately." But
now Jong's daughter rails at *her* as *she* did once at *her* mother.

There is the novelist and columnist Anna Quindlen, mourning,
"My mother died when I was nineteen. For a long time, it was all you
needed to know about me." She muses, "Perhaps it is at best difficult,
at worst impossible, for children and parents to be adults together. But
I would love to be able to know that." Mary Gordon, lovingly and
critically, watches her mother's deterioration.

Natalie Angier, the science writer, wittily writes of her mother as
that then rare full-time working mother, who didn't want to be home
full-time for her children. "We weren't captivating; we were kids. We

liked kiddie stuff, we read kiddie books, we read comics, and Mad magazine....We didn't live to entertain our mother and she, with all due courtesy, returned the favor." And so, in the terms of her era, Angier writes, her mother was, "a bad mother. Which is why I salute her..."

There is Maria Hinojosa's laughing, proud questioning of her mother and asking her mother what happened when she bawled out presidential candidate Bob Dole. "I just told him he was wrong," said her mother, when Dole blamed violence against women on welfare.... This is the same mother in Hinojosa's childhood, who kept her out of school to honor Cesar Chavez at a rally. For Hinojosa, "the struggle for justice became central in my life."

Consider the Haitian writer Edwidge Danticat, whose mother shocks her by appearing on Madison Avenue and Fifty-fifth Street, she who never leaves her Brooklyn apartment. The daughter follows the mother on her surprising journey, finding herself as heavy with love for her as a sack full of salt.

Nonprofessional writers, the high school students who won the Barnard contest also write about their mothers feelingly, including those mothers who can, as Joy Buchanan 16, writes, do everything at once: "I . . . have to learn that trick where she talks, does her hair, puts on make-up, and gets dressed at the same time." And Yu-Lan (Mary) Ying, 16, writes of her mother who, because she knew no English, worked in a Chinese restaurant from "late afternoon until late at night"—yet, "Although her job exhausted her, my mother still woke up early in the morning to cook breakfast for my brother and me. Like a hen guarding her chicks, she never neglected us ..." Nor did the mother fail to recognize Yu-Lan's difficulties in learning English. And the mother, instead of resting before work, began to study, with her daughter, "reading and memorizing five new words a day." This was until the mother could pass the post-entrance exam and the daughter could "comprehend what everyone was saying, and people could understand me."

Another daughter, Trezia Jean Charles, also 16, speaks of her mother as "a woman of courage and dignity," despite growing up "in a world of hatred, violence and disloyalty, in Haiti, under the regime of Papa Doc."

Whether the mothers were Victorian wives but professional in their fields, lay abed in a quilted bed jacket, or organized the projects and fought violence against women, marched against unjust governments, each provided the way.

At this time, in this nation, through the memories of the writers, Judith Shapiro's words come true: "In some societies, women are accorded great respect for being mothers." They become, as Yu-Lan Ying wrote, "truly the guiding light of my life."

This book is literary, heart-breaking and heart-enlarging, appropriate for reading with pleasure or reading in the academy and learning with pleasure.

E.M. Broner
Professor Emerita, Wayne State University
Author of *A Weave of Women* and *The Telling*

M is for..........

In some societies, women believe that heaven is a place where they will be reunited with their mothers, freed from the cares and burdens of their lives as married women. In some societies, women are accorded great respect for being mothers.

In other societies, mothers are viewed with suspicion. In the middle class world of the United States during the 1950s, for example, mothers were caught in a particularly fierce double bind: on the one hand, marriage and motherhood constituted women's major legitimate life career; on the other, women who channeled too much of their energy and ambition into motherhood were viewed as predators who lived, like vampires, on the life energy of their children and kept them emotional prisoners. The daughters of mid-century, middle-class American women have themselves often had to navigate a complicated set of feelings about their mothers—mothers who conformed to a restricted set of expectations and opportunities and mothers who rebelled against them; mothers who were too different, mothers who were not different enough.

Today, many of us feel that we are living in a social world that is hostile to all enduring social bonds, that puts powerful pressures on ties to all of our significant others—parents, siblings, spouses, and children. In a society that values individualism and autonomy above all else, mothers are especially suspect. If ties to our mothers are the ties that bind most closely, then the project of growing up is first and foremost a project of escaping from the relationship that most threatens our belief of self creation.

The legacy of Freud and psychoanalysis has also taken its toll on our relationships to our mothers. We now know to look beneath the surface of love. Archaeologists of the heart, we find the buried strata below: anger, fear, resentment, the inevitable ambivalences of deep feeling and profound attachment.

But I must take care in talking about who "we" are and what "we" feel. As I look around at the students who currently populate the classrooms and residence halls of Barnard College, as I look also at the past generations of students whom I have come to know as Barnard alumnae, I see a great diversity in how women experience their mothers, which is reflected in the pages that follow.

I see this diversity of experience reflected in the results of an essay contest that Barnard has been sponsoring since 1991, in which girls who are in the 11th grade of the New York City public school system are asked to write about "A Woman I Admire" and in which many choose to write about their mothers. Each year, I read the essays of daughters writing about mothers from China, from Korea, from California, or New Jersey; from Haiti, from the Carolinas, from Astoria, or Flatbush—daughters of many worlds with mothers of many worlds. Daughters bringing their disparate traditions to bear on how we can understand and talk about our mothers.

As I read the student essays, as well as those contributed to this volume by Barnard alumnae, I am reminded that successful women have often either had fathers who treated them as if they were sons or mothers who themselves broke through the constraints that limited how much women could achieve and how satisfied they could feel in those achievements. I fall into the second category myself. Enjoying the great good fortune of continuous support, love, and encouragement from both of my parents, I benefitted especially from a mother who always understood what I was reaching for, who never placed on me or on herself the limits that defined the lives of most women of both of our generations.

In the excerpt from her autobiography, *Blackberry Winter*, that is reprinted in this volume, Margaret Mead speaks of her mother's "unfailing and ungrudging generosity." "In my life," she writes, "I realized every one of her unrealized ambitions, and she was unambivalently delighted." So, too, is it with my own mother, a high school Latin teacher and librarian, who has seen one daughter become a university professor and college president and another daughter become a doctor and a lieutenant colonel in the Army medical reserves. Like Zora Neale Hurston's mother, she was always encouraging us to "jump at de sun." She instilled in us "a sense of unlimited possibilities," as Joyce Purnick's mother did for her. Like Madeleine Stern's mother, she always supported our life decisions, however strange or risky they may have appeared at the time.

This collection is dedicated to many mothers; I am proud and grateful to dedicate it to mine as well.

Judith Shapiro
President, Barnard College

About this book

In the fall of 1991, Barnard College in New York City created an essay contest to highlight the voices and literary talents of the young women in its local public high schools. The contest required eleventh grade girls to write about a woman they admire.

The response was remarkable. Scores of essays arrived, one more moving than the next. The students' choices ranged from Eleanor Roosevelt to Rosa Parks, Tina Turner to Mother Teresa. But mostly, and with special feeling, these young women wrote about mothers and grandmothers, aunts and foster mothers—women who have wrestled with poverty, violence, illness, or alienation—and survived; women who have achieved, not only in the home, but also in the world at large.

The contest has grown over the years and become a New York City tradition. And each year, one thing remains the same: about one-half of the essays celebrate mothers, or those women who play the role of mother in the lives of these students.

It is out of these poignant and inspiring personal tales that this book has emerged. As the first liberal arts college for women in New York City, Barnard has historically seen its mission as one that supports the talent, vision, and spirit of women throughout their academic, social, and professional lives. Its alumnae, who have become leaders in all walks of life, include some of this country's most prominent writers.

This book joins the work of some of these writers with a selection of winning essays by the high school students—all on the subject of "mother." The alumnae voices are as varied as those of the students. For the alumnae, too, "mother" is a powerful magnet. But while the students all write from the vantage point of teenagers, the alumnae have written at many different stages in their adult lives. And since they span the century, starting with Zora Neale Hurston, born in 1891, they speak to us from many different eras as well. The combination of perspectives provides a rich kaleidoscope of potent perceptions for *The Source of the Spring: Mothers Through the Eyes of Women Writers.*

ONE OF THE LEADING ARTISTS AND INTELLECTUALS of the Harlem Renaissance, ZORA NEALE HURSTON (1891-1960) was a novelist, anthropologist, folklorist, and champion of black heritage, and the first African American woman to receive a Guggenheim fellowship. Her work includes four novels, including *Their Eyes Were Watching God* and *Jonah's Gourd Vine*, numerous short stories, essays, and plays, and her autobiography *Dust Tracks on the Road*, for which she received the Anisfield-Wolf Award. This is an excerpt from her autobiography.

MY MOTHER WAS THE ONE TO DARE ALL

Our house had eight rooms, and we called it a two-story house; but later on I learned it was really one story and a jump. The big boys all slept up there, and it was a good place to hide and shirk from sweeping off the front porch or raking up the back yard.

Downstairs in the dining-room there was an old "safe," a punched design in its tin doors. Glasses of guava jelly, quart jars of pear, peach, and other kinds of preserves. The left-over cooked foods were on the lower shelves.

There were eight children in the family, and our house was noisy from the time school turned out until bedtime. After supper we gathered in Mama's room, and everybody had to get their lessons for the next day. Mama carried us all past long division in arithmetic, and parsing sentences in grammar, by diagrams on the blackboard. That was as far as she had gone. Then the younger ones were turned over to my oldest bother, Bob, and Mama sat and saw to it that we paid attention. You had to keep on going over things until you did know. How I hated the multiplication tables—especially the sevens!

We had a big barn, and a stretch of ground well covered with Bermuda grass. So on moonlight nights, two-thirds of the village children from seven to eighteen would be playing hide and whoop, chick-mah-chick, hide and seek, and other boisterous games in our yard. Once or twice a year we might get permission to go and play at some other house. But that was most unusual. Mama contended that we had plenty of space to play in; plenty of things to play with; and, further-more, plenty of us to keep each other's company. If she had her way, she meant to raise her children to stay at home. She said that there was no need for us to live like no-count Negroes and poor white trash—too poor to sit in the house—had to come outdoors for any pleasure, or hang around somebody else's house. Any of her children who had any tendencies like that must have got it from the Hurston side. It certainly did not come from the Pottses. Things like that gave me my first glimmering of the universal female gospel that all good traits and leanings come from the mother's side.

Mama exhorted her children at every opportunity to "jump at de sun." We might not land on the sun, but at least we would get off the ground. Papa did not feel so hopeful. Let well enough alone. It did not do for Negroes to have too much spirit. He was always threatening to break mine or kill me in the attempt. My mother was always standing between us. She conceded that I was impudent and given to talking back, but she didn't want to "squinch my spirit" too much for fear that I would turn out to be a mealy-mouthed rag doll by the time I got grown. Papa always flew hot when Mama said that. I do not know whether he feared for my future with the tendency I had to stand and give battle, or that he felt a personal reference in Mama's observation. He predicted dire things for me. The white folks were not going to stand for it. I was going to be hung before I got grown. Somebody was going to blow me down for my sassy tongue. Mama was going to suck sorrow for not beating my temper out of me before it was too late. Posses with ropes and guns were going to drag me out sooner or later on account of that stiff neck I toted. I was going to tote a hungry belly by reason of my forward ways. My older sister was meek and mild. She would always get along. Why couldn't I be like her? Mama would keep right on with whatever she was doing and remark, "Zora is my young'un, and Sarah is yours. I'll be bound mine will come out more than conquer. You leave her alone. I'll tend to her when I figger she needs it." She meant by that that Sarah had a disposition like Papa's, while mine was like hers.

Behind Mama's rocking-chair was a good place to be in times like that. Papa was not going to hit Mama. He was two hundred pounds of bone and muscle and Mama weighed somewhere in the nineties. When people teased him about Mama being the boss, he would say he could break her of her headstrong ways if he wanted to, but she was so little that he couldn't find any place to hit her. My Uncle Jim, Mama's brother, used to always take exception to that. He maintained that if a woman had anything big enough to sit on, she had something big enough to hit on. That was his firm conviction, and he meant to hold on to it as long as the bottom end of his backbone pointed towards the ground—don't care who the woman was or what she looked like, or where she came from. Men like Papa who held to any other notion were just beating around the bush, dodging the issues, and otherwise looking like a fool at a funeral.

Papa used to shake his head at this and say, "What's de use of me taking my fist to a poor weakly thing like a woman? Anyhow, you got to submit yourself to 'em, so there ain't no use in beating on 'em and then have to go back and beg 'em pardon."

[...]

When I began to make up stories I cannot say. Just from one fancy to another, adding more and more detail until they seemed real.

People seldom see themselves changing.

So I was making little stories to myself, and have no memory of how I began. But I do remember some of the earliest ones.

I came in from play one day and told my mother how a bird had talked to me with a tail so long that while he sat up in the top of the pine tree his tail was dragging the ground. It was a soft beautiful bird tail, all blue and pink and red and green. In fact I climbed up the bird's tail and sat up the tree and had a long talk with the bird. He knew my name, but I didn't know how he knew it. In fact, the bird had come a long way just to sit and talk with me.

Another time, I dashed into the kitchen and told Mama how the lake had talked with me, and invited me to walk all over it. I told the lake I was afraid of getting drowned, but the lake assured me it wouldn't think of doing me like that. No, indeed! Come right on and have a walk. Well, I stepped out on the lake and walked all over it, it didn't even wet my feet. I could see all the fish and things swimming around under me, and they all said hello, but none of them bothered me. Wasn't that nice?

My mother said that it was. My grandmother glared at me like open-faced hell and snorted.

"Luthee!" (She lisped.) "You hear dat young'un stand up here and lie like dat? And you ain't doing nothing to break her of it? Grab her! Wring her coat tails over her head and wear out a handful of peach hickories on her back-side! Stomp her guts out! Ruin her!"

"Oh, she's just playing," Mama said indulgently.

"Playing! Why dat lil' heifer is lying just as fast as a horse can trot. Stop her! Wear her back-side out. I bet if I lay my hands on her she'll stop it. I vominates a lying tongue."

Mama never tried to break me. She'd listen sometimes, and sometimes she wouldn't. But she never seemed displeased. But her mother used to foam at the mouth. I was just as sure to be hung before I got grown as gun was iron! The least thing Mama could do to straighten me out was to smack my jaws for me. She outraged my grandmother scandalously by not doing it. Mama was going to be responsible for my downfall when she stood up in judgment. It was a sin before the living justice, that's what it was. God knows, grandmother would break me or kill me, if she had her way. Killing me looked like the best one, anyway. All I was good for was to lay up and wet the bed half of the time and tell lies, besides being the spitting image of dat good-for-nothing yaller bastard. I was the punishment God put on Mama for marrying Papa. I ought to be thrown in the hogslops, that's what. She could beat me as long as I last.

[…]

I knew that Mama was sick. She kept getting thinner and thinner and her chest cold never got any better. Finally, she took to bed.

She had come home from Alabama that way. She had gone back to her old home to be with her sister during her sister's last illness. Aunt Dinky had lasted on for two months after Mama got there, and so Mama had stayed on till the last.

It seems that there had been other things there that worried her. Down underneath, it appeared that Grandma had never quite forgiven her for the move she had made twenty-one years before in marrying Papa. So that when Mama suggested that the old Potts place be sold so that she could bring her share back with her to Florida, her mother, urged on by Uncle Bud, mama's oldest brother, refused, Not until Grandma's head was cold, was an acre of the place to be sold. She had long since quit living on it, and it was pretty well run down, but she wouldn't, that was all. Mama could just go on back to that yaller rascal she had married like she came. I do not think that the money part worried Mama as much as the injustice and spitefulness of the thing.

It was not long after Mama came home that she began to be less active. Then she took to bed, I knew she was ailing, but she was always frail, so I did not take it too much to heart. I was nine years old, and even though she had talked to me very earnestly one night, I could not conceive of Mama actually dying. She had talked of it many times.

That day, September 18th, she had called me and given me

certain instructions. I was not to let them take the pillow from under her head until she was dead. The clock was not to be covered, nor the looking-glass. She trusted me to see to it that these things were not done. I promised her as solemnly as nine years could do, that I would see to it.

What years of agony that promise gave me! In the first place, I had no idea that it would be soon. But that same day near sundown I was called upon to set my will against my father, the village dames, and village custom. I know now that I could not have succeeded.

I had left Mama and was playing outside for a little while when I noted a number of women going inside Mama's room and staying. It looked strange. So I went on in. Papa was standing at the foot of the bed looking down on my mother, who was breathing hard. As I crowded in, they lifted up the bed and turned it around so that Mama's eyes would face the east. I thought that she looked to me as the head of the bed was reversed. Her mouth was slightly open, but her breathing took up so much of her strength that she could not talk. But she looked at me, or so I felt, to speak for her. She depended on me for a voice.

The Master-Maker in His making had made Old Death. Made him with big, soft feet and square toes. Made him with a face that reflects the face of all things, but neither changes itself, nor is mirrored anywhere. Made the body of Death out of infinite hunger. Made a weapon for his hand to satisfy his needs. This was the morning of the day of the beginning of things.

But Death had no home and he knew it at once.

"And where shall I dwell in my dwelling?" Old Death asked, for he was already old when he was made.

"You shall build you a place close to the living, yet far out of the sight of eyes. Wherever there is a building, there you have your platform that comprehends the four roads of the winds. For your hunger, I give you the first and last taste of all things."

We had been born, so Death had had his first taste of us. We had built things, so he had his platform in our yard.

And now, Death stirred from his platform in his secret place in our yard, and came inside the house.

Somebody reached for the clock, while Mrs. Mattie Clarke put her hand to the pillow to take it away.

"Don't!" I cried out. "Don't take the pillow from under Mama's head! She said she didn't want it moved!" I made to stop Mrs, Mattie, but Papa pulled me away. Others were trying to silence me. I could see the huge drop of sweat collected in the hollow at Mama's elbow and it hurt me so. They were covering the clock and the mirror.

"Don't cover up that clock! Leave that looking-glass like it is! Lemme put Mama's pillow back where it was!"

But Papa held me tight and the others frowned me down. Mama was still rasping out the last morsel of her life, I think she was trying to say something, and I think she was trying to speak to me. What was she trying to tell me? What wouldn't I give to know! Perhaps she was telling me that it was better for the pillow to be moved so that she could die easy, as they said. Perhaps she was accusing me of weakness and failure in carrying out her last wish. I don't know, I shall never know.

Just then, Death finished his prowling through the house on his padded feet and entered the room. He bowed to Mama in his way, and she made her manners and left us to act out our ceremonies over unimportant things.

I was to agonize over that moment for years to come. In the midst of play, in wakeful moments after midnight, on the way home from parties, and even in the classroom during lectures. My thoughts would escape occasionally from their confines and stare me down.

Now, I know that I could not have had my way against the world. The world we lived in required those acts. Anything else would have been sacrilege, and no nine-year-old voice was going to thwart them. My father was with the mores. He had restrained me physically from outraging the ceremonies established for the dying. If there is any consciousness after death, I hope that Mama knows that I did my best. She must know how I have suffered for my failure.

But life picked me up from the foot of Mama's bed, grief, self-despisement and all, and set my feet in strange ways. That moment was the end of a phase in my life. I was old before my time with grief of loss, of failure, and of remorse. No matter what the others did, my mother had put her trust in me. She had felt that I could and would carry out her wishes, and I had not. And then in that sunset time, I failed her. It seemed as she died that the sun went down on purpose to flee away from me.

That hour began my wanderings. Not so much in geography, but in time. Then not so much in time as in spirit.

Mama died at sundown and changed a world. That is, the world which had been built out of her body and her heart. Even the physical aspects fell apart with a suddenness that was startling.

My oldest brother was up in Jacksonville in school, and he arrived home after Mama had passed. By then, she had been washed and dressed and laid out on the ironing board in the parlor.

Practically all of the village was in the front yard and on the porch, talking in low tones and waiting. They were not especially waiting for my brother Bob. They were doing that kind of waiting that people do around death. It is a kind of sipping up the drama of the thing. However, if they were asked, they would say it was the sadness of the occasion which drew them. In reality it is a kind of feast of the Passover.

Bob's grief was awful when he realized that he was too late. He could not conceive at first that nothing could be done to straighten things out. There was no ear for his excuse nor explanation—no way to ease what was in him. Finally it must have come to him that what he had inside, he must take with him wherever he went. Mama was there on the cooling board with the sheet draped over her blowing gently in the wind. Nothing there seemed to hear him at all.

There was my sister Sarah in the kitchen crying and trying to

quiet Everett, who was just past two years old. She was crying and trying to make him hush at the same time. He was crying because he
sensed the grief around him. And then Sarah, who was fifteen, had
been his nurse and he would respond to her mood, whatever it was.
We were all grubby bales of misery, huddled about lamps.

I often wished I had been old enough at the time to look into
Papa's heart that night. If I could know what that moment meant to
him, I could have set my compass towards him and been sure. I know
that I did love him in a way, and that I admired many things about
him. He had a poetry about him that I loved. That had made him a
successful preacher. He could hit ninety-seven out of a hundred with
a gun. He could swim Lake Maitland from Maitland to Winter Park,
and no man in the village could put my father's shoulders to the
ground. We were so certain of Papa's invincibility in combat that
when a village woman scolded Everett for some misdemeanor, and
told him that God would punish him, Everett, just two years old,
reared back and told her, "He better not bother me. Papa will shoot
him down." He found out better later on, but that goes to show you
how big our Papa looked to us. We had seen him bring down bears
and panthers with his gun, and chin the bar more times than any man
in competing distance. He had to our knowledge licked two men who
Mama told him had to be licked. All that part was just fine with me.
But I was Mama's child. I knew that she had not always been happy,
and I wanted to know just how sad he was that night.

I have repeatedly called up that picture and questioned it. Papa
cried some too, as he moved in his awkward way about the place.
From the kitchen to the front porch and back again. He kept saying,
"Poor thing! She suffered so much." I do not know what he meant by
that. It could have been love and pity for her suffering ending at last.
It could have been remorse mixed with relief. The hard-driven force
was no longer opposed to his easygoing pace. He could put his poten-
tialities to sleep and be happy in the laugh of the day. He could do
next year or never, what Mama would have insisted must be done

today. Rome, the eternal city, meant two different things to my parents. To Mama it meant you must build it today so it could last through eternity. To Papa, it meant that you could plan to lay some bricks today and you have the rest of eternity to finish it. With all time, why hurry? God had made more time than anything else, anyway. Why act so stingy about it?

Then too, I used to notice how Mama used to snatch Papa. That is, he would start to put up an argument that would have been terrific on the store porch, but Mama would pitch in with a single word or a sentence and mess it all up. You could tell he was mad as fire with no words to blow it out with. He would sit over in the corner and cut his eyes at her real hard. He was used to being a hero on the store porch and in church affairs, and I can see how he must have felt to be always outdone around home. I know now that that is a griping thing to a man—not to be able to whip his woman mentally. Some women know how to give their man that conquesting feeling. My mother took her over-the-creek man and bare-knuckled him from brogans to broadcloth, and I am certain that he was proud of the change, in public. But in the house, he might have always felt over-the-creek, and because that was not the statue he had made for himself to look at, he resented it. But then, you cannot blame my mother too much if she did not see him as his entranced congregations did. The one who makes the idols never worships them, however tenderly he might have molded the clay. You cannot have knowledge and worship at the same time. Mystery is the essence of divinity. Gods must keep their distances from men.

MARGARET MEAD, WORLD-FAMOUS ANTHROPOLOGIST, author, and public figure, was born in 1901 in Philadelphia and died when she was seventy-seven years old. She published nearly thirty books in her distinguished career, including *Coming of Age in Samoa, Male and Female, Rap on Race* (with James Baldwin), and her autobiography *Blackberry Winter*. In addition, over a thousand of her articles have appeared in diverse publications, from scholarly journals to *The Nation*, the *New York Times*, and *Redbook* magazine. She was frequently invited to television talk shows and as an expert witness to Capitol Hill. A curator of anthropology at one of America's oldest and most venerable museums, the American Museum of Natural History, she was also a dedicated teacher, researcher, and public speaker. This is an excerpt from *Blackberry Winter*.

THE ORIGINAL PUNK

I was a first child, wanted and loved.

When I was fifteen, I asked my mother whether she had planned her children. She answered, "Goodness, no! There are some things that are best left to the Lord!" In fact, "the Lord" was only a figure of speech. She did not believe in a personal God, but she had an abiding trust in a generally benevolent providence.

Before my birth, my mother kept a little notebook in which she jotted down, among other things, quotations from William James about developing all off a child's senses, as well as the titles of articles on which she was working for various encyclopedia, and here she wrote, "When I knew baby was coming I was anxious to do the best for it."

Pictures of me as a baby show me in the arms of my mother or grandmother, with their hair down and wearing wrappers, dressed in a way I have no memory of seeing either of them. Only now, after so many years, I realize that it was for her children's sake that my mother pinned up her hair so carefully every morning as soon as she got up. Earlier, when I was too young to notice, she let it fall softly around her face—but later, never. In turn, the first thing I do in the morning is to comb my hair, and when my daughter was young I put on something pretty—as I still do when I am staying in a house where there are children.

Another picture shows me, a three-month-old baby, prone and head up, in a Morris chair. Years later we still had the Morris chair, and by the time I could think about it, I knew both that the chair represented some kind of revolution in furniture design and that it was somehow a good thing to have slept in a Morris chair instead of a crib, like other babies.

I was the first baby born in a new hospital, so Mother had the attention of the entire staff. She made a modern choice, but when I began to read school poetry—including "I remember, I remember the house where I was born" and "Over the river and through the wood,/ To grandfather's house we'll go"—I felt somewhat aggrieved that I had no house where I was born and no grandfather's house to go to on Thanksgiving Day, because both my grandfathers were dead and my paternal grandmother lived with us in our house. [...]

My father was six feet tall, which was very tall in 1901. He called my mother, who was just five feet tall, "Tiny Wife," and that was what I called her, too, when I first learned to talk. She was slight and had very blue eyes and golden hair, and I delighted in her gentle beauty. However, she seldom allowed herself to enjoy pretty clothes or elaborately dressed hair. Life was real, life was earnest—it was too serious for trivial things. She had babies to care for and a house to manage. She also felt it was important to continue her own intellectual life and to be a responsible citizen in a world in which there were may wrongs—wrongs to the poor and the downtrodden, to foreigners, to Negroes, to women—that had to be set right. Long afterward, near the end of her life, when she was recovering from a stroke and allowed herself to take pleasure in pretty bed jackets, she confided in her son-in-law, Leo Rosten, "Margaret wanted a little rosebud mother." When she died, we dressed her in pale blue with a spray of sweetheart roses. Then, for those last hours, my father felt that his young wife had been given back to him.

[...]

My mother grew up on the shore of Lake Michigan. Her Chicago childhood was so real to her that I, too, thought of the past as "before the Fire"—in 1871—from which my grandfather's house on the North Side just escaped destruction, or "before the Fair"—the Chicago World's Fair in 1893. One of my treasures, as a child, was a miniature can of Van Houten's cocoa that came from the Fair. For years I kept it carefully on my prayer desk—the prie-dieu my mother had bought at a sale, not realizing what it was. "Someday," I thought, "someday I will open that little can and actually taste the essence of the World's Fair contained in it." Meanwhile, since this could be done only once, I kept the can standing next to a miniature jar made from the clay of the Holy Land.

For all her slightness and delicate beauty, my mother had been a determined and impetuous young girl. She told us stories of how she led the whole high school out on the streets to celebrate the election of Grover Cleveland and how she had refused to kiss a boy, who was later lost on an expedition to the interior of China, because, instead of kissing her, he had said, "Emily, I am going to kiss you!"—and so, of course, she had said he couldn't. Father countered with the story of how he saw Mother sitting in the front row of a class at the University of Chicago and sat down beside her, announcing (probably only to himself, but we never knew for sure), "I am going to marry you." Fifty years later, an elderly lady, the mother of a colleague, came up to me after a lecture and announced in a menacing voice, "I am responsible for your existence. I introduced your father to your mother."

Mother wore a wedding ring, but she never had another ring until, thirty years after their marriage, Father gave her a turquoise ring. Turquoise is my birthstone, and as a small child I learned to say, "December's child shall live to bless the turquoise that ensures success." But I didn't find out about being a Sagittarian—someone who goes as far as anyone else and shoots a little farther—until I was sixteen, when we learned about astrology from the physicist husband of one of my mother's college friends.

It was always difficult to give Mother a present. She felt that the money would be better spent on a good cause. Once Father, in a fit of remorse, I suspect, about some fancied infidelity and remembering how Mother had often said she would like a string of blue beads, went to Tiffany in New York, where he bought her a lapis lazuli necklace for ninety dollars. Mother reacted to this flamboyant gesture with horror and insisted that the necklace be taken back. The credit was given to me to use when I got married. And so, ten years later three undergraduate friends and I rode down from Barnard on the top deck of a Fifth Avenue bus to pick out Tiffany teaspoons and coffee spoons and an unappreciated gravy spoon that was not shaped like a ladle.

Whenever a question arose about how money was to be spent—should we buy a new rug or give the money to a fellowship fund of the American Association of University Women?—my mother always tried to capture the money for the more worthy purpose. Between the quotations of sheer delight, from Wordsworth and Browning, that came so readily to her lips, there were also the stern phrases of her American forebears and the impassioned declarations of early feminists, for example, about freeing women form the ignominy of being classified, along with criminals and imbeciles, as incapable of voting.

Mother's vehemence was reserved for her causes she supported and her fury was directed at impersonal institutions, such as political machines—the Vades of Philadelphia or Tammany Hall—the Telephone Company, Standard Oil, or the Chicago Stockyards. As a matter of principle, she never wore furs; and feathers, except for ostrich plumes, were forbidden. Long before I had an idea what they were, I learned that aigrettes represented a murder of the innocents. There were types of people, too, for whom she had no use—anti-suffragettes (women who probably kept poodles) or "the kind of woman who comes down at ten in the morning wearing a boudoir cap and who takes headache powders." But these were never people whom she knew.

For actual, living people she only had gentleness and generosity and a radiant smile that lives on in the memory of those who knew her and of everyone who turned to her for help. Her vehemence was wholly disinterested, and so she could argue with an intensity that upset my grandmother, who had been used to quieter family meals.

The lack of any contradiction between my mother's ardent support of good principles and her fury at injustice, on the one hand, and her deep personal gentleness, on the other, came out clearly in her response to the advice given mothers in a baby book that was published just about the time I was born. The author, L. E. Holt, was an advocate of the kind of regimen, such as schedules for bottle-fed babies, that ever since has bedeviled our child-rearing practices. She read the book, but she nursed her babies. She accepted the admonition about never picking up a crying child unless it was in pain. But she said her babies were good babies who would only cry if something was wrong, and so she picked them up. Believing that she was living by the principles of the most modern child-rearing practices, she quite contentedly adapted what she was told about children in the abstract to the living reality of her own children.

All her life she kept a kind of innocence that we all too readily interpreted as an inability to appreciate humor. Once, on Groundhog Day, she reported that she had seen in Doylestown a barrel with a sign on it that read, "Ground hog, just caught." When she looked inside the barrel, she found that it contained sausage. "Why sausage?" she asked, very puzzled. Or quite seriously, she would make some intellectual conversion, as when she transformed "pep" into a lament, "This horse has no pepper!" By putting the promptings of the senses and of the unconscious at a distance, she also distanced humor.

In fact, she had no gift for play and very little for pleasure or comfort. She saw to it that we had wholesome food, but it was always very plain. It was only toward the end of her life that I began to suspect that both the plainness of our food and, in some measure, her own fastidiousness were due to a sensory deficiency of smell and taste.

She herself conscientiously filled the eighteen lamps we needed in our house in Bucks County, but she let me arrange the flowers. Indeed, she gave far less attention to the flower garden than to the vegetable garden. Changes in style—giving up tablecloths for doilies—were made not for the sake of fashion, but to save work for servants. Her two younger sisters were far more pleasure-loving and often criticized my mother for her austerity. But she easily accorded her sister Fanny McMaster a sense of beauty and style which she felt she herself lacked. Yet any room in which she lived, filled with books and papers, had lamps that were good for the eyes and an air of welcome. It never gave one the sense that here were things among which children had to walk warily. The few precious things we had—the Wedgwood coffee service and the Meissen "onion pattern" china, which everyone in my mother's family was given by Great-aunt Fanny Howe—were always used and only briefly regretted when a piece was broken or lost in one of our many moves from one house to another. My mother did, however, reserve a little impersonal rage for the unfair way long-dead ancestors had distributed the family silver.

As she had no real gift for play, she also could neither tell nor make up stories, and there was always a touch of duty in the parties and games she planned for us. By the time I was eight, I had taken over the preparations for festivities. I made the table decorations and the place cards, filled the stockings, and trimmed the Christmas tree, while Mother sat up half the night finishing a tie for Father's Christmas present. She could neither cook nor sew, although intermittently she did a little cross-stitch embroidery or some enjoined knitting. What household skills she had were primarily managerial—providing a safe and comfortable home in which children were fed nutritionally, book salesmen and nuns collecting for charity were invited to lunch, other people's children were welcomed and treated as people, and in which there were rooms large enough for committees to meet.

In many ways she shared the intellectual snobbishness of the tradition that was so characteristic of families of New England origin, Unitarian or once Unitarian, college-bred, readers of serious novels and deeply imbued with the attitudes and imagery of the nineteenth-century essayists and poets, especially Robert Browning. The world, as she saw it, was divided into "people with some background"—a charitable phrase which accorded neither credit nor blame, but somehow divested them of privilege—"ordinary people," and a special group for "fine people"—a term that was most often applied to "fine women."

Ordinary people let their children chew gum, read girls' and boys' books, drink ice cream sodas, and go to Coney Island or Willow Grove, where they mingled with "the common herd"—a phrase we never let Mother forget she had used. They also read cheap paperback novels and were riddled by prejudice—prejudice against Labor, against foreigners, against Negroes, against Catholics and Jews.

In contrast, fine people were highly literate and had taste and sophistication. Even more important, they engaged actively in efforts to make this a better world. They fought for causes and organized community efforts. Mother believed strongly in the community, in knowing her neighbors and in treating servants as individuals with dignity and rights. In fact, by insisting on their rights, she often alienated servants who might well have responded more easily to expressions of warm but capricious affection.

Her involvement in causes carried with it a fixed belief in the value of walking. She gave walking as her main avocation in her listing in *American Women*. For years she was famous in Bucks County because, during the summer we moved there, she walked to Plumsteadville to attend a sale and back home again, a journey of some fifteen miles, and also because she herself painted the kitchen ceiling—two strange and, in local terms, unfeminine activities. It was a kind of criticism she did not mind.

All these things were part of my consciousness of my mother, but for me she had two outstanding characteristics. One was her unfailing and ungrudging generosity. In my life I realized every one of her unrealized ambitions, and she was unambivalently delighted. The other was that she was absolutely trustworthy. I know that if I had ever written to her to say, "Please go and wait for me on the corner of Thirteenth and Chestnut Streets," she would have stayed there until I came or she dropped from sheer fatigue.

But I, as the eldest—the original punk, the child who was always told, "There's no one like Margaret"—had the clearest sense of what she was. When my youngest sister Priscilla was twenty-two, she prepared an autobiographical account for one of my social science projects. In it she wrote, "Dick was Dadda's favorite, Elizabeth was Grandma's favorite, Margaret was everybody's favorite. I was Mother's favorite, but Mother didn't count for much in our house."

Priscilla wrote this in the days when she, the last child, was leaving home and Mother was struggling, unhappily, to pick up the threads of graduate work she had dropped twenty-five years earlier. And Priscilla was one of the children born after the death of my nine-month-old sister Katherine, my parents' third child. It was a death that drove a wedge between my father and my mother and made my father vow never again to give his heart so wholly to a child.

[...]

The way in which one's parents grow old matters a great deal. My mother had a severe stroke and had to learn to talk and walk and relate to the world again. It took her a year to do it, and once she had fully recovered so that she could find any book in the house and locate any name we wanted to know, she died. Her death left my father free because he would not have wanted her to make the long, wary recovery again.

For many years, **Madeleine Stern** has led a double life as a writer and an antiquarian bookseller. She has fourteen books to her credit, including biographies of Margaret Fuller, Louisa May Alcott, and Mrs. Frank Leslie; she has edited an equal number of volumes, most of them collections of previously unknown thrillers by Louisa May Alcott. She has been a partner in the rare books firm of Leona Rostenberg and Madeleine Stern, located in New York City, since 1945. With her partner Dr. Rostenberg, she has coauthored six books including the most recent, *Old Books, Rare Friends: Two Literary Sleuths and Their Shared Passion,* from which this piece is taken. In 1997, she received a Distinguished Alumna Award from Barnard College, from which she graduated in 1932.

MY MOTHER: LILLIE MACK STERN

This year especially I wished her back, here with me. It was a banner year, 1997, what with Doubleday's publication of *Old Books, Rare Friends,* a dual autobiography written jointly by my partner Dr. Leona Rostenberg and myself. The volume was extremely well received and in addition, at the time of its publication, a Distinguished Alumna Award was conferred upon me by Barnard. Yes, my mother would have relished both events and shared in the rejoicing.

We shared so much during the forty-six years we spent together. She set me on my way and then loosened without breaking the connections that tied me to her. She kept her anxieties to herself, told me often and in deep earnest: "You must lead your own life, not mine." With her almost instinctive understanding of youth, she joined in our pleasures. When Leona and I went to the theater and afterward to Schrafft's for dinner, she was often a welcome third. She bound my life together. When I was a child she swept the floor while she recited poetry as I watched and listened. Later on, after I had earned some small success, she would say with eager anticipation, "Now tell me all about it."

I did tell her all about it, and I wish I could still do so. What she was to me is part of the joint memoir *Old Books, Rare Friends*. She lived much of it with me, though she could never read it. Here are the passages she would have dwelt upon. They attempt to recapture both her identity and her unbroken connection with me:

"My father met my mother, Lillie Mack, in a bowling club in 1901, when bowling, like cycling, was a popular pastime for men and women, and they were married in 1902. My mother was a woman of extraordinary wisdom and understanding. She had graduated from Normal College—later renamed Hunter College—and as long as she lived she would be the auditor and perceptive critic of everything I wrote. She could also turn out the best apple pie in America with a minimum of effort. She was a twin, and her family, named Mack, moved to New York [from Cincinnati] when she was six months old. The story was that my grandmother had decided she would rather be a lamppost in New York than the mayor of Cincinnati.... Both families—my mother's and my father's—were comfortable, though not wealthy, and had much in common."

[At the time of my first paid job, "manning" a newspaper stand opposite our house one summer when I was seven or eight]:

"The relatives fumed. In fact they sent delegations to assure my mother she would be hauled to court if she allowed me to take a paid job. She was as adamant as I. She understood my desire to command that corner post. More important, she knew that she would be able to determine exactly where her often wandering daughter was—by merely glancing out her window. I got the job—and held it. Newsprint filled my nostrils and my soul. . .

One halcyon day, while 1 was superintending the stand in my khaki bloomers, a man put down two cents for a daily paper. I handed it to him. Then he put down a dime. I asked him what it was for, and he answered, 'That's for you'. . . I raced home later to tell my mother, and I think from that day on I became an optimist."

[During my Hunter College High School years, when Helen Keppler was a close friend]:

"When Helen suggested we go to see *Cyrano de Bergerac* on Broadway, my mother immediately expressed her approval: 'If Helen Keppler wants to see *Cyrano*, she must be a very nice girl.'"

[In 1930, at the time of my father's death]:

"My loss could in no way be measured against my mother's. I had lost the father who took a little girl sledding. She had lost her companion of thirty years. One of my mother's first acts after my father's death was to throw his letters away. She wanted no inquisitive eyes interpreting her love. My immediate and persistent reaction was gratitude that it was not my mother who had died. I knew I could not have borne her loss. . . It seemed natural now that my mother and I should turn spontaneously to each other and become even closer."

[After college]:

"At no time did I ever feel any parental pressure to marry. I am sure that my mother would have liked to see me married—but married to the 'right' person, who would be a companion in an understanding and permanent relationship. Marriage for the sake of marriage meant nothing to her, any more than any of the 'shows' of life did."

[Regarding my first book]:

"I dedicated *We Are Taken* to my mother, who had listened with what seemed like appreciation to my readings from it. In 1935 the novel was published by a small firm, the Galleon Press, with offices in New York's Flatiron Building, at 175 Fifth Avenue. My mother had seen in a New York newspaper the press' announcement that it was looking for manuscripts, especially novels. A few prior attempts at placing *We Are Taken* had been unsuccessful, so when my mother suggested I try Galleon, I did."

[During the writing of a biography of Louisa May Alcott, whose relationship with her mother often reminded me of mine]:

"I sought to track down the changing episodes of her life and the changing aspects of her work in a sequence of articles that were invariably read aloud to my perceptive mother and—usually over a table at Schrafft's—to my perceptive friend [Leona Rostenberg]."

[When suddenly, on April 9, 1945, I resigned from teaching to become a partner in Leona Rostenberg-Rare Books]:

"When I reached home [from school that day] I phoned my principal and my head of department, informing them of my decision. I mailed back my keys. When my mother came home, I greeted her with the explosive statement, 'I've resigned from school.' She sat down quickly and then said, 'Something terrible must have happened.' Her mind was filled with protective impulses. Through the long Depression and the course of the war she had taken comfort in the thought that, as a tenured teacher, I would forever be secure, financially independent, able if necessary to walk alone. She must have been devastated, though she refrained from further comment. She would be, as she had always been, as supremely supportive as she was loving."

[Regarding the early rare books partnership and the letters received from all over the world; my mother's death]:

LILLIE MACK STERN

"Our mothers took as much pleasure in such letters as we did. They chuckled over them and recognized them as tokens of our expanding reputation. By early 1957 Leona's mother... began to withdraw. In early March she suffered a fatal heart attack. Her great loss left ... Leona heartsick for months to come.... Gradually she felt a sense of freedom and spent much time with my mother and me.

[I realized now even more keenly that] my mother had been far more than a mother to me. She had not only made a home that spread a warm and loving protective cloak around her daughter; she had been for me an intellectual companion, a sounding board for my writings, a creative source. She may have pushed me forward, but she never demanded anything else from me. 'You must lead your own life,' she had always insisted. Then, in 1958, after a brief illness, she died. Her shocking loss, the end of such a relationship, left me feeling like an amputee. Even during our brief book hunt abroad in the fall of 1958, that feeling persisted. The return home was especially difficult, since there was no mother at the dock to greet us.

There was never any real question as to our future.... The partners and friends now became companions for the life to be. Now we were on our own—but too we were truly together."

Had she been able to read this, she would not have wept—my mother was not a woman for tears—but she would have felt it deep within her heart. Today, forty years after her death, I have come to realize that it is not necessary for her to read it. She knew it all without reading it because she made it happen.

Observing with her wry smile, commenting succinctly, imparting her fortitude and her wisdom, rejoicing in my rejoicing, she lives again in this dual memoir. She was a very human being indeed, with her circle of admiring friends, her love of cards and poetry, her contagious laugh, her gusto, her affirmativeness, her strength, her love of life. And now I know that she who shaped me still resides in me.

JUNE BINGHAM IS AN AUTHOR AND PLAYWRIGHT. Her most recent plays are *Eleanor and Alice: A Play About the Roosevelts*, and *The Ballad of Mary Todd Lincoln: A Dramatic Musical*. She is currently working on her fifth book, *The Hill Top and the River: Growing Older Without Growing Old*. Her four great-grandchildren will probably be old enough to read before it is completed, she remarks. In 1990 she founded the Trained Liaison Comforter Program at Columbia-Presbyterian Hospital in New York City to assist the families and friends of patients in the Intensive Care Units. She and her husband, Robert Birge, still volunteer there once a week.

SHOULD MOTHER'S DAY
BE MATRIARCH'S DAY?

A funny thing happened to mothers on the way to the twenty-first century. In the early twentieth century, middle- and upper-class mothers ruled the roost with unchallenged, even unquestioned, power. Growing up as I did under three generations of matriarchs, I used to wonder why Tyrannosaurus Rex had not been named Tyrannosaura Regina.

Yet today young women who opt to stay home as full-time mothers may feel downgraded, not only in the old sexist manner by some men, but also by some of the new career women. Paradoxically, within the home, many a senior mother is voluntarily relinquishing the kind of power wielded by her female forebears in favor of modern democratic power sharing.

This phenomenon became vivid to me when I read the 244 autobiographies of my college classmates of our fiftieth reunion. They exhibit a tentativeness, humility, and humor toward their offspring that would have caused their female progenitors to say, "You're forgetting your place."

Like many of my classmates, I stem from an unbroken line of matriarchs: mother, grandmother, and great-grandmother. These ladies (they would have scorned the word "woman") were not expected to go to college nor, in the earlier generations, to have a volunteer job.

Each lady, perforce, focused her potent intelligence and personality on her family members. Like a flower in the sun under a magnifying glass, some shriveled. My own maternal great-grandmother had seven children. Every one paid a call on her every day. Or else!

When she came to inspect my newborn older brother, she announced, "That one won't live." This so infuriated my mother that she hovered unrelentingly over him. He made it through to seventy-two years.

My grandmother had only three children and they phoned her every day. Or else! My mother also had to lunch with her twice a week and listen to reports on whomever her mother had selected to be insulted at that day. The only exercise my grandmother got was by lifting her hand to ring for a meagerly paid servant, or by stepping from her car to her dressmaker's.

My mother, too, had three children. But though she tried, she was unable to make the phone rule stick. Still, my brothers and I, together in time with spouses and children, had to have lunch with her every weekend. Or else! When I tried to extricate myself from this fifty-two-times-a-year engagement, she was not simply insulted but deeply hurt: "Well, of course, if you don't even want to be with your own mother. . . ."

These command reunions were not inherently unpleasant—my four children reveled in the lavishness of food and attention—but the visits came around so fast that I never had a chance to build up any desire for them.

Now that I'm a grandmother, there are moments when I yearn to revert to old-fashioned matriarchy, so that my preferences would more often be acceded to. But most of the time I enjoy being egalitarian with my married offspring, their four spouses, and their ten no-longer-small children.

When we have our semi-annual get-togethers, I seek their opinions on menus, rooming arrangements, and gift-giving. The rest of the time, communication among us is intermittent and, I believe, spontaneous.

While my offspring were students, they were expected to phone home every Sunday night. Or else. But after they became fully adult, they began checking in only when they felt like it, or had something to discuss. Today this may mean two phone calls in an hour or two in a month. I don't keep track, and I don't suppose they do either.

A daughter in her mid-twenties once hesitantly confessed that whole days go by without her thinking of me. She was startled when I burst out laughing: "Whole days go by without my thinking of *you*." She and I did a little dance of liberation.

Of course, if a family member is in need, we know that the rest will be there—on the double. A senior grandson volunteered to return early from his junior year abroad when his grandfather was gravely ill. His mother asked if I thought it a good idea. I did. And he came.

Although I'm happy to oblige when asked for advice, I'm wary about offering the unsolicited kind. For one thing, too many changes have occurred in society since I, at twenty, was parentally informed that if I were to become pregnant outside wedlock I'd be disinherited and never able to come home again.

For another, I'm far less sure than my parents were that a senior necessarily knows more than a junior. When I was young, we were told, "You can't teach your grandmother to suck eggs," and seniors were described as our "elders and betters." Today a teenage grandson instructs me patiently on how to operate my word processor. Doubtless he wonders how anyone as adept as he is can be descended from such a klutz.

Yet some female seniors are still matriarchal, both in imposing their advice and checking to see if it is followed. This fosters deference on the part of their offspring that startles those of us who do not believe in adults trying to control adults. A married man in his late twenties was asked to be guest of honor at a fundraiser. He said, "I have to ask Grandmother. If she says it's OK, I'll do it." But she did not, so he did not.

In contrast stands the grandmother who fears to offer any opinion to her offspring no matter how dire the situation. When they do things of which she disapproves, she suffers in silence—silence, that is, toward the offspring. But she is vocal about it to other people.

Perhaps such indirect criticism is necessary for her sanity, since no one can keep all emotions under wraps forever. But it makes me wonder if she should not, at least once, level with her offspring. The opposite of domination need not be abdication.

While my generation, willy-nilly, had matriarchs to advise us, those matriarchs, in turn, had long uninterrupted traditions to advise them. Today there are no traditions or authorities that everyone recognizes nor even any generally agreed upon criteria by which to make value judgments.

What is happening, I believe, is that the information explosion has eroded the old "mother knows best" without providing anything in its place. In fact, it comes as a surprise to some young people when mother, or grandmother, knows anything at all.

Before the time of print, knowledge was handed down by word of mouth. And because little changed from generation to generation, the ancient truisms continued to apply. But in today's world of instant change, what wisdom can a senior female offer?

MARBEL ROSSBACH

Experience is the harvest we have garnered—together with the ability to spot the type of pattern that repeats over the years. To speak from these is not to set ourself up as superior, which the old matriarch did. I can remember my mother saying when my brother disagreed with her, "How dare you be so impertinent?" Harder to believe even than her phrasing is that my brother was then fifty years old.

If a female elder's perspective has more depth and breadth than that of the young, then we deserve to be listened to at least once on each issue. I do not approve of nagging but, at the same time, I do not believe in biting my tongue when an offspring, or even a good friend, seems headed for preventable disaster. Speak once, and then, as the marriage service advises, "forever after hold your peace."

A younger friend listened as I described some dilemmas that arise when our family reunions are at my house and I try to accommodate the carnivores and vegetarians, the teetotalers and boozers, the three-squares-a-day folk and the nonstop snackers. "You know what you are: a matriarch."

"Wash your mouth out with soap," I commanded. Laughing, we agreed that it should be possible to be a *mater familias* without being a martinet.

Still, the line is not always easy to draw. Recently a teenage grandson was torn as to whether to go off to boarding school. I debated with myself about speaking up—and finally, nervously, did so. Rather than resenting my interference, he seemed to relish being the focus of any attention. And, to my surprise, he took the advice.

But how to judge when to speak up? One factor is how much one cares about the issue. Another is whether one happens that day to have stamina enough to bear the juniors' potential rage at what they may think is interference. A third is whether one has the self-control to remain silent when the problem appears transitory, thus reserving one's ammunition for the kind of long-term problem where the patterns learned over the years may still be applicable to the younger people whom we love as irrevocably as our mothers and grandmothers loved us.

BETTY JEAN LIFTON, PH.D. IS A WRITER, lecturer, adoption counselor, and children's rights advocate. She is the author of several books on the psychology of the adopted, including *Journey of the Adopted Self: A Quest for Wholeness, Lost and Found: The Adoption Experience,* and *Twice Born: Memoirs of an Adopted Daughter.* Her other books include *The King of Children: The Life and Death of Janusz Korczak* and *A Place Called Hiroshima,* for which she received the SHALOM Center Brit HaDorot Peace Award for contribution of work to world peace, and *Children of Vietnam,* which was nominated for the National Book Award. She is married, has two children, and currently resides in New York City. This excerpt is partly adapted from *Journey of the Adopted Self.*

THE ADOPTEE'S TWO MOTHERS

Have you met your "real" mother? I am often asked.

The word real makes me flinch—as I know it would have made my adoptive mother, who thought of herself as my one and only mother.

Yet the truth is that I, like all adoptees, have two mothers: the one who was bestowed upon me by law, and the one who was banished from me by law. I was to learn that while the law could replace my "birth mother" (the politically correct term), it could not prevent her from stowing away in some remote area of my unconscious waiting for me to find her.

And when that time came—when I was able to make conscious the unconscious—I searched for and found that lost mother, who had gone on with her life without me. As a thirty-year-old married woman, I could understand my unmarried seventeen-year-old mother's inability to hold on to me, even though the abandoned child in me would never understand. As a writer, I tried to give form to what I had experienced in my memoir of growing up adopted.

I went on to write about the unresolved grief and loss and anger of other adopted people as they struggled to understand who they were and why their mothers have given them up. I came to see that being cut off from one's origins—especially from one's birth mother—has traumatic effects on the adoptee; that it is unnatural for members of the human species to grow up separated from and without knowledge of their blood kin. Such a lack has a negative influence on a child's psychic reality. Adopted children are asked, in effect, to disavow reality, to live *as if* they were born to the woman who raises them, to play the role of the imposter, or what I term the "artificial self."

No matter how loving their adoptive parents, adoptees feel cut off from the genetic and intergenerational source that gives everyone else roots. They have, to quote one psychologist, "fallen out of the cradle of history."

When adoptees ask Who am I?, they come to the primal question Who is She, the mother who gave me birth? And then they begin the journey that I have described in *Journey of the Adopted Self: A Quest for Wholeness*—parts of which are excerpted below.

The Mothered/Motherless Self

No one is more romantic about mothers and mothering than the adopted. They are like a blind person who tries to envision the radiance that nature has bestowed upon a flower he will never see. Those who know their mothers cannot imagine what it is like not to know the woman who brought you into the world. What it is like to be forbidden by law to see her face, hear her voice, know her name. No one can imagine it because it is unimaginable.

The adoptive mother who feels threatened when the child she is raising asks quite naturally, about his own mother—the "other mother," who gave birth to him—does not stop to consider that she knows her own mother, just as the legislator who approves sealing the identity of the adopted child's mother knows his own mother, and the lobbyists who work to keep adoption records sealed know their own mothers. How can any of them understand what it is like to be among a select group of people who have been chosen by destiny, and by society, not to know?

Yet, just as the adopted are more romantic than anyone about mothers and mothering, they are also more disillusioned. Where is this mother for whom the child secretly grieves and fantasizes, and for whom the adult child still yearns? What kind of mother gives up her child and disappears without a word? What kind of mother surrenders her child out of love? What kind of mother is able to part from her child?

What is a mother, anyway?

A mother, according to the venerable *Oxford English Dictionary*, is a woman who has given birth to a child; a woman who exercises control like that of a mother, or who is looked up to as a mother. Motherhood is the condition or fact of being a mother; the spirit of a mother; the feeling or love of a mother.

No dictionary can define a mother as well as a mother herself. An Abyssinian noblewoman speaks to us through the centuries:

> The woman conceives. As a mother she is another person than the woman without child. She carries the fruit of the night for nine months in her body. Something grows. Something grows into her life that never again departs from it. She is a mother. She is and remains a mother even though her child dies,

though all her children die. For at one time she carried the child under her heart. And it does not ever go out of her heart ever again. Not even when it is dead.

The adopted child, who must grow up as if dead to his mother, has the need to believe that the woman who carried him in her body still carries him in her heart; just as he needs to believe that the woman who did not carry him in her body, but who cares for his daily needs, carries him in her heart. The task of adopted children is to reconcile these two mothers within them—the birth mother who made them motherless and the psychological mother who mothered them.

Both Your Mothers

I have learned over the years that there are many ways to have a mother, and many ways to lose one. While I was researching my biography of Janusz Korczak in Warsaw, Bieta Ficowski took me aside and confided the secret that her mother had kept from her until shortly before she died. On her deathbed she confessed that Bieta was not really her daughter.

Bieta's mother told her that during the war she had agreed to find hiding places for Jewish babies smuggled out of the ghetto. They were to be hidden for the duration of the war and then returned to surviving members of their families. However, she fell in love with Bieta and decided to keep her for herself. When the war ended, she could not bring herself to turn the child over to the Jewish authorities who were taking orphans to Palestine. She felt particularly guilty about hiding Bieta indoors on the day Jewish officials came into their courtyard inquiring about children. Only now, as she lay dying, could Bieta's mother reveal the truth.

Bieta was deeply shocked, but she forgave the only mother she knew. During her search for her Jewish family, Bieta learned that her mother and father, and all of her relatives except for an uncle now in

America, had perished in the death camps. She had to absorb the fact that she was not who she thought she was. She had two mothers: one who abandoned her in order to save her and one who rescued her but withheld her identity from her. Bieta was still trying to work through her feelings of grief and anger for her loss and to reconcile her two mothers in some loving way within herself. Her husband, the well-known Polish poet Jerzy Ficowski, helped her do this with a poem, "Both Your Mothers," that brought these two women together against a background of history:

> *. . . But the mother*
> *who was saved in you*
> *could now step into crowded death*
> *happily incomplete*
> *could instead of memory give you*
>
> *for a parting gift*
> *her own likeness*
> *and a date and a name*
>
> *so much*
>
> *And at once it happened*
> *that someone hurriedly took care*
> *of your sleep*
> *and then stayed for a long always*
> *and washed you of orphanhood*
> *and wrapped you in love*
> *and became the answer*
> *to your first word*
>
> *That was how*
> *both your mothers taught you*
> *not to be surprised at all*
> *when you say*
> I am.

To discover that one has two mothers may not be as dramatic for adoptees who are not Holocaust survivors, but it is just as shocking and difficult to come to terms with. Yet everyone has two mothers, if we believe the psychological theory that we all split our mothers into the good one and the bad one. The psychological task, we are told, is eventually to realize that they are one and the same person, both good and bad. Some professionals believe that adoptees make one of their mothers the good mother and the other the bad one. But I think we could say that adoptees tend to split each mother into good and bad. This means that they have two good mothers and two bad mothers—four mothers in all who must be reconciled within themselves.

Think of it like this.

The adoptive mother is good in that she rescued the child, but she is bad in that she may have stolen the child. The birth mother is good in that she gave the child life, but she is bad in that she abandoned the child.

The adoptive mother is the authentic mother because she raised the child, but she is inauthentic because she is not the mother whom Mother Nature chose.

The birth mother is the authentic mother because she bore the child, but she is inauthentic because she did not mother it.

The child is attached to his adoptive mother by social history: she is the repository of his life experiences. He is still attached to the birth mother by his prenatal experiences: she is the repository of his original self.

What are adoptees to do with this conflicting imagery of good and bad mothers who rescue, steal, love, and abandon them? Who alternately stand in opposition and merge is one? To whom are they to be loyal? Which one of them is real?

Who Is the Real Mother?

From biblical times we have been asking who is the real mother, the one who bears the child or the one who raises it? King Solomon settled a dispute between two women claiming a child by ordering that he be cut in two by a sword so that each woman could have half. When the woman who had given birth to the child gave up her claim so that the child could live, she was declared the real mother. Blood was clearly thicker than water.

But in his play *The Caucasian Chalk Circle,* Bertolt Brecht changed the verdict. The judge placed the child inside a chalk circle and instructed each woman to pull on an arm until the child was forced out to one side or the other. When the adoptive mother refused to take part in what would only tear the child apart, she was declared the real mother. In this case, adoption was thicker than blood.

So, who is the *real* mother? To be *real*—turn to the dictionary again—means to have an existence in *fact* and not merely in appearance, thought, or language. Both mothers *are real* by that definition for both do *in fact* exist. The problem is that there is no definition in the dictionary for a *real mother.* We have to make up our own. For me, a real mother is one who recognizes and respects the whole identity of her child and does not ask him to deny any part of himself. This is difficult to do in a closed adoption system that requires the child be cut off from his heritage, and that pits the original mother against the replacement mother. If one mother is real, the other must be unreal. The stakes are high: the real mother has the power to cancel out the unreal mother, as if her motherhood never existed.

The adoptive mother believes that she is the *real* mother because she is the one who got up in the middle of the night and was there for the child in sickness and health. The birth mother believes that she is the *real* mother because she went through nine months of sculpting the child within her body and labored to bring it forth into the world.

They are both right.

The adoptive mother who loves and cares for the child is the real mother. And the birth mother who never forgets her child is the real mother. They are both real, and yet, because the child will remain burdened by the mystery of mothers, they are both unreal—as is the child.

Who Is the Real Child?

By denying that adoptees have two real mothers, society denies them their reality. And so it should not surprise us that adoptees do not feel real. They expend much psychic energy searching for the elusive *real child within*, only to find that child's identity hopelessly entangled in the reality and unreality of the two mothers. For deep inside every adoptee there is a chalk circle where he or she is pulled this way and that by two competing mothers. By the one who is there and by the one who is absent. (The fathers are still shadowy figures in this terrain.) The adopted child lives in fear of being torn apart by these two mothers, by divided loyalties, which is another way of saying that the child lives in fear of fragmentation.

Barry, a forty-three-year-old man adopted when five days old, described feeling he was in the middle of a "no-man's land," with his adoptive mother and birth mother on either side: "In different ways I was a part of both families, yet belonging to neither. My adoptive parents raised me, sacrificed for me, and loved me as much as they were able to. I was grateful—and hated them at the same time. I yearned to be with my birth mother with a passion unequaled in my life before or since. How could she give me birth and then give me away? I couldn't make sense of it. All I knew was that I needed that blood connection and didn't have it. I was stuck in that 'no-man's land.'"

It is still difficult for adoptive mothers and fathers to understand that the secrecy around the adoptee's blood connection can sentence their children to a no-man's land. Love is enough to forge the bonds between them, the adoptive mother thinks while the child is young and cuddly. But love based on a mother's own gratification at having a child to raise, rather than empathy for the child's inner struggle to cope with the mysteries of his existence, is not enough. It may not even be love, if we think of Janusz Korczak's and Alice Miller's concept of mother love as unselfish and putting the psychological needs of the child first. An adopted child can feel love and gratitude to his adoptive mother and father for their nurturing, and still feel resentment, as Barry did, for their keeping his heritage a secret.

Adoptees often find a way out of their no-man's land by escaping to a mythic realm beyond it. For here is the paradox: when one lives in no man's land, one can invent and reinvent oneself at will. Not being entrapped by roots, the adopted can become anyone or anything they want, both real and unreal. Both mythic and divine.

It seems only natural that the adopted child, whose mother has mysteriously disappeared, would identify with a mythic hero who has also lost his mother at birth. Child heroes, such as Moses, Oedipus, Sargon, and Romulus and Remus, were all abandoned to fate before being found and rescued by kindly people. They were forced to endure many trials, but had the superhuman resilience to survive. Carl Jung points out a striking paradox in child myths: while the *child* seems in continual danger of extinction, he possesses powers far exceeding those of ordinary humanity. Jung relates this to the psychological fact that though the child may be insignificant and unknown, a "mere child," he is also "divine."

Adopted children feel akin to the children in fairytales too: motherless babes who are suckled by animals; crafty changelings who replace human children; and magical children found in forests or on riverbanks. They identify with Starman, who is at home in the skies, and with Superman, who, after falling from another planet, lived a dual life much as they do—pretending to be a *real* person in everyday relationships and then disappearing on secret exploits that he shared with no one. One adopted man remembers not being able to read at grade level until he discovered that Superman was adopted. He began collecting and reading every issue of Superman's adventures, and he's been reading ever since.

But while the hero has a clear mission to fight for good over evil, to save maidens from dragons, or to found cities, adoptees can't help but wonder why they were put on earth. Searching for some meaning in their strange fate, they often feel they are connected to the divine mysteries of creation, are destined to do great things in the world.

"Everyone is a child of God who gets lost," a Jungian analyst tells me. "Usually one attaches to the parents who become the main care-takers. But the adoptee makes the God connection, and develops a nonhuman relationship to the cosmos." Because of the ambiguity of their origins, it is not unusual for adoptees to feel split in their iden-tity between human beings and the gods—much like the legendary twins Castor and Pollux, one of whom was mortal and the other immortal.

Adoptees, then, live with a dual sense of reality: wanted and unwanted, superchild and monsterchild, immortal and mortal. One part of the self is tied to an earthly existence, while the other is in touch with a higher destiny. One part is real, the other unreal. One part is chosen, the other abandoned.

The mother who relinquishes her baby for adoption, for whatever reason, does not perceive it as an act of abandonment, but rather as a way of giving the child a better life than she can offer. She is opting for what the Romans called "the cure for chance"—the chance to make up for a hapless birth.

But the baby, vulnerable and helpless, is not ready to start gam-bling on chance. It wants its own mother and can only perceive of her disappearance as an abandonment. This sense of abandonment and mystery about origins will shape the adoptee's life.

The Search

Prenatalists believe that the beginnings of awareness and early mem-ory can be traced back to the womb. What does the adopted baby remember from back there? I wondered as I observed the intense need of some adoptees to find and be reunited with the mother they were merged with in the womb.

We could say that from the time they are separated from their birth mother, all adoptees are consciously or unconsciously in search. Each time an adopted child wonders whose tummy she was in, what her mother looks like, why she was given up; each time he has a fantasy or a dream, looks on the street for someone who looks like him, the adoptee has taken a small step toward becoming a searcher.

Adoptees are often not clear what they want when they finally make the decision to search. Some say they just want to find medical information, or the reason they were given up, or someone who looks like them. Others that they want to know their family history, to look into the eyes of someone of the same blood, to say thanks to their mother for giving birth to them.

Adoptees may deny that they expect to find anyone special in their birth mother, but unconsciously everyone hopes to discover a soul mate—someone strong and independent who will reach out with unconditional love. At the moment of beholding her, they expect to be instantly transformed into the whole self they were meant to be.

No matter who adoptees find—the All-Loving Mother, who flings open the door; the Mother from Hell, who bars the way; the Ambivalent Mother, who swings back and forth; the Mother who Married Father—they will learn that the mother who left them behind has done her own kind of disavowing to survive. Her response will be influenced by how she dealt with the shame and humiliation of her pregnancy; the pain of losing the innocence of her youth; her feelings about the father; and the trauma of giving up her child. It will also be influenced by how much denial she has done for emotional survival, the secrets she has kept, the guilt she has felt, and the new life she has made.

Here is the paradox: The adoptee who returns is both the beloved lost baby for whom the mother once pined and the dangerous enemy who wreaked havoc on her life once and could do it again. The mother cannot embrace one without confronting the other.

This is true for the adoptee, too. Although the adoptee's adult psyche is bound up with the lost mother as profoundly as the fetus' archaic psyche was bound up with her in utero, the mother is perceived as both goddess and witch, representing both life and death. The adoptee cannot embrace one without confronting the other.

Two Mothers and None

We could say that the reclaimed birth mother has risen as if from the dead, for her absence has made her as if dead to the child. Still, her reappearance in the adoptee's life does not necessarily undo the loss that was created by her absence. The phantom mother has been flushed out and then fleshed out, yet this actual birth mother with whom one has had no prior relationship may not fulfill the promise of the fantasy mother.

To witness the psychological confusion that many adoptees experience after reunions of any kind is to realize the critical importance of fantasy in the early structuring of the self. When this structure is shaken or toppled, one's identity is threatened. One is faced with a loss of dimensions that parallel the original loss, for the fantasies were the link not only to the "motherself" but to the magical, omnipotent part of the self that made one unique.

Eventually, most adoptees come to realize that they cannot be fully their birth mother's child any more than they were fully their adoptive mother's child.

Between Two Mothers

Where is the adoptive mother in all this? While the adoptees were growing up, the birth mothers were the invisible ones in their lives, but during search and reunion it often seems that the adoptive mothers become invisible. But visible or not, on stage or in the wings, the adoptive mothers are always there in the adoptee's psyche, and have an influence on the reunion process.

Reunion could be described as a tale of two mothers. The birth mother originally relinquished her child to the adoptive mother, and now the adoptive mother feels that she is being asked to relinquish the child back to the original mother.

Each is flooded with regrets. The adoptive mother regrets that her child is not biologically related, and the birth mother regrets that she relinquished her child. The adoptive mother regrets that the birth mother has come back, and the birth mother regrets that she ever left. These two women, who have always been invisibly linked, try to cover up their feelings as they maneuver from their designated places on either side of the adoptee. "I know there are times she resents my closeness to our daughter," an adoptive mother admits to me. "And there are times I resent her being biologically related to our daughter."

Some adoptive mothers insist on meeting the birth mother, and some birth mothers insist on meeting the adoptive mother. The issue of status is at play here. The adoptive mother may feel a need to protect her role as mother, and the birth mother may feel a need to be acknowledged by the adoptive mother. Each needs the other to establish the authenticity of her slightly tarnished credentials, for, on some level, the adoptive mother does not feel she is entitled to claim the adoptee, just as the birth mother does not feel she is entitled to reclaim the adoptee. Each mother is threatened by the other. The adoptive mother worries that the birth mother will be critical of what she did or did not do for her child; the birth mother worries that the adoptive mother will be critical of her for giving up her child.

There is a lot of primitive energy going on between these two women, not unlike the kind that passes between women who love the same man.

Healing

As complex as reunion is, eventually some kind of healing is experienced by everyone. Once the denial and secrecy are lifted, everyone has a chance to be liberated. And no matter how the reunion works out, the adoptee has been empowered by the decision to search, and take control of her own life.

It is healing for the adoptee to see the birth mother, freed from the burden of her guilt and shame, continue her life from where it stopped at surrender. She may begin a new career, end a loveless marriage that had been entered as a place to hide, and reconcile with her own mother, as she resolves the unfinished business between them.

It is also healing to be able to share one's feelings with one's adoptive mother, after hiding them for so many years. To renegotiate the relationship as an adult child, and to be able to shed the old fear and guilt that one is being disloyal and ungrateful. Once they get over their initial shock and resistance, adoptive mothers are often transformed. The lifting of secrecy frees them as well as the adoptee.

Accepting One's Existential Fate

One impulse behind search and reunion is the adoptee's desire to modify the past. To deny the loss. To restore the mother. To rewrite the script that might have been. Part of the healing process takes place when adoptees are able to accept that what happened happened: it was their existential fate to be surrendered by one mother at birth and raised by another. It was their fate to have two mothers.

My birth mother RAE, four years after relinquishing me.

My adoptive mother HILDA, a decade before adopting me.

ANNE BERNAYS IS THE AUTHOR of eight novels, among them the award-winning *Growing Up Rich* and *Professor Romeo*. She has also published numerous short stories, poems, essays, travel pieces, and book reviews. Her most recent book, coauthored with her husband Justin Kaplan is *The Language of Names*. She has taught fiction writing since 1975, is a co-founder of PEN/New England, and is on the Advisory Board of the National Writers Union. Born in New York City in 1930, she has three daughters, five grandsons, and one granddaughter.

DORIS E. FLEISCHMAN

A woman once told me that, as a child, her worst anxiety was that when she grew up she would turn into her mother. I think a lot of us have this need to inoculate ourselves against the maternal virus, the idea being that we would like to be self-invented, self-maintained. But for better or worse, our fears are often realized.

I never consciously modeled myself on my mother and, in fact, resisted incorporating or repeating anything about her for the longest time. I was a mother myself before I began to see that she possessed some habits of mind, some attitudes I positively admired. Let's say her influence on me started when I was quite young but, like one of those capsules that releases tiny beads of a drug over an extended period, it didn't kick in until I was past my prime.

I think what kept me resisting so long and so energetically was that from a time I can just barely recall, I never wanted anyone to tell me what to do—still don't—and the minute they do, I resist. Stubborn. But also impressionable. My mother, like most mothers, was always telling me what to do, citing her experience, her wisdom, and her status as back-up argument. This went over inefficiently. I must have been a tough little person to manage.

My mother embodied paradox, an ultimately painful condition I must have been aware of even before I could talk. Beyond the domestic hearth she was an out-and-out feminist, beginning when she was at Barnard, where she was a member of three varsity teams and captain of one of them, namely softball. After graduating in 1913 she went to work for the *New York Tribune* as a reporter. She was the first woman to cover a boxing match (though, ironically, her father refused to let her go alone and accompanied her himself). Later, she was promoted to Assistant Editor of the Women's Page. In the early twenties she went to work as a writer for my father, known today as the "Father of Public Relations," and worked with and for him for the rest of her life. She was the first American married woman to get a passport under her own name. (When I tried the same thing thirty years later they wouldn't give it to me; I had to go under my married name.) A member of the Lucy Stone League, a group of East Coast professional women who kept their names after marriage and tried to persuade the rest of the female population to do likewise, she went by "Miss Fleischman" until her seventies when she, somewhat inexplicably, took my father's name for the first time.

This biography underscores the contradictions in my mother's life, and confused me thoroughly: did I want to be like her or didn't I? Inside the rather grand houses in which I grew up, my mother was the very model of a Victorian wife (like her own mother, who was born in the 1860s). She let my father make most of the large and at least half of the small decisions involved in running a household. Let him decide on what scale they lived, and where; who and how they entertained (they did a lot of this, as my father socialized with his clients);

what schools my sister and I would attend; and all in all, determine the shape and texture of their life together, visible and invisible. So what did I see: a woman with the proven strength to be original, independent, curious, willing to risk and take chances who was, ultimately, the biddable creature of a man with an attitude about almost everything and a bright streak of narcissism. A few days before I married, she told me "Remember, Annie, if you have an argument with your husband, he's always right." It took me years to even begin to slough off this advice and correct the balance in my marriage.

The double message my mother sent me over and over again did nothing, of course, but confuse me, not only about myself but about her. It was too long, then, before I realized that the Lucy Stone women had a point: when you drop your birth name abruptly, after the wedding ceremony, you're slicing off a part of yourself as important as a limb, and allowing yourself to be swallowed whole by someone else. Even if you love the guy to pieces, there's no excuse for this act of self-mutilation. Do I sound like her? Absolutely, except I don't say it as prettily as she did; she had better manners.

When I was growing up, my mother went to the office every weekday and wrote, triple-spacing every draft but the last. I don't have an office but I go to my desk every weekday and try to write. She was wonderfully disciplined, a real pro when it came to turning out an article or news release, a careful researcher and speller. She valued the precise and the clear. While she didn't have the best sense of humor, she had other virtues: directness, discrimination, wit, stoicism, and a kind of authenticity that even her own confusion over what it meant to be a wife in the twentieth century couldn't shake.

I'm not, never have been, the kind of person who, on seeing someone wonderful, thinks, "I'd give anything to be like her!" Over the years I picked up and ingested a little of this, a little of that from my mother. It added up. And as a mother myself, I've passed along to my three daughters some tips on the art of living that she, no doubt, got from her mother—the thread unwinds unto the *nth* generation. Tips

DORIS E. FLEISCHMAN

like: Don't sit around in a wet bathing suit. Never buy cheap shoes Always take a sweater along. Don't complain if it hurts. Don't waste your god-given gifts or talents. Practice your art, whatever it might be, until you get as good at it as you can.

FRANCINE DU PLESSIX GRAY'S PUBLISHED WORK
includes *Lovers and Tyrants, Rage and Fire,* and *Soviet Women.*
She is a frequent contributor to the *New Yorker,* and lives in
Connecticut with her husband, the painter Cleve Gray.

GROWING UP FASHIONABLE

My mother enjoyed claiming direct descent from Genghis Khan. Having asserted that an eighth of her blood was Tatar and only seven-eighths of it "ordinary Russian," she would go on to drop a few names in the chronology of our lineage: Kublai Khan, Tamerlane, and the great Mogul monarch Babur, from whose favorite Kirghiz concubine my great-grandmother was descended. And voilà—our ancestry was established.

Tatiana du Plessix Liberman could have set all human history on its head and you wouldn't have dared argue with her. In her prime, she was five feet nine and a half inches tall and a hundred and forty pounds. The majesty of her presence, the very nearsighted, chestnut-hued, indeed Asian eyes that fixed you with a brutally critical gaze through blue-tinted bifocals, had the psychic impact of a can of Mace. Her alleged kinship to the great Khan was symbolically fitting: draped in shawls and adorned with blazing costume jewelry that recalled insignias of archaic cults, she strode into a room like a tribal war goddess, and she moved through life with a speed and fierceness that recalled the howling wind of the steppes. Tatiana was a force of nature—one of the most dazzling self-inventions of her time—and we who loved her may remain under her spell until the day we die.

By profession, my mother was a designer of hats, and, for twenty-three years, she had her own custom-design salon at Saks Fifth Avenue, where she instructed thousands of women on how to lure their men, keep their husbands, and enchant their luncheon companions through the proper tilt of a beret or the sly positioning of a little black dotted veil. "Tatiana of Saks" was hailed by the *Herald Tribune* as "the 'milliner's milliner,'" and was perhaps best known for her ethereal spring hats: casques of pastel-shaded veiling; leafy pillows of tulle specked with violets; turbans of frothy gauze swirled beehive style; bonnets of silk surah displaying bundles of silk roses underneath their rolled brims.

Though Tatiana was one of a handful of professional women who were looked on as New York's most commanding fashion presences—others were the editor Diana Vreeland, the designer Valentina, and Hattie Carnegie's designer Pauline Potter (later Pauline de Rothschild)—she herself did not abide by the seasonal caprices of haute couture. Soon after arriving in the United States, in 1941, she hit upon a uniform, and she stuck to it for the next half century: she wore black, except in summer or at balls; she wore tunics, of wool or linen by day, of satin or velvet at night; and the skirts she reluctantly wore to work were switched for slacks the second she got home. She kept her hair tinted a dark-golden blond, parted on the side, and simply rolled. Her eyebrows—plucked and archly lined with a light-brown pencil—and her ruby-red nails and vampishly drawn mouth, tinted with Arden's Rose Aurora, remained equally unchanged. Yet no canon of fashion did she transgress more violently than Diana Vreeland's decree "Elegance is refusal." One might say that Tatiana perfected the art of too-muchness: the great hunks of fake jewelry she flung on herself included eight-inch-wide imitations of preColombian breastplates, four-inch stretches of rhinestone bracelets, candelabras of paste earrings, and—her most famous logo—a massive ring of quasi-rubies (garnets, actually, I later learned) resembling the top of a bishop's crosier.

Elegance is in fact a matter of consistency; and Tatiana's gestures, her speech, her entire manner were absolutely in line with the maximalism of her getup. She was brazen, brusque, intolerant, blatantly elitist, prodigally generous, and as categorical in her tastes as a Soviet commissar. She did not converse but proclaimed, and many of her decrees had to do with deriding conventional symbols of affluence. "Diamonds are for suburbs," she said, and "Meenk is for football." Tatiana took such pride in a forty-five-dollar set of Macy's garden furniture with which she equipped our first little New York rooms, on Central Park South, that it followed her wherever she lived for almost fifty years. In the sixties, when her fortunes had risen considerably, she furnished her entire weekend house in Connecticut for a thousand dollars, with white plastic furniture from Bon Marché. ("Plastic ees forever.") She probably owned fewer couture clothes than any other fashion personality in New York, copying all her tunics, over the years, from a few originals of Dior's and, later, Saint Laurent's, which had been gifts from the designers.

The world had to come to Tatiana; she made very few steps toward it, particularly toward the United States. At the time of her death, in 1991, she was still getting her news from French periodicals and New York's Russian-language newspaper *Novoye Russkoye Slovo*. The faux pas she made in English were epic: she once went to F.A.O. Schwarz, flanked by my eight- and ten-year-old sons, and announced to the salesman, "I want to buy kike." "*Kite*, Grandma, *kite*," the children pleaded. "I want *kike*!" she insisted. She had a Nietzschean faith in success ("One does not argue with winners") and cultivated an old-fashioned brand of Russian elitism, in part corny and in part humanistic; it was indifferent to money and geared instead to pedigree and public achievement. The penniless Soviet émigré Joseph Brodsky, whose Nobel Prize she predicted nearly two decades before he received it—and within an hour of meeting him—was perhaps the most glorious star in her firmament.

How paradoxical she was! Tatiana was the only mother I can

remember of any student in my class with a full-time job, yet she was militantly opposed to women entering the professions, because she believed that "women's brains are smaller than men's" and she was appalled by anyone's going to a woman doctor or lawyer. Like most members of the Russian gentry, she was intensely puritanical, unable to discuss sex even with her closest friends; she never underwent a gynecological examination after the day I was born. But she grabbed attention by making some of the lewdest remarks in New York society. "What kind of orgasm she has?" she inquired of a friend who had brought a dewy-eyed new girlfriend to one of her cocktail parties. "Vaginal or clitoral?" "Put logs in fireplace," she commanded my future husband the first time she came to his Connecticut house. "Fireplace without logs is like a man without erection."

It was part of Mother's dictatorial largesse that she wanted to impose her enthusiasm and preferences on her friends and loved ones. Arriving at a beach on the first day of vacation—she was a sun worshiper and a crack swimmer—she would walk ahead of us very fast, her slender arms clanging with tribal gold, and examine the quality of the sand, the clarity of the water, the status of the population. Then she would holler to her group, *"Venez ici tout de suite! C'est le seul endroit!"* ("Come here at once! This is the only spot!") And we would all troop along, knowing that she was usually right, and fearing that if we didn't follow her orders the arrival of a busload of noisy nudists would subject us to her derisive "I told you so." Yet beneath Tatiana's despotic manner and her exhibitionism was hidden a deeply private, self-demeaning child-woman, whose complex character was forged in the terror of the Russian Revolution.

I have photographs that show my mother in the Russia of 1912. She is six, an assertive tot with long blond curls and dressed in a Paquin frock. ("Now you know why there was a revolution," she often quipped about that picture, pointing to the lavish Parisian dress.) Tatiana Iacovleva was born in St. Petersburg but brought up in Penza, a district capital some three hundred miles southeast of Moscow. She came from a family of intellectuals who displayed that craving for French culture and luxuries from which few upper-class Russians were exempt. Living with her mother and sister in one room of their boarded-up house, she barely survived the Revolution and the great famine that swept parts of Russia in the early 1920s. Although she had only a year of traditional schooling, she had a gift for memorizing poetry, a talent she retained throughout her life. Able to declaim by heart hundreds of lines of Lermontov, Pushkin, Blok, Yesenin, and Akhmatova, she helped feed her family by standing on street corners and accepting hunks of bread from Soviet soldiers in exchange for her verses.

In 1925, Tatiana was found to be tubercular, and relatives who had already fled to France managed to get her to Paris. She arrived there at the age of nineteen—a gorgeous, unwashed savage, as one of her kin described her—and lost no time in announcing her craving for the best clothes, invitations to the most brilliant parties and literary salons, and (a particularly Russian fixation) a title of nobility.

Within four years, she had achieved her goals: she acquired legendary status through the poet Vladimir Mayakovsky, then a frequent visitor to Paris, who fell insanely in love with her, dedicated some of his finest late poems to her, and vainly tried to bring her back to the casteless anarchy of Russia she had fled. Instead, she married, in 1929, my father-to-be, Bertrand du Plessix, a diplomat and the dashing youngest son of an impoverished French viscount. By that time, Tatiana had been to art school briefly and had studied with an Armenian-émigrée milliner, mastering the profession that would sustain her for the next forty years. (Among the exiles who have fled great historical upheavals, the milliner's trade has always been looked on as one of women's most honorable occupations. After the Revolution of 1789, many French expatriates supported their families by making hats in cottage-industry settings, where duchesses might find themselves working in fifty-woman ateliers.)

There was a brief hiatus in Mother's hatmaking career, for the first two years of my parents' marriage were spent *en poste* at the French Embassy in Warsaw, where I was born. There Tatiana learned the intricacies of diplomatic protocol—"the papal nuncio *always* at the hostess's right," she would instruct me. But, however much she enjoyed this hierarchic folderol, Tatiana loathed living away from Paris, which remained for her the center of world civilization, and she particularly hated Warsaw. She forced my father to abandon the diplomatic corps, and it was a move he never recovered from, avenging his botched career through rage and innumerable liaisons.

Back in Paris, I was left totally in the care of my possessive father and a tyrannical governess while Tatiana attended swank parties—with a variety of aspiring but inevitably rejected lovers—at which she could recruit new clients. She opened her own salon in our Paris flat, where she received clients in her bedroom, hurriedly making up the beige damask cover of her sofa bed upon rising, so that she could start welcoming ladies by ten.

And that is how I first remember Mother: seated at the dressing table, brushing her marcelled dark-golden hair. The tabletop displays a fourteen-piece set of sterling-silver brushes and bottles, each engraved with the crest of my father's family and my mother's initials, T.I.P. I crouch on a little stool in a corner of the bedroom (I am between six and nine now), terrified that any movement will trigger her annoyance and my dismissal. The silence she maintains with me is all the more wounding because with the rest of the world she is loquacious and exuberant, the life of the party. I've heard a story about her climbing on a table in a very crowded bistro and walking the length of the room, from table to table, to join her friends at its far end. Mother the magical table-walker—this is part of the legend I weave about her. And as I crouch in the corner she blows me a few kisses with her fingers. There is only one phrase I remember her speaking to me, *"Tu es très jolie ce matin,"* and throughout my childhood I wondered whether she would have found me less boring if I'd been more *jolie.*

Once she is dressed, I follow her like a puppy to a small chamber off her bedroom, where she crafts her hats with the aid of an assistant, a melancholy, round-faced émigrée with the difficult name of Nadezhda Romanovna Preobrazhenska. Nadezhda Romanovna, whose husband works as a taxi driver, often kisses and hugs me during bouts of émigrée tears: "Ah, the beloved country we left behind, the dachas and the meadows and our own staff of servants, and now reduced to this, *dushenka!*" She sits at one end of the table, which is heaped high with rolls of felt, tulle, and lamé; with spools of grosgrain and satin ribbons; with aigrettes and peacock feathers and pink cloth roses—the whole heap surmounted by the large round steam press that will force felt and straw to take on the shapes of bretons, casques, or berets. At the other end of the table, Mother sits in front of a large oval mirror again, sculpting velours, draping organza or satin onto her head. She never sketches her hats, but uses her own reflected head eight hours a day, three hundred days a year, as the medium of creation. Mirrors were the central metaphor of her life.

Throughout the day, in between my lessons (at my eccentric father's wish, I do not go to a regular school but am tutored at home by my governess), I spy on my idol, peeking through the keyhole of her fitting room as she holds a bunch of globe-domed pins in her mouth, adjusting models of jerseys and moirés to the head of the Baronne de Rosières or the Duchesse de Gramont.

In the evenings after she has departed on yet another client-hunting trek in the haut monde, I seek Mother in her closets, studying her cashmeres and velvets and silks, most of them given to her by the designer Robert Piguet. I recall feeling an exquisite sensation—as close to masturbation as anything I can remember from childhood— while stroking a particular Piguet evening dress of electric-blue satin, which carried the scent of his dry, terse perfume, Bandit. The texture offered a powerful sensual consolation, as if the cloth that had lain against Mother's skin were the equivalent of her longed-for embrace.

Then came the war, and my father's death in the first months of fighting with the Free French, and our flight to America. Mother got her first job three days after we arrived in New York, in January of 1941, through friends of a fellow Russian émigré who had married an American heiress. It was arranged that, for seventy-five dollars a week, Tatiana would design hats at Henri Bendel's, which was particularly renowned for the excellence of its hats, as attested by Cole Porter's "You're the top!... You're a Bendel bonnet, A Shakespeare sonnet." At Bendel's Mother was known as Countess du Plessix. (The P.R. gambit of popularizing European titles seemed to suit the taste of wartime New York; witness Countess Mara shirts and ties and Princess Marcella Borghese cosmetics.) Hats were big business then—one of *Vogue's* fashion editors during the forties and fifties, Babs Simpson, estimates that she and her colleagues acquired a minimum of ten new hats each season, giving the previous year's bunch to their maids—so Tatiana was in great demand.

A year after she started at Bendel's, her designs came to the attention of Saks Fifth Avenue's founder and president, Adam Gimbel. In the forties and fifties, no center for custom-made clothes in Manhattan—with the exception of Bergdorf Goodman—more epitomized American high style than the glamorous Salon Moderne, on the third floor of Saks. A suite of rooms walled with Louis XV boiserie and pale-blue damask, it was dedicated to custom-made women's fashions and directed by a willowy blond designer known as Sophie of Saks, who was Gimbel's wife. Throughout the thirties, the Salon Moderne had been a showcase for Paris imports, but, with the cessation of trade imposed by wartime, Sophie started to design a line of her own, and was having trouble giving it the proper cachet. Both she and her husband were entranced by Tatiana's European flair, and in 1942 Gimbel offered Tatiana a job making hats for the Salon, at a salary of a hundred and twenty-five dollars a week. "Don't ever learn English, you'll sell more hats that way," Gimbel told Mother, and she would more than amply follow his advice.

Within a few years, Sophie's only competitors in American made-to-order clothes were Mainbocher and Hattie Carnegie, and Tatiana's principal rivals were Lily Daché and John Fredericks. Sophie and Tatiana's customers included stars like Claudette Colbert, Marlene Dietrich, Irene Dunne, and Edith Piaf; the socialites Mrs. E. F. Hutton and Mrs. Pierre du Pont; assorted magnates like Estée Lauder, Betsy Bloomingdale, Mrs. Darryl Zanuck, Harriet Deutsch (an heiress to the Sears, Roebuck fortune), and Anita May (a great-granddaughter of the founder of the May Company).

Texas-born Sophie was a perennially cheerful woman whose fashion philosophy was somewhat like Tatiana's: to make a woman look as sexy as possible and yet like a perfect lady. She was particularly noted for the superb tailoring of her suits and coats, always made with matching blouses and linings, and for the lush fabrics of her evening dresses. Tatiana's creations added a dash of spryness and wit to Sophie's traditional, *comme-il-faut* elegance. (A typical touch of her whimsy was to put a thermometer or a tiny revolving weather vane on a winter hat in place of a feather.) And after a long week of working side by side the two women played cards together every weekend. "The three of us lunched every day in Sophie's office," says Helen O'Hagan, the former vice-president of public relations at Saks Fifth Avenue, who joined the store in 1955 as an assistant press officer. "Both Sophie and Tats loved to talk, but Tatiana had to remain the center of attention. She carried on about whom she'd met at dinner parties that week, and then the two would discuss their canasta game for the following Saturday and Sunday. When Tatiana had hogged the stage a bit too long, Sophie would lean over and poke her knee and say, 'Tats, enough! Let someone else speak.' And, of course, Tatiana always sat facing the door, so that she could quickly jump up and catch any customer who wandered into the Salon at lunchtime."

Tatiana the Dictator allowed no fingering or perusing of models: she immediately imposed her preference, and that was that. "Tatiana simply brought something out and said, 'Thees ees hat for you,'" Ethel Woodward de Croisset, a Parisian who frequented the Salon Moderne in the mid-forties, says, "And then she put it on your head and made a loud one-word comment in French, such as *'Formidable!'* or *'Divin!'"* But my mother's success was based on cultural and social skills that far transcended her craft as a designer. Her stint in the diplomatic service had enabled her to master a code that was still central to mid-century elegance—the appropriateness of each chapeau for a particular social occasion. And she was a gifted lay psychiatrist: she was able to convince plain women that they were beautiful. "I listen to problems and solve by putting flowers on heads," she used to say about her customers. "They parade out of salon full of confidence, like prize racehorses."

By the time Tatiana had become Saks' star milliner, I was settled at the Spence School, in New York, one of the few foreigners and scholarship students there, shrouding my anxieties under the mask of the successful, outgoing girl. The war, my father's death, and my deliverance from the governess had literally thrust my mother and me into each other's arms, and as I was approaching puberty I came to sense the great shyness that lurked under her noisy, tyrannical facade. Although I was not yet ready to forgive her failings, I was beginning to realize that she had been too ambitious, too deeply involved in her climb to success, to "mother" me properly when I was a small child. But nothing brought us closer together than her marriage to Alexander Liberman, a fellow Russian émigré, whom Mother had first met decades earlier in France. He became the guardian angel of my youth, blending paternal and maternal roles and performing the duties that Mother was too impatient or bored to undertake. He dealt with report cards and dentists, imposed curfew hours and taboos on lipstick, and, later, warned me of the dangers of adolescent sex and informed me about the mysteries of birth control.

Mother's love for Alex, whom she called Superman, was of a mystical, obsessive kind, and he was entirely devoted to her. His first job in the United States was a modest post in the layout department of *Vogue*, and although he eventually became editorial director of the entire Condé Nast publishing empire, he is the first to emphasize that in our early years in the United States my mother was the family's principal breadwinner.

The Libermans' swift rise in New York's fashion and media worlds was made possible by their ever shrewd choices of who might be "useful" to them, and by their hospitality, which came to be proverbial. At our first Christmases, when we were barely able to pay grocers' bills, they gave huge parties—forty, fifty people squeezed into our flat—at which everyone received a small but beautifully wrapped gift. Friends of friends were welcome. There was food enough for hundreds, and music—a wheezing Russian fellow called Zizi perpetually playing the march from Prokofiev's *The Love for Three Oranges* on our rented upright.

However opulent the customers of the Salon Moderne, my mother's workroom at Saks was akin to a Dickensian sweatshop. It was a dark, low-ceilinged space with little cross-ventilation. At two long worktables sat some twelve seamstresses. Tatiana had to produce sixty models a year—thirty for the spring collection, thirty for the fall—and the atmosphere of her atelier was made electric by her concentration and her speed of execution. But somehow it was also serene. She was thoughtful with her assistants, sending them home when they were getting a cold or had child care problems; they were awed and endlessly amused by her. My most striking memory of Mother at work has to do with the uncanny swiftness of her fingers. Her right hand was crippled and clawlike—the result of a nearly fatal car accident in 1936—but it flew over the cloth, sculpting the most delicate pleats, flutings, and tucks with the deftness of a microsurgeon.

It was from this corner of Saks that Tatiana went out to wage a battle familiar to all mothers: the struggle over her daughter's adolescent body. Mother's comments on my changing shape were biased by the numerous hangups she had about her own body, particularly about her breasts, which had been direly misshapen—or so she repeatedly told me—by nine months of nursing me. ("What else could I do, in *Warsaw?*") From my thirteenth year on, her sartorial commandments went something like this: "You and I can't wear belts, *chérie*, our breasts are too big. We can't wear red shoes, our feet are too wide." Such scrutiny reached a critical point at those moments, both longed-for and dreaded, when we had to shop for my clothes, which we bought exclusively at Saks, where Mother had a large discount.

When I was a freshman, my school suggested that each member of my class acquire a long evening frock for her initiation into East Coast-preppy puberty—the Groton-St. Mark's Christmas dance. As I arrive at Saks to meet Mother, I have already created the dress of my dreams, pink or blue, a tulle skirt perhaps scattered with a few paillettes. Leaving orders with her assistants that she be instantly paged if a customer should appear, Mother clutches my hand and pulls me down the grim gray service stairs toward the Junior Misses department. "Psst! Psst!" she goes as we emerge. "Salesgirl! Queeck!" She is known throughout the store, and help instantly appears. "She must have a dress for evening, long, black!" she commands. "But *Maman*, I don't want black," I gasp. "*Ridicule!*" she answers. "Black is *only* color for evening." "But *Maman*—" She is already at the rack, going speedily through the garments, pushing back dresses that I crave, crave to try on—but, alas, Mother is triumphantly holding up her definitive choice. It minimizes the bosom, all right—bodice of stark black velvet, sad little skirt of black-and-white plaid organdie, with cap sleeves to match. It is *mannish*; it is *nunnish*—in sum, it's a lemon. "*On essaye!*" she orders. She rushes me into a dressing room, and as she exclaims "*Quelle élégance! Divin! Un rêve!*" I stare at myself dejectedly in the mirror. I plead, "*Maman*, can't I try the—" "*Ça y est*, again you want to try on the whole store!" She is off, black and white monstrosity in hand, and I pliantly acquiesce, for her love has been so hard won that I fear the smallest confrontation could destroy it. Over time, I have often thought back to my mother's imposition of her own blackness on my first evening frock: Was she refusing me my femininity, because it made me into a rival? Or was she, on the contrary, speeding me into adulthood, into a sexual elegance akin to hers?

I did not menstruate until I was sixteen. My classmates, one after another, began to host the "visitor," as we called it at Spence, while I played a delicate make-believe game, every four weeks dropping the excuse card into the little black box in the gym, expertly chatting about cramps. I had no one with whom to share my dreadful secret. Mother had never approached the issue, and my stepfather had offered some vague information, but I could not bring myself to tell him my worries—worries that I could never have children, was doomed to be barren and useless to society. And then one day, in my junior year, my period arrived, directly after basketball practice. I rushed home to the little brownstone on East 70th Street that we had been sharing with another Russian family. I ran into my bathroom, pulled down my pants, and sat on the toilet, admiring the strand of pink. Mother came in from Saks and opened the bathroom door, staring at me, as she did most days upon returning from work, with that shy, inquisitive glance which was meant to ask, "Is everything O.K.?" "*Maman*, I have my period!" I exclaimed. But I don't know how to handle it, I added, explaining that most of the girls used pads, some used tampons, but that idea kind of scared me. Do you, have you ever used tampons, is that what I should try to use? She stared at me, deadpan, and said, "Oh, sure, I can put anything up there—tennis balls, anything!" And then she fled the bathroom, terror in her eyes.

By now I was a precociously literary, symbol-savvy teenager. What was that business about "balls"? Men had balls; was she trying to tell me how many men could get in there, or that she was the one in the family who had the balls? Or was she trying to prove how "progressive" she was, liberating me to accept my sexuality forthrightly and have fewer problems with it than she had? (If so, she succeeded.)

It was around this time that Mother bought me my first pair of trousers. She had always looked upon herself as "emancipated," because she had started wearing pants in the twenties, and her idea of the chicly liberated woman was frozen around the notion that "she wears pants." So, as I stood in the dressing room trying on my first

pair of slacks, Mother stared at me with that gaze of unmitigated ado-
ration which it was my highest goal in life to gain, and said, *"Divin! Tu
dois toujours porter les pantalons!"* She carried on about my skinny hips, so
much more elegant than her size 16—why ever bother with a skirt?
For the next half century, "You must always wear pants" was Mother's
repeated refrain—her version of the mantra with which every mother
attempts to keep her daughter in her control, be it "You're killing me,"
"I won't argue anymore," or the aria in the second act of *The Magic Flute*
through which (as I see it) the Queen of the Night tries to keep her
daughter Pamina under her spell.

But we did have some good times, Mother and I. The best
moments came when I was on school vacation, and picked her up at
Saks to go to lunch at the Hamburger Heaven on 51st Street, across
from St. Patrick's. "Twenty-five minutes!" she would proclaim as we
rushed down the service stairs. We sat on the childlike high chairs and
winked at each other conspiratorially as the waitresses snapped the
little trays over our knees. Food was very important to Mother, and,
unlike most fashion plates, she was not much concerned about
remaining svelte. We both ordered our hamburgers extra rare, and
lathered them with the wonderful American junk—pickles,
ketchup—that still symbolized the paradise of our adopted country,
topping it all off with lemon meringue pie. I tried to stretch out our
time to forty, forty-five minutes by questioning her about who was
coming for fittings that afternoon. Very important, she'd answer,
looking at her watch. Marlene and Claudette! We never discussed
school, for she always feared that such talk would reveal her igno-
rance of educational matters, and though I went to Spence for seven
years, she never visited the school until my graduation day.

"The attachment to the mother is bound to perish, precisely
because it was the first and was so intense," Sigmund Freud wrote
about daughters and mothers. Freud never did give us girls much of a
chance to bond. His writings on this issue, however, have helped me

to realize that the complexity of daughters' struggles for independence from their mothers is especially byzantine. A boy achieves the necessary separation from his first love object—Mother—by identifying with Father. But a girl faces the paradoxical task of detaching herself from her mother while continuing to identify with her to some degree. This ambiguous process of disentanglement is the more arduous if the mother is a high priestess of the very rite that every teenager wants to master above all others: seduction.

In the years before I left home for college, I passed canapés in my mother and stepfather's living room to fashion arbiters like Christian Dior, Adrian of Hollywood, Coco Chanel, and Irving Penn; to assorted sex symbols and media celebrities like Marlene Dietrich, Claudette Colbert, Janet Gaynor, Salvador Dali, and Ray Bolger; to a variety of world-class fashion plates like Babe Paley, Gloria Guinness, and Patricia Lopez-Wilshaw; and to the assembled membership of *Vogue's* glamorous editorial staff. Black-clad Mother whipped through her blazingly white-furnished rooms, bullying her crowd with imperious decrees: "Dostoyevski ees *terrible* writer, nothing but journalist," or "Take off British dress, it look like tablecloth." Not many professional women had children in those days, and as I grew older Mother increasingly wished to show me off. Just before the guest arrived, she would peruse every inch of me— "Your face is too *wide* for straight hair"—and then propel me into the living room with a small shove in the small of my back, commanding, "*Charme.*"

Well into my twenties, I whirled through contradictory cycles— periods of servile obedience to my parents' swank monde, followed by periods of rebellion against it. During my last years at Spence, I spent my weekends looking for contraptions—chest-flattening bras, foot-shrinking shoes—that would purge me of those bodily details my mother so emphatically criticized. I followed diets that might help me to resemble the meticulously starved models who flocked to her parties. (One called for three days of buttermilk and soda water, another for three days of stewed prunes and tea.) I suppose I was both emulating the standards of style for which mother was a conduit and fashioning my body to be as different as possible from her voluptuous one. What tormented misunderstandings occur between mothers and daughters! Compared with Tatiana and her ravishing friends, I felt dreadfully plain, but her growing affection for me signaled that I was becoming more and more "presentable," as she put it, and also turning into what *she* would like to have been—a school-smart, tomboy-skinny "intellectual."

So I was a divided soul: while continuing to smile graciously and pass canapés to Elsa Maxwell and Pierre Balmain, I was carving out an imaginary future for myself that would be radically unlike my parents' lives. I, Francine Ludmilla Pauline Anne-Marie du Plessix, wanted to marry someone who would liberate me from all this shit. I dreamed of settling down with a scholarly, somewhat mystical gentleman farmer who wrote poetry or novels on the side. I yearned for a Tudor-parsonage-like home, with dark wood paneling, ottomans tufted in deep burgundy, and a cozy kitchen where I would put up blackberry jam while listening to my husband talk about St. Paul's view of the Resurrection and the eschatology of the Church Fathers.

But first I had to go to school. I spent two years at Bryn Mawr College and two at Barnard, flirting with a variety of careers as different from my parents' as possible. I began as a medievalist, dallied with physics and premed, and ended up majoring in philosophy and religion. I went to night classes at the Art Students League with the notion of becoming a painter, and later I came close to entering Union Theological Seminary. After my junior year, I spent a summer session at Black Mountain College, a community whose zeitgeist—rebellion against every form of established order—thrust my antiparental cycle into high gear. I smoked an early-vintage pot (this was 1951), sat entranced through John Cage's Zen-anarchist events, played strip poker with Robert Rauschenberg, and particularly appalled my mother by wearing a leather motorcycle jacket and chopping my hair short and jagged. ("She has *shaved* herself!" Mother cried, and our friend Leo Lerman moaned, "You look like Port Authority Terminal.") The summer after graduation, I lived in New Orleans, where I drank bourbon with jazz clarinettists and played poker with a Communist cell. (The experience was salubrious: the members' humorlessness quickly inoculated me against the C.P.) I returned to New York and worked for two years as a reporter on the overnight shift at the United Press, writing "World in Brief"s on murders, earthquakes, corn futures, and the latest developments in the Joseph McCarthy hearings. I was the only woman on the graveyard shift, and I relished the Martinis consumed with my male colleagues at 8:00 A.M. in Third Avenue bars, going home to a basement room whose address, in the West Village, so appalled my mother that she never deigned to visit it.

During the feminine, unquestioning Eisenhower fifties, Tatiana's career flourished as it never had before. Her hats were so popular that in 1955 Saks decided she should produce a ready-to-wear line alongside her custom designs, and sent her on the road to promote her creations in the Midwest. "Tatiana—so much the vogue!" a Saks ad in the *Times* announced. "Charming for Easter but prophetic for summer... the Deep-Mushroom, shadowy sheer or all-velvet." In the meantime, I, at the age of twenty-three, had moved to Paris, and was emulating the life *she* had led at twenty-three. I got a job with *Elle* and sat in the showrooms of Chanel, Patou, Givenchy, Dior, taking notes on the tweeds and tulles paraded at collection time. Down to a near-anorexic hundred and ten pounds, I pinned dresses on models and wrote fashion captions that said, "Balenciaga's newest chemise surprise! False double hem, single-breasted buttoning down the side." Just as my mother had done in the thirties, I scrambled to get invited to the Baroness So-and-So's dinners, and borrowed dresses from couture houses to attend them.

My correspondence with my parents reflected my fear that their success and their bonds with important friends far superseded their need for me. "*Maman adorée,*" one letter from the spring of 1955 reads.

"I am crazed, crazed with joy at the prospect of accompanying you to Rome this summer . . . I beg you not to change your mind. I'm not so much thrilled by the prospect of Rome as by the notion that it will be the only way we can be *quietly* together. You are as you always have been the crux of my existence." And then there were missives in which I stated my solidarity in practicing *their* trade—one for which I felt increasingly unfit. "Monday the major hustling begins," I wrote. "Three major collections a day to cover and then sittings late into the night. I'm in the photo studio where I'm going to live through the rest of the week, preparing the color pages, which are made before the collections begin in an atmosphere of atomic secrecy, a messenger just arrived from Dior in an armored truck, pistols in each hand, with the suit we're using on the cover."

My frequently caustic descriptions of Paris high society seemed to impress Mother. Her crippled hand had always served as an excuse for not writing more than a few phrases, usually at the end of my stepfather's missives. But in the fall of 1955 I received a typed three-page letter in which she hinted that I might be "a writer": "Your long letter on . . . the Île Saint-Louis is, quite simply, a chef d'oeuvre of contemporary prose. And you're totally mistaken if you think that it was too long, for I had Alex read it to me three evenings in a row."

But nothing delighted Mother more than the man I was going out with in my last year in Paris: an alcoholic prince. No A-plus college exams or creative writing awards won at Barnard evoked such a surge of maternal approval as I received during my affair with that particular cad. And what was I doing with that ridiculous prince, with my borrowed finery and my mannequin's body and a fashion career that sent me into deep depressions? I was running as fast as I could toward my mother's approval and love; I was shouting, "I'm just like you now! Please pay attention! Pay attention at last!"

And then one morning in the middle of that race I woke up delirious, with a temperature of 105° and internal hemorrhages. I had an extreme case of mononucleosis. Doctors prescribed total rest for two months and partial rest for at least a year. I returned to the United States in the fall of 1956 to pursue my convalescence, and, as I stood on the boat deck waving to my parents, who were waiting on land below, I wore a Chanel suit of pink-and-gray tweed they had given me as a present for my twenty-sixth birthday. The first and last item of haute couture I would ever own, it marked the end of my life in fashion. A few weeks later, it was in this particular costume that I met my future husband, the reclusive, contemplative painter Cleve Gray, and soon I began to live that quiet country life in the snug, dark house I had dreamed of as a teenager. Here's a sign of my unmodish attitude toward clothes, and of my sentimental concern for any present my parents ever gave me: I so lovingly maintained the jacket of that Chanel suit that, in the fall of 1994, I wore it to the christening of my first grandchild.

What was remarkable was the degree to which my mother seemed to approve of my marriage and my new life. My husband, who revered her, immediately became "world's best son-in-law." It helped that he spoke fluent French and was a Princeton graduate, the acme of my mother's simplistic hierarchy of American Values. We had two sons, born sixteen months apart, and, as meticulously as I had crafted a quiet country life, radically different from Tatiana's, I attempted to give my children all that I had not received from her in my youth: I drove daily car pools, ate dinner with them six days a week, gave them their first skiing and tennis lessons, tried to offer them constant companionship. My relations with Tatiana reached an unprecedented level of serenity in those years, maybe because I was continuing to fulfill a secret wish of the most loving mothers—the desire that their daughters not repeat their mistakes.

Tatiana was in the deepest sense a family person, with a Confucian devotion to most of her blood kin, and she adored her grandchildren. An abiding memory: Mother rushing up the stairs upon coming home from Saks, when I brought my first baby to her New York house, shouting, *"Il est là! Il est là!"* and sweeping the six-week-old into her

arms, repeatedly cooing, *"Joli garçon! Joli garçon!"* She grew to be hilar-
iously competitive about my children, and they worshiped her. At the
age of three, my older son announced, "I'm going to marry Grandma
when I grow up." How she delighted in that: "He wants to marry *me*,
not his mother."

Still, our friendship was not without its difficulties. Unable to
master more than a few paragraphs in English, Tatiana could never
read or discuss my writing, except what was translated into French;
she grew proud of me solely on the basis of reports that I was achiev-
ing "a reputation." Moreover, I had to keep my frontiers guarded. My
husband and I visited my parents almost weekly at their house on East
70th Street, staying in my childhood room. But if Mother had her way
we would have been constantly under her thumb, attending the same
parties she and Alex attended, joining them in their summer sites—
Saint-Tropez, Ischia, the Lido. I politely said no to most of her offers
and demands. No, we cannot come to the April-in-Paris ball next
month; no, *Maman chérie*, don't make a copy of your Dior suit for me,
it is simply too formal for my kind of life. "Why do you always say no
to your mother?" asked my husband (whose life would have been far
easier if he had said no early on to his own invasive mother). Within
two years, he understood enough to cease asking the question. And,
over time, Mother came to realize that my happiness depended on my
ability to carve out a realm of my own. So we visited across our bor-
ders, both of us still somewhat on guard, yet able to discuss the children's education, whatever books we'd both read in French, and the
illness and death of old friends.

It is ironic that my career took off the very year Mother's declined.
In the spring of 1965, just as I was placing my first pieces with *The New
Yorker*, Saks' management decided that the hat department was losing
too much money. And, with no great ceremony, Tatiana was fired by
her friend Adam Gimbel. Owing to the waning interest in custom-
design fashions, Sophie, who, miraculously, remained Mother's close

friend, was to shut down the Salon Moderne altogether four years later, in 1969.

What I find most curious about Tatiana's twenty-three-year tenure at Saks is that she never dared ask for a raise. This timidity was part of her Old World culture, her grande-dame quality: for her, talk of money was taboo. The timidity also had to do with her self-demeaning modesty. However well she sold, Mother never thought she was selling *enough*. ("I'm not *worth* more than they're giving me," she told my stepfather whenever he urged her to ask Adam Gimbel for a raise.) And so the fabulous Tatiana of Saks ended her career receiving virtually the same salary she had been offered two decades earlier as a refugee—a little more than eleven thousand dollars a year. Nor did she receive a pension. "She's a countess," Gimbel told my stepfather when he got up his courage to raise the issue. "And everyone knows you're well off now."

The demise of Tatiana's calling in the early and mid-1960s had deep roots in the culture at large: by the late 1960s, the only people showing enthusiasm for headgear were members of the counterculture, and they wore symbolic hats—coonskin caps, Che Guevara berets, gypsy scarves, Native American headbands—to express their sympathy with oppressed political and racial minorities, with all that was tribal, ethnic, primitive. Tatiana's aesthetic had been one of quietly elitist moderation, of seductive yet tamed femininity. And nothing could have been more abhorrent to her than the forthright, egalitarian sensuality that accompanied the end of the hat and was reflected in the fashion magazines that had been her bibles since her youth—Helmut Newton's lascivious Valkyries, Deborah Turbeville's shots of seemingly masturbating girls. A few years before her death, Tatiana shyly brought out an album of her press clips and photographs to look at with me—flattering, Horst-like shots of daintily groomed Jean Patchett modeling Tatiana's exquisite boaters, bretons, toques. "Don't women still want *becoming* fashions?" she asked me wistfully.

Mother was only fifty-nine when she was fired, and was still filled with volcanic energy. If I had my life to live over again, I could see to it that I visited with her more often in those first years of her retirement, and praised the valor of her career—to make her know that her sometimes intractable daughter was also her most loyal admirer. I would have tried to be a pure *friend* of Tatiana, to cultivate a comradeship uncluttered by the debris of mother-daughter relations. What a gigantic appetite and gift for friendship she had! Her ardent attachments extended far beyond the "useful" women of New York. They included dozens of friends from the 1930s, and a number of charity cases—down-and-out Russians, meek little ladies from the Midwest— whom she fed and sheltered because they had been put in her care, sometimes decades earlier, by an acquaintance.

But I was at home in Connecticut, raising my children, writing about and working for political causes. In the late 1960s, my involvement in the antiwar movement created new sources of tension between Tatiana and me. Like most Russian émigrés, she was militantly opposed to any détente with the Communist world. During Connecticut weekends, she would watch me while I was designing Eugene McCarthy posters or making phone calls about some forthcoming peace rally. A lifelong teetotaler, she had begun to drink in her retirement, and she would growl at me over her glass of Bordeaux, "You sell out to Hanoi? You play into hands of Viet Cong?"

Can we ever invent an ideal parent? Returning from an antiwar demonstration in Washington with the photographer Richard Avedon, I mused, "What would I have been like if I'd had a mother who could *understand* me . . . like Hannah Arendt, say?" Avedon replied, "You'd have become a fashion model."

In her new idleness, Mother read more than ever—an average of four or five books a week in French or Russian. She went to Kenneth's every few days to have her hair dressed. She now played canasta every afternoon. She received and counseled former clients, who continued to pour out their hearts to her. She became a cultural icon to the many Russian artists and poets who were beginning to arrive in the United States: Voznesensky, Yevtushenko, Brodsky, Baryshnikov, and Rostropovich all flocked to admire Mayakovsky's muse, to hear her recitations of Russian verse. Yet Mother soon lost the marvelous dynamism that had characterized her when she was Tatiana of Saks. In photographs taken of her after 1965 her formerly searing gaze is replaced by a haunted, sorrowful stare, as if she were looking back at a lost treasure, a lost purpose—her work.

Her physical decline began in 1976. She had a mild heart attack, and then, in 1981, she endured a five-and-a-half-hour gallbladder operation, which kept her in the hospital for nearly two months. She became addicted to powerful painkillers and was never able to shake them off. She stayed in bed much of the day, and received only a few of her very oldest friends for tea. She still played canasta once or twice a week, but friends reported that she was too muddled to think her way through a game, and in order to keep her spirits up they purposefully lost several games a month to her. (How Mother could fake! She pretended to me that she always won!) In 1985, she fell and broke her hip, and she stopped going out altogether. She became a near-invalid, her life valiantly prolonged by my stepfather's attention, and by the care of the remarkable nurse-companion of her last ten years, Melinda Pachengo.

Mother and I began a curious new sartorial relationship: whenever I visited New York to spend an evening with friends, I dressed for dinner and then went to her room to say good night: *"Montre-toi!"*, she would command, scrutinizing me through her bifocals and offering some comment like "Can't you put some curl in your hair?" or "What would we do without *shawls*?" I chafed under her gaze, but what else did I have to offer her? I was now her surrogate fashion plate—the only body, the only style she had left to exhibit.

Toward the end, Mother regressed into a deep, exclusive Russianness. She wanted to see only Russian friends, watch only

Russian films, taste only Russian food. In the span of two years, my stepfather hired thirty-two different chefs in the hope that one of them might reawaken her waning appetite, but to no avail. Three days before her death, in the spring of 1991, I came to see her. She had been in bed for months and in the hospital for many weeks. She weighed ninety-eight pounds. She was lying on her bed in a white bathrobe and had a book in her hand, which I knew she was only pretending to read, for she did not even have her glasses on. She showed no emotion and no sadness—just an immense lassitude. I sat down on her bed and talked to her quietly, mostly about the children, telling her not to speak, for she had barely any voice left. Her eyelids were fluttering, and I kissed her good night. "Wait, " she said weakly. "Pass me my glasses. I want to see you." I obeyed. She motioned for me to rise, and gave me one very long, exhaustive stare. I was wearing a black silk pants suit that she had given me some years before, after she stopped going out. The closest thing to a smile that she could summon crossed her face, and she managed to whisper, "*Très jolie. Tu dois toujours porter des pantalons.*"

She is buried a mile from my house, in our family plot in the Warren, Connecticut, cemetery. I take flowers to her grave every few weeks when the weather is warm. She has returned to me in several dreams, but never more powerfully than in a dream I had recently, the night before the third anniversary of her death. It went this way:

I am living quietly in a simple country house with two women companions—kindly, neutral presences, both slightly older than I. Our house is on a hill overlooking a valley, within view of another hill of equal height. Suddenly, a message arrives from Mother saying that she is living across the valley and wishes me to come to immediately live with her on "Atlanta," the hill opposite ours. (Clever subconscious! Change the "l" to an "i," and you get an anagram of Tatiana.) Mother's message annoys me. I send her back the message "I am very happy where I am, I do *not* wish to go live with you in Atlanta." Next,

Photo by Constantine Joffe

TATIANA JACOVLEFT DU PLESSIX LIBERMAN, 1943

there arrives a wizened graying man, a Father Time figure. *No*, I say again to Mother as Father Time brings me another imperious message from her. No, I shall *not* join you on the other side. No, I shall stay where I am. You're telling me that *your* side of the valley is better—the *only* place to be, but I'm not going yet! Whereupon Mother appears at the house of my two women companions to join me on my own hill. She is the radical opposite of the mother I knew: a tiny, smiling old lady, wearing a timid black hat—a submissive little toque, the kind of hat Mother might have designed for a client who had a family funeral to attend. But Mother smiles merrily and waves and blows me kisses from across the room, and I blow kisses back, and there is a sense of serenity, of mutual approval, of understanding between us more total than we ever shared in life.

Upon waking, I phoned a friend who is very keen on filial issues. "What does it mean?" I asked after telling her the dream "It means you won," she answered. The answer was a trifle too Yankee, too competitive for me. "What does it *mean?*" I pestered my husband. "It means she loved you," he said.

That morning, as I brought Mother my flowers and tended her grave, I said, Thank you, *Maman chérie*, for the dream. Thank you for this wondrous life, which I've crafted in opposition to you, and in the spirit of your grace.

JOYCE JOHNSON IS THE AUTHOR OF *Minor Characters*, which won a 1983 National Book Critics Circle Award for autobiography. Her other books include *What Lisa Knew: The Truths and Lies of the Steinberg Case, In the Night Cafe, Bad Connections,* and *Come and Join the Dance.* She teaches in the Graduate Writing Program at Columbia University.

DEPRESSION GLASS

Remember how Daddy used to joke, "Music makes me relax too much," his funny stories about falling sound asleep at the operas and concerts to which he escorted you during your courtship? And how he'd manage to wake up in time to enthusiastically join in on the applause—even shouting, "Encore! Encore!" You, he said, were so considerate, you'd pretend he hadn't missed a thing.

You certainly seem to have been an awfully good sport. Once Daddy rashly took you to lunch at a very fancy hotel. You looked over the menu and saw that the prices were way beyond his means. After all, he was only a bookkeeper, though always a perfect gentleman. When the waiter came, you smiled and said, "I'll have the graham crackers and milk."

I have the feeling Daddy lacked experience with women. He should have made you change your order, but he was too cowed and impressed. "It's my favorite dish," you said without batting an eye, the sentimental heroine of some O'Henry tale. The funny thing was, they served it to you very smartly in a crystal bowl, surrounded by a silver one filled with cracked ice.

I loved to hear about you and the graham crackers and how that was the night Daddy got up the nerve to pop the question. Consideration, you used to endlessly point out to me, was the most important thing in marriage. By my teens, of course, I thought passion was. I'd even begun to equate passion with truth—nothing had ever seemed realer. Didn't your lifetime of consideration require too much acting? You got so little of what you wanted.

Daddy wanted you and me to have all the art we needed, but the voice of Red Barber from Ebbets Field was more moving to him than any aria from *Traviata*. He had the capacity to forget himself and everyone else during baseball season, stretched out on the couch with his vest unbuttoned, his cigar between his teeth, his head next to the radio.

Baseball gave you sinus headaches. You'd seal yourself in the kitchen, but the roar of the game would seep in under the door, with a swell and a fade like the surf at Brighton Beach, carrying whiffs of Daddy's Muriel Panatellas. I loved that smell, and the smell of Burma Shaving Creme that mixed with it whenever I sat on Daddy's lap. I wore cigar bands on my wedding finger.

I'd feel lonesome on those baseball Saturdays and Sundays. Every now and then I'd go and perch next to my father on the couch. Whenever he remembered me, the hand he wasn't smoking with would come down and squeeze my arm, pretending to feel for muscles like Popeye the Sailorman's, whose adventures he'd read me from the Sunday paper, even though you said it would be better not to. But I could never get him to answer my questions once the game was on. "Don't be such a chatterbox, Honeybunch," was all he'd say, so I'd give up and go back to you.

Once I heard you talking on the phone to one of your sisters about some grown man who had his mind on chasing little white balls when he should have been thinking about why he wasn't getting anywhere.

I think you'd made up your mind to live, Mother, as if sex had no importance—as if you could somehow just rise above it. Daddy may have felt differently, lying on the bed separated from yours by the night table—an erotic distance of two and a half feet. The bedroom set was maple, ersatz Colonial—none of that jazzy stuff of the period, those vanities wide as Cadillacs where women with long red finger-nails painted themselves for men. For you, a little powder to take the shine off, a touch of Tangee lipstick, did the trick.

Walking in on you and Daddy one Sunday morning, I was sur-prised to find him in your bed; he had one arm folded around your shoulders; both of you were sitting up, reading the paper. I'd thought beds were like toothbrushes, not to be shared. "Go get some orange juice," you said quickly. When I returned, Daddy was back where he was supposed to be; you'd disappeared into the shower.

When he died, you gave his bed away, moved yours to the center of the room. You said, "It looks larger here now, doesn't it?" not real-izing how it sounded. It wasn't like you to break up a set. You mated for life, better or worse.

Your sisters stayed manless to the end. I remember Aunt Leona exhausting herself playing tennis or golf on the weekends; bringing her trophies home from Van Cortland Park, lining them up on the dresser in her chaotic bedroom, child-size like mine. She cut her hair short like Buster Brown's, had it dyed auburn; Aunt Anna's was already gray. There was always some "girl" Aunt Leona was falling out with, some intense friendship gone sour. You made it known you didn't think much of a person who devoted her life to the giddy pur-suit of pleasure. Aunt Anna said Aunt Leona would always burn the pot, even when she was only boiling water. You were horrified by the ephemera Aunt Leona left behind at eighty-five: suitcases of garish nylon dresses suitable only for Florida, boxes of broken costume jew-elry, tennis rackets in need of restringing, senior-center canvases of cabbagey, tropical-looking flowers. Was this the sum total of a life?

You threw most of it away, saving those maladroit paintings. Art did not belong in the garbage. You stuck them in your linen closet and never hung them.

I always knew you wanted to share me with Aunt Anna much more than you did with Aunt Leona. "Your Aunt Anna has a broken heart," you told me once when I said I wanted to stay with Daddy and not go upstairs. I remember staring at Aunt Anna's chest, wondering if there was a crack under her clothes like the crooked black line on the red vase you'd glued back together so at least it could hold dried flowers. "Kiss Aunt Anna goodnight," you'd prompt me. My aunt was so undemanding, she'd be willing to let me off—"Aw, maybe she doesn't want to"—but then I'd feel so bad about the crack in her heart, I'd throw my arms around her. Aunt Leona, on the other hand, would just grab kisses whenever she felt like it, swooping down on me and tickling me under the arms or the chin until I screamed for her to stop. But I knew it was my job to kiss her, too; without me, after all, the aunts would have been utterly kissless.

You always called them The Girls. "Let's go up and see The Girls," you'd say after you'd dried the dinner dishes.

Some nights Aunt Leona would come downstairs by herself and everybody would start whispering about the crack in Aunt Anna's heart. I remember you saying "Excuse me" during one of these conversations and rushing out of the room, returning a little later with your proud look of smiling through tears.

Soon after that, Aunt Anna suddenly went away on vacation in a big white car that came for her early in the morning. You said she was staying at a lovely hotel.

We took a long ride on the subway and went to visit her there because she'd called up and said she missed me very much. The hotel was a grey building with many floors and hundreds of windows. It was such a quiet place, no children were allowed to go inside because they might get boisterous and wake up the guests. I remember a little park where I stamped my footprints in the snow while you stood looking up at the rows of windows. Suddenly you said brightly, "There she is! There's your Aunt Anna!" You picked me up around the waist and told me to wave and blow kisses."More," you said urgently. "Keep doing it! Don't stop!"

I saw an old woman in a bathrobe and blew my kisses to her, although I wasn't so sure she was Aunt Anna and she didn't blow any back. I was glad when we finally went home because I didn't think much of the hotel.

Eventually Aunt Leona told me Aunt Anna had been married once. Her husband was a Trotskyite printer, who disappeared with all her money while she was in the hospital, recovering from a miscarriage. That explained the broken heart and something else I'd often wondered about when I was little: why most of the furniture in the apartment upstairs, all the books in the plain gloomy bindings and the lamp with the sunflowers on it and the tiny blue enamel clock and the prints of snow-covered villages from Russia seemed to belong to her; why I was told, "Don't bounce on Aunt Anna's couch" and knew I couldn't drink my milk from one of her good pink glasses.

You had the identical set in green, proof that your older sister's marriage and yours had truly overlapped in the void before my birth, because Girls did not buy sets. Maybe there was a sale on at Macy's and the two brides—one already middle-aged—made their simultaneous purchases in a burst of mistaken optimism, anticipating all the entertaining permanently called off by the Depression—celebrations demanding sherry, wine, ice water, cordial, in glasses with stems and feet. When I took you to a flea market a few years before you died, you surveyed the goods with an indignant expression, as if you'd suddenly realized that thousands of other American housewives had been similarly taken in. "Don't buy anything here," you said, looking at me meaningfully.

When I was three or four, I was convinced Aunt Anna's valuable pink glasses were made of candy, and I remember feeling bowled over and confused when Aunt Anna used one of them to serve me lemonade one Saturday night when I'd been lent to her. She didn't seem aware she'd made a great mistake. She even let me have the matching pink candy straw with the tiny spoon at the bottom. I couldn't resist taking a small bite out of that. I was so astounded by all the blood that gushed from my lip, I forgot to howl for a moment.

When Aunt Anna died, you gave me seven pink cordial glasses, although I never serve cordial, and I asked you for something else—Aunt Anna's blue glass girl, the first adult item I can remember coveting. This girl was Deco and distinctly not Aunt Anna's taste. All I can think is that her vanished husband, whose name oddly enough was Roman Blueglass, must have brought her into their house. The blue girl seems related to the books on socialism he forgot to pack and the illustrated copy of *Candide*, which I read when I was eight, finding it very different from other books for children—I was awfully puzzled about where exactly in her body a lady could hide her jewels.

I've seen Roman Blueglass in one ancient photo of a family gathering; he was actually handsome. Curly grey hair; a thin, sarcastic, un-American wolfish face—just the type I've always been attracted to. Perhaps Roman Blueglass leaned over my cradle, before he cracked Aunt Anna's heart.

The blue girl lived on Aunt Anna's coffee table just as she now does on mine. Was it her saturated blue that first attracted me, the way she kept generating sparks of light in my aunt's foggy living room where all the browns and doleful greens were dissolving into the gray rising up from the carpet?

Invariably my hand would reach for her, and yours, intercepting, would move her aside.

"Oh, let the child touch her," Aunt Anna would say. "What's the harm?"

ROSALIND GLASSMAN,
CIRCA 1945

"One touch—that's all." And there'd be something agonized glint-
ing under your sternness, as if you could have laughed from sheer
embarrassment.

Rhapsodic on my aunt's coffee table, the blue girl arced herself,
tiny head thrown back, naked breasts tilted upward, her feet submerged in pure blue water. Ripples in her rectangular pool where
Daddy thoughtlessly stubbed out his cigar lapped around her ankles.
She had your haircut and almost your face, so I knew her blue hair was
really blond. Why was she waiting on the edge of her pool with that
intent look of smiling somewhere inside herself?

I touched the top of her head with one finger. I touched her belly,
which made two touches.

"She's looking forward to a nice warm bath," I heard you or Aunt Anna attempt to explain.

Midnight blue—that was her color. A blue that had nothing to do with us, like the smoky blare from the radio when someone turned on the wrong station.

JUNE JORDAN IS AN AWARD-WINNING POET, novelist, and political writer. Her published work includes *His Own Where*, a young adult novel nominated for the National Book Award, *Civil Wars*, a highly praised collection of political essays, articles, and lectures, and her most recent collection of poems *Kissing God Goodbye: Poems 1991-1996*. She is Professor of African-American Studies at the University of California at Berkeley, where she also directs Poetry for the People Project.

MANY RIVERS TO CROSS

When my mother killed herself I was looking for a job. That was fifteen years ago. I had no money and no food. On the pleasure side I was down to my last pack of Pall Malls plus half a bottle of J&B. I needed to find work because I needed to be able fully to support myself and my eight-year-old son, very fast. My plan was to raise enough big bucks so that I could take an okay apartment inside an acceptable public school district, by September. That deadline left me less than three months to turn my fortunes right side up.

It seemed that I had everything to do at once. Somehow, I must move all of our things, mostly books and toys, out of the housing project before the rent fell due, again. I must do this without letting my neighbors know because destitution and divorce added up to personal shame, and failure. Those same neighbors had looked upon my husband and me as an ideal young couple, in many ways; inseparable, doting, ambitious. They had kept me busy and laughing in the hard weeks following my husband's departure for graduate school in Chicago; they had been the ones to remember him warmly through teasing remarks and questions all that long year that I remained alone, waiting for his return while I became the "temporary," sole breadwinner of our peculiar long-distance family by telephone. They had been the ones who kindly stopped the teasing and the queries when the year ended and my husband, the father of my child, did not come back. They never asked me and I never told them what that meant, altogether. I don't think I really knew.

I could see how my husband would proceed more or less naturally from graduate school to a professional occupation of his choice, just as he had shifted rather easily from me, his wife, to another man's wife—another woman. What I could not see was how I should go forward, now, in any natural, coherent way. As a mother without a husband, as a poet without a publisher, a freelance journalist without assignment, a city planner without a contract, it seemed to me that several incontestable and conflicting necessities had suddenly eliminated the whole realm of choice from my life.

My husband and I agreed that he would have the divorce that he wanted, and I would have the child. This ordinary settlement is, as millions of women will testify, as absurd as saying, "I'll give you a call, you handle everything else." At any rate, as my lawyer explained, the law then was the same as the law today; the courts would surely award me a reasonable amount of the father's income as child support, but the courts would also insist that they could not enforce their own decree. In other words, according to the law, what a father owes to his child is not serious compared to what a man owes to the bank for a car, or a vacation. Hence, as they say, it is extremely regrettable but nonetheless true that the courts cannot garnish a father's salary, nor freeze his account, nor seize his property on behalf of his children, in our society. Apparently this is because a child is not a car or a couch or a boat. (I would suppose this is the very best available definition of the difference between an American child and a car.)

Anyway, I wanted to get out of the projects as quickly as possible. But I was going to need help because I couldn't bend down and I couldn't carry anything heavy and I couldn't let my parents know about these problems because I didn't want to fight with them about the reasons behind the problems—which was the same reason I couldn't walk around or sit up straight to read or write without vomiting and acute abdominal pain. My parents would have evaluated that reason as a terrible secret compounded by a terrible crime; once again an unmarried woman, I had, nevertheless, become pregnant. What's more I had tried to interrupt this pregnancy even though this particular effort required not only one but a total of three abortions—each of them illegal and amazingly expensive, as well as, evidently, somewhat poorly executed.

My mother, against my father's furious rejections of me and what he viewed as my failure, offered what she could; she had no money herself but there was space in the old brownstone of my childhood. I would live with them during the summer while I pursued my crash schedule for cash, and she would spend as much time with Christopher, her only and beloved grandchild, as her worsening but partially undiagnosed illness allowed.

After she suffered a stroke, her serenely imposing figure had shrunken into an unevenly balanced, starved shell of chronic disorder. In the last two years, her physical condition had forced her retirement from nursing, and she spent most of her days on a makeshift cot pushed against the wall of the dining room next to the kitchen. She could do very few things for herself, besides snack on crackers, or pour ready-made juice into a cup and then drink it.

In June 1966, I moved from the projects into my parent's house with the help of a woman named Mrs. Hazel Griffin. Since my teens, she had been my hairdresser. Every day, all day, she stood on her feet, washing and straightening hair in her crowded shop, the Arch of Beauty. Mrs. Griffin had never been married, had never finished high school, and she ran the Arch of Beauty with an imperturbable and contagious sense of success. She had a daughter as old as I who worked alongside her mother, coddling customer fantasy into confidence. Gradually, Mrs. Griffin and I became close; as my own mother became more and more bedridden and demoralized, Mrs. Griffin extended herself—dropping by my parents' house to make dinner for them, or calling me to wish me good luck on a special freelance venture, and so forth. It was Mrs. Griffin who closed her shop for a whole day and drove all the way from Brooklyn to my housing project apartment in Queens. It was Mrs. Griffin who packed me up, so to speak, and carried me and the boxes back to Brooklyn, back to the house of my parents. It was Mrs. Griffin who ignored my father standing hateful at the top of the stone steps of the house and not saying a word of thanks and not once relieving her of a single load she wrestled up the stairs and past him. My father hated Mrs. Griffin because he was proud and because she was a stranger of mercy. My father hated Mrs. Griffin because he was like that sometimes: hateful and crazy.

My father alternated between weeping bouts of self-pity and storm explosions of wrath against the gods apparently determined to ruin him. These were his alternating reactions to my mother's increasing enfeeblement, her stoic depression. I think he was scared; who would take care of him? Would she get well again and make everything all right again?

This is how we organized the brownstone; I fixed a room for my son on the top floor of the house. I slept on the parlor floor in the front room. My father slept on the same floor, in the back. My mother stayed downstairs.

About a week after moving in, my mother asked me about the progress of my plans. I told her things were not terrific but that there were two different planning jobs I hoped to secure within a few days. One of them involved a study of new towns in Sweden and the other one involved an analysis of the social consequences of a huge hydro-electric dam under construction in Ghana. My mother stared at me uncomprehendingly and then urged me to look for work in the local post office. We bitterly argued about what she dismissed as my "high-falutin'" ideas and, I believe, that was the last substantial conversation between us.

From my first memory of him, my father had always worked at the post office. His favorite was the night shift, which brought him home usually between three and four o'clock in the morning.

It was hot. I finally fell asleep that night, a few nights after the argument between my mother and myself. She seemed to be rallying; that afternoon, she and my son had spent a long time in the backyard, oblivious to the heat and the mosquitoes. They were both tired but peaceful when they noisily re-entered the house, holding hands awkwardly.

But someone was knocking at the door to my room. Why should I wake up? It would be impossible to fall asleep again. It was so hot. The knocking continued. I switched on the light by the bed: 3:30 a.m. It must be my father. Furious, I pulled on a pair of shorts and a t-shirt. "What do you want? What's the matter?" I asked him, through the door. Had he gone berserk? What could he have to talk about at that ridiculous hour?

"OK, all right," I said, rubbing my eyes awake as I stepped to the door and opened it. "What?"

To my surprise, my father stood there looking very uncertain.

"It's your mother," he told me, in a burly, formal voice. "I think she's dead, but I'm not sure." He was avoiding my eyes.

"What do you mean?" I answered.

"I want you to go downstairs and figure it out."

I could not believe what he was saying to me. "You want me to figure out if my mother is dead or alive?"

"I can't tell! I don't know!!" he shouted angrily.

"Jesus Christ," I muttered, angry and beside myself.

I turned and glanced about my room, wondering if I could find anything to carry with me on this mission; what do you use to determine a life or a death? I couldn't see anything obvious that might be useful.

"I'll wait up here," my father said. "You call up and let me know."

I could not believe it; a man married to a woman more than forty years and he can't tell if she's alive or dead and he wakes up his kid and tells her, "You figure it out."

I was at the bottom of the stairs. I halted just outside the dining room where my mother slept. Suppose she really was dead? Suppose my father was not just being crazy and hateful? "Naw," I shook my head and confidently entered the room.

"Momma?!" I called, aloud. At the edge of the cot, my mother was leaning forward, one arm braced to hoist her body up. She was trying to stand up! I rushed over. "Wait. Here, I'll help you!" I said.

And I reached out my hands to give her a lift. The body of my mother was stiff. She was not yet cold, but she was stiff. Maybe I had come downstairs just in time! I tried to loosen her arms, to change her position, to ease her into lying down.

"Momma!" I kept saying. "Momma, listen to me! It's OK! I'm here and everything. Just relax. Relax! Give me a hand, now. I'm trying to help you lie down!"

Her body did not relax. She did not answer me. But she was not cold. Her eyes were not shut.

From upstairs my father was yelling, "Is she dead? Is she dead?"

"No!" I screamed at him. "No! She's not dead!"

At this, my father tore down the stairs and into the room. Then he braked.

"Milly?" he called out, tentative. Then he shouted at me and banged around the walls. "You damn fool. Don't you see now she's gone. Now she's gone!" We began to argue.

"She's alive! Call the doctor!"

"No!"

"Yes!"

At last my father left the room to call the doctor.

I straightened up. I felt completely exhausted from trying to gain a response from my mother. There she was, stiff on the edge of her bed, just about to stand up. Her lips were set, determined. She would manage it, but by herself. I could not help. Her eyes fixed on some point below the floor.

"Momma!" I shook her hard as I could to rouse her into focus. Now she fell back on the cot, but frozen and in the wrong position. It hit me that she might be dead. She might be dead.

My father reappeared at the door. He would not come any closer. "Dr. Davis says he will come. And he called the police."

The police? Would they know if my mother was dead or alive? Who would know?

I went to the phone and called my aunt. "Come quick," I said. "My father thinks Momma has died but she's here but she's stiff."

Soon the house was weird and ugly and crowded and I thought I was losing my mind.

Three white policemen stood around telling me my mother was dead. "How do you know?" I asked, and they shrugged and then they repeated themselves. And the doctor never came. But my aunt came and my uncle and they said she was dead.

After a conference with the cops, my aunt disappeared and when she came back she held a bottle in one of her hands. She and the police whispered together some more. Then one of the cops said, "Don't worry about it. We won't say anything." My aunt signaled me to follow her into the hallway where she let me understand that, in fact, my mother had committed suicide.

I could not assimilate this information: suicide.

I broke away from my aunt and ran to the telephone. I called a friend of mine, a woman who talked back loud to me so that I could realize my growing hysteria, and check it. Then I called my cousin Valerie who lived in Harlem; she woke up instantly and urged me to come right away.

I hurried to the top floor and stood my sleeping son on his feet. I wanted to get him out of this house of death more than I ever wanted anything. He could not stand by himself so I carried him down the two flights to the street and laid him on the backseat and then took off.

At Valerie's, my son continued to sleep, so we put him to bed, closed the door, and talked. My cousin made me eat eggs, drink whiskey, and shower. She would take care of Christopher, she said. I should go back and deal with the situation in Brooklyn.

When I arrived, the house was absolutely full of women from the church dressed as though they were going to Sunday communion. It seemed to me they were, every one of them, wearing hats and gloves and drinking coffee and solemnly addressing invitations to a funeral and I could not find my mother anywhere and I could not find an empty spot in the house where I could sit down and smoke a cigarette.

My mother was dead.

Feeling completely out of place, I headed for the front door, ready to leave. My father grabbed my shoulder from behind and forcibly spun me around.

"You see this?" he smiled, waving a large document in the air. "This is an insurance paper for you!" He waved it in my face. "Your mother, she left you insurance, see?"

I watched him.

"But I gwine burn it in the furnace before I give it you to t'row away on trash!"

"Is that money?" I demanded. "Did my mother leave me money?"

"Eh-heh!" he laughed. "And you don't get it from me. Not today, not tomorrow. Not until I dead and buried!"

My father grabbed for my arm and I swung away from him. He hit me on my head and I hit back. We were fighting.

Suddenly, the ladies from the church bustled about and pushed, horrified, between us. This was a sin, they said, for a father and child to fight in the house of the dead and the mother not yet in the ground! Such a good woman she was, they said. She was a good woman, a good woman, they all agreed. Out of respect for the memory of this good woman, in deference to my mother who had committed suicide, the ladies shook their hats and insisted we should not fight; I should not fight with my father.

Utterly disgusted and disoriented, I went back to Harlem. By the time I reached my cousin's place I had begun to bleed, heavily. Valerie said I was hemorrhaging so she called up her boyfriend and the two of them hobbled me into Harlem Hospital.

I don't know how long I remained unconscious, but when I opened my eyes I found myself on the women's ward, with an intravenous setup feeding into my arm. After a while, Valerie showed up. Christopher was fine, she told me; my friends were taking turns with him. Whatever I did, I should not admit I'd had an abortion or I'd get her into trouble, and myself into trouble. Just play dumb and rest. I'd have to stay on the ward for several days. My mother's funeral was tomorrow afternoon. What did I want her to tell people to explain why I wouldn't be there? She meant, what lie?

I thought about it and I decided I had nothing to say; if I couldn't tell the truth then the hell with it.

I lay in that bed at Harlem Hospital, thinking and sleeping. I wanted to get well.

I wanted to be strong. I never wanted to be weak again so long as I lived. I thought about my mother and her suicide and I thought about how my father could not tell whether she was dead or alive.

I wanted to get well and what I wanted to do as soon as I was strong again, actually, what I wanted to do was I wanted to live my life so that people would know unmistakably that I am alive, so that when I finally die people will know the difference for sure between my living and my death.

And I thought about the idea of my mother as a good woman and I rejected that, because I don't see why it's a good thing when you give up, or when you cooperate with those who hate you or when you polish and iron and mend and endlessly mollify for the sake of the people who love the way that you kill yourself day by day silently.

And I think all of this is really about women and work. Certainly this is all about me as a woman and my life work. I mean I am not sure my mother's suicide was something extraordinary. Perhaps most women must deal with a similar inheritance, the legacy of a woman whose death you cannot possibly pinpoint because she died so many, many times and because, even before she became your mother, the life of that woman was taken; I say it was taken away.

And really it was to honor my mother that I did fight with my father, that man who could not tell the living from the dead.

And really it is to honor Mrs. Hazel Griffin and my cousin Valerie and all the women I love, including myself, that I am working for the courage to admit the truth that Bertolt Brecht has written; he says, "It takes courage to say that the good were defeated not because they were good, but because they were weak."

I cherish the mercy and the grace of women's work. But I know there is new work that we must undertake as well: that new work will make defeat detestable to us. That new women's work will mean we will not die trying to stand up: we will live that way: standing up.

I came too late to help my mother to her feet.

By way of everlasting thanks to all of the women who have helped me to stay alive I am working never to be late again.

JANET BURROWAY WAS RAISED IN PHOENIX, Arizona, and attended Barnard College, Cambridge University, England, and the Yale School of Drama. She has taught at the University of Sussex, England; the University of Illinois; and the Writers' Workshop at the University of Iowa; and has been a Lila Wallace/Reader's Digest Fellow. She is the author of plays, poetry, children's books including *The Giant Jam Sandwich*, and seven novels including *The Buzzards* (nominated for the Pulitzer Prize), *Raw Silk* (nominated for the National Book Award), *Opening Nights*, and most recently *Cutting Stone*. She reviews regularly for the *New York Times Book Review* and writes a quarterly column, "In a Certain Light," for *New Letters* magazine. Her text *Writing Fiction*, in its fourth edition, is used in more than 300 colleges and universities in the U.S. She is the Robert O. Lawton Distinguished Professor at Florida State University in Tallahassee.

EMBALMING MOM

"I want to put you in a story," I say. "Apparently it's a matter of some importance."

It must be about 1941. She is ironing and her back is to me. She says nothing and does not turn around, but she licks her finger to test the iron. Her spit sizzles like bacon and I can see her hand. Long strong fingers, violet veins, amber freckles. Under the taut freckled flesh of her forearms her narrow bones roll with the maneuvering of the iron.

"I don't mean professional importance," I say, "but psychological. Spiritual, if you like." She rolls the iron along the board.

Things have not been going too well with me lately —a number of breakages, and not all of them for the first time. The compressor on the air conditioner broke down again. The left earpiece of my reading (writing, sewing) glasses split at the hinge and I can't see to tape it together without my glasses on. Both of my teenaged sons had their hair cut again, for opposing reasons. I got divorced again, and moved again, or at least, I must not have moved, since I live in the same house in Florida, but it seems to feel as if I have moved again.

She rolls the iron along the board, wide end to narrow end in a serpentine path from her belly toward the window sill. It occurs to me that nobody ever sees her own bones, and that she has therefore never seen these bones that twist and roll under her skin, the forearm bones of a bony woman, their mineral and marrow.

"Well," I say, "important to my soul, if you want to put it that way."

"Hmmph," she says. Does she say, "Hmmph?" It seems unlikely. Perhaps what she says is, "Hah!" I think she sighs. Once my brother Bud pointed out to me that when things fall apart you always run home to Mom. He pointed this out because I was fleeing a threatening lover (again) and he thought I wasn't very well hidden in the breakfast bay. But I told him safety is not the point; the point is feeling safe.

She is ironing the skirt of the pima cotton dress with the white and purple pansies, the pintucked yoke, the puffed sleeves edged in eyelet. The pansies part at the point of the iron, swirl left and right under the heel of her hand and wheel down the board behind the butt of the iron. I do not, however, say "butt" in her presence. That much is clear.

I cross my legs, sitting at the breakfast bay, which is covered in some orange substance, a precursor of Naugahyde. I am wearing the trouser suit made out of handwoven amber tweed that I bought off the bolt in Galway at an Incredible Bargain. The trouser suit was stolen out of a parked station wagon in New York in 1972, but it is apparently important that I should be wearing it now, partly because it was such a bargain and partly because I designed and made it myself. I feel good in it: cordial, cool. I think of something I can pass on to her. I laugh.

"Do you know what a friend of mine said the other day?" Cordially rhetorical. "He said: Hell is the place where you have to work out all the relationships you couldn't work out in life."

It's all right to say *hell* in this context, not as a swear word but as an acknowledgment of a possible place. My mother's not narrow-minded about the *nature* of hell. I laugh again, and so although she laughs I don't know if she laughs with me; I miss the tone of her laugh. "Haw, haw!"? I hope it's that one, the swashbuckling one.

"I'd rather work this one out here," I say, but am conscious that I mumble and am not surprised that there is no response. I am sitting on the orange plastic of the nook in the bay window, which my father designed and made, watching my mother at the ironing board that folds up into the wall behind an aluminum door. This also was designed and made by my father, who is not here because he is living in the mountains with his second wife although he was true to my mother right up to the end. And beyond. Outside the desert sun slants through the oleanders, illuminating minute veins in the fuchsia petals. The pansies on the ironing board I remember wearing in the sandbox under the oleanders before I started school, which means that my mother is about thirty-five. I am forty-five and three months by the calendar on the window sill to the left of my typewriter.

"What friend was that?" she asks, eventually, with a palpable absence of malice and a clear implication that any friend who goes under the designation "he" is suspect. It was all right to say *hell* but not *he*.

"Nobody in particular; just a friend."

"Your father gets sweeter every day," I think she says, and I am sure that her head angles to one side, a long neck made longer by the tight poodle cut of her hair, already greying, already thinning, the corrugations of her neck where it arches no wider than the spine of a hardbound book.

"Yes," I say. "Well." She takes the edge of one puff and twirls the eyelet, arching the iron into each semicircle on the board, expertly smoothing it so that when she releases it each arch buoys into a perfect wave. It occurs to me that I can do this, too.

"You know, I'm not sure I feel too well," she says, as if surprised, mumbling now, but she is an old hand at the audible mumble, and I will not rise to it.

Instead I say, "All we need to do is embark on a minor conflict. Anything will do, any of the old ones. My posture, for instance, or the state of my room. Smoking will do. Or that my hair needs cutting."

My elder son has joined the navy and writes that he has had his hair cropped; it never occurred to me before that a crewcut makes one a member of the crew. My younger son has scissored his blond thatch so short that it also seems to have erupted out of World War II, but for him it has an altogether different ideological significance. He does not, however, want it called *punk*. I am so anxious he should like me that I pay to have his left ear pierced and offer him a diamond-chip stud of which I have lost the mate. He accepts it cheerfully, but most days he wears a diaper pin through the punctured lobe.

She deals with the eyelet of the other sleeve, and she turns to me. I am so startled by this success that I reach into my Italian handbag for a cigarette, and my glance catches no higher than the hand she splays protectively over her stomach; I concentrate on the lighting of my cigarette, and can only suppose the shape of her mouth, narrow-lipped but open wide in the friendly "hah" shape, large straight teeth except for the crossing of the two lower incisors that I encounter in my own mirror every day of my life. I hear her say, nasal on the vowels, "I just don't want you to be indis*creet*, sissy."

This confusingly hit home. I recognize the authenticity of it: the plaint, the manipulation, but also the authenticity. Because I am indiscreet; it is my central fault. I confess to freshmen students, junior colleagues, anyone with a dog smaller than a bread box. I expose myself by telephone and telegraph; I say it with ink. I betray the secrets of my friends, believing I am presenting their cases. I embarrass clerks in K-Mart.

But she has her back to me again and all I can see is the parting of the pintucks left and right as she deftly presses them away from the pearl shank buttons. Because she didn't mean the right thing and has no notion that she has hit home.

"What does that mean, indiscreet?" I ask, a little shrill, so that I deliberately draw the smoke in after I've said it, feeling the depth of my lungs, my verbal bottom. "Do you mean sex? Do you mean: lie better?"

"I'm not going to be sidetracked into a discussion of words," my mother says, a thing she would never say.

"It's not a sidetrack," I nevertheless reply. Her forefinger sizzles.

I need an ashtray. I know there are no ashtrays here but I'm willing to choose carefully among the things I know are here: the amethyst-glass pot with calico flowers set in paraffin; the Carnival glass cup with her name, "Alma," etched in primitive cursive; the California Fiesta pottery in the lurid colors of the zinnias along the front walk. I cross to the cupboard and take the little Depression glass fishbowl because I know it best, because it currently houses a tiny goldfish on the windowsill to the left of my typewriter in my house in Florida.

"It's true that I'm indiscreet," I confess, indiscreetly, "but it's not entirely a fault." I tap my ash, and my hair prickles hot against my turtleneck. Both of my husbands liked my hair long, although the second one did not smoke and the first blamed me for indiscretion. The convolutions of authority are confusing. "It's also simply the way I am, it's a negative side of my strength. The thing I want most of all is an understanding audience, a teaching one. The best thing is to tell and be understood. Do you understand?"

"*I've* never looked at any man but your father," she replies, to the oleanders, to the waffle iron, to the pique collar that she designed and made and which she now parts into two perfect eyelet-edged arches of Peter Pan.

"*Mama!*"

No, that won't do. I must not put myself in the hysterical stance because if anything is clear, the clear thing is that she is the hysterical one and I'm the one who copes, deals, functions, and controls. I am the world traveler, the success.

I continue in a more successful tone. "We could start with Dad if you like, but I don't think it's the best place because it's so hard to be honest."

"I *hope* I brought you up to be honest!" Back to me still, she whips the dress from the board and holds it up for her own inspection.

"I mean that there are so many ways of lying, apart from words, especially where marriage is concerned. I think it would be better if we just kept it between you and me."

"There's lying and there's telling the truth, especially where marriage is concerned!"

This strikes a false note. She is not speaking to me as she must speak to me because I am not speaking to her as I must speak to her. I tap my ash into the fishbowl while she takes a copper wire hanger and buttons the now-perfect dress onto it at the nape. With one hand she holds the hook and with the thumb of the other she flicks one neat flick at the button while index and middle finger spread the hand bound buttonhole and the button pops into place. I can see the gesture with magical clarity; I can do it myself. Once when I was caught playing doctor in the tamaracks with crippled Walter Wesch she sat me in the basin and spread my bald pink *mons veneris* with the same two fingers, soaping with the flick of her thumb, scourging me with her tongue in terms of Jesus and germs.

"Mama, look," I say, "the reason I *want* to do this—try to understand—is that I want to tell the truth. I want to capture you ... as you really are." I squirm on the plastic, hair hot at the nape, and add despairingly, "As a *person*."

Does she say, "Hah!"?

"I've tried before, and you come out distorted. I know you're a remarkable person...."

Now she is doing one of Daddy's Arrow shirts, a plain white one with a narrow stitched collar. The point of the iron faces one point of the collar, then the other. The long strong far hand stretches against the stitching so the hot collar lies perfectly flat without any of the tiny corrugations that even a laundry leaves these days. I can do this. My two sons can do it.

She turns again, one eyebrow raised and a mocking smile, "What, then, am I the most unforgettable character you've met?"

Not like her, neither the eyebrow nor the words, which have the cadence of a British education. I'm the one with the British education. I try again. She turns back like the film run backwards, the point of the iron faces one point of the collar, then the other, she stretches with the strong far hand, the bones of which she has never seen, and turns again robot-like, profile gashed with a smile, "Honey, write for the *masses*. People need to *escape*. They need to *laugh*."

This is closer. My fist is too big to go into the goldfish bowl and I have no way to stub out my cigarette. I have to hold it while it burns down to the filter and out. So it turns out to be me who says brightly, "Okay, why don't I do you up as The Most Unforgettable Character I've Met?"

To which, against my will, try as I might, she replies, "Why me? Hah, hah, there are plenty of fish in the sea."

"No!" I slam the bowl down dangerously, but it doesn't break. How could it, when it houses the goldfish next to the calendar on the window sill? Dangerously shrill, I say, "That's exactly what I don't want you to say!"

She hands me a shirt out of the basket, a blue one with the same narrow Arrow collar; I understand that I'm supposed to sprinkle it. I fetch a pan from under the stove and fill it with warm water, holding the hot cigarette in the hand that turns on the tap. I run water over the filter, which sizzles, and reach for the garbage bin under the sink, ashamed because my back is to her now and I am doing this in full view. The bin is of the step-on sort, chrome lid on a white cylinder adorned with a bow-tied posy of photographically exact nasturtiums. *Nasty urchums*, Bud and I used to call them in the sandbox years, though I don't remember if we dared to say this in front of Mama. I toss the cigarette in the bin and, when the lid slams, curb the impulse to take the garbage out.

My last love affair was trashed over the question of taking out the garbage. It's a common story. He said, "What can I do to help?" and I said, "Thanks, I'd appreciate it if you took out the garbage." He said, "It makes no sense to take it out now; it isn't full. Do you want the sausage sliced or mashed?" I did not want the sausage sliced or mashed, and so, forcefully, I said, "The garbage." He said, "What are you on about?" and I was, I admit, a trifle eloquent; it's my job. I put myself in the hysterical stance and he put himself in the imperturbable stance, but it was he who slammed out and that was that. It's common. My mother used to say: common as an old shoe. She meant it for praise, of people who didn't stand on their dignity.

I carry the pan back to the table. "D'you remember when Bud came up the phrase, 'Mama's Homey Canned Platitudes'?"

At this she swashbuckles; the whole haw-haw comes out and I can hear it from the bottom of her lungs but cannot look at her again because she misses the point; she can laugh at herself but she doesn't know there was real grief in it for us, Bud and me, to whom honesty comes so hard except for money. All I can look at is the linoleum, which is annoyingly and irreverently clear, the black outlines of rectangles on a flecked grey ground, the absurdly marbled feather shapes at the upper left corner of each rectangle: it is not the linoleum I want to see.

"Look, you don't understand," I stumble, splashing points of warm water from the pan to the shirt on the table, each spot an instant deeper blue as if I were splashing paint. "The point is that it's become a kind of platitude for us, Bud and me. It's easy to remember your cliches but they prevent us from remembering you; they only conceal something we never saw because we were kids and kids have to . . . see . . ."

The telephone rings rescuingly. She crosses from the ironing board to the phone, which she pulls through the little sliding door that my dad designed and made so that it, the phone, can be both reached from and closed into both the kitchen and the den; she answers, "Hello?" and swashbuckles the laugh. How can it be that the laugh is false and the pleasure genuine? Can I do this myself? "Why, Lloyd!"

It's the preacher, then. As she stands at the telephone I notice what she wears, which is a green cotton cap-sleeved house smock edged in black piping, sent her one Christmas by Uncle Jack and Aunt Louellen and which has, machine embroidered over the flat left breast, a black poodle dog with a rhinestone stud for an eye. I can see this though her back is to me, and I can see the sharp shadow of the wingblades underneath the cotton, the bones she has never seen. I cannot see her face.

"Lloyd Gruber, how nice of you to call! Oh, as well as can be expected for an old lady, haw haw. Yes, she's home, fat and sassy, you know she's got another book out and she's on a *tour*, well, I wouldn't want to tell you I'd pass it around in the Women's Society for Christian Service but you know it's *those* words that sell nowadays. What? Oh, no, that broke up ages ago. Why, Lloyd, I'm not the least bit worried about her, you know I was twenty-three myself before I married, yes I was, she's a spring chicken. . . ."

"*Mama!*"

Discouragement appears on me as wrinkles in the elbows of the Galway tweed. My mother can embarrass clerks in Kress' five-and-dime. I leave the rolled shirt on the table and escape to the dining room, eight thousand miniature distortions of the sterile orange tree outside, a bough bobbing under the weight of its puckered fruit. I can taste the acrid taste of these oranges from the time Bud tricked me into lagging a tongue across the wet pebbles of their useless flesh. I think I have changed my mind. I think I will simply cross the living room and thread my way down between the zinnias that line the walk...

But there she is, crossing toward the living room herself, with the dress and the shirt flapping from the hooks over her hand. She is there, of course, because she is the pushmi-pullyu of the psychic Midlands. If I go to touch her she will recoil, but if I walk away she will be at my heels. I can do this, too. Somewhere are two teenaged boys and a half dozen former husbands and lovers who will attest that I can do it, too.

She has hooked the hangers on the knob of the corner cupboard to inspect a possible inch of misturned eyelet, a possible crease in the French seam of the Arrow armhole. She says, "Now *what* is it you want, honey?"

Home is the place where, when you have to go there, they don't understand why you've come.

"I want to put you in a story," I say evenly.

Back to me she presses a hand over her stomach, she makes a little clucking sound of pain, her back arches in the instinctive position of a Martha Graham contraction and releases, rolling upward from the flat buttocks that I do not mention in her presence. I will not mention Martha Graham, Martha Quest, Billy Graham, Billy Pilgrim, Janet Pilgrim. I may mention graham crackers.

"Sissy, I don't want to fight with you."

"Not a real fight, mom. That's just a device to get us started. What I really want to do is catch your essential..."

The ironing has apparently passed muster because she picks up the two hangers again and carries on through the living room. The grape-cluster pattern of the threadbare carpet passes before my eyes, the inset knickknack shelf that my father made, the gilded miniature watering can that I broke on the way home from the fourth grade hobby fair and lied about; the big blond console TV that can't have appeared before I was in high school; the bookcase with *Hurlbut's Stories of the Bible* and the complete works of Edgar Guest. I follow at her heels, black patent Cuban heels, from which emerge the graceful corrugations of the quadruple-A ankles she is so proud of and of which, having the same ankles in spite of my big bone structure, I am so proud. We pass the bulbous, sagging couch, the oversized chartreuse fronds and magenta flowers on the slipcovers that she produced in an awesome lapse of taste, the impossible flowers into which I flung my hot face on the occasion of my first heartbreak: Ace Johnson, yearbook editor, senior class counselor, and jilt. My face sizzles in the flowers as she pronounces the phrases of impossible misunderstanding: "Why, sissy, cheer up, haw, haw, there'll be another one along in a minute; there are plenty of fish in the sea."

My elder son is on a boat, seeking discipline and the romance of comraderie. My younger son is the lead singer in a band called Beloved Children, which plays in bars he is legally too young to enter. I am on occasion invited to hear this group, and I do. I sit wondering at the sweet demonic presence of these children, who wail a noise that I like and envy. As a girl I knew nothing better to do than sit a sizzling wallflower and pray that someone would ask me to dance. The Beloved Children crop their heads and embrace freakdom. One of their lyrics praises masturbation, "the central occupation, generation to generation," but they do not have the courage of their erections because one by one the members of the band come by to warn me that I will be shocked. To which generation do they think I belong? I politely assure them that I can take it.

Now we're into the hall, the cupboard where the Bible and the Ansco camera are kept, the laundry cupboard that my father designed so you could put the clothes in from the bathroom or the hall and which we called a chute though nothing chutes from anywhere to anywhere.

"Let me tell you about something," I say, hurrying after her. The trouser suit is an insane thing to be wearing in this heat, long sleeved and cuffed, lined and turtled at the neck. My hot hair prickles; I was thirty-four and living in England before I had the courage to assert to her that I could wear my hair straight and long. "Once I went back to a house I'd lived in years before. Not this house, you understand, some other house. I went back, and it hadn't been sold, the real estate market was bad, and it was a white elephant of a house, so it was being rented, and a lot of my old things were still there. I went in, the tenant was very nice, and we fell into conversation, and I lit a cigarette..."

I wish I hadn't got into this. I remember the first time she caught me with a cigarette, she and Daddy together, and Daddy said, "Aha! Caughtcha!" but Mama said, "You're trying to kill me!" She hangs the dress and the shirt, both, in the long closet with the sliding doors, which makes a kind of sense because when I was five this was my room but later it was hers and Daddy's, and I see from the set of her shoulders that she has drawn in her chin, but I don't know if it's because I mentioned a cigarette or not.

"He set an ashtray in front of me. It was a cheap, simple glass ashtray in the shape of a spade, like the ace of spades."

She probes her stomach. I think she sighs again.

"I'd bought a set of those ashtrays in a little country market some dozen years before and had used them daily for—what?—four or five years—and in the intervening time I had not thought of them once, they did not form any part of my memory. When he set this one down I flicked my ash in it, and I recognized the way the cigarette sounded on the edge of the glass."

She is at the bureau with her back to me, her face averted even from the round rimless mirror, and she begins to lay out things from the drawer, as if for my inspection: the ebony-handled nail buffer, the little pot of waxy rouge that I once stole and lied about, the porcelain doll that sits now on the sill to the left of my typewriter in my house in Florida.

"I was flooded with a whole sense of the reality of that house, and of my life there. I know I'm not explaining myself very well." And I'm not, but I'm not going to make any reference to Proust. "I was homesick, Mama."

She slides the nail buffer along the bureau top toward the window sill where the oleanders nod. The milk of the oleander leaves is poison, Bud and I were taught, as I later taught my boys that the pods of the laburnum were poison, in the garden of the English house that held the glass spade ashtray.

"There's a story," I blurt, inspired, "by John Cheever. In which one of the characters says that fifty percent of the people in the world are homesick all the time."

"Which marriage was that?" she asks, and smiles at me in the mirror while she is putting on her vermilion lipstick so that her mouth is stretched and distorted over the cartilage and the bones.

"Which marriage was what?"

"In that house." She takes out the powder box decorated in peach-colored feathers and opens it in a minor explosion of peach-colored ash, arranges it in front of the buffer, the pot, the doll on my windowsill beside the calendar and the goldfish. It was indiscreet to use a name she doesn't know. I should have quoted Edgar Guest, how it takes a heap o' livin' to be homesick all the time. I should have said that Jesus said life is one long longing to go home.

"Which marriage was it in that house?"

"My first. Look, what I'm trying to say. . . Mama, sometimes—usually when I'm driving, for some reason—I think about something that has happened in my life, good or bad, and I think, 'I can't wait to tell Mom,' or else I think, 'I can't tell Mom. . . .'

And suddenly I am driving alone the street toward my house in Florida; my third marriage has collapsed although it has not yet occurred, or my dozenth affair although I don't know with whom, and into the angst of its collapse comes the shame, *I can't tell Mom. . . .*

"And then," I say, "it's like waking up from a dream, a good dream

ALMA MAY MILNER BURROWAY

or a nightmare, the sadness or the relief. Do you understand?"

Facing herself in the mirror she places a finger on her nose and deforms it slightly to the right while with the index finger of her same hand pressing downward and the other index finger pressing upward, she produces from her pores several dozen live curling worms of ivory-colored wax. I avert my eyes in the old embarrassment and then in the old fascination focus again on the one specific section of the mirror where she places a finger of the other hand on her nose and deforms it slightly to the left. Everyone who grew up in America in the fifties can do this too.

"*Will* you understand?"

She takes the puff and dabs the peach-colored ash over her nose and cheeks. Minute clogs of powder catch in the emptied pores. She smiles at herself in the mirror, chin tilted, a smile for the PTA or the Women's Society for Christian Service, and as I avert my eyes in the old embarrassment she says, nasal on the vowels, "All I want is your happiness, sissy."

I put my head in my hands. Through my fingers I can see the knees of my trouser suit, baggy and crushed, with the stains of crushed grass on them. My hair is hot and heavy. I will confess to her. I confess, "Nobody knows better than I do how hard it is to make words say what you mean. But it's taken me all these years to know it was just as hard for you."

"All I *ever* wanted was your happiness," she says for the PTA.

"It's not so!" I adjust my tone and say more successfully, "It isn't so." I go to her and try to take her insubstantial shoulders, try to force her toward the mirror and the crossed lower incisors, but am uncertain whether I see her grimace or mine, the powder in her pores or mine. "You wanted me to be happy your way, by your rules: don't smoke, don't wear pink with red, marriage is sacred, the wages of sin. . . . And the truth is you were holding onto a bunch of phrases just like me. You knew they didn't work. The truth is. . . ."

The truth is that my elder son is a romantic militarist and my younger a punk rocker. I laugh to my friends: I don't know where they came from! But I know at least one place they are headed, somewhere years hence, to seek for themselves why they are so much, and so threateningly, me.

"Mommy isn't feeling very well, dear. I think the old ulcer is acting up again."

"Don't go to bed. Please don't go to bed."

But she is out of the smock, which she hangs on the brass hook over the shelf of shoes. She raises a modest and protective hand to her collar bone above the peach satin slip, over the rosily mottled V of flesh below the collarbone she has never seen.

"Don't go to bed!" I say. "It doesn't fool me, I can do it, too. It's a way of getting what you want without asking for it, you've got ulcers and high blood pressure and adrenalin flux, I've got a fibrolated coccyx and chronic otitis and atopic dermatitis, it doesn't fool me, Mama. I can do it, too."

But I notice that my trouser suit is also gone; it has disappeared from my body as abruptly as it disappeared from the parked station wagon in New York in 1972. I am standing in nothing but my ivory satin teddy. My hand goes to my collarbone and the mottled V of flesh. She reaches into her end of the closet for the polished cotton housecoat in stripes of pink and grey sent to her one Christmas by Uncle Jack and Aunt Louellen; she sizzles the zipper up, and I reach into my—later Daddy's—end of the closet for the puffed-sleeved pansy dress, which I disengage from the hanger with a deft flick of my thumb at the button at the nape and of course it does not fit; it binds at the armholes and breast, its handstitched hem is above my knees; and yet, it fits so much better than it ought.

"Would you get me some milk, sweetie? Funny thing, I always hated milk, and now it's the one thing I can have for my ulcer."

"Don't go to bed."

But she slips under the rose chenille bedspread and lays her tight poodle cut back on the pillow, producing minute wrinkles in the perfectly ironed pink pillowcase, smiling with eyes closed, arms folded over her flat breast. I pull the puffed footstool to her and sit clumsily, crushing the pima pansies as I try to cover my knees, which are stained with grass and tamarack.

"There'll be a brighter day tomorrow," I am almost sure she says. On the nightstand is the photo of her taken on the morning of her wedding day, which now sits beside the doll in my house in Florida. Distractedly I tap my ash; the goldfish attacks it for food. In the photograph she stands beside a mirror in a simple twenties shift of pintucked chiffon, her hair marcelled into a shelf so that the profile is half obscured and the mirror image is full-faced, the strand of pearls breaking over the collarbones, the mouth pensive and provocative, the eyes deeply sad. Daddy used to call them bedroom eyes.

"Mama, look at me."

"Sissy, let me tell you, there are so many people in the world worse off than we are."

"Oh, Jesus, Mama, the starving in China, the man who had no feet."

"Don't take the name of the Lord in vain."

"It's the way I talk, for Christ's sake."

"No child of mine ever talked that way!"

"Don't be an ass, Mama, it's only words."

"I'll wash your mouth out for you!"

"Will you, will you?"

"It kills me to hear you talk that way."

"Does it? Then let me give you something to wash out of my fucking mouth. Daddy's remarried. He's married again!"

Her eyes have been fluttering and slit but now they open. I have got her now. She glances away and back, her smile parts on the gash of the crossed incisors.

"There are plenty of fish in the sea, haw haw!" I say.

She says, eyes averted, "Your daddy gets sweeter every day."

"Jesus Christ, don't you understand anything? I saw your bones!"

The pima dress is wrinkled, sweaty, and has sand in the pockets. It will have to be washed again and ironed again. The compressor on the air conditioner will have to be replaced again. "We carried your ashes up to the top of Marble Mountain, Daddy and I, we flung them over the quarry and the foundations of the house you lived in, over the roof of the general store. And do you know, Mama, they're rubble, the marrow looks like dry dog food. I saw the mineral in your bones, blue melted mineral in the chunks!"

Now her eyes widen, the melted hazel and amber of her eyes speak terror, and I know that mine will do this too.

"We scattered them, Daddy and I!"

"You're trying to kill me," I know she says.

"No!" I grip both her long strong hands in my own. "No, I'm trying to keep you!" I finger the veins and freckles, feel for the bones of her hands and see my own hands long and strong on the black bones of the typewriter keys. I avert my eyes. Beyond the calendar—the fish, the doll, the photo of her bedroom eyes—tropical sun slants through the azaleas, outlining the veins in their fuchsia petals. I hold her eyes.

"Let me see you, Mama!"

But the hands go limp in mine and the eyes begin to close. The lids are delicately veined. I grip her hands. "I've got you now!"

"Not altogether so," my mother says.

A thing she would never say.

Her hair is blued, purpled, and her pores have disappeared. There is an odor of pansies, oleanders, roses, orange blossoms, peach. The planes of her face have been expertly ironed. All the ruckles of her cheeks are gone, and her mouth, closed, seems fuller in repose. Deep buttoning makes symmetrical creases in the rose satin on the coffin lid. The people passing speak of her; they say: *dear soul*, and *always cheerful*, and *devoted wife and mother*, and *a lady*. Her hands, crossed, are delicate and smooth. There is about her a waxen beatitude.

I don't know how they do this, but everyone says it is an art. Everybody says they have done a splendid job. They have caught her exactly, everybody says.

ANNE LAKE PRESCOTT WAS BORN IN 1936 in New York City. Since graduating from Barnard in 1959 she has worked at the college, first as a teaching assistant and, after 1974, as a tenured professor of English. She is the happy parent of two children and two books (the second, *Imagining Rabelais in the English Renaissance*, is forthcoming from Yale University Press in 1998). She and her husband divide their time between Connecticut and New York, with occasional trips to New Jersey and Vermont to visit their new grandchildren.

MOTHER/ELEANOR

My mother, Eleanor Hard Lake, died a few hours before I was asked to write something for this volume. She was ninety-two, almost as crisp-minded as ever, and even more willful. After the risky surgery meant to save her life she refused to leave her bed at the rehabilitation center because it hurt to get up, because the operation itself, despite her consent to it, had struck her as "a foolish waste at the tag end of a long life," and mostly because she just damn well didn't want to. "She has always had a will of iron," I said apologetically to the various nurses and doctors who spoke to me with various degrees of exasperation. "Trying," one of them called her, although most who cared for her were also charmed by her grace and gallantry as death approached. "Well," said one Irish nurse when I told her that my mother's maternal family had come from County Cork, "that explains why she won't do what she's told." Toward the end she wouldn't even eat what was set so lovingly before her; I imagine she felt, although she never quite said so, that it was time to move on.

Alerted to the gravity of her situation by the wise and kind doctor who like so many had come to love her, I had raced back from New York to the town where we both lived so I could be with her. I found her with her always plain and now decaying face turned upward, the penetrating eyes shut, and the prominent nose, thinned by illness and age, pointing sharply toward the corner of the room. As I studied her, or rose to touch her and tell her I was there, or put a new disk in the CD player so she would die to music and not to the broken silence of the care center or the noise of a rented TV, she looked like a figure on the prow of a ship sailing the dark waters toward (I like to believe) some approaching and larger light. "She's putting up quite a battle," remarked the nurse who came to check on her. But some minutes later the labored breathing stopped. "She's gone," said the nurse gently in confirmation when she came to check again, and I found myself, against all my own expectation, bursting into tears. The tears were less of grief than of astonishment that she could, after all, really and truly and actually die. Even on her deathbed she had seemed permanent. If one can live for almost ninety-three years, why not forever?

She had been, unsurprisingly, the chief influence on my childhood and adolescence, from early days in Manhattan to wartime Washington (where I first learned about growing vegetables thanks to the Victory Garden program she helped run in our part of the city) to post-war Connecticut. When I was an adult, long since graduated from Barnard and reading essays by high-school students hoping to come to my alma mater, I would find touching tributes to mothers. I too owe mine a great deal. An accomplished journalist and editor, she could turn a phrase: "Whatever she wears," she once wrote of a friend, "Martha looks as though she has been gardening in a high wind," and she once remarked of ambition and its disappointments that "after all, most of us are destined to play in the outfield of life." She taught me how to make pot roast, how to read out loud, how to pick the suckers off tomatoes; she even paid me hard cash to memorize poems I can still recite. And in her role as a journalist she taught me to strive for clarity and precision, not for sesquipedalian pomposity or obfuscation. When she read my prose she would halt at such words as "heuristic" or "hermeneutics," although she knew what they meant, and under her stern editorial eye and poised blue pencil I would feel I had to justify them or send them crawling away on their overgrown syllables. An editor at The Reader's Digest Condensed Books (and a reader for that organization until she died), she passed on to me a taste for landscaping prose—any prose, including my own—by pruning prepositional phrases, uprooting repetition, draining verbal overflow, planting fresher metaphors, shooing away weasel words, and bringing relief to sentences lying prostrate under the weight of passive verbs.

I was glad that she so loved my husband, our children and our grandbabies, that she took such pride in my brother Tony and my sister Lydia, and that she produced among those who knew her such sustained admiration and love. When she died I got letters or calls from the tearful minister, the woman in charge of finding jobs for local high school students, the grieving doctor, old classmates from Smith, former servants, an articulate young woman who had been one in a long series of teenagers hired to run errands (she was always getting postcards from them with news about school, travel, marriage), the retired grocer at whose store we had long shopped, and even the President (although, to be sure, only because my brother had worked for him).

And yet ... what a difference between so many of the essays I have read by Barnard students and my own feelings! You probably cannot be from the class of 1959 and think about your mother with a rush of unmodified love and gratitude on the one hand or, as a classmate put it to me recently, with a rush of battery acid such as she would have sensed two decades ago. Time eats everything except, perhaps, ambivalence. That it lets grow and grow. There is the personal ambivalence bred by the inevitable confusions of daughter-hood: the suspicion one is being misread (no, I'm not that person, the one you want and think I might somehow be—I'm somebody else, somebody who will never be the belle of the ball, the soft one, the easy-going one, the nice one, or even the one who remembers to empty the dishwasher; can't you hear me, see me, as I really am?). An old tale, that, and often told. More specific to some of the class of 1959, I think, is a moment in history that must have had an impact on how we related to our mothers. There had been a time before World War II when many women, especially the sort whose daughters might go to Barnard, had jobs, adopted liberal or radical causes, and, as P.G. Wodehouse phrased it somewhere, would "step out high, wide, and plentiful." My mother, after all, had been a flapper in the 1920s, had worked for Fortune and been offered a job as editor of *Life* magazine's "*Life* Goes to a . . ." series, and had partied at or near the edges of the Algonquin crowd brightened by Dorothy Parker and her like.

After the war, though, many women—without, so far as I can recall, needing direct instruction by their husbands—had retrenched. My clever, talented, and determined mother, the one who had wanted to fight Hitler with her bare hands, who had helped my father perjure himself on official documents so as to rescue several Jews from Germany, who had worked for the republican side of the Spanish civil war, was now reminding me that boys like you more if you let them win at cards, that I might be more popular if I didn't speak up in class so often, and ("What's the matter, Anne, don't you *like* boys?") that I would please her more if I dressed better, did something about my hair, smiled a lot, and spent less time in the woods like some virgin goddess of the hunt. Luckily for my future happiness—and career—I did as my mother did, not as she said.

Eventually we became good if somewhat wary friends. After all, when I was still a student in college a boy did like me enough to marry me, and my bookwormishness led to a paying job at one of our top colleges. Mother was not one to quarrel with success. I have even

ELEANOR HARD LAKE

begun to look more like her—the face that peers from my latest driver's license and Barnard ID now has more Hard and less Lake. I hear her in my voice when I answer the phone (that same "social voice" I had despised for its insincerity when I was growing up) and I see her in my signature when I make those "n's" so like her own.

Yet I never fully knew my mother, and that, I think, is an aspect of the mother/daughter tragicomedy that appears most vividly only after the daughter has herself become older and, perhaps, a mother herself. Many years ago when I was going through some papers I found one of her childhood drawings: a dancer, not unlike Isadora Duncan in floating trails of gauze, moves alone through pillars, not going anywhere in particular but clearly yearning for something. There was also a fragment of prose describing a cobbler in a faraway kingdom who would gaze out of his window and tell himself, "Someday I will go there, to those distant mountains, and see what they hold." After that, when my mother was at her most irritatingly efficient or woundingly critical, I would occasionally remember even as I raged or wept that there might be another person inside her whom I might like and who was, like me, lonely and longing for something indefinable. I never dared ask to meet this other Eleanor; daughters seldom invite their mother's inner children over to play. Then, when my mother was old and I was a middle-aged professor and we were "doing lunch," as they say in New York, the time never seemed quite right to request an introduction. There would always be another day for that, I must have thought. Or did I fear that if I inquired after the girl who drew the picture and began the story I would learn that she had died young, buried beneath the wife, mother, widow, writer, editor, tomato-grower, and maker of pot roasts? I hope not. Indeed, now that it is too late for what might in any case have seemed to my mother an intrusion into her well-guarded inner world, I hope that the romantic little Eleanor I never quite met survived—still young—to ninety-two, that that she dances on, no longer alone or pained by desire, amidst what Edmund Spenser called "the pillars of Eternity," and that she has reached those mountains, and that she likes what she has found there.

ROSELLEN BROWN IS THE AWARD-WINNING AUTHOR of nine books, including four novels, three collections of poetry, and *The Rosellen Brown Reader*, a collection of short stories, essays, and poetry. For her novel *Civil Wars*, she received the Janet Kafka Heidinger Prize in literature. She currently lives in Chicago with her husband, where she teaches in the graduate writing program of the School of the Art Institute.

Dear Mama,

It's a little discouraging writing to you these days, when your mind is like a sea dotted with the tiniest green islands of memory. I'm not sure anymore what you are hearing. I'm not sure, either, what matters: the depredations of age call everything into question. Nothing I can say about it is original—how the losses make our active, striving years more valuable at the same time that they lay over everything a dense veil of futility. How I've never felt humbled by anything the way your slow dwindling has humbled me and made everything seem, yes, Ecclesiastes had it right, vanity.

So, adding up the "totals"—accomplishment, achievement, all the "a" words, starting with ambition—feels a little beside the point. You are here. You are what you are just now. A minute, since you've passed ninety, is as short or as long as it was years ago when you were the girl in that photo with a butterfly of a bow in your hair or the young woman with a baby in your arms. Only, no longer remembering that past and without much future, this moment, the present, isn't what it's cracked up to be. My brothers and I swim into your line of vision and out again. We seem to visit your awareness the way we visit the city you live in, intermittently, leaving almost no residue behind.

There isn't a lot unsaid that I feel needs saying now, and I suppose that's lucky. We never worked up a long list of recriminations, voiced or unvoiced; I never even "rebelled" in the true sense of the word— not all in a rush, visibly (by which I mean audibly!), insisting that attention be paid my grievances. I only drew away my absolute loyalty, my eagerness to agree with you, defend you to others, your sufficiency as arbiter of my taste and my desires, gradually, as my life defined itself. Early on, I think, more protective than defensive, I felt enough of what it was to *be* you, your vulnerabilities clear to me and unthreatening, that I didn't enjoy hurting you. In fact it cost me something to cause you pain, just at the point when a lot of my friends loved to turn the knife in their mothers' flesh. I don't know why I didn't feel the need; maybe I should have, maybe I'd have grown up faster? Too late to wonder.

But the "differentiation" accomplished itself willy-nilly. How could it not have come about when I lived a life so different from yours? You, Russian born, the poor girl who had to go to work after the eighth grade, at fourteen; who took courses at night school, always hungry for the education you couldn't have; who, once your first baby was born, never went to work again—the common immigrant scenario. I, the middle-class girl of my very different generation, who also did the expected, with your blessings: college, graduate school, travel. The values were yours, their fruition mine. You never understood why the women I grew up with, at least those who had children (and what was the matter with those who didn't choose to have them?), needed to work outside their homes, or even why as a writer I had to work *in* mine, my children nearby but never, from your point of view, sufficiently tended. You thought it was wonderful that I wrote and published and won prizes but you searched, always, for proofs of my maternal derelictions. I remember once, angry, telling you that I wouldn't let you take pride in my achievements if you wouldn't respect what it took to accomplish them.

It was not your experience to need such accomplishments for yourself, however. Even though it was clear to me that, given your energy and acuity, born in a later generation you'd have been right up there with the high achievers, I've never been able to make it very clear to you that if you send women to college, they will likely want (either early or late) to use their educations in the world. You didn't have the tools to understand that—with some notable exceptions we are only the children of our times.

But here's the crazy thing: You should have been the writer in the family.

You are the one with the most audacious talent, the ability to leap, to make undreamed-of connections, to work your way through the most complex and rewarding syntactical branchings. (Eighth-grade educations were worth more in those days.) Your writing's got rhythm, vision, smarts—I use the present tense: it's too painful not to. I've never seen a natural gift like yours, though all of it went into letters and, for one short period, into a volunteer organization newsletter whose editorials you sweated out as if they were meant for the Op Ed page of the *New York Times*.

And you—you disparaged that talent as I finally learned you disparaged so much in yourself, and I don't know why. When it came to your remarkable verbal gifts, the first and easiest thing was for you to bow in deference to my father, who had a fine way with light verse. He published letters to the editor on political controversies and clever poems in the New York newspapers around the time of the end of World War I, and he sent you marvelous, witty love poems. Supple and funny but never profound, they were crowded with what we always called the "fifty-cent words" of a self-taught man who also never went to high school (though few would have guessed it) but who grew up on the formal rhetoric of the early century. "Oh, Daddy's the one who can write," you'd say, laughing, "not me." But always, when you said "Who, me?" so dismissively, I could see your eyes shine with a kind of wonder, a hunger for praise, a delight at the compliment. You loved it that I, your writer daughter, could insist on your serious talent but you never took it in, never made it part of yourself. "I always had such respect for the real writers, the ones I read, that I never allowed myself to think I could do what they did!" you'd say. "I was never deserving...."

Nor were you deserving, in your mind, of a lot of things. Once, I remember, though I can't recall the specific thing you were speaking about, your eyes filled with tears as you told me how you never thought you had the right to—and here my memory fails me. (The memoirist never admits to a forgotten climax to a story, but I'm no memoirist.)

It may have had something to do with daring to go to the head of the supermarket line with a single stick of butter—something like that, some instance of a poisonous, self-destroying modesty that appeared to come down over your whole being like a sack that closed around you and wouldn't let you breathe. I remember thinking that my own, and my own children's, lack of boldness began right there in that panicky self-obliteration.

I asked you why you thought you didn't deserve more—in the small claims and the large, I meant—and you couldn't tell me why. One of your sisters, you always said with awe, was very intelligent, the other very beautiful, but in spite of that you were your father's favorite and the only one of them who really lived a fulfilled and relatively happy (though extremely sheltered) life. Why did you think you deserved so little? What did you miss along the way of ego-strengthening self-respect that builds daring the way early fluoride builds strong teeth?

If your unschooled adolescence made you self-conscious, I never saw that; most of your girlfriends also lacked formal schooling. But I often wondered if your shaky, even willful, reasoning might have been disciplined by a longer education. Your lack of trust, for example, in scientific method led you into bizarre assertions about how the body works—you treated cause and effect, when it suited you, as a casual, even a foolish, fiction. But that's not the kind of mystery one ever solves—there are no controlled experiments to answer it.

Or was it really, as you liked to describe it, too scrupulous an over-valuing of others, those you knew and those distant luminaries like the writers you didn't dream you could emulate?

Fortunately for me, I am not so scrupulous and have written in the face of a lifetime of my betters, innocently clamoring to join them. But the mystery, Mother, that has already disappeared into the diffusion of your memory, is not so much why you never had the will to use your talent—there are plenty of people who are good at something: dancing, singing, puzzle-solving, high jumping, yet have no desire to put it to formal use. But you, whose will was always so vigorous, who kept our family moving and harmonious in a hundred ways, why did you feel you deserved so little for yourself? Your timidity, though you seemed bold, I suspect, to others, made you a Mrs. Bridge, the Kansas City matron in Evan Connell's devastating novel— a woman who shivered at the need to make choices, indecisive, prey to the opinions and accusations of others with or without merit. You lost sleep over every purchase—we used to laugh at the memory of having found you once at three o'clock in the morning, sitting halfway down the stairs considering a chair you'd just bought—and, of course, it went back to the store the next day. More painfully, you took to heart every unkind thing anyone ever said to you and harbored it close to your heart, guilty beyond anyone's defending.

The paradox of ambition, of course, is that no one can maintain with perfect certainty what it is that will make us happy in our lives. By my standards, you could have used your enormous gifts to more satisfying advantage. Yet you—you continued to insist, you insisted even recently in one of the brief remissions of the sleep you seem to be practicing for the longest sleep of all, that one of your greatest accomplishments was simply having me, as if I was the pot of gold at the end of the rainbow. But it's been one of the best gifts any mother could have bestowed for me to have grown up on this story that you loved to tell and retell: How, after you'd given birth to two boys and desperately wanted a girl, your doctor bet you a bottle of champagne that I'd be your girl. How, coming up out of the anaesthetic they used so prodigally back then, you heard the nurses murmuring, "Oh, Mrs. Brown loses!" How you struggled through the mists of semiconsciousness to remember that this time losing meant winning—how joyously you put it all together and knew you had your girl. That story was like a fairy godmother's blessing on my head, and it protected me all through my childhood from the slightest envy of my older brothers.

This is the now-mythologized tale you whispered to me, eyes misting over, from your bed when I saw you last time. (It alternates with the set-piece tale of how you met my father one bewitched weekend in the country and then and there changed your name from Bertha, which had been the corruption of your Yiddish name, Blume, to Blossom, which was its far more palatable translation.) How dare I try to define for you what ought to have been your need, your satisfaction? I suppose I should be grateful for the writing gene, and the family gene, and the will you used on so many other things, but which I've combined with your love of words and made my work life. If I wish you'd had both, family and work, it's because, loving and admiring you, I wish I could have seen what you'd have made of your intersection with the world. The wish may be anachronistic, but I can still think it would have been a good encounter.

Meanwhile, how complex you continue to be, even in this limbo without much memory of what you've said three minutes ago. When we were settling you into the nursing home where you live now, after another confrontation with your many incapacities I said to you without much hope (two nurses standing at the foot of your bed intro-

BLOSSOM (LIEBERMAN) BROWN, 1930

ducing themselves), "Mom, while they're here, do you have anything you want to ask them?"

And you, gazing out the window, not at a loss for words or for syntax more complex than most can handle at the height of their powers, said contemplatively, smiling a little, "Well, I don't suppose I can ask them if it would be possible for anyone to make a sky lovelier than that!"

No, I said, I guess you can't. What a writer you would have been, Mama, if you'd wanted to, or dared to, or, like your stubborn daughter, needed to be one.

With all my love,
Rosellen

NANCY KLINE IS THE AUTHOR OF, among other books, *The Faithful, Lightning: The Poetry of René Char*, and *Elizabeth Blackwell: A Doctor's Triumph*. Her short stories, essays, and translations have appeared widely. She is a recipient of a National Endowment for the Arts Creative Writing grant, and has been a finalist in playwriting and in nonfiction in the Massachusetts Artists Fellowship Competition. She is the director of the Writing Program at Barnard College and is currently at work on her next novel whose working title is *The Mother Lode*.

OUT OF TIME

My eighty-seven-year-old mother is singing me off-color French songs.

It is almost noon. We two are seated on my parents' deck in the late June sun.

"Ah, vous dirai-je, Maman—?" she sings, her slim voice as quavery as the oriole's, her feathery hair a fragile shade lighter than the sunlight, palest yellow, white.

"Au clair de la lune, mon ami Pierrot—" sings my mother. "Or there was one, how did it go? In Italian. They always asked me to sing it at parties." She hums a few bars, then sings: *"Viva la figa, viva la figa!"* She pauses. "I don't speak Italian, I never knew what it meant, exactly. It was a real crowd-pleaser."

I smile at her. "What a character you are."

"Yes," she says, and looks pleased with herself. "I'm so old. People don't know what to make of me."

I laugh and turn my face up into the warmth of the summer day. "Wasn't there one about a fortune-hunter?"

"The one who marries the rich old maid!"

And my mother launches into the ballad of their wedding night. She takes off her clothes. She turns off her hearing-aid. She takes out her teeth. She takes off her wig. She takes out her eyeball and puts it in a glass of water.

"I'm becoming her," my mother says.

"No you're not."

"Well, my parts are certainly wearing out. And your father's."

Daddy has driven into town, despite his cataracts, to get the Sunday papers. This late morning moment is my mother's and my own.

"How is he?" I ask.

She doesn't answer right away. Then says, "I'm furious at him."

"For dying?"

"I worry about him all the time."

"I'd like to punch him in the nose," I say.

"Yes."

His heart stopped three years ago, for a full two minutes, before they brought him back.

How can somebody you love so much cease to exist?

Despite the doctors' dark prognosis, he seems to be amazingly himself these days, just slower and slower. What isn't the same, what will never recover, is how we think about time.

We stop to listen to it now, slipping in and out between the shimmering aspen leaves, around the dark green holly bush whose branches click on one another, out beyond us, at the edge of the yellow field.

"So," my mother says, "are you still—sitting down?"

I've been meditating, recently. "Yes. Every morning."

Just the slightest whiff of disapproval floats in my direction.

Mother is a Marxist, has always been. As such, she lifts her skirts instinctively away from anything that might smack in the least of mysticism.

"I lift weights every morning," she says. She pauses, reconsiders. "Well. One weight. A two-pounder."

She flexes her left arm. Sure enough, a bump is visible beneath the poignant falling folds of wrinkled skin.

"A powerhouse!"

"Do you remember," she says, "the time we were on our way to Albany and Ben got lost—"

Daddy always gets lost on the way to Albany, it is inevitable.

"—and drove by accident into the Buddhist monastery? How appalled we all were by that lady who was bald?" She gives me a long penetrating look. "You're not planning to shave your head?"

"Not today. But Buddhism makes sense to me. I don't know why. I'm an agnostic. At best."

"You and your father," she says. Like some bad gene we share.

"He's agnostic?" I look at her speculatively.

"Actually, now that you mention it, he told me recently that he talks to God."

"He does?!" I say.

"He was on his third Rob Roy when he told me."

"What does he say to God?"

"According to him, he says," she takes a beat, then says in my father's diffident, friendly, optimistic voice, "'I hope you're there!'"

We laugh, the two of us. The tears spring to my eyes. And I'll bet to hers. But we look away from one another so as not to see. Somewhere down the road the dogs are barking.

"Would you like more coffee?" she asks.

"Sure."

She stands up and leans for a moment against the wooden railing of the deck, looking out at the fragile green mountains that rise in the distance.

"Daddy and I are both getting smaller," she remarks, scientifically. "Have you noticed?" She sounds genuinely interested in the discovery.

"I have." They are both shrinking, growing down, before my very eyes.

My internist tells me you can lose as much as an inch a decade after the age of thirty. A daunting thought, especially when your full height measures four feet eleven and three-quarters, as my mother's does.

Did.

Once, she turned to me with fire in her eyes and said, "My whole life would have been different if I'd been five feet tall!"

Now she remarks, "I have a fantasy these days."

"Oh?"

"Wouldn't it be nice," my mother says, "if we could all just get smaller and smaller until we simply, finally, disappeared?"

Fifty is coming, my fifty, I am living out my fiftieth year right now, and though I struggle not to feel this as a desert, I do. I feel it as a loss, a starkness: I have lived more than half my life, it's gone, how is that possible? Where is everybody going so fast? Running out of time.

I have no patience with this feeling, but it gusts around the edges of my life right now, like driving across the desert, buffeted abruptly by high winds you cannot see. The car swerves suddenly, unnervingly. I take hold of the steering wheel so hard my knuckles whiten.

One of the knuckles on my right hand is arthritic. I have my mother's arthritis, as she had her father's at my age.

My son asks if am I going through a midlife crisis. Well yes. But what is that?

He called me on the phone last night.

He is driving across the country this week, back to the East Coast from the West Coast, where he goes to college. He is heading to his grandparents' house, to spend the weekend. By prior agreement, he telephones every two days. On my nickel, of course.

"Hi, Mom," Gabriel said, last night. "The Rockies were awesome."

"Where are you now, Sweetie Pie?"

"Missouri," he said.

"How's Missouri?"

"Endless."

"Don't fall asleep at the wheel!"

"Be cool," he said.

I took a deep breath. "Oh all right. I'll let you be a grown-up."

Gabriel said, in my voice, my cadence, he didn't miss a beat, "But, who will worry? If I don't?"

I laughed. "I'm glad we understand each other."

We have the same hair too. At a certain crisis moment in the hair-cut cycle, our dark curls abruptly spring out away from our heads in exactly the same wild shape and pattern, like a formal hedge gone haywire. We are both known for this. His best friend calls him Fuzzy; mine calls me something even worse. The last time Gabriel came home, before visiting his father's barber, he put on my eyeglasses and smiled a middle-aged smile for the camera. If he'd flashed my passport at the Frequent Flyer desk, they'd have awarded him my miles.

This isn't always easy. Gabriel is majoring in Psych and feels the need to tell me, every time he calls, about his need to separate.

"I'm very angry at you," he explains, in a neutral psychoanalytic tone of voice. "I love you enough to tell you that. I'm really furious at you, for the divorce."

His father and I were divorced ten years ago.

"Still?" I say.

"There's no time in the unconscious."

"How about Henry?" I inquire. "Are you mad at him?"

"No, Dad and I don't have enough of a relationship yet. The day I know he loves me, I'll get angry at him. I'm working on it right now. That's why I have to spend more time with him than you this summer."

"Because you and I like each other."

"Yes."

"That's why we can't spend more time together and you're mad at me."

"You got it."

"Great."

After conversations like this one, I seek my parents out to apologize for having been so irritating all these years.

"Mom?" said Gabriel, last night.

"Yes?"

"Where's the Mississippi River?"

"Somewhere along in there," I said.

Geography has never been my strong suit, or his.

He will have found it—crossed it—by this afternoon.

Imagine. My firstborn child is driving a car, all by himself, across the United States of America. So he'll have time to think, as he explains it.

It wasn't till we'd hung up that I suddenly remembered I was his age when I sailed for France. I crossed the ocean, I had a life at twenty.

He has a life, my son. Astonishing.

I found myself singing Woody Guthrie:

Passing through, passing through!
Sometimes happy, sometimes blue,
Glad that I ran into you!
I'm so happy that I met you passing through!

Then burst into tears.

Because it turns out our children are just house guests, visitors in our lives. When they arrive, and for a long time after that, they seem so permanent, all interwoven. An illusion. They prove themselves to be the man who came to dinner. One day, years after we've forgotten how to have a private life, they graduate from high school and they're gone. The population shifts, another room becomes available.

It felt to me last night as though my son had driven through my life and out the other side—like that tunnel you can take straight through the Alps—as though the whole time I was under the illusion he was stationary, he was really moving.

And right on his heels my seventeen-year-old. Lovely Miranda. Watch her dust.

In another year my daughter will go away to college. This year, she is taking her SATs, and dieting.

"I'm so fat!" she is always lamenting, and believing it. "Just look at me!"

She is gorgeous. She has the breasts I've always wanted, she is tall and slim, her wavy blonde hair falls in a cascade around her shoulders.

"Disgusting," she says belligerently, into the full-length mirror.

Just last week, she managed, one night, right after we'd gone out for Chinese food, to get into the dress she'd worn three years before, to her eighth grade graduation dance.

The dress was a little tight.

"Mom?"

The problem is that I'm her mother. There's not one thing I can say to her that won't misfire. So I try to keep my mouth shut.

"Mom?"

Good luck.

"What?"

"Am I fat?"

I was lying on my bed, attempting to digest my moo shoo pork.

"No."

"Are you sure?"

"You look great."

"I can hardly close this zipper."

"Maybe that's because you were a child when you bought that dress."

"So?"

"So you're not, now. You're four inches taller. You've changed shape. In addition to which, you've just eaten Special Diet Steamed Vegetables with Rice."

"But I have such fat thighs! They're disgusting—look at them!"

"They're not," I said, and tried to banish the image from my mind's eye of my wavery own. I never thought that I'd be jealous of such things, not me. I'm not that kind of mother.

I'm green with envy.

"And my butt!" Miranda said.

"It's just right," I said.

"You're just saying that. Look at it! It's fat!"

"It's not."

"And my calves!"

"They're beautiful."

"They're not!"

And then I blew it. "Go for a run, if you feel that way."

"See!" My daughter whirled around to face me. "I knew it, I am fat, you were lying all the time, I'm going on a diet, I'm fasting, I won't eat anything ever again!"

"Miranda," I said, "could you do this in your own room for a while?"

Sometimes, of course, we go shopping together. We stop for a salad and iced coffee. We cross the Park to look at the Impressionists. "Cezanne," I say. "Monet," she says. We rendezvous at Van Gogh's sunflowers.

On the other hand, I am sometimes the most embarrassing mother in the East:

"How could you call me 'Snooky' in front of my friends?!"

Slamming out of the kitchen.

"Mother. You're not going to wear those pants. Are you? They're practically bell-bottoms!"

Then there are more complicated moments still, when looking at me she sees some distorted, funhouse image of herself, and she strikes out to smash the both of us. She calls me names, she judges my life. We are both raging, shouting, hurt. We hate each other.

Half an hour later, Dr. Jekyll is back.

She makes a batch of popcorn in her hot-air popcorn popper, sans butter, sans salt, sans everything, and we watch a rerun of *The Brady Bunch* together.

And vice-versa.

Sometimes I find myself in such a fury of dislike for her—her narcissism, her impatience, her opinions—that I want to pummel her out of existence. Until I suddenly realize it is myself I am looking at, unmediated. Excruciating.

I hope when this part is through that Miranda and I will choose to be friends. Already she knows things that I don't know. Like her brother before her, she is outdistancing me. Impassioned about the structures of government, she reads me essays I don't understand about the Constitution, then explains them. I expect she'll be a lawyer. Or an opera singer. She will not be me, that much is clear. Sometimes.

Sometimes, despite our twin confusion, it is obvious to both of us that we are not identical. Then we forgive each other.

What a roller coaster ride, and the two of us hanging on by our fingernails.

A door slams somewhere in my mother's house.

"Your granddaughter must be up," I say.

It is now high noon, which seems to register as early morning on her internal adolescent clock.

My mother turns toward me. "Miranda's very tall," she says, accusingly.

"Don't look at me," I say.

I'm five foot one, my mother's daughter. And shrinking.

"She has her father's height," I say. "But she's really not, you know. Very tall. Her generation is huge. She's only five foot seven."

Out onto the sunlit deck steps a blinking Miranda, still fluffy and bewildered with sleep. She is wearing orange boxer shorts with Princeton Princeton Princeton written all over them and a maroon Wisconsin T-shirt featuring a vicious badger.

"Good morning," we say.

"Hi," she says, and plops into a chair.

My mother's pale blonde skin has leapt me like a forest fire, tree-top to treetop, to settle on my blonde fair daughter. I have my father's darker skin, but they look alike, my mother and my daughter, except for the disparity in their heights. Two blue-eyed blondes whose chromosomes have floated to the surface in that dreamy milky complexion.

Not that I covet such skin, which has caused my mother such grief.

"Did you put on fifteen?" I say to Miranda, who groans in response.

The damage was done to my mother in her early childhood, when her family lived for four years out in Colorado. There was no fifteen then. The sun burned down around her daily, monthly, four years' worth of fire to make her skin blaze, incandescent, unprotected. And then, at the other end of her life, to make the cancers bloom. Small growths, nothing to write home about, they appeared when she was in her fifties—two on her back, one a few years later on the back of her left hand, then two at five year intervals on her arms. These were removed each time without fanfare, to leave white scars not nearly so dramatic as the other colorful benign bumps she'd begun to sprout, with age.

One day, when she was seventy, she saw a spot that didn't look right, midway up the fine firm bridge of what she called her Alcott nose. My daughter has inherited that too.

"I'll have to have this spot removed," my mother said, but refused to be accompanied to the hospital. "He told me it would take an hour," she explained. "Then I get in a cab and come home."

Had she foreseen the truth, she would still have objected to company. She does not ask for help. Her blood is too proud for that, too Puritan. Her mother, my grandmother, moved out to the frontier in a covered wagon as a child. When she was my daughter's age, she taught in a one-room schoolhouse, where her older students, great big frontiersmen, ruffians, all chewed tobacco in class and spat the juice out on the floor. To protect her long skirts, my grandmother drew a huge chalk circle around herself, into which her pupils were forbidden to spit. Then she taught them how to read.

On the day my mother reported for the operation that she didn't call an operation no one came along.

"Are you okay?" I asked on the phone that night.

Her voice was changed, unrecognizable. "No," she said.

"What do you mean?"

My mother had never told me before, not ever in my life, that anything was wrong with her.

"Mother, what's the matter?"

I heard her in the silence struggling to regain control.

She said, "My nose is gone."

"What?"

"Half of it. Half of my nose is gone," she said. "They have destroyed my Alcott nose."

They had kept her ten hours in the hospital, then finally released her. In the recovery room, the nurse in charge of home care took her bandage off and had her look in the mirror: "I want you to see what it looks like, so you won't be surprised when you change the dressing."

My mother looked.

"Now, honey, you were just operated on," said the nurse. "It will heal real quick. Here's how you bandage it."

Then she told my mother she was free to go.

"Sue the bastards!" I said. "I'll be right there."

"My nose is gone," she said, dazed, incoherent.

In fact, it remained, but twisted. Violence had occurred, visible as a twisted scar with a small red puncture at its center.

She joked, "When I get the flu, it's double trouble."

Small children asked her what was wrong.

She always answered them with careful courtesy: "I had an operation," and explained, so they wouldn't be afraid.

But she was.

When we suggested reconstructive surgery she refused. And though she said, "I'm too old to care about my looks," it wasn't indifference we saw in her eyes.

And it was more than skin that was restored when finally, at eighty-two, she obeyed her family doctor when he ordered her to mend her ways—"It's affecting your sinuses," he said—and permitted a plastic surgeon to take a tiny piece of her left cheek and graft it over her scar.

When the bandages came off, she telephoned to tell me that her Alcott nose had risen from the dead.

"Hurray!" I said. "That's wonderful."

"Isn't it?!"

"Although I thought you were too old to care."

She laughed.

"At least I'll be intact for my funeral," she said.

I am always asking her lookalike grandchild if she has put on her fifteen, all over.

"Oh, Mom," my daughter's always sighing. "It takes forever!"

I tell her she might try wearing a bigger bathing suit.

Because today more of her surface area is covered than usual and the pale June sun seems mild enough, I do not press the point. Warmth filters down around the three of us, the distaff side. The men are out driving their cars.

"Guess what?" my mother says. "I discovered the meaning of second childhood last week!"

"Oh?" I say. "Uh-oh."

"What do you mean?" says Miranda, lazily. Her eyes are closed against the sun.

"It's like this," my mother says. "You see and hear and smell and feel the world around you, and in you—without relation to time. There's no past, there's no future."

The Buddhists have a name for this; it isn't second childhood.

"It was the Library Fair," she says. "Last weekend. We were walking up Tinker Street. Beautiful—late afternoon, everything sparkling and moving. Throngs, you know. Everybody in shorts: fat ladies, skinny ladies, men with knobby knees. I've never seen so many knees. Kids standing sideways in the walk, transfixed at the sight of other kids' balloons." She pauses. "One little boy stopped right in front of me and said, 'I'm almost as big as you are!'"

Miranda opens her eyes to take a look, blinks, puts a hand across her forehead like a visor.

"Then I saw," my mother says. She looks at me. "How many Library Fairs have I been to—fifty? Suddenly, last week, I saw it was the first fair I had ever felt, and the last one I would see."

"What do you mean?!" I say.

"It wasn't that I wouldn't live to see next year," she says, putting out a hand in my direction. "There was no sense of doom—it was entirely joyful. I see! I will not see like this again. The sudden sense that all of it was beautiful. And new. And would never be duplicated."

A breeze comes up, to ruffle us.

"The point is," she says, "that the beginning of life can happen even to someone at the end of it. That's the second childhood part."

"Enlightenment," I say.

"What?"

"That's what the Buddhists call it."

"Sounds very grand," she says, and shrugs it away, then takes the gesture and transforms it into the neck exercise she has been trained to do, throughout the day, for her arthritis.

Miranda, who is an exercise neurotic, watches her with interest. "How do you do that?" she asks. And the two of them launch into a joint training session.

Beyond them suddenly I see a lithe brown deer as silent as a shadow come nibbling into view, at the edge of the woods above us.

"Look!" I say.

The lovely creature raises its head to look, sees us—a frozen instant—bolts. White tail like a handkerchief. Gone.

"That was Florabelle," my mother says. "Have you met her twins yet, Miranda? Deerlet A and Deerlet B?"

Miranda laughs and stretches.

"They are the most charming, tiny replicas. They're teaching themselves to bound. We both talk to them, when they come out of the woods for lunch."

"Aren't they scared of you?" asks Miranda.

"Not a bit. They don't have the good sense of their mother. I expect to meet them on the screened-in porch any day now."

"How about the wild turkeys?" I say. "Have they come back?"

"Oh yes! As extraordinary-looking as ever."

And abruptly, my mother is up and out of her chair, all four-foot-six of her, and into her world-class impersonation of the passing flock, the male, pinheaded, fatly feathered, magnificent, a-strut, puffed-up with wild turkey testosterone, and then the faceless brood of docile, self-effacing, browny wives, who trail behind him at a distance, coughing every now and then like courtiers.

My daughter and I fall back against our chairs, filled up with laughter.

"Such bounty," Mother says, and straightens out her pale blue blouse.

In the silence that follows, we can hear the brook running over stones. It is not the season yet when all the water has dried up.

Mother says, "Our books are another bounty." She pauses. "Do you know what I found last weekend, at the 3-For-10¢-Table? A first edition of *Stuart Little.*"

POLLY EDDY KLINE

"Really?!" I say. That was my favorite book when I was very young and it was our ritual for her to read me a story every night.

Every night, when I was just beginning, when the dark had fallen, Mommy came and sat down on the edge of the itchy brown plaid blanket I had pulled up to my chin, and, when she opened the book and began to read to me, she took me to some other place. Wherever it was that Stuart Little slept in his matchbox and got lowered down the drain on a string to salvage Mrs. Little's wedding band. Wherever it was that Pooh ate too much honey and Peter Rabbit too much lettuce, wherever Captain Hook terrorized the neighborhood and fled in terror himself from the ticking of a clock.

This place my mother took me when she read to me was out of time.

She turns to her grandchild now and says, "How would you like a poached egg on toast?" As if the idea had just occurred to her.

Miranda smiles and nods.

This is their ritual. For two decades now, whenever the children have come to visit, this is the food their grandmother has offered them.

"Orange juice?" she says.

It occurs to me that she has lived on this planet seventy years longer than my daughter. I have been here nearly fifty. My daughter will outstay me and my mother by who knows how many years. Will Miranda remember us, the three of us, out on the deck together in this suspended instant, in the quiet country noon?

I marvel at our intersection.

I wonder will it last, if I record it here.

Poet, novelist, and essayist **Erica Jong** is best known for her seven bestselling novels: *Fear of Flying, How to Save Your Own Life, Fanny: Being the True History of the Adventures of Fanny Hackabout-Jones, Parachutes & Kisses, Shylock's Daughter* (formerly published as *Serenissima*), *Any Woman's Blues*, and *Inventing Memory*, but she is also a widely published and anthologized poet who has published as many books of poetry as novels.

Her work is translated into twenty-seven languages and has been awarded the Premio Internationale Sigmund Freud in Italy and the United Nations Award of Excellence. Known for her commitment to women's rights, authors' rights, and free expression, Ms. Jong is a frequent lecturer in the United States and abroad.

MY MOTHER,
MY DAUGHTER, AND ME

All we know of love comes from our mothers. Yet we have buried that love so deep that we may not even know where it comes from. If we have been wounded and have grown scar tissue over our hearts, we confuse the scar tissue with the heart itself forgetting the wound that caused it.

My first memories of my mother come from the year my younger sister was born. I do not remember *ever* being the center of the universe because when I came into the family, my older sister—four-and-a-half to my zero—was already there.

I am four-and-a-half when my younger sister is born and my mother lies in bed like a queen receiving guests, children, parents, friends. She is beautiful and brown-eyed with reddish-brown hair and she wears a padded silk bed jacket over a silk nightgown. The women in my family only wear bed jackets in times of great ceremony—childbirth, illness, death—and we rarely spend daylight hours in bed. We are all so energetic that we clean up after our housekeepers, type for our secretaries, and instruct caterers in how to cook—though cooking is not exactly a family talent. So if my mother is in bed wearing a bed jacket, it *must* be important. And it is: daughter number three has just been born.

The baby has a cold caught in the hospital and four-and-a-half-year-old Erica has ringworm caught from her best friend's cat. She is forbidden to touch the baby—who is guarded by a dragon-like baby nurse. She feels contagious to the point of leprosy, so superfluous she thinks no one will even *care* if she runs away. At four-and-a-half she can only conceive of running away to her best friend's house on the floor below—but that is where she *caught* the ringworm in the first place. (In later days she might have run around the corner to the candy store—though every time she did *that* she ended up using one of her sweaty nickels to call home from the musty, cigarette-smelling phone booth. Invariably the adults wheedled her into saying where she was. She wanted to be found so badly she always *told*. She let them convince her to come home though it meant crossing the street like a big girl). So she stays in the apartment—a rambling dilapidated West Side palace whose double-height front windows give north light because so many of the people in the family are painters.

Erica's mother will not remain in bed wearing that quilted bed jacket for long. Pretty soon she will be up and running around, doing a "quick sketch" of the baby in her crib, telling the nurse how to care for the baby, stuffing the chicken to be roasted and cutting together the butter and flour for the crust to enclose the apple pie she has told the housekeeper to make. Then she will dash to ballet school or the park or the ice skating rink at Rockefeller Center with her two "big girls."

But the time—a day? two days? a week?— her mother stays in bed seems endless to four-and-a-half-year old Erica. Especially after the dragon screams at her:

"Don't you dare touch the baby with that hand!"

Baby Erica has never forgiven her mother for this abandonment. Pointless to explain that the obliviousness of the baby nurse to the teachings of Freud was hardly her mother's fault. Useless to say that the baby nurse was probably a poor soul who earned her meager living going from household to household, from baby to baby, without hope of a household or a baby of her own. It was an abandonment and abandonments are, by definition, always your mother's fault. In my grown-up mind I am strong and successful. In my baby mind, I am an abandoned child.

These are merely *my* memories of my younger sister's entrance into the world. Surely my mother's are entirely different. My older sister's are surely different too. And as for the baby, what does she remember of those days but what we tell her? But somewhere in the most primitive part of my brain lies the fierce betrayal my baby sister's birth provoked. I have never quite forgiven my mother for it. Even after years of lying-down analysis and sitting-up therapy, I still, at times, feel like that abandoned four-and-a-half year old with ringworm all over my arms and torso.

My mother and I have long since reached a truce. She turned eighty-six this year and I have endured and surpassed my fear of fifty, so we are very tender with each other like glass unicorns who might break each other's horns by kissing too passionately.

Now that I have a nineteen-year-old daughter myself I understand all my mother's difficulties with us. I have even been moved to fall to my knees before my mother and say: "You are my heroine simply for *surviving* three daughters!"

My daughter now rails at me as I once railed my mother. When Molly monologues, sparing no one with her barbed wit, my mother and I look at each other and smile.

"Tell her you're sorry you were such a dreadful mother," my mother says, her voice dripping with irony. " And *apologize.*" I even *listen* to my mother now.

"Molly," I say, "I only did the best I could. I'm sure I made plenty of mistakes. I *apologize.*"

"Yeah, yeah, yeah," says Molly, impatient with me. She looks at me with the sheer contempt that is grounded in excessive love. To myself I may sometimes be a four-and-a-half-year-old with ringworm, but to her I am Kali, the giant statue of Athena that once stood in the Parthenon, Medusa guarding the Golden Fleece. *"Just wait till you have a daughter,"* I think. But I am too wise to say it. And my mother and I grin at reach other like co-conspirators. Raising a daughter requires superhuman patience. Raising a daughter is definitely tougher than writing.

I have just completed a novel about mothers and daughters. In *Inventing Memory*, I trace the mother-daughter daisy chain through four generations, showing how we are shaped both by our mothers' yearnings and our own desperate need to break free of them. The dynamic between these two powerful forces is largely what molds our lives as women. Yes, our fathers and grandfathers matter, but what we learn from our mothers and grandmothers stays in the bone marrow. It surfaces as soon as you become a mother yourself. And what you sow as a daughter, you will inevitably reap as a mother.

Inventing Memory has absorbed me more than any book have ever written. It has given me the chance to study how great-grandmothers influence even the great-granddaughters they never meet. It has allowed me to explore the process by which mothers seed their daughters with their own dreams.

In writing *Inventing Memory* I rediscovered my truest subject and plumbed it to new depths. I find few things as fascinating as the way mothers and daughters affect each other. And though I have written of mothers and daughters before—particularly in *Fear of Flying* and

Fanny—I have never before been able to show the mother-daughter dynamic duplicating itself, with subtle variations, over the generations. By chronicling a whole century in the lives of the women of a family, I permitted myself a large enough canvas to show how the mother-daughter dance repeats itself, shaping the aspirations of the dancers. Since we still unfortunately live in a society that requires good-girlism of women, mothers can either give their daughters the precious permission to be free—or they can fetter them with their own inhibitions.

My mother was brilliant in setting me free. Or maybe I was brilliant in demanding my freedom. With mothers and daughters you never really know *whose* is the initiative. We are so interwoven, so symbiotic, that you cannot always tell the mother from the daughter, the dancer from the dance.

Of course I barely understood any of this about my mother and me in my teens or twenties or even thirties. I was locked in mortal combat with her, denouncing her both to her face and behind her back, pillorying her in my novels—even as they betrayed my passionate love for her. Of course I thought I was the first daughter in history to have these tumultuous feelings. Of course I thought my mother was oblivious of my needs, hypocritical in her life and in her art and desperately in need of enlightenment by me. I must have been insufferable. But she greeted most of my excesses with love. And it was her love that set me free.

For how is the gift of freedom bestowed *except* by love? By never letting me doubt that I was loved, my mother fueled my books, my life, my own parenting. Though I was fiercely independent and refused to take financial support from my parents from college graduation onward, I always knew I *could* go home again. When I wrote painful things about my mother in my novels, she simply said: "I never *read* your novels because I consider you a poet." I knew I could write whatever I had to write and still be loved.

My mother had a benign relationship with her mother but a

tortured one with her father. He was a brilliant artist who was a relentless taskmaster to his two painter-daughters. And because he considered my mother the more talented one, he drove her mercilessly. He pushed her so hard that, after she married my father, she escaped into the primal pleasure of having babies. By the time her art surfaced again in middle age, she had three Amazons—us—to distract her. It cannot have been easy to go on painting and also mother us all. But she did it. She still paints nearly every day of her life.

In our house, draftsmanship was held to my grandfather's relentless standards. You had to draw from life before venturing into the world of the imagination. You had to master charcoal and Conté crayon before indulging in color. You had to do hundreds of still lifes before you could draw "the model." And you had to be able to draw a creditable nude before you dared paint people with clothes on. I found all this regimentation so daunting that I gave up painting (despite being considered talented by my teachers). From the age of eleven, I spent every Saturday at the Art Students' League in New York, drawing alongside professional artists and holding myself to such impossible standards that I always felt like an abject failure. Though I painted all through high school and much of college, I relinquished painting with great relief when I discovered myself as a writer. Being an artist was too fraught with conflicting feelings for me. I needed something I could call my own. Writing belonged to me as painting never could.

So I empathize with my mother's struggle to enter her father's profession. She never stopped painting but she expressed her ambivalence by not promoting her work to the public. She was afraid to compete, afraid she might succeed and kill her father. As with so many women, her courtship of failure had a purpose: to please a man.

My daughter Molly may well be the bravest of our Amazon clan. At eighteen, she is writing her first novel. She reads me chapters every few nights and in her book my role is clear: I am the mother-monster.

"Mommy, I hope you don't mind," my daughter mischievously

says, "but I've made you a total narcissist and a hopeless alcoholic in my novel...." She laughs provocatively, hoping to get me mad. I think for a minute, remembering what my friend, novelist Fay Weldon, says about teenagers: never react to *anything* they say except with a neutral "I see" or "hmmm." Teenagers exist to provoke their parents, Your only defense against them is not to be provoked.

It's true that I don't *recognize* myself in the character Molly calls "my mother" in her blisteringly funny first fiction. But who am I to censor her? If *I* don't understand that fiction is not fact, who the hell will? I've been using *my* family as comic material for twenty-five years—how can I deny that basic right to my daughter?

"You're sure you're not insulted, Mommy?" Molly asks, hoping I am.

"I'll laugh all the way to the bank with you," I say, hugging her.

In a family of artists, you early come to understand that what you have at home is what you paint. That pumpkin may be intended for pie, but it's fated first to pose for a painting. The tiny baby in the crib is simply the family's newest model. My mother and grandfather both stand over the crib sketching, sketching, sketching. My sister is born with a golden frame around her face. In truth, we all were. And if your family is unavailable to pose? Well then, you paint *yourself*. My grandfather kept a mirror opposite his easel so when he had no other model, he could always paint himself. He painted himself in every stage of life and he did the same for us. There are dozens of portraits of me at all ages, in various costumes. In one portrait of me at five, I wear a black velvet dress with an ivory lace collar and a floppy black velvet hat with black marabou pompons. I look as if I were sitting for Rembrandt—my grandfather's favorite painter. In another portrait—done by my mother—I am seventeen and wearing a Japanese wedding kimono with an antique obi. My hair is done with lacquer combs as if I were a blonde geisha and my face is powdered white with rice powder. A crimson dot of lipstick adorns my lower lip. Whenever I look at the portrait I remember the summer spent in Japan when it was done.

All these portraits have empowered me in various ways. Some may not be to my taste and some are hardly flattering, but I am certainly glad they *exist*. *I* exist more richly because they exist. My memories are captured by a wall of portraits in my mother's house.

So throughout my childhood, I was the subject of works of art. I came to feel that art was as natural a process as breathing. It is.

But the process of art is also the process of metamorphosis. I may be an ogre in Molly's first novel, but I am sure to be an angel in her last. My mother may have sharp edges in *Fear of Flying;* in *Fear of Fifty*, those edges are soft as a scarf of cashmere and silk. I have many more mothers than one. And each of those mothers parallels a particular phase in my life. Each represents a change in *me* more than a change in my mother. As I grow more confident of my identity, I fault my mother less and less. As I grow older, my mother grows mellower along with me.

There is no end to this story. As long as I live I will be redefining my daughterhood in the light of my motherhood. Because I am a writer, I will write about the process since writing is my way of staying sane. But there will never be a final incarnation of my mother, of my daughter, of me. We are all works in progress.

What is constant is the metamorphosis itself. Kurt Vonnegut said in one of his novels that people are like centipedes wearing different faces as they make the trek from infancy to old age. I have always loved that image: each of us as a centipede, marching through time.

My mother is a centipede and so is my daughter. Sometimes our paths intersect as we trudge along on our three hundred feet. But we have already marked each other in millions of ways. We share the same DNA, the same dreams, the same daring. If Molly is destined to be the most daring of all, it's no less than I expect. So many generations of women have empowered her. So many mothers and grandmothers have gone into her making. May she dare to follow her dreams *wherever* they lead! Without daring, what use are dreams? Without daring, what use are all the struggles of your mother, your grandmother, your great-grandmother? Make no mistake, these ancestors are watching you. If you disappoint them, you disappoint yourself.

"We think back through our mothers if we are women," Virginia Woolf said. And through us, our mothers think forward into the future.

MARY TANNEN HAS PUBLISHED THREE children's books and four novels, including *Loving Edith*. She is a regular contributor to the *New York Times Magazine*, and also writes for *Vogue*. Her fiction has been published in the *New Yorker*. She has a son and a daughter and lives with her husband in New York City.

DORIS/NOT-DORIS

In middle age I am very much like her: same size, same coloring, same temperament. A friend I hadn't seen in a long time laughed when we met. "You've become your mother," she said. Recently I came across a dress of hers that I had saved. It was one she'd worn at my age. (Beige cotton, eyelet lace shirtwaist.) I was tempted to try it on but resisted and threw it away. All my life I've been comparing myself to her: what was she doing at my age? Sometimes she is the standard I try to reach. At other times—lately—she is the opposite of who I want to be.

She was a doe-eyed country girl with small bones. She came to New York City during the Second World War, to live in a walk-up apartment in a brownstone on West 73rd Street. It was not on a whim that she came, or out of a sense of adventure, but for my father, who was an officer on a submarine chaser patrolling the Atlantic coast. She came so that if he had any time free, they could spend it together. She did not know anyone in the city. She brought a two year old and a newborn (me.) She had to pull the baby carriage up and down flights of steep stairs. It was so hot that at night she would walk around the apartment in her underwear, and look out the window and see her neighbors in their underwear. No one cared.

When she told me the part about the underwear, years later, she still seemed amazed. She had never lived in a city before, and after those few months, never lived in one again.

After the war she had twin daughters. She hauled laundered diapers out of the basement and hung them on two pulley lines out the kitchen door. Four lines of diapers. Every day we came home for lunch—my father too. She made soup, or chicken à la king, or welsh rarebit, with homemade cake or cookies or fruit for dessert. She had a system for keeping house: Monday wash, Tuesday iron, Wednesday vacuum downstairs, and so forth. She sewed the curtains and slipcovers and all our clothes, even the coats.

The first day the twins went to school, she got into bed and read and read. She went through novels fast and only vaguely remembered what they were about.

In the afternoon, she would put her hair up in pin curls. When my father came home at five o'clock, her hair would be combed out and she would have lipstick on. Dinner would be ready.

She taught me how to set table, iron, dust, cook, and sew. She taught me how to hop, how to skip, and how to do the Charleston— in the kitchen, while she was cooking. She did not go out much, except with my father. They saw other couples, for dinner and bridge. After an evening at someone's house, she would call and thank the hostess. She would sit down by the phone and light a cigarette before she called.

She was quiet. She and my father considered this one of her chief virtues, that she did not call attention to herself. She chose for me what she believed to be a quiet name. It was understood that I would be just like her.

The print of her foot in the sand was narrow and curvy. Mine was fat and square. Her fingers—when I brought my botched sewing for help—were clean, dry and tapered. Mine were grubby, moist, and blunt. She didn't need attention. I did.

She married at twenty-one. I married at twenty-two. By the time I was thirty I had two children and was sewing curtains and slipcovers. I would have had four children, but my husband objected. I think he was puzzled that I had turned into a domestic goddess. At the time he married me, I had affected a more independent, adventurous persona. I had been about to leave for Washington D.C. to go into the United States Information Agency, with vague plans of living a picaresque life as a writer. But I married him and began changing into Doris.

I felt as if I were surrendering to something, to my fate as woman, which was ridiculous, as I was living in New York City, in the 70s. where no one surrendered to anything. The women's liberation and zero population movements were raging all around me. Maybe I was afraid that unless I did it just like Doris, I couldn't do it at all. I would have affairs and lose my husband. I would get caught up in work and neglect my children. At the same time I felt as if I had fallen down a long hole, that I had lost the person I had wanted to be and that I would never get her back.

When my youngest turned three I made my first attempt at being not-Doris. I adopted two kittens. My husband hated cats. I didn't like them much myself, but Doris was terrified of them. (She accepted my cats good-naturedly. No screaming and jumping on chairs. But I could see they made her nervous.)

A few years later, I left the kids with my husband for a week and went to Ireland to research a children's book. When the book was published, I felt that it was the first project that I had consciously undertaken and completed, that my whole life before had been but a walking dream. Publishing a book is a monstrously egotistical act—to presume that you have something to say that even strangers would be interested in. It was profoundly not-Doris.

It's been almost twenty years since I first committed the act of publishing, and I've been tugging at the reader's sleeve ever since. I never see my name in print without feeling embarrassed, at being so noisy, so needy. But more and more I am giving in to my not-Doris side—taking up sports like rock climbing and kayaking, socializing occasionally without my husband (he doesn't mind), wearing clothes that call attention to myself (never beige).

A few years ago I helped Doris pack. She and my father were moving into a retirement apartment. It was not a move she would have chosen for herself. She dreaded taking meals with others in the dining room. But my father couldn't live on his own. If she were to die first, her children would have the burden of caring for him. She didn't want that. She had already had one heart attack, which had left her weak and pale, yet she insisted on taking her complete dinner service for twelve (which she had painted as a teenager) with her to the new apartment, so she could entertain the family at Christmas.

She didn't make it to Christmas, or even Thanksgiving (although she had the ingredients for pumpkin pie ready in her cupboard).

In our last conversation, over the phone, I told her that I had dedicated my latest novel to her. "It isn't about me, is it?" was her response. I assured her that it wasn't. She would not like it that I am writing about her now.

Two days after our phone conversation, she had a stroke while making lunch for my father, and died before I could reach her. I believe that when she realized that she had become the center of a bedside drama that could go on for weeks or months, she exited in hasty silence. She was capable of that.

Almost three years later I still find myself saying, "I need to call Mom." I wonder what I need to tell her.

I want to do something for her: give her more attention, lavish her with praise, but I know that she would deflect it, as she always did. She was a self-effacing heroine, a woman who sacrificed for her family. And yet her very strength and nobility kept her apart. I wanted to get closer, to violate her privacy, to ease my guilt of never doing enough.

DORIS AND I, 1943

Whenever I did something not-Doris, it would worry her, and yet I think she was secretly pleased when I got away with it. I miss relating my adventures to her. I always felt I was acting as much for her as for me—finding the not-Doris for both of us. I would like to tell her that even though I am happily engaged in being not-her, I still appreciate, admire, and greatly miss the woman who was Doris.

JUDY MANN'S BOOKS INCLUDE *Mann for All Seasons* and *The Difference: Growing Up Female in America.* A *Washington Post* columnist, she has also contributed to *Ms., Working Women,* and *Reader's Digest.* She is a frequent guest on radio and television talk shows, and lectures on gender and political issues at forums across the country. She lives with her husband in McLean, Virginia, and on Gender Gap Farm in the Shenandoah Valley.

WATCHING A PARENT SLIP AWAY, A LITTLE AT A TIME

For more than a decade, I have shared in my column some of the joys, triumphs, and simple passages of life that have occurred within my family, not because they were unique, but because they happen, in one form or another, to so many families. It is in that same spirit that I share now the greatest sorrow that my family has known, for this too will happen to all of us.

Early on the evening of March 28, 1989, I received a call from the Powhatan Nursing Home in Arlington saying that my mother had died. Her name was Margaretta Warden, she was eighty-seven years old, and she had been living in the shadow of death for more than a year. As anticipated as that call was, there are no words to describe the sense of loss I felt then, and feel to this day. The closest physical sensation I can think of is having the wind knocked out of you, again and again and again.

There were a number of themes that ran through my mother's

long and productive life, and one of the most constant was that of
teaching. Mother's heritage reached deep into the earliest days of the
Society of Friends in Chester County, Pennsylvania, and from those
roots she brought forth an enduring appreciation for education, pro-
ductivity, frugality and, above all, a gentleness and sense of courtesy
toward her fellow human beings that guided her every action. Mother
was a classmate of Margaret Mead's at Barnard College and delighted
in reminding us from time to time that she, Margaret Mead, and
someone whose name long ago dropped out of the story were the
only three students exempted from their anthropology final exam.
After college, mother taught at and later ran the first Arthur Murray
studio in New York. Years later, she taught French, and she was a
stickler for correct grammar.

Mother would not have scripted her final years the way they
occurred. One of the enduring lessons she taught us in the end is that
there are some things we simply cannot control, and we simply must
do the very best we can. Mother was independent and self-reliant—
she prized those qualities highly—and they were taken from her mercilessly. I can remember her saying fifteen years ago, when the debate
over life-support machines first surfaced, that she did not want to be
hooked up to any kind of artificial machine. "Just let me go," she said
firmly. But for most of her last year the only nourishment she could
get was from a feeding tube and for much of that time she received
assistance in breathing from an oxygen tank.

A great deal of attention is being paid now to the problems of
aging parents, who cares for them, and the pressure this puts on their
sons and daughters who are working themselves and also raising children. To call this the "sandwich generation," the current term, trivial-
izes the crushing emotional, physical, and financial stress that takes
place when a family is caring for an aged, incapacitated member. Our
family was far more fortunate than most: my father, Charles Warden,
was torn apart by grief and worry during the years of Mother's
decline, but he was there to oversee her care. He was there to hire the

health care aides and physical therapists, to take her to the doctors and the specialist who, in the end, ruled out Parkinson's disease as the cause of her problems but came up with no alternative diagnosis, or, more to the point, no way of helping her recover.

My father, their housekeeper, and several home health care workers took care of my mother at home until a year ago, when she got pneumonia. By then she was bedridden almost all the time and eating was a terrible ordeal. She had lost a great deal of weight.

On St. Patrick's Day, 1988, their housekeeper called and told me Mother was dying. I had been at their home the night before and realized then how heartbreakingly close the end was. When I went to their home the next day, I knew she had pneumonia and I knew her death was imminent and that her wish to die at home could soon be fulfilled. My father knew on one level how grave the situation was, but in his heart he could not admit it; and his heart always ruled where my mother was concerned.

I could have made the decision then not to call my mother's doctor and not to call the ambulance and not to have her taken to Arlington Hospital. But I could not do that. These quality of life arguments become meaningless when we have to make the decisions for those we love. I felt a year ago, and I feel today, that she deserved every chance to live that we could give her. With the agreement of my father, however, I told her doctor in the emergency room that we wanted no heroic measures and no code blue lifesaving procedures to start her heart if it stopped. That is a terrible decision to have to make.

Mother had no chance to fight the pneumonia without nourishment. My father and I agreed that a feeding tube should be inserted through her nose, if it could be done without causing her pain. She began receiving antibiotics, but within days the doctor gave Mother twenty-four hours to live. My brother and his wife arrived from Massachusetts. Their daughter and my older son spent the night in Mother's room with their grandfather. My sister and her husband came from Michigan. My younger son spent the next day by his grandmother's side, instead of going to school, and urged me to bring his little sister to the hospital so that she, too, could be with her grandmother. There were times during her struggle when Mother woke, and when she saw her grandchildren she smiled and reached for their hands.

We made decisions about what funeral home would handle arrangements, and the cemetery plot, and my brother and sister-in-law selected the casket. We spent the hours comforting my father, who was inconsolable, and ourselves, and we made sure that Mother was never without a family member by her side. The hours passed into days. Mother's lungs began to clear. We brought in heart and lung specialists and began respiratory treatments to help her. Mother had survived double pneumonia, but it left her weakened beyond measure. The hospital was ready to discharge her.

We made the hard decision to put her into a nursing home because she needed the skilled nursing care and physical therapy that could never be managed at home. My father could tolerate the idea only by thinking that it was for a short period of time to help her regain her strength so she could come home. She never did. For the last half year of her life, she was at Powhatan, which is close to my home and that of my father. He saw her every day. The two health aides who had helped her at home continued to care for her while she was in the nursing home.

The last day that I saw her when she was awake was New Year's Day. My father and I visited her, and when I saw how alert she was, I went home and returned with my daughter. Mother's face lit up when she saw her granddaughter. That smile and the way they held hands are a memory I will always cherish.

I will not deny that this past year has been hard on my father and hard on all of us. We ran headlong into the staggering costs of nursing homes and the patchwork of Catch-22 federal health care and private insurance regulations that often seem designed more to save money than lives. We explored every possible medical hope. We also

MARGARETTA WEED WARDEN

discovered the kind of love and care that exists in a good nursing home. We saw genuine respect for human life.

And we saw a love affair that lasted nearly sixty years. Toward the end, when Mother seemed to be sleeping most of the time, my father visited her very afternoon and read her poetry. He took her roses. He spent the last evening with her. My family and I have taken comfort in the idea that the last year was a way of letting us prepare for Mother's death. Father could not have handled it a year ago. He was not ready to let go until a couple of days before the very end. We think of the last year as her final gift, her way of giving us time to get ready.

But we were not.

NAOMI FONER IS A HIGHLY SUCCESSFUL WRITER, producer, and director. Her motion picture screenplays include *A Dangerous Woman,* and *Running on Empty,* for which Foner was nominated for an Academy Award for Best Original Screenplay and received the PEN West Screenplay Award and a Golden Globe Award. She also wrote and produced *Losing Isaiah,* starring Jessica Lange, which was directed by her husband Stephen Gyllenhaal. Active in various political groups, Foner has served on the Board of Directors of the Writer's Guild of America-West, and has taught and lectured extensively. She lives in Los Angeles with her husband and two children.

RUTH AND NAOMI

When I knew my mother was going to die, I went out and cut off all my hair. It surprised us both. My mother Ruth, who had named me Naomi.

By then, I had stopped going to school at all. After the great blackout, when I had stumbled my way through the dark city to learn that she was going to lose both her breasts, I had lost interest in anything else. I was caught behind a curtain of Saran Wrap. I could see out, but nothing passed through the membrane, and the soup of my own feelings soured behind that clear impregnable barricade. I was dying too. Like my mother. We both gave off the same rotting smell.

She shrank in the tilting hospital bed to the flat-chested baby sister she once had been. I tried to grow into the hugeness of body and spirit that had been my lion-breasted grandmother. We had done the dance and passing back to back, switched places.

We did things women did for each other. I walked her to the bathroom and up and down the linoleum-floored hallway. I combed her hair and plucked black hairs out of her chin. I read out loud from books she used to love, but she wasn't listening to anything but the sound of my voice. Sometimes, I lay next to her on the hospital bed and neither of us spoke. In those moments, she was almost my mother again.

Eventually, the plastic overtook us. It was everywhere. We slid off it. We stuck to it. We drank from it. The magic material of the fifties. I slept on the green plastic armchair with the unforgiving metal arms. I poured water for her from the brown plastic pitcher by her bed into a cup and then held it for her to take small sips through a plastic bending straw.

I was doing penance. I wanted to get sick too. That would be easier than watching her waste away, hope shining from her eyes. Her belly swelling with the pregnancy of death. She was a doctor. She knew better. But still she hoped. That was the hardest thing to watch.

There had been so much hope. Miracles even. The magic rays that let us see through ourselves. But they had turned on us. My mother lay in the hospital bed because she had believed in them. The fluoroscope in her office had exacted its toll on her flesh.

I was growing old watching her die. She knew it. She tried to help. She would never really be gone, she said, because she was somehow in me. Part of me. I didn't understand that yet. It would take having my own children. But I knew she meant it as comfort.

She had been so strong. So vibrant. Almost too large to live with. Would there be space for me too? And now she was becoming her death. Leaving me alone. I sat in her hospital room and remembered the trips to the Jewish market between house calls. The sweet

RUTH SILBOWITZ ACHS, 1946

Muenster slice. The sour pickle for the doctor's daughter. Sitting in the Chevrolet with my brother while she went to give "a shot" to an immigrant baby. "For money you could get honey," one of those mothers had told her when she came a few minutes late on a spring afternoon. Where was the "honey" now?

"Be angry. It's alright. I feel it too." I let her hold my hand. I looked at the loose skin and the rings I had seen from so many angles since childhood and wondered how she had gotten so brave. There had been so much fear. But when the worst came, she let go of it and walked into each day with her eyes open. Sometimes tears streamed from them. But she never looked away. It would have meant missing something in what little was left.

There were days spent looking back. With her sisters. How they had loved each other. They sat in the dark living room with my mother stretched out on the couch and remembered out loud. Their immigrant parents. Pumping gas at the corner station their father had run next door to the black coated orthodox congregation in the Bronx. The rabbi yelling in Yiddish if they stayed open on Saturday. They laughed about the mink coat my grandmother would have when the pair of minks my Grandpa Benny had brought home had enough offspring. They remembered the food and the fights and the fat cousins. It was almost, but not quite enough. It's hard to die at forty-eight. With a daughter and a son not yet grown. With so much left to do. With your own mother and sisters watching.

When she was gone, I sat with her things. The sheets hand-stitched by a patient who couldn't pay for the penicillin. The dresses from Loehmann's where she shopped while I sat on the golden lion in the lobby with my brother. The dishes that only came out for the dinner parties we watched from the second floor landing. The books. The rings that were too big for my fingers. I cried for what I would never have. I refused to visit her grave. She wasn't there I insisted. I knew.

She had told me she was some part in me. And at her funeral I understood she was some part in all that she had already done in her short life. They couldn't take that away and put it in a hole in the ground. They couldn't touch it. It was mine forever. Along with her expectation, so strong it remained unspoken, that I would make something of myself. I would carry her with me to the top of the mountain. She would see the Promised Land. And somehow, my daughter, when she came, would know her grandmother. Ruth, Naomi, Ruth, again. The whole greater than the sum of the parts.

DELIA EPHRON IS THE AUTHOR OF, among other works, *How to Eat Like a Child, and Other Lessons in Not Being a Grown-Up, Teenage Romance; Or, How to Die of Embarrassment*, and *Hanging Up*, her first adult novel. She has contributed articles to numerous magazines, including the *New York Times Magazine, Vogue, Esquire, Glamour, Redbook, Cosmopolitan*, and *New York*. Born in 1944, she lives in New York City with her husband. This is excerpted from *Funny Sauce*.

MOM IN LOVE

Dear Diary,

You would not believe my algebra teacher, Mr. Brickley. His hair sits on top of his head like a bushel. Every time he says something, he writes it on the blackboard. I'm not kidding. Like if he says, "There will be a test Monday," he turns and writes "Monday" on the board. Also, he wears short-sleeved shirts and the flab on his arm waves when he writes. Oops—the phone.

It was for Mom—a guy. I hope he's better than the hypnotist she brought home from the Sierra Club. Maybe Mom should marry Mr. Brickley. What a totally nauseous idea. Personally I am saving myself for Sting.

9/15

> *Coffee with Sosa. Believes getting a Marxist in dept. is essen.*
> *Pro*
> *Is our only sig. gap in. Euro. field. Am. hists. will secure app't. if we don't.*
> *Con*
> *Fritz covers the field adequately. As regards Am. hists., so what?*
> *Met a woman. A therapist.*

DD,

I just finished talking to Kristy on the phone for three hours. A total and complete record. She says that Mr. Brickley never writes his name. He just puts M. Mr. M. Brickley. Do you believe that? I think the M stands for Moss! Wouldn't that be a riot. Kristy looked "moss" up in the dictionary and it said, "A spongy bog." That is Mr. Brickley to a T.

Poor Mom. She had this date tonight and she couldn't decide what to wear. It really cracked me up. She put on this dress and it's like, How do I look? So I go, "Okay." I really didn't want to tell her but nobody wears dresses like that anymore. But anyway she got it 'cause then she put on these pants, which were a lot better, and I loaned her my Guess shirt. But then I just had to say something. "I can't believe you're wearing those shoes." So she changed them.

I just sat there watching her run around deciding what to wear and cracking up. My mom's kinda cute sometimes. I guess 'cause she's a therapist and always thinking what everything means, she goes into a spaz when she has to look good. So then this guy arrives. Joel. I couldn't believe it. He was so little and round. She went to all that trouble for a little round guy. I just said hello and got out of there fast. Once she wasn't ready and this guy kept saying things to me like, "What are you studying?" So lame.

9/30

Cooked dinner for Anne. Osso buco. Told her about Scotty—he changed his major for 3rd time. A. said: Can't be easy for him to have mother who's Scientologist; father who's medvl. hist. Found myself trying to explain why married to L. 13 yrs. when knew all along was wrong person. A. said I probably didn't think I deserved it—love and hap., that is.

A. very different from L. A Ph.D. in clinical psych., a successful practice, a 14-year-old dgtr. she's close to. A. said, unlike L. she's "terrific" to be divorced from (i.e., doesn't take alimony). Ironic sense of humor. Warm. Said her prob. with ex was—cd. never tell him what she thought. Hard to believe. Apparently has changed a lot.

Heavy wk. Quartet rehearsal. Drinks with Heller—Sosa wants me to lobby him. Said she'd never seen a kitchen as org. as mine. Hope wasn't a criticism.

10/3

Stopped by Anne's today on spur of moment. Unlike me. Went bowling, which I haven't done since age 10. Worried about scoring lower than she. Am I doomed to spend life worrying about lack of athletic ability? Shades of h.s. Ridiculous. We took Anne's dgtr. Jenny with us. Every time her mother bowled, Jenny said, "Oh, Mom," as if it were the most embarrassing moment of her life. Seems sweet. Also shy. Couldn't even get her to let me buy her a Coke. It's funny—I even like it that Anne has a dgtr.

Started a diet today. Didn't plan to. Found myself refusing dessert.

DD,

I know you'll think I'm crazy but I think Mom actually likes that butterball. I was talking to Kristy about it and she said, "No way," but I don't know. He stopped over the other day without calling—I really don't think Mom should put up with that—and we all went bowling. I was really embarrassed for them that they wanted to go bowling, and Mom kept saying that she once bowled 150 when she was fifteen. I mean, really, who cares? But anyway, she kept giggling all the time and dropped the bowling ball on her foot and the butterball was rubbing it. It made me sick but she liked it.

I sorta miss my dad tonight.

DD,

Right in the middle of Kristy and me making up a song, "One Great Moss," Mom burst in spazzed because I forgot to tell her Joel called. I don't see why she was upset. It's not my fault I forgot.

10/11

Difficult day. Anne didn't return my call. Suddenly thought it was over. A realization: I couldn't imagine life going back to what it was before Anne. Turned out Jenny was busy and forgot to tell her I called.

Told Sosa I don't give a shit about this Marxist thing.

10/12

Quiet dinner with Anne. She pointed out how much I tend to isolate myself. Might even have picked medvl. hist. as profession because it is cerebral and, for most peop., inaccessible.

10/15

Anne's in love with me. I am flying.

DD,

Mom's really furious with me but I don't care. Butterball was over again!!!!!!!!!!! and I didn't say hello. Just 'cause someone says hello to you doesn't mean you have to answer. Why should I be having these fake conversations if I don't want to.

The main problem with Joel is he's always being so nice. And he's sooooooooo nosy!!!!!!!!!! He just comes into my room and goes hi. Do you believe that? He brought me one of Sting's albums. He said he heard I liked him. I suppose *Mom* told him. If she talks to him about me, I'll never forgive her. Dad would never discuss me with some strange person. Anyway, so then I'm supposed to say thank you for something I don't even want.

10/25

Seems Jenny's reacting a little to the fact there's a man in her mother's life. Last night I brought Anne a pint of her favorite tofutti and I brought a Sting album for Jenny. Jenny wouldn't say hello. In general she hasn't been too friendly lately. Usually I arrived and she retreats to her room. But this time I went into her room to give her the present. She wouldn't look at me. Literally refused to meet my eye. Anne suggested she say thanks. She did. To be precise she said, "Thanks. Now can I go back to what I was doing?" Anne was pretty upset about it. Actually I find the whole thing amusing. She's just a kid. It'll pass.

DD,

Something really terrible happened today, diary. I came home from school and opened the freezer and there was tofutti there. Ever since it's been just Mom and me, since I was five, Mom always made this big deal—we should never have ice cream in the house 'cause it was sugar and fattening. If you wanted ice cream, Mom said you should just go out and buy one scoop for a treat. I've always eaten junk at my dad's and good food at my mom's. That's the way it's always been. And now Joel's bringing in mountains of tofutti like it's a normal thing to do so they can eat it together.

You know what I hate the most? When I can hear them laughing.

11/15

Difficult that Anne leaves at 3 A.M. to go home. Said I'd be happy to stay at her place. (Surprised to hear myself say that.) Anne doesn't want to upset Jenny more—amazing, but in 9 yrs. Anne's never let a man sleep over. Told her I'm not any man. Anne said she'd think about it. Am so crazy about her.

DD,

Last night I slept over at Kristy's and I got the feeling Mom was really happy I did.

DD,

Mom and Joel are having problems. They spent all day sitting out back talking about their relationship like total geeks. Talk, talk, talk, talk, talk. I feel sorry for Joel for falling in love with a therapist. Maybe he'll realize what a mistake he's made.

11/20

Told Anne she has to let me into her life completely. I can't be in halfway. We're acting like teenagers sneaking behind Jenny's back. A couple of nights ago, Jenny slept over at a friend's and I felt as if it were the warden's night off.

Anne and I spent the day going over and over it. She says she feels caught between me and Jenny. I told her I'd do anything for Jenny—I'm buying the whole package, not just Anne. I'm sure Jenny's a lovely kid when she isn't around me. I've always wanted a daughter. Told Anne to trust me—she said she's always had a problem with that. I know Jenny's being difficult but I can handle her.

11/26

That kid's a monster. I arrived for Thanksgiving, and walked into the room where she was watching television, and said, "Hello. What are you watching?" Nothing. I might as well have been invisible. So I said, "Oh, really. That sounds like a good show," just to tease her, and she turned the TV off, walked out, went into her room, and slammed the door. Wouldn't come out to eat.

Anne was furious. She went in to talk to Jenny and came out very upset.

DD,

Thanksgiving was disgusting. If Mom wants to invite Joel, fine, that's her decision. That doesn't mean I have to be with him. I told her I thought on holidays you were only supposed to invite people you really care about. Mom asked what I have against him. I swear it is not personal. Totally objectively I really don't know what she sees in him. I know he's a professor but big deal. Medieval history is a dumb thing to be a professor of. I told her I didn't want to hurt her feelings but I don't think he's good enough for her. She said I should give him a chance. Actually what she said, which was really, really disgusting, was, "Jenny, I think you should try to open your heart to him." I asked her if she ever listens to the noise he makes when he chews.

Mom would be better off with Mr. Brickley. Maybe even a lot better off, which is totally depressing if you think about it.

P.S. I'm so glad I'm spending Christmas vacation with my dad!
P.P.S. Maybe I shouldn't leave Mom and Joel alone?

12/15

The monster leaves in three days. Thank God.

DD,

If I don't talk to you before, Merry Christmas!!!!! and pray Mom and Butterball break up for New Year's.

DD,

Do you believe this? On my first night home, Mom tells me Butterball is moving in. We were at a restaurant having tacos and she told me. IN PUBLIC! How could she do that? I would never say something like that to her in public. That is so insensitive. I will never forgive her. And on my first night, too. She didn't even have the decency to wait a night. She thinks she's a shrink but she doesn't even know how to do anything. I asked her why she and Joel couldn't wait to live together till I'm out of high school. Then I'll be gone. She said it was too long. It's only three and a half years.

I think she's being desperate. She couldn't possibly love him. Mom says she knows it's hard for me. She said, "Jenny, change is scary." Well, she doesn't know. She doesn't know anything.

Joel is disturbing my entire life. I do not see why he doesn't see that Mom and I do not need him. There is no room for him at our house, and I don't know why he doesn't get it.

DD,

What I want to know is, what about his stuff? Where's he going to put it? He has this dog. And, diary, I haven't told you 'cause I didn't want to upset you, but he has this son! He's twenty (and fat!) and he lives in Chicago, but suppose he changes his mind and moves here!!!!!!????

I don't think Mom understands. This is *my* house. Just point to a spot, diary, any spot, and I can tell you everything about it. This house is not supposed to be for more people. Where will I fit??????????

1/10

Anne's furniture modern; mine mostly antiques. Will they go together? I expressed this concern to Anne, who said I was probably worried about how she, Jenny, and I would go together, as opposed to the furniture. It's very comforting being in love with a therapist—she always tells you what you really mean. I think Anne's most worried about how neat I am, though she hasn't said it. Anne, for instance, throws all the utensils in a drawer. She does not use a plastic separator.

DD,

He's coming, diary, and I don't want him. I want my mom! I want my whole mom!!!!!!!!

DD,

I gave Mom a list. He is not kissing me good night, ever. I want my mom to come into my room alone and do it. He is never calling me Jennikins. That is Mom's name for me and no one else's. There is no way he is going to see me play Calpurnia in *Julius Caesar.*

DD,

Joel is even weirder than I thought. His furniture is about 400 years old. Mom and I like new stuff. I knew he didn't belong here. Maybe after she lives with one of his ugly wood tables for a while, she'll realize what a mistake she's made. Also, he puts everything in jars. I mean he puts noodles in jars and raisins and rice. Everything! He opens all the cereal and mixes it together in a jar. I do not like my cereal mixed up. One thing's for sure, Sting would never do that. Anyway, every time I pass a jar, which is practically every second, I just unscrew the top and take it off.

2/9

I put the top on a canister. The monster takes it off. I think she actually bumps into my coffee table on purpose. She's given her mother a list. I am not allowed to kiss her good night. I am not allowed to use her telephone—this is something I'm very interested in doing, of course. I am not allowed to call her Jennikins. She should know what I call her. I am not allowed to see her play Calpurnia in Julius Caesar. *All very funny if it weren't infuriating.*

I really don't know why she hates me.

2/14

I think I hate her! Now every time I say something she waits two minutes and says, "Excuse me, what did you say?" She's 14 years old, how can I hate her??????? How can I hate Anne's daughter!!!!!!! Oh, Christ. I certainly can't discuss this with Anne.

DD,

Either I'm moving in with Dad or I'm moving in with Kristy. I've got to do something. I feel so out of it. Tonight Mom came home from work really upset and was talking to Joel about something that happened at the clinic. She used to talk to me about those things. (Also, I don't really think he gives the best advice.) What I feel like has happened is before Joel I was not a kid to Mom but I wasn't exactly an adult either. Now he's here and I'm knocked down a peg.

Sometimes when they're in their room, I think they're talking about me. I bet they're plotting to get rid of me. Then they can live happily ever after.

3/1

Happily ever after was invented by someone who did not have a stepchild.

DD,

Here's what happened tonight. Mom wanted chicken for dinner and I'm thinking of becoming a vegetarian. So I was saying that I really didn't want to eat what she was making. So then Joel butted in and said, "I'm sure we can have a compromise here." That was so dumb. I just screamed at him, "KEEP OUT OF IT!" If I am arguing with my mom then I'm arguing with my mom. I stomped out to call Kristy and heard him say, "What's wrong with her now?" I yelled "Don't talk about me!"

Then Joel came downstairs and said, "I need to talk to you." I just screamed, "I hate you!" So then he put on this sad face which made me even madder. "Look Jenny," he said, "it hurts me when you talk to me like that."

"Well, how do you think I feel? You're ruining my life."

"I don't want to ruin your life."

"Ha."

Then he said, what nerve, "Jenny, I know you have a really special relationship with your mom and I don't want to interfere. I've never had a daughter—"

"I'm not your daughter!!!!!!!!!!!!!!" I knew that's what he wanted, diary, I knew it!!!!!!!!!!!!

3/6

Still can't figure out what happened. Jenny suddenly decided to become a vege-tarian, and Anne had been planning to cook chicken. I suggested we compromise. Jenny blew up and stormed out.

I went to talk to her. She was screaming she hates me, she's not my daughter. I was just trying to tell her I was sorry she was so upset. I've never had a daughter so I might make mistakes sometimes. I don't know why I wanted to tell her that. I don't know why I was being nice. She's a pain in the ass and I'm sick of her. Why does she exist? I had to go out for an hour to calm down.

Anne's beside herself. How could her happiness be causing her daughter this much pain? She said, in a way, it's her fault. By not being with a man all these years, she's led Jenny to believe there would never be anyone but the two of them. Anne also thinks Jenny is protecting her father. Apparently he hates to buy anything that isn't on sale and it makes Jenny worry about him.

Anne thinks if only Jenny would let herself, she could get so much from me. (It was sweet of her to say that.) Anyway, we've made a pact. We're going to stop discussing Jenny.

DD,

Mom thinks I should see a shrink. I AM NOT SEEING A SHRINK. In my opinion the only reason shrinks have business is that other shrinks send them their kids. Mom said, "You're obviously feeling a lot of upsetting things. I know my being with Joel has been very difficult for you." At least she's right about that. I asked her if she was going to forget my birthday. She said she thought I was really worried that she was going to forget *me*. It drives me crazy that she's always telling me what I really mean. But then, you know what, diary? She started crying. "Couldn't you try to like Joel a little? He's so nice." Maybe I've hurt her. Maybe she's crying like crazy right now. Good.

Last night I had a dream that I found Joel kissing someone else and poor Mom was so upset, I had to kick him out.

3/15

A splitting headache. Told Anne I didn't think she should allow Jenny to mistreat me. A. said I was the adult, Jenny the child, I should handle it—can't make her choose between us. Told her I was not making her choose. I simply thought she should be stricter with Jenny. "Don't tell me how to raise Jenny!"

"I live here too."

"She's not your child."

"Oh, I get it. First I'm supposed to handle it; now I'm not supposed to handle it. If I can't discipline her, you do it. You're not strict enough."

"Don't judge me."

"I'm not judging you!"

"You're watching how I treat Jenny and judging it. I can't have you watching me all the time."

"Me watching you? That's a joke, coming from a shrink. You're the one who's always telling everyone what they mean. I can't live here if I have nothing to say about your daughter."

"Fine, don't live here. We were fine before you came, and we'll be fine after you leave."

"Fine."

3/16

Anne and I have decided to get married.

3/24

Set the date for May 21 and found myself pouring lentils into my cereal bowl this morning. Jenny pointed out, if I didn't put things in jars, that wouldn't have happened. I guess with Jenny around, I'll never be too far from reality.

4/4

Anne says she's sure getting married is a character flaw. (I'm glad she's flawed.) She can't think of a reason why it makes sense. She even suggested she's getting married because she likes to keep up with trends and getting married is now fashionable. She was kidding, of course. I know this sounds odd but the reason I want to get mar-

ried is, when we're dead, I want it to be that husband and wife was what we were to each other. Is that morbid or romantic? Anne says it's appropriately medieval. Jenny said, yuck.

DD,

I know I haven't written for a while 'cause I've been major depressed. Tomorrow Mom and Butterball are getting married, only he's not Butterball anymore 'cause he's lost some weight. Kristy calls him dietball. Anyway mom bought this white dress—it's not long but it's so inappropriate. I'm really embarrassed for her. I'm supposed to be in the wedding, but maybe I'll get paralyzed tomorrow and not be able to get out of bed.

Suppose I have to take Joel's last name? I asked my dad. He said no one could ever change my name, but suppose they make a special case? I bet Dad's really upset but not showing it. I bet he's a wreck. I swear the word stepfather will never cross my lips. I'll call Joel stepshit.

P.S. His son is here and fatter than his picture! Butterball II.

5/20

No wedding bells but we'll have quartet music in our living room. Actually it will be a trio since they'll have to do without yours truly. Anne's childhood friend who's a defrocked priest will perform the ceremony, and the university chaplain will sign the license. Jenny has had the decency to suffer quietly. Told Anne I really appreciate that. There is one hopeful sign. Jenny's stopped taking the tops off the canisters.

I sat Jenny down tonight and told her I had no intention of trying to take her father's place. I know she has a father. I hope she heard me.

DD,

The wedding was awful. Mom was just glowing all the time and Joel was racing around trying to make everyone comfortable as usual. Kristy came and we made this pact. After they got married, we kept hugging each other over and over so no one would notice I wasn't hugging Joel, especially Joel. But then he asked me to dance. I had to dance with him 'cause it was his wedding, but I just looked down all the time. People were taking pictures. I wanted to die.

Kristy has decided that her plan for this summer is to get a boyfriend. So we went to get T-shirts with our phone numbers printed on them. It was so hysterical. She did it but I was too embarrassed. I put my zip code on instead.

DD,

Joel bought me a helmet to wear when I bike-ride. At first I couldn't decide whether to buy this purple helmet with silver flecks on it even though I loved it, 'cause the color didn't exactly go with my bike. Also I might look weird riding down the block with purple on my head. But Joel said, "Go for it."

P.S. I was really surprised when Joel said, "Go for it." He never seemed like the type.

6/3

Jenny hugged me.

DD,

Tonight was dress rehearsal for *Julius Caesar*. Mom helped me make my toga out of a bed sheet. It kept falling off till Mom fastened it with about fifty safety pins. She swears it will stay up.

Mom and Joel are going AND my dad is flying in. That should be strange. Suppose I have to introduce Joel? "Uh, Dad, this is the man mom married." Get me out of here! Kristy is stage manager and she swears that if my toga falls down, she'll drop the curtain.

6/8

Heller wanted to know if I was going to teach Tomas à Becket again next fall. Said yes even though I'll probably have six students. Am beginning to accept that what I like is never going to be fashionable.

Met Anne's ex. He looks older for his age than I do for mine.

DD,

The play was so incredible, diary, but you wouldn't believe it. Moss Brickley was there with his wife, and if you saw her, you'd faint. Oh, rats, gotta go. Mom and Joel are taking me out for pizza, then I'm sleeping at Kristy's with Debra, who's becoming my second-best friend. Ta, ta, as they say in Rome.

JOYCE PURNICK BECAME THE FIRST WOMAN to head the Metropolitan Section of the *New York Times*—the paper's largest news department—in the spring of 1997. She came to the *Times* in 1979, was its first woman City Hall bureau chief, and covered several classic beats, ranging from education to politics. Among the many awards she has won are the Meyer Berger Award from Columbia University's Graduate School of Journalism, a George Polk award for excellence in metropolitan reporting, and the Peter Kihss Award for outstanding reporting on New York City government. She has been honored by the Associated Press, the Newswomen's Club of New York, and the Newspaper Guild. She is married to Max Frankel, media columnist for the *New York Times Sunday Magazine* and former executive editor of the *Times*.

THE ACCIDENTAL FEMINIST

This is my mother's favorite story. She never actually said it was her favorite story, but I always knew it was because she told it many, many times, and every time it was with an air of triumph that said more than the words.

The story is a simple one, about her maternal grandmother's arrival in this country, and this is how I remember it:

In the late 1800s, when she was in her early twenties, my great-grandmother Pauline emigrated from Poland with her husband

Samuel. Like most Jewish women from the old country, she wore a wig, just as many Orthodox Jewish women do today. Once married, the custom goes, a religious Jewish woman is supposed to cover her hair rather than risk distracting men from prayer or study. Hence the wig, or *sheitel* (rhymes with *title*) in Yiddish.

Sheitels have never been the most comfortable of accouterments. They are much improved today, but in the nineteenth century they were hot and itchy, and not very attractive. They limited a woman's sense of freedom and, detractors have argued, reinforced a woman's presumed inferiority. Men—the students, the scholars—had to be protected from a woman's crowning beauty. Her hair.

So, my mother used to tell me, when her grandmother caught her first glimpse of the Statue of Liberty from the prow of her ship, she ripped the sheitel right off her head, threw it into the East River, declared her freedom, and that, thank you very much, was that. This was, after all, America. Great-grandmother Pauline never wore a sheitel again nor, as far as I know, have any of her descendants.

As I get older and try to figure out the reasons why my life took the course it did, that story keeps popping into my mind. I have a career, that I love. Of course I do. Of course I never felt impelled to marry, though I was lucky enough to find my match at the age of forty. Of course, of course. Because—environment and timing and happenstance notwithstanding—could the daughter of Charlotte Leah Schrader and great-granddaughter of the rebellious Paulia have done anything else?

I suspect my mother would have been stunned had I ever said this to her directly, but she really was a feminist—an accidental feminist, perhaps—but a feminist nonetheless. I know that from more than family fables. But since my mother often spoke indirectly, there is one more story to tell: one afternoon, when my mother was already failing in her bout with cancer, we were talking about a friend of hers. I noted that the woman's abusive husband had walked out on his young bride. "No," said my mother, barely audible. "*She* walked out on *him*."

The voice was weak but the message loud and clear. Women should be strong, determined, direct. Never passive. And they should never allow themselves to be the victim, not of cultural norms or circumstances or of a man.

This often reinforced message came from a seemingly improbable source—a red-haired, green-eyed beauty who wore dresses and heels even to the A&P (it was the fifties, remember) and was a loyal, supportive wife to my father—a man as strong in his way as she in hers. My mother was feminine in the traditional sense of the word, but in the age of Donna Reed and Doris Day, she never held out marriage as a woman's ultimate accomplishment, or even hinted that a man and only a man completed a woman.

She so instilled in me a sense of unlimited possibilities by seeing to it that I was exposed to every opportunity, that to this day I am impatient with women who shy from competing with men, who hide their intelligence to avoid threatening men or bruising their egos.

In fact, as naive as this will sound, it wasn't until I was in my early twenties, working as a reporter and reading about the nascent women's movement, that I realized society had different expectations for men and women. My mother didn't, nor did my father. And so I didn't.

My mother was not impelled by politics, I am sure. What drove her was her own experience. She never had the chance to do what she wanted. The Depression got in the way. And so did her gender.

I learned about my mother's life incrementally over the years, and, as always, indirectly. She didn't talk much about herself but children figure out how to fill in the blanks. My mother wanted much more than she ever got, and got much less than her younger brother did. She was the girl, she was older, and when she was still in her late teens, her father died.

She had a model's figure and carriage so she went to work in the garment industry, as many Jewish men and women did in those days, and modeled coats in a New York City fur market. That helped support the family, and her brother's college education. He went to a free city college, but there were books to buy, and lunch and transportation money. The sister and the mother worked to make sure the boy got the education. That is the way it was.

When she was about twenty-nine, my mother married her boss, my father, had me and my younger brother, and submerged what remained of her dreams. Instead she was a wife, mother, showroom model, and business partner with my father. Once my brother and I were old enough—when I was in college and he in high school—my folks started a fur manufacturing company together. They struggled awhile, but finally they did all right. And then my mother took ill and died at the age of sixty-seven.

She died without ever getting the education her brother did, or the dance lessons she longed for because that is what she dearly wanted—to be a great dancer. She might have been one, too. Or at least found out if she could have made it. If it hadn't been for circumstances and custom. And living in a time and place when women took second best.

That is, I am certain, why my mother loved to tell the story of Great-grandmother Pauline. To make sure—indirectly of course—that her daughter would always know she descended from a woman with the courage to send her sheitel to the bottom of New York Harbor.

CHARLOTTE LEAH SCHRADER

A CHINA SCHOLAR TURNED CHINESE COOK, **BARBARA TROPP** is the author of *The Modern Art of Chinese Cooking*, widely regarded as the classic text in English on Chinese cooking techniques, and the best-selling *China Moon Cookbook*, winner of the prestigious Julia Child Award for Best International Cookbook. For eleven years, she owned and operated the acclaimed China Moon Cafe in San Francisco. An elected member of Who's Who in Food & Wine in America, she teaches widely, has been profiled in the PBS series *Great Chefs of San Francisco*, and is founder and past president of Women Chefs and Restaurateurs.

THE FRUITS OF MOM'S TREE

I inherited from my mother her guts, her smarts, her perfectionism, and her ovarian cancer. At age forty-nine, I'm now a year older than she at the time of her death. Mom died silent, in a coma, having never shared her pain. She carried it all, from the start. It literally ate her up.

Mom was part conservative, part renegade. She married at twenty-four, a relatively old age for women of her time and class. In a conventional mode, she married a paternal-seeming man of her own religion and background, and immediately conceived kids. Unconventionally, she went into her marriage one of the few women in the country with a podiatry degree. She tried a route that didn't work. Bored with a housewife's life, she set up her doctor's shop on the ground floor of our split-level house on the very day her youngest child began school.

Mom was a caged bird longing to sing. Inscrutably tailored, she kept at the end of her Spartan closet a single, wildly patterned dress. I yelped like a threatened dog when she dared to wear it. Laced into space shoes by day, she made the occasional, delicious foray to Mr. Gregory's for spike heels so thin she had to walk on tiptoe lest she slip through the Jersey boardwalk. Mom's marriage wasn't charmed. She saw a marriage counselor—unusual for her time and our town—and might have flown away had she lived.

Mom's ideal for her daughter was a life of travel and achievement. When I was not yet a teen, she announced with uncharacteristic glee that Hope Cooke had married the Prince of Sikkim. Was it the dream of the child or the hope of the mother that made me soon after study Chinese?

Mom never traveled, never in body and I suspect rarely in spirit. Asphyxiated by her life, I exploded out of the house the minute I was able. When I returned from a four-month trip to Europe following my junior year at Barnard, she met me at Newark Airport, eyes gleaming with pride and imagined adventures. I told her of Turkey and Greece, Prague and Budapest, and for a moment she was there. Just a moment. Then she was trapped in a hospital, caught in the hot web of pain that was to be her death.

Like many women of her time (and mine), Mom was a prisoner of diets. Struggling always with five pounds of forbidden, lusty pleasure, she projected her fat onto her daughter. I was subjected to grapefruit diets one week and butter-less toast the next. What to lose but my identity? Hungry and craving, I instead became a chef. I ate mightily for my mother and turned slim.

Looking back on my mother and ahead to my stepdaughter—now fourteen and towering over me with her full-breasted figure—I see how I've gathered the fruits of Mom's tree. Some I've eaten with

EDNA KROLL TROPP

pleasure and thankfulness. Others I've spat out like poison. Such is the mixture of blessing and curse. On the family table, some dishes will surely kill.

How strange it is now, at the age my mother never reached, to look back in the mirror and see her—first in her prime (the photo from her school years), later in her death throes (the image burned in my brain). Strange too to carry her genes and her urges. Delicious to be free of the bulk of her pain. Wonderful to have eaten the feast that was forbidden. My marriage is blissful, my life deeply pleasurable. My passport is full, my cup runneth over.

My death, should it come early, will not be like hers. My mother granted me the gift of knowing what I'd need to survive her. I embrace you, Mom. I love you. I strive to overcome you.

Recipe For Good Mothering

Marinate your daughter in ample amounts of love and tenderness, tempered with distance so she can grow. As she does, give her realistic boundaries and the joy and discipline of making her own choices. Add a dash of fantasy to the mix, so she can dance as well as walk.

When she's old enough, inspire her with the example of fulfilling work and healthy relationships. Teach her about hard choices. Keep adding love, always.

If you die before her, set a great example. She'll be left with the taste of your dying, so make it as sweet as you are able.

NTOZAKE SHANGE IS AN AWARD-WINNING PLAY-WRIGHT, novelist, and poet. Her play *for colored girls who have considered suicide/when the rainbow is enuf* received the Obie Award, the Audelco Award, and a Tony nomination. She has received the Guggenheim, Cubb, and the National Endowment for the Arts for Playwriting fellowships, and a MacDowell Colony fellowship. Her novels include *Sassafrass, Cypress, & Indigo, Betsey Brown,* and *Liliane,* and her published poetry collections include *nappy edges, A Daughter's Geography,* and *The Love Space Demands.* Her most recent books are *White Wash* and *If I Can Cook/You Know God Can.* She teaches at Prairie View A & M University in Texas where she is Associate Professor of Drama and English.

ELLIE, WHO IS MY MOTHER

"In the fullness of time, we shall know why we are tried and why our love brings us tears as well as happiness."

—The Torah
(My mother's favorite quotation from childhood)

There is a memory of the swish-swishing of skirts, the smells of powders and coffee, my father's cologne seems to seep from her skin and the pillow I nestle my head, my whole body curved again as in the beginning. I am the only one. This is my mother, Eloise, who married Paul who was my father and that's how she became my mother.

Mirrors. Small delicate bottles. Dresses with pearls and lace from Paris I knew this. I saw it on the globe that lit up at night like the neon signs across the way, letting me know we were colored in the colored part of town. Yet the movies and photographs were black and white. Not fitting all the different shapes and odors of folks who came to see my mother. Laughter from the kitchen. Laughter up the stairs. Aunt Emma was here, Uncle Jimmy was here with Aunt Margaret. So were my grandmothers. My mother had a special greeting for each one, as if there were something in her soul that let her know what touch or hug a body needed. My grandmother hovered like Billie Burke. I couldn't distinguish my mother from Jean Seberg, Marilyn Monroe, Kim Novak, or Dorothy Dandridge. I remember her eyes glowed as mine widened when Carmen DeLavallade danced.

The lindy hop was not the only vernacular activity my mother mastered. There were collard greens and smothered pork chops. There were the nights when sleep came dragging its heels and my mother had a rhythmic pat that was so soft yet steady that sleep gave up staying away from me. Let my mother calm my soul so that when my dreams came, I dreamt in color.

I liked to hide in the back of my mother's closet with her dresses and smells. Now I realize many, many other little girls did the same. Even my own daughter waltzed about in my robe, wrapping my scent about her like some kind of magic.

Once we all wore the same color blue dresses, my sisters, my mother, and I. We were one for a long time. I could not tell long after I should have known better that I was not my mother. I wanted to be my mother. I liked her. I liked that way people liked her. I liked my father. But I could not be him. I could be her. I could deep-sea fish, play baccarat, sing like Marian Anderson, defend the race. We were a vulnerable people. I could tell from the stories my mother told with her friends when they played inscrutable games of cards for hours. Bridge. What did I know then about mother, this bridge called my back. What do I know now about my mother?

I live with the myth of her, my indisputable legend of her. Executing intricate steps of the cha-cha-cha in La Habana, dressing us all for The March on Washington, surviving diseasetrous lover after lover that I chose for myself, since I was not my mother. Since I was not my mother, I am still learning to mother myself which Alta and Adrienne told me years ago. But, I couldn't give up the black-and-white films of Ellie, who is my mother, to another time or other places. I see horizons sometimes and think of what she saw for me. I am guilty of spending days under huge oaks imagining myself as my mother when I became a mother, yet I am not. I really know I am not my Mother, but if I were to ever lose my myth of this woman of independent thought and chutzpah during the fifties, who actually demonstrated the meaning of "each one teach one," I would be less a woman than I am, less a mother than I am becoming. I respect Ellie. Then, sometimes I feel sadly for her because as colorful and colored as we were, our world was defined in black and white. Our world was featured in *Ebony, Jet, Sepia*. Now when I look at us, Ellie, and then me and my daughter, something is awry, I become uncollected. I never saw my mother "uncollected." She was not one to accept or expect to survive on Blanche's risky kindness of strangers, nor was she "invisible." But, I'm saving all my images, all the touch recollections I can sustain because the depth of Ellie's presence in me is antidiluvian, fierce, and infinite. So unlike what she appears to be, all of which she gave to me.

MARY GORDON IS THE BESTSELLING AUTHOR of five novels—*Final Payments, The Company of Women, Men and Angels, The Other Side,* and *Spending*. She has also published a book of novellas, *The Rest of Life,* a collection of stories, *Temporary Shelter,* a book of essays, *Good Boys and Dead Girls,* and a memoir about her father, *The Shadow Man*. Winner of the Lila Acheson Wallace-Reader's Digest Writer's Award, a Guggenheim Fellowship, and the 1996 O. Henry Prize for best short story, Mary Gordon is a professor of English at Barnard College. She lives with her husband and two children in New York City.

MY MOTHER IS SPEAKING
FROM THE DESERT

M y father is dead, but I do not live among the dead. It is among the living I must move, even when they are touched by him, or the idea of him. It is their words I must respond to and to them I must speak.

There is, for example, my mother. My father's wife.

When I speak about my father, people often ask me, "But where was your mother in all this?" I don't know what to say. She was there, of course. And yet, she wasn't with us. I don't know where she was.

As I don't know where she is now. She seems to be speaking from the desert. Everything she says now is spoken from the desert, a desert she has in part created. But only in part. Mostly, I suppose, the desert was created because she is eighty-six, and something has hardened, or broken, or worn out. The part she made came about through a dark will and sense of worthlessness. Believing she deserves nothing, she surrounds herself with empty air. The sun gleams in her eyes. Her eyes can sometimes seem colorless, as if they were ruined by looking at the sun. Sometimes she looks blind. Her eyes are very beautiful. The rest of her face is gaunt now and so you must look at her eyes: you can't look at anything else.

When she hasn't combed her hair, when she has lost a tooth she won't have attended to, when she won't cut or file her nails, or change her clothes, she is distressing to look at. She used to be a very buoyant person, fleshy, with a wonderful skin that always made you think of the inner flesh of fruit: an apple or a peach. When she wore sleeveless dresses in summer, the cool thick muscles of her upper arms made you want to rest your hot cheeks against them. The freshness and crispness of those dresses was a miracle. Their colors were the colors of nature: sea green, sky blue. It was as if she were wearing the elements themselves—the limitless sky, the refreshing sea—instead of a dress made of material whose shade was only a reminder of sea or sky.

In winter she wore hats with feathers and tailored suits made of men's fabric, with shoulder pads and serious straight skirts. She "went to business." She was a legal secretary. She worked for one lawyer from 1931 to 1970 when he died, then she became his partner's secretary. She was proud of her business clothes, different from the clothes of other mothers who had nothing at stake in what they wore; they could slop around the house wearing anything, and what would it matter? In her handbag she carried a gold compact, lipsticks that smelled like nothing else except themselves but I knew would taste delicious if I could only taste them. I wanted to taste everything: her skin, warmed or cooled by a light dusting of freckles, her light dresses, her lipstick, her perfume.

But underneath this freshness, this crispness, this robust, delightful not only health but healthfulness, there must always have been a secret devotion to rot. Perhaps it was connected to her polio, with which she was stricken with at the age of three. Buried beneath her grief and shame about her body, and beneath the stoicism that conceals her grief and shame like a softening tuber underneath a field.

Now the healthfulness is gone; she has burrowed down to a deeper place, a darker place, perhaps a one she feels to be more truthful. Or, perhaps, thought of another way, it is a place she goes to in the desert. The place of carrion. She lies down beside it, she makes her home in it: there she is at peace.

I failed to keep her from this place because my attempt to keep her from it was not an act of love but of terror and hatred. My mother's rotting body has taught me things I would otherwise never have known. About myself and the world. My mother's body, rotting at the center of my history, is the tight heart at the center of everything I know.

If I could understand how she changed from the fresh, lovely mother to the rotting one, what would I understand?

Everything. The darkness.

Or perhaps not. Perhaps I would only understand my mother.

Or perhaps not even that. Perhaps only something, but only one thing, having to do only with her.

She has lost her memory. As I am obsessively involved with bringing back my father from the past, she is letting the past slip from her hand, a fish into dark water. She is letting it drop through a scrim of tissue paper into the night air. She is allowing it to disappear in snow.

I believe she is doing this in part because of a great sorrow. A sorrow I can do nothing to help, a sorrow I probably helped bring about because of my hatred of her body. Because I abetted her in a project that would enact her hatred of her body. She yearned for its corruption because she believed, above all else, in its degradation. I sense that she thinks what she is doing now is nothing more than telling the truth.

She is in a nursing home now because of her desire to rot. There is no way around it, you cannot devote yourself to rot and have a place in the civilized world. Something must be done for you, to you. And I was the one to do it.

I had been living in a small town along the Hudson River. When my mother retired, at the age of seventy-five, I bought her a house two blocks from mine. I thought it was a perfect plan: she could stop working and be with her grandchildren. When Anna, my first child, named for her, was little, she was an enchanting grandmother: inventive, doting, amusing and amused. She said it would be a privilege and a pleasure to see the children growing. She'd worked every day except for six weeks off when I was born since she'd been eighteen. I sensed that her competence was slipping, that they were getting impatient with her at the office. I wanted her to leave of her own accord; the idea that they should force her to retire would have been the worst possible disgrace for her.

But bringing her to the country was a disaster. She didn't want to do anything. Take courses at the college, I suggested—Italian, opera, your father sang opera, and you could learn his language. Tutor children. Take in typing. Volunteer at the rectory. No, she said, I've worked long enough. She only wanted to be served. Five weeks after my second child was born, she had a fall. Or something: it was some sort of grotesque physical mishap. She told me that her brace and shoes were off, she wanted to go to the bathroom, so she simply crawled in. But she fell out of bed trying to get onto the floor. I knew that she'd been drinking. After that, she was confined to a wheelchair for six months and she never regained much mobility.

Six years later, when I moved to New York, I decided to leave her in the country. My husband would be there most of the week and we would be there on weekends. I hired a Taiwanese woman to live in. She'd been a nurse in Taiwan; she was getting a master's degree in psychology. She was a pretty, boyish, sharp-witted person, with an excellent sense of humor. After a month, she told me she wanted to quit; living with my mother was too depressing. I begged her to stay 'til Christmas. But around Halloween, when I took my mother to her regular semiannual physical, I discovered she hadn't taken her shoes off since the end of the summer. She'd slept in her shoes—high, built up, tightly laced boots—for three months. The doctor forbade her to take her shoes off in his office. He said he'd come to the house later. When she took off her shoes, the room was filled with the stench of rotting flesh. He said if she'd waited much longer, gangrene would have set in.

This made my decision: she'd have to go into a nursing home. An evaluating nurse, sent by the state, determined that my mother met the criteria to be in what was called a primary care facility. Most of the criteria had to do with piss and shit. The mind, the abilities of the imagination and the spirit, had almost no weight in these questions. I pulled every string to get my mother into a first-rate Catholic nursing home quite near where I lived. When I told her, she got blind drunk, cursed me and cried. Li, the Taiwanese nurse, wept. She said she couldn't live without my mother. I stood firm. "You can go to Mass every day," I told my mother. "Soon I'll be dead," she said, "then I won't need to go to Mass."

If I come upon her now and she isn't expecting me, I find her sitting with her head buried in her hands. There is no need for her to do anything now but adopt this formal posture of grief. Yet I don't think she would like to die. She will not, I believe, die soon. She has, I have been told by many doctors, the heart and blood pressure of a teenager.

If I were an allegorist, if I decided to do something in the manner of Giotto embodying the virtues in a living figure, I would paint my mother in her wheelchair, her head in her hands, wearing her magenta sweater (the only one she wears although there are a dozen in her cupboard). I would call it The Death of Hope.

She hopes for nothing, and because I believe that nothing can be done for her, because I have given her up, I hope for nothing on her behalf. Now everything in her life points out the futility of hope. But if I had wanted to paint hope, the embodied virtue, I would have painted my young mother in her sea green or sky blue dress, her lovely arms, her white skin and her strong and useful, perhaps rather dangerous teeth. Because hope can be dangerous. In that it leads to the death of hope. But it does not lead in a straight path to death. There is the animal, with the animal's hope. This is not human, it is not our own. It is something, but it is not ours.

There is a link between hope and memory. Remembering nothing, one cannot hope for anything. And so time means nothing. It is a use-less element. Living in time without memory or hope: a fish in air. A bird in water. Some unfortunate creature doomed to the wrong medium. Yet not, alas, to death.

I don't know what my mother does all day. She eats her meals. She sleeps. In the time that she's been in the home she's made three friends; one died, one is her roommate, whom she bullies. When the roommate rebels, she refuses to speak to her. She was making her roommate empty her bedpan until the nurses interfered. She has one friend who is completely charming: intelligent, loving, and aware. I don't know why she likes my mother; but she says my mother means the world to her, that if anything happened to my mother she doesn't know what she'd do. I know it would be rude to ask the reasons for such a statement, but I'm genuinely puzzled. I want to tell my mother's friend, "But you're too good for her. You can do much better than my mother. Find somebody else." Then I cover my mother with kisses, atoning for my betrayal. She doesn't know why I'm doing it, and, wisely, she doesn't respond.

I know that she prays. But I don't know what she's doing when she prays? What is she saying? Where is she? Is she in a blank silence, the presence of God, where there is nothing without meaning and she knows she is where she has always belonged, perhaps where she has always been? Is she silent, or is she saying words to God? Her own words or the formal words of prayer? Or is she having simple conversations, too banal to repeat, yet placing her exactly at the true, safe center of the universe? She says she prays for me. She says she prays for me and my family all the time. I believe her. But I don't know what she is thinking of us when she prays. Or even who, since she sometimes forgets that she has grandchildren.

I think she must be happy, praying. Or at least not suffering, in a place beyond memory. With God, since both of them are outside time, memory is irrelevant. So I can think of her praying, be both admiring and calm. Praying, she is in the place where she belongs. A place where she is still what she so often was: outstanding. I believe she sees the face of God. But who can see the face of God and live? Who can see the face of God and remember it? Perhaps that is the point. Perhaps it is the point most especially for my mother, for the way she must live now. The way she has no other choice but to live. Praying, she comes alive. Free of her body. Beautiful again: a spirit. Joyous. Not weighed down. Not even tragic. Partaking of greatness. Great.

I take her to a doctor at Mount Sinai to see if there is anything she can do that might reclaim her memory, return her zest for life. The doctor asks her questions.

She answers with words from the desert. "I don't have my memory any more. I don't think about things. They were all sad."

The doctor, who is beautiful, and lively, and wonderfully intelligent, says gently, "What about the happy things? Do you think about your mother? You had happy times with her."

She says, "That's sad too. Because everything is lost."

There's nothing I can say when she speaks like this because everything she says is true.

Is everything for my mother in the present? Does she live like God?

No, she still experiences fear and loss.

The dreadfulness that this should be the last to go. One day, when I arrive at the nursing home, she's trembling. A bishop is going to say Mass for them on the next day. She's been selected to read the Epistle. She's afraid she won't be able to do it. She's afraid she won't know when to come in. I find the nun who's in charge: she assures my mother that she'll hand her the microphone when the time comes. I go over the reading with her. She's letter-perfect. I say I'll come the next day to be with her for support.

She reads the Epistle. She reads out Philippians 3:22:16 as Philippians, March 22nd, 1916. She doesn't know she's made a mistake. After Mass, the bishop is extravagantly warm, full of praise. She doesn't respond to him. She doesn't know what he's talking about. The forty-five minutes of Mass is enough time to have erased the experience for her. But she was able to experience thirty-six hours of anticipatory anxiety and dread.

But she doesn't seem to dread the M.R.I. Perhaps because I've underrepresented its discomfort. The technician tells her to lie completely still, or the pictures will be useless. After a few minutes, I see her beginning to thrash. Through a microphone the technician tells her in an accusing voice that she is ruining everything. Instantly, I know what to do. I jump up, run over to the hole her legs are sticking out of, and thrust my head in. "We're going to say the Rosary," I tell her. And into the hole I shout, "The five sorrowful mysteries, the first mystery, the Agony in the Garden." Our Fathers. Hail Marys. The second mystery. The third. She settles down and lies quietly. The test is done. I realize that for me, who claims to live by words, there are no words that could automatically take away my terror. No poetry, no passages from great novels could be shouted at me and cause me to lie still. She is, in this way, more fortunate than I.

When we get to the doctor's office, on the other side of the

Medical Center, the doctor asks my mother if the test was difficult. What test?, she asks. The doctor describes the M.R.I. I don't remember anything like that, she says.

Another piece of good fortune; without memory there is no reliving of terror. The past no longer haunts. It is finished, and for good.

But if a loss of memory spares pain, it also vexes questions of pleasure. How is pleasure judged if it cannot be relived, recalled? It seems, from a capitalist stance, a bad investment. What yields pleasure yields it at some cost. Time, effort, money. Particularly in her case, since she is immobile, she must be brought to things or things brought to her. If she is brought to something the effort is enormous. When I think of doing things that might please her, I often find myself asking: "Is it worth it?" Worth what? The effort. Also, the resentment the effort entails. The capitalist's resentment for a bad investment.

What is something worth if it doesn't lodge in memory? Take, for instance, the situation of my son's Christmas play. I'd had a meeting with the social worker, the nurse, the doctor, who are in charge of her. We'd all agreed that she'd been less responsive than formerly. We agreed, as a team, to be more hopeful, more inventive, more persevering in suggesting things that might bring her "out of herself." None of us asked where she might be when she was in herself. As I leave the meeting, I'm inspired to ask my mother if she'd like to see her grandson as the star of the Christmas play. Usually, she says no to everything; she hasn't been out of the nursing home in three years. But for some reason, she says yes.

I move with extreme efficiency. No ambulette is available. An ambulette means she can be wheeled into a van, she doesn't have to get out of her wheelchair. But we're not lucky; all that's left is a regular ambulance which, I find, requires that she be lifted off her wheelchair onto a stretcher. The two attendants, both very young, one a slight Hispanic with an even slighter moustache, the other a chunky, opulently permed Italian, are both charming, helpful, and kind. My mother likes them; she flirts with the young man; she tells the young woman she's half Italian. We go up Broadway, sirens flashing. We arrive at the school and she's wheeled in on a stretcher. The sea of parents parts for us. The attendants switch her from the stretcher to a wheelchair. David, my son, introduces her to his teachers, the head of the middle school, and all his friends. When the play begins, the drama teacher says that David has asked that the play be dedicated to his grandmother. She loves everything: the Christmas carols, seeing her grandson with a major role (as Chico Marx), the dedication, all the attention. She glows with happiness as she is transferred from the wheelchair to the stretcher. We sing Christmas carols in the ambulance on the way home. I leave her at her room; she says she'll certainly sleep well tonight.

I am in love with her, with myself, with everyone connected with the evening. I tell myself that I have to do more things like this, all it takes is imagination, and hopefulness, and a little thought. What a difference can be made by things like this, I say, as I fall blissfully to sleep.

In the morning. I call her. I say: "Did you wake up thinking about last night."

"What happened last night?" she asks.

"The play," I prompt her. "David's Christmas play."

"I don't remember. I don't remember anything," she says.

My first thought is that she's done this to make a fool of me. No, to make a fool of hopefulness. Then I think that it was such a wonderful experience for her, and she knew how rare it would be, so she had to forget it, so as not to long for more things like it. Then I think that it doesn't matter, the experience is lost, it is worse than if it never happened. All the effort, all that expense. I vow I won't tell my son. I hope he doesn't bring it up if he sees her, or that she'll have the sense to fake it. With all my will I remind myself that she was happy at the time, that that's what matters, that it's not important that she doesn't remember it. For the moment, it was of great value; I tell myself we live for moments only. But I don't believe it for a second.

My desire, my need to punish my mother is very great. I am conscious of no need to punish my father. This is because of the totally different histories of their bodies in relation to me. If I force myself, I can call up his toothless mouth, his ripped trousers, but when I think of his body, automatically I first think of his beautiful hands with their silver ring, the buttons on the sleeves of his suit jacket. I think of the place in the center of his chest where I could rest my head, the place of comfort and safety I will yearn for till the moment of my death. I can call up the fresh young arms of my still young mother, but only with effort. When I think of my mother's body, I think first of degradation, rot. That is my first landing; I have to push myself past that place to the place of the refreshing mother, who is wonderful to be around.

Because of her polio, my earliest vision includes the vision of a damaged female body. For many years, the only adult female body I saw unclothed was, it must be said, grotesque, lopsided, with one dwarf leg and foot, and a belly with a huge scar biting into and discoloring unfirm flesh. She'd point to it and say, "This is what happened when I had you."

For many years as a child, much longer than I should have, I imagined that all women had this slit belly and when I had children I would too.

I had many chances to look at my mother's body over the years, but I saw my father's only fleetingly, in stolen glimpses, in the nature of a crime. But it is a whole body: strong legs and back, dark nipples that match his maroon bathing suit, a raised mole on his chest I finger like a talisman or toy. At the same time, a ruined mouth. I learn to take in bodies in a fragmentary way, because both my parents' bodies bear witness to a damage I would rather avert my eyes from. I must ignore my father's toothless mouth and everything about my mother except her beautiful hair, skin, eyes, fine teeth, and buoyant upper arms. But my father's damage can be corrected; all he has to do is put in his teeth. This causes me to believe that the miracle of prosthesis applies only to men. Clothed, with his teeth in, my father can become entirely desirable. My mother never can. She always limps; she is always unable to do most ordinary things. She can't walk more than a few steps. She can never carry me.

I am ashamed, as a woman, that when I say the words "My mother's body," I have feelings of revulsion, and when I say "My father's body," I have feelings of joy and peace. It's an old story. The love of the absent, of the not. The elegant beneficence of early death. An existence in memory, which has no smell. Or in photographs, where the flesh is not subject to rot.

I should feel more loyalty to the body more like mine. Because, if I hate my mother's body, what can I feel about my own?

But my body is not like hers. She is crippled; I am not. It shaped the way we lived: this difference between us. What was always in the front of both our minds was that the crucial thing was that she must not fall. We lived both our lives in terror of her falling. It was like living on a fault line or on the top of a volcano. The anxiety that the thoughtless move, the too-forceful move, the unexpected move would cause calamity. My mother's falling seemed like a natural disaster. The crash, the crying out. Then the immobility. I never remember her rising up after she fell. She had to be brought to bed. Where she would lie and weep with her eyes closed. Sometimes she would moan aloud. No sense of when she might get up again. Perhaps never.

I learned quite early that it is my fate always to be the most able-bodied in any room. That is the way I have always lived, alert for the scar, the concealed false limb, the tremor, the flicker of anxiety at the prospect of uncertain terrain, the slurred speech, the hesitant, reluctant gesture. I always find it and I always know that because of this I am called upon, not only to act, but also to find a solution for the damage that must be accommodated to, made up for, got around. I believe that I will always find a solution and that it will always be right. This is the source of my worst qualities: arrogance, self-right-eousness, also intense self pity, then resentment and contempt.

I used to believe all these could be traced to my mother's body. I have learned it had another source: my father's body and my understanding that it is only by my efforts that he stays alive. The other thing I learn quite early: his death means I have failed.

My mother will live for many years, but I have failed her too. I cannot keep a living spirit in her body. I cannot make her remember. I cannot keep her from a living death, a rock-like existence, almost without consciousness. I cannot keep her from a life in which death would make very little difference.

I have failed them both.

When you are with my mother, it is best to have conversations that don't require a reference to the past. No interpretation. Narrative is second best, a far second after description. Plain description is what's called for.

Our best visits consist of my taking her to the garden in Riverside Park. I wheel her chair down the hill. I have to struggle to keep the momentum from hurtling her to disaster. I bend my legs and strain my body to keep her safe. The next day my back always hurts. But I keep my posture easily because of the horrifying vision of what would happen if I did not. My mother, hurtling forward. Her head gashed on the pavement. I see the bloody forehead, the wound with pebbles imbedded in it. Inattentiveness could bring about a tragedy: I must be hypervigilant about everything, every variation of the surface.

We wheel around the enclosed garden. We say the names of flow-ers or colors. Peony, we say, foxglove, lily, pansy, phlox. The words are beautiful in themselves. And we say the names of colors: red, yel-low, purple, blue, deep rose. Sometimes we sing. She remembers the words to songs. Doing these things, we are both happy.

When we are doing these things, I wonder, "Is it possible I still have a mother?"

"Of course," I say, "how could it not."

But then, how can it be.

A mother without memory of the stories of the past means that I must accept the possibility that I have never been a child.

Does she remember my childhood, my babyhood. Who am I to her? Someone she doesn't remember giving birth to, who is, somehow, fully grown. A daughter with a lost childhood. My father is gone, my mother has misplaced my childhood. So what? Why the importance of these images? To whom do they matter? The shocking insistence, the narcissism of asserting the importance of memory. Perhaps it is always only in order to be able to say: "This is where I am. Magnetic North."

Where is my mother? Where does she think she is?

My mother is speaking from the desert where she would like to disappear. But how can she disappear there, when there is no place to hide? Perhaps by the sheer force of something whose name I do not know. Perhaps it is her sorrow, creating a fog in which she will disappear. Yet she is visible to me, partly because I have ineradicable memories of her vividness. She was, above all, a vivid creature. She raged so people were careful not to cross her. She kissed men right on the mouth, she'd grab the microphone at public gatherings to sing. She laughed so loudly in the movies that people she knew would meet her in the lobby afterwards and say they knew just where she had been sitting. She loved foods that she could crunch and chew: particularly nuts; she would indulge herself in an extravagant purchase of cashews and almonds every year at the end of Lent. Just as no one alive remembers my father's body, no one remembers my mother's freshness and her vividness because no one else now alive had a stake in it.

She was always admirable, attractive, enjoyable. Even when she was committed to a course of degradation, to her love of rot, the vivacious animal held sway.

She was the life of the party. Now she is barely alive.

For many years, she used alcohol to allow herself to fall into the pit of shame, of stupor, of oblivion. Now she can enter it without chemical aid. Age provides her with a stupor from which she has no desire to escape, even if she could. For years I have stood at the edge of the pit, trying to keep her back. The same muscles I use when I push her wheelchair down a hill, holding her back from hurtling forward. Now I realize that her desire for stupor is stronger than my ability to keep her lively. I give in to her need for darkness. I give her up. I turn my back on her. And go off, as I always did, with him.

For three weeks, at any time during the day when my mind is not taken up with the business of living—reading, writing, caring for children, shopping, cooking, speaking to friends, calling insurance companies or the Super—what I am thinking about is my mother's fingernails.

She has given up attending to her nails, at the same time that the head nurse on her floor has taken three weeks vacation. This woman oversees her charges with a benevolent general's intelligence and interest in the welfare of her troops. While she's away, things slip a bit. My mother's nails are not quite claws yet; they haven't begun to turn under. I know she's waiting for me to cut her nails. Everyone is waiting for me. The substitute nurse says they have no nail scissors, it's up to me to produce some. And do I? Three weeks in a row I forget. She refuses to file her nails, the nursing home says it cannot, and

I forget to bring clippers. All of us joined in an insistence that my mother will appear more animal than she needs to.

They care for her body in a way that is better than most. But it is up to me to keep an eye on the details. She is a difficult patient for them because she refuses to take a shower. I tell them that she has never taken showers, because she has never been able to walk without her shoes. As I tell them that I realize what an extraordinary thing it is: my mother has never taken a shower. Very few people in the modern West can say such a thing. Occasionally, perhaps once a year when she was younger, she would, with great difficulty, and requiring much assistance (my father's, her mother's, and then, after her mother's death, mine) take a bath. Would the nurses believe me if I told them that for most of her life she was exceptionally clean? That she reminded me of sheets hung out in the wind, of the white flesh of apples? Would they believe me, or would they say, quite properly, what does that have to do with now?

When I have to say the words, "Her hair is dirty, her teeth are falling out, she has a rash," I am covered over in rage and panic that literally takes my breath away. I can hardly speak. I want to cry. I want to say, "She had wit and dash and beauty. She asked things of life in a world where no one dared to. You must understand that she does not deserve this. Because you don't understand it, I would like to punish and humiliate you in the way that she is punished and humiliated." At the same time as I am her advocate, I want to scream at her, and say, "How can you allow this to go on?" It makes me want to end her life. At the same time I want to sit in her lap and say, "Don't you understand that I'm your child and a child shouldn't have to do this." And have a transformed mother, fragrant, buoyant, say what she was almost never able to say, "Don't worry about anything, I'll take care of everything."

Although my sense of her ability to care for me was always partial, there were times when I yearned for her presence as purely as
Proust's Marcel longed for his mother's kiss in his bed in Combray. It
happened only irregularly while my father was alive. I remember one
of his few moments of annoyance (he was never really angry at me)
when my mother was at a meeting one night and I expressed my sense
of missing her. "You're never satisfied," he said. "When I'm not here
you want me, when your mother's not here you want her." It didn't
occur to me to defend myself on the grounds that what I really wanted
was both my parents, and that was actually rather a normal impulse.

When my mother went to work and my father went to the city I
was left with a woman from the parish whose idea of child care was
to let me wander around the dark house all day, unamused, unspoken
to. I was afraid of everything there: the black-out shades, the too-
sharp flowers in the night-colored garden, the cat who slunk under
the leaves and would appear, suddenly, from underneath them, her
eyes baleful, a dead bird in her jaws. For hours in good weather, I sat
on the porch waiting, not for my mother, but my father. And on the
first, miserable days of school, it was my father that I missed. He
would stand on the other side of the schoolyard's chain-link fence,
and I would touch him through the diamond-shaped links till the last
possible second. Then the bell would carry me away to that doom-
laden room, smelling so agonizingly of half-sour milk, half-eaten
lunches, paste, the spearmint leaves the nuns sold, two for a penny,
during recess.

But in the summers after my father's death, when it was determined that it was good for me to get away, to get out of myself, to
quit the moping, the thought of being separated from my mother's
freshness, from her firm, fragrant arms and lovely clothing, was
unbearable. I lived in anguish the last days of school, knowing what
was to come.

The first summer after my father died, I was sent away to my
mother's friend in the Bronx. She took me to museums every day. But

they were the wrong ones. There was only one real museum: the Metropolitan, with its grand staircase, its Madonnas, its huge statues with their smooth, high flanks. My mother's friend took me to the displays in the Museum of the American Indian and the collection of antique dolls in the Museum of the City of New York. She took me to the Museum of Natural History where I was frightened of the huge skeletons I thought at any moment would come to life. There was only one successful outing, to the Hayden Planetarium, where I lay back and looked at the model of the heavens, convinced that once again my father and I were seeing the same thing.

Although I knew on principle I was too old for missing my mother—the appropriate time for that having passed with my first communion, when I achieved the Age of Reason—I didn't dread what would happen to me if I cried in front of my mother's friend. I knew she would understand. The shame would emanate from a standard held only by me: my helplessness at keeping intact the thin skin that contained my tears like an overstretched balloon. But when I was with my aunts and uncles, my mother's family, it was their response, not something coming from myself, that was the thing most to be feared.

They had an ideal called "toughness" whose dark opposite was "sensitivity." "She's so goddamn sensitive," I always heard them say about me. "You have to watch every word you say." One day, when I'd been caught crying, my aunt and uncle decided they were going to try an experiment to toughen me up. They told me to stand at the opposite end of the room. They shouted insults about me, mostly about how big my stomach was. If I cried, I had to go into the bathroom and compose myself, then come out and start again. I never won, or they never lost. I don't know what made them stop. Probably, it was mealtime, or there was something they wanted to watch on television.

I cried again during the last half-hour of that visit. My endurance was simply at an end: like an exhausted runner, I couldn't go the last steps. "Are you crying because you're remorseful?" my uncle asked. "Yes," I said. I was sure I had something to be remorseful about, or he wouldn't have used such a serious word. They didn't like "big words." Finally, I assumed that what I had to be remorseful about was the fact of my crying.

The second summer after my father's death, I was sent to a camp run by my aunt, my uncle, and their spouses. It was a boys' camp; I was the only girl. I wasn't allowed to join in most of the activities. It was the last thing I would have wanted anyway. I was quite unathletic and anything but a tomboy. I spent the day looking at old magazines, *Good Housekeeping* and the *Ladies Home Journal.* I cut out pictures of women. I tried to read the boys' classics that were around. It was my first experience of reading a book that bored me: *The Last of the Mohicans.* And *Oliver Twist* was the first book I put down because it made me too afraid.

I cried for my father, I cried for my mother, I cried out of sheer wretchedness and boredom. My aunt, my mother's sister, who was the camp nurse, bought me a picture of Alfred E. Newman, the gap-toothed hero of *Mad* magazine. Underneath his foolish face were the words "Keep smiling." Every time she saw me starting to cry, she'd point to the spot on her front teeth where Alfred's gap would be. That would make me cry even more. One day she did it and my grandmother, who was usually anything but sympathetic to me, banged down a pot and said to her, "Leave her alone, for God's sake, can't you see her little heart is broken?" She never did anything like that again, but it made clearer than ever to me how my mother failed to protect me. She would never stand up to her brothers and sisters. When I complained about her siblings' insulting me from across the room she said, "They're just doing it for your own good. Let's not make waves."

But however partial her protection was, I missed her terribly, I knew she loved me. More; I knew that she admired me. I knew that from the moment of my birth.

I think her admiring me combined with her sense of her own unworthiness to make her feel she always ought to be giving me up. She perceived, at a very early stage, that I was more like my father than like her. So she stood back and let him take me.

On one of our walks to the garden she says, "I don't remember your father's face but I remember he was crazy about you. Sometimes I felt I could hardly get near you." "That must have been difficult for you," I say. "No," she says, "because I realized how important that made me. I was the mother of the person who was so important to him. I was the stupid one. But I was the one that brought you forth." While she uses words like "brought you forth," I realize all she was deprived of because of having to work so early. She wanted to be a teacher, but was rejected because of her handicap. Rejected in a particularly cruel way. She'd been accepted on the basis of her test score, but when the people at the normal school saw her they were surprised. They put her through a series of humiliating physical tests; they made her do squat thrusts. Then they told her she had to understand that in case of a fire she wouldn't be able to get the children out of the building fast enough. She said she understood. With the same stoicism that she understood that I belonged to my father.

When I think about these things, I am filled with love for her, and I remember how lovable she was, and how intensely I missed her in the times we were apart. What I missed most was the sense of rightness, of right choices, that she represented, her crispness, her business acumen, the fact that up and down the street and all around the parish, people asked her advice about "letters from the government," or tax returns, or wills. She put her blue-framed glasses on and within minutes solved their problem. Or she would get on the phone. She was brilliant on the phone. She prided herself on having "a good telephone voice." How irresistible she was on the telephone, of course no one could resist her. And she was delightful around anything having to do with money: at the bank, where she was immediately given pride of place because her boss was the bank's attorney (she never had to stand in line; she could get any check approved). Or even in the butcher shop, the vegetable market. As long as she was touching coins or bills, or something representing them, she was at ease, and powerful, and, most of all, effective. Yet she didn't care about money, in the sense of accumulating it for herself. She liked, only, being involved in its movement.

I understood very well that my father's death had only enhanced her social position, therefore mine. She had been the unfortunate wife of an unfortunate husband: now she was the noble widow and I the gallant orphan. There was no place where we went that this was not immediately legible. But never more so than when we entered our pew in the front of the church, always getting there early so my mother wouldn't be jostled by crowds and thrown off balance. There was a terrible crush at Sunday Mass in those days. The whole congregation had an admiring eye on us. We were consistently admired.

And she would occasionally, though sparingly, use her status as a noble and competent cripple for my good. There was the memorable incident that occurred when I was thirteen, the only one in the class with a working mother. I invited some boys and girls over one afternoon to dance. It was a disaster. The boys stood on one side of the room and smoked. The girls danced with each other. One boy, trying to be cool and light his cigarette from the gas stove, set his hair on fire. Another burned a hole in the rug. A third opened the storm door with such force that it broke off its hinges. One of our neighbors reported all this to the Rosary Society; it spread through the parish. The principal threatened me with not being allowed to graduate publicly. My mother went up to school. She made a point of how difficult it was for her to walk down the long corridors, and that she had to take time off from work. She said to the principal, "What do you think those kids were doing? I don't think they were doing anything. It shows the difference in our minds." She never blamed me, which was unusual for her. I was tremendously proud of her—none of the other parents stood up to the nuns—but it made me feel unworthy. And I was aware I had been spared punishment because she was a cripple and a widow.

But that was only part of it. I was also spared because she was daring and articulate. When she knew she was right, she was fearless. Part of the pride she felt she had to give up as a cripple transformed itself into something morally positive: she didn't care what people thought about her. She took pride in appearing outrageous, vulgar even, in saying *hell* and *goddamn* freely and in all company. When I went through a squeamish phase, at about the age of ten, she said that she'd never trust anyone who was afraid of the word *shit*. And when, in early adolescence, I dreaded changing clothes in front of other girls she said, "If you see anyone with anything you don't have, throw a shoe at it."

But it was this same lack of regard for public opinion which allowed her to stop grooming herself, to give in to her love of rot. Looked at in this way, a regard for the opinion of the world, a consciousness of and concern for how one is seen, seems infinitely precious and humanizing. But my mother's dashing lack of regard for public opinion gave her, when she was younger, a richer and fuller humanity, more fun, more scope for self-expression and satisfaction of her strong nature. And it was a great gift to me: I never had to endure what many girls did, the blunt hoof of propriety crushing my chest, the beast mother, with her blood-red eyes, enforcing the implacable rules of the household gods. She was not afraid of being in the world, as the mothers of many of my friends were. She took me into it.

When we went to restaurants—only two of them, but they were important ones in the place we lived—she was always given the best table, and always waited on by someone she knew. After my father died, she made a little home for us in restaurants. No, not a little home. A vacation spot. A resort.

I understood that all the food I was eating on these occasions came to us because of my mother's relationship to money. She made it; she could spend it; she was willing to spend it on fun. I don't know if it was because of this that all the food connected to my mother on these occasions seemed extraordinarily delicious. Bright colors, good textures, satisfying, clear, unclouded tastes. Many foods frightened me to the point of panic in those years. Mayonnaise, cocoa, fat and gristle on meat, the smallest spot on the skin of a tomato. I thought they would poison me or choke me; they would, in some way, be the cause of my death. My mother seemed magically able to avoid all these disturbing food elements on our outings together. She assured, by her assurance in ordering, that we would come near none of these things. She made it so that they didn't exist, a distant memory from a deprived past. Everything she suggested we eat was festive, modern, possibly unnourishing, but full of the electric joy of life I knew when she and my father lived alone. None of her family knew anything about things like that, and I hugged our superior skill to ourselves, as I folded my menu, unfolded my napkin, took the paper off my straw.

In the local luncheonette we were waited on by her friend Tess, an iron haired, thin-lipped woman who seemed to come to life around my mother. She always said, "God bless her" to me, always brought us our orders without having to ask for it. She knew what we wanted: "The regular." Grilled cheese sandwiches, chocolate milk for me, coffee for my mother. For my dessert the specialty of the house: lemon ice cream.

Every time I got a good report card (and I always did) she would drive to the next town to a bar and grill called the Brick Cafe. It was owned by a man named Charlie, an ex-prizefighter who had briefly been one of my mother's beaux. It is rather unusual that my mother—a cripple, though a beautiful one—had one beau who was a prize fighter and another who was a rodeo cowboy. These are the only two she ever spoke of, but I think they were the only ones. Except for John Gallagher, a widower, an undertaker. John wanted to marry her. The cowboy and the prizefighter, I think, did not. My father must have had the slightly illegal appeal that the prizefighter and the cowboy did, but he was sanctioned by the priests she worshiped. And he did, remarkably, want to marry her. People who knew them when they were courting say they were publicly, almost embarrassingly, amorous. They kissed on the subway. And he wrote her poetry. He would buy her greeting cards, then cut or rip out the printed verse on the inside and substitute one of his own. In 1945, her birthday message included the words: "Never in all the annals of recorded time/existed such sweet pretext for a rhyme."

I'm sure Charlie the boxer didn't write her poetry. By the time I was born, he'd long retired. He tended bar at the Brick Cafe; his brother Paul, a morose, dark, heavy German, cooked in the back. He was never visible except when he came out to say hello to my mother in a filthy white T-shirt and grease-spattered pants. Here again, we never had to ask for what we wanted. My mother had Welsh Rarebit, which Paul made miraculous by generous lashings of beer and luxurious slatherings of butter on the toast points. I was brought a shrimp cocktail with Russian dressing. The coral colored stripes of the shrimp beautifully matched the orange pink of the dressing and the polite green understatement of the lettuce cut what would have been too rich for a young palate to bear. I drank a Shirley Temple and my mother a Manhattan. We were the only unescorted females in the place. Charlie would whisk us to our car, to see that we got home safely. We were on top of the world, a place far exalted above her brothers and sisters. I always wished we were living by ourselves on those nights, in our own apartment, but I know she felt she needed her family's help. I know they didn't understand our exalted position: they thought we were somehow pathetic, somehow beneath them, needy dependents. I knew we weren't. But as it turned out, they were right—my mother and her family—and I was wrong.

Because, as it turned out, my mother needed her family's support. She wasn't very good at being only a mother. It wasn't her widowhood—being without my father, no longer being a wife—that diminished her capacity; I don't believe she minded being without my father at all. But when her mother died and she was no longer a daughter, she couldn't be a very good mother to me.

My grandmother died, without a will, after a long illness during which my mother and I took care of her virtually by ourselves. After my grandmother's death, the family split in half, some taking my mother's side in her claim to deserve the house, on the grounds that she paid the mortgage entirely from 1929, the beginning of the Depression, to 1941, the year of her marriage. I don't know what my aunt's claim to the house was, perhaps that she had always lived there. She left—ran out—to get married at the time my grandmother was dying, coming home only after the deed was done to tell my mother and me. My mother was undone; she blamed my aunt for abandoning her and her mother; she called her a liar and a sneak. My aunt, withholding, silent, won the day. Half my mothers brother and sisters (there were nine of them) no longer spoke to her after this time. So all at once my mother was both orphaned and bereft of the idea of herself as a person inviolably protected by the inviolable carapace of family life. This dipped her nature in a bath of acid. She began to disintegrate. She began to drink.

This coincided with the ascendancy of polyester, which I tie to her physical decline. She drank every night, she no longer ironed. The bread-like smell of the iron on the damp cloth was no longer part of the evening air. The smell of alcohol took its place.

The fragrant mother, the dappled mother, turned into a horror. And I was left alone with her: what I had dreamed of, what I had wanted since my father's death. At twelve, I had to clean up after her, pick her up when she fell, listen to her lament about her hardships at the hands of her brothers and sisters.

But she wasn't like this all the time. She wasn't like this before dark. She got up fresh and ready to work each morning. How could she be an alcoholic, she would say, when she got up every day and worked like a horse. And she did. But at night, she took her work clothes off, put on pajamas, and by nine was a blubbing, slobbering mess. A mess I had to clean up.

Having won the house, she let it go to ruin. It was never possible to be proud of our house. I was glad when it was sold, twenty-one years after we began living there alone. I will never go near it again.

The details of the house's disintegration are almost unbearable for me to recall. First, she let things pile up. Books, newspapers, mail. She didn't replace what broke or faded. She allowed her dog to sleep on the furniture so every piece was stained and covered with hair. Unable to walk him, she tied the dog to the side porch railing, giving him only a foot or two of leeway, so that he had to piss and shit in the same spot for fifteen years. She picked up his shit but did nothing about the urine smell by the staircase against which he lifted his leg many thousands of times. I wonder why I didn't walk the dog. I don't know the answer, only that I did not.

For five years I lived alone with her, ashamed of her, proud of her, thinking I had no other choice. Then I went to college, a non-Catholic college, an Ivy League college, somewhere no one we had ever known had gone, although it was only twenty miles from where we lived. Barnard. Columbia. Morningside Heights. I had to live at home for the first two years, it was considered unthinkable that I should leave her alone. But then after two years, I earned the money to live in a dorm, promising to come home every weekend. A month before I was to leave, my mother fell and was confined to a wheelchair for six months. Heartlessly, I kept to my original plan, leaving her to the care of her cousin's wife, a plain and dour German woman who despised me and adored my mother. Throughout her life, my mother was always able to draw to her dark-hearted, intensely practical, yet secretly yearning women who saw in her immense vitality the font of life from which they had been kept.

After I left for the dorm, my mother closed up the upstairs part of the house, separating it from the rest by many plastic cleaning bags which she kept together. They flapped horribly. They were as unsightly as eczema, but she claimed they cut the heating bill way down. They also made it necessary that I sleep with her in her bed when I was home. I know we both enjoyed that, watching late movies and eating junk food like roommates, then curling into each other's bodies. "Sleeping like spoons," we called it, "the big spoon, the little spoon," perfectly suited for repose.

I left New York to go to graduate school in Syracuse, and for three years I came home as little as I could. On holidays, if there was no other choice. Then I got married to a man she didn't like. She wouldn't pay for the reception, although she allowed me to have it in the house. Three years later, when I came home to tell her I was leaving my husband, I decided, for some reason, to thoroughly clean her house. It had been an issue in my marriage; at one point, my husband declared that I didn't deserve to live in a house. I ripped down the plastic bags, weeping in fury. "These are horrible, horrible, horrible," I kept saying. My mother said, "Why didn't you just tell me you didn't like them? I would always have taken them down." I called in a man to make a set of heavy curtains to close off the upstairs. I paid for it, but then I gave up on the house. My mother was sympathetic to my divorce, defended me to all her family. I was the first in the family to be divorced. When I told her that my husband's tidiness drove me mad—I didn't tell her that the real reason for the divorce was that I had fallen in love with someone else—she said, quite casually, "All I ever wanted was a man to clean up after me."

Who are "you," my mother? How could I find a "You" as I tried to find one for my father? What is your humanity? Are you still human?

It is, perhaps, now even more crucial than it was for my father for me to try to find a "you" that corresponds to his. I knew that in his case, I would be involved in a process of search, remembrance and invention. I didn't know that it would be the same for you. I didn't know that in the year when I was taken up with finding my father, you would be slipping away. That some surface, some responsive, vibrant material, would turn to stone. And the past would become something I had access to, like power of attorney, a legacy in your name you were prohibited from spending. A legacy suddenly taken from you and sent—where? Where has your memory gone, my mother? It was not an object; it was spirit, and the spirit, like the flesh, it seems, can be entirely consumed.

I don't know what it means to you to use language. When you speak, you sound like a machine, a computer voice or a tape recorder. You reproduce the words you somehow sense have been called for in a situation whose defined marks are no longer legible. So when you say how much you love me, what, exactly, does that mean? I always knew what my father meant each time he said it. Or wrote it. I have nothing that you wrote.

I don't know if you suffer.

I imagine you in the desert, but a desert covered in fog. The landscape has been laid bare; you don't know by what. Only that this bareness is final, and is all.

I keep trying to bring you to life. I think that if I bring you to the garden and we can use words to describe flowers, if we sing songs, you are alive again. But it isn't very much and some days, if I'm tired or overworked, I ask myself if it's worth it. And some days I say no. I sometimes go more than a week without seeing you.

On the days I decide not to see you, I think I would prefer if you were dead. I have never lived a day not wishing my father was alive.

This is, I know, entirely due to the difference between the ideal (dead) body and the actual (living) one.

I think regularly about the desirability of your death. Yet if anyone did anything to cause you even the slightest discomfort, did anything to show you even the smallest disrespect, I would raise my voice and strike them to the heart.

At the very same moment when I find the sight of you unbearable, the same moment when the sound of my voice, the tone of it which you very well understand, may be striking you to the heart.

My mother's eighty-sixth birthday. I have brought her what is pleasant to the senses: roses, flavored tea, a whipped cream cake.

Every year before she went into the nursing home, every year, that is, since my grandmother died when I was twelve, I made her a peach shortcake for her birthday. She took a pride in not liking sweet things, in caring nothing for chocolate. The tartness of the peaches pleased her, the plainness of the underlying cake. This year I don't make her a shortcake, I buy it, and it is not peach, but strawberry. At the Metropolitan Museum, I buy a postcard of a Byzantine icon and an expensive frame in which to place it. This is her birthday gift. I have collected people who are well disposed towards her. One gives her back a book she borrowed. It is a book about a saint he says he was attracted to "on account of his perseverance." She says, "Yes, I miss having this book near my behind." What she means is that she shoves it between her back and the back of the wheelchair. I'm sure she'd never read it, but the man doesn't realize that. Or perhaps he does. During the party she sits like a stone. One of her bottom teeth is rotting, in a way so that it is gradually turning into a splinter or a fang.

The temperature is nearly 100 degrees and, after I leave her, I can do nothing for the rest of the day but lie in my bed, paralyzed by what I can only call despair.

Her power over my life is enormous.

I want to take her to the garden this morning because I started the day having such terrible thoughts about her. I have to do something for or with her that has in it some semblance of pleasure, something that lifts me from the unbearable state of rage and responsibility and shame.

The social worker in charge of my mother's case has written to tell me that I must sign a DNR form. Do Not Resuscitate. Do not use unusual means. Don't keep her alive. Let her die.

I sign a piece of paper that authorizes that someone will look on while my mother dies.

After I do this, I go to her floor, to check and see if anything has been done about her nails. Nothing has. Full of righteousness, I hand the nurse, back now from vacation, the nail clippers that I have, after waiting three weeks, finally remembered to bring.

She says that whoever told me there were no nail scissors was wrong: someone could always have cut my mother's nails. She doesn't like it that an error has been made. But she is on the side of her staff. She says I have to understand that my mother resists grooming. The podiatrist, standing behind her, filling in charts, chimes in that she resists him also. I lose my temper. "It's not third grade," I say. "You don't get your feet attended to as a good conduct award." I address my comments to the podiatrist, because it would take more courage than I have to meet the head nurse's eyes. I have thought of her as a friend. Her humor, her intelligence have carried me through many situations which would have been unbearable to me except for her.

I wheel my mother to the elevator. I tell her we are going to the garden. When we are in the elevator, she tells me the towel she always sits on is stained with pee. I ask her why she doesn't ask the staff to change it. She says, "I forget to ask them. I'd rather have you change it." I say nothing, but I know that no force on earth will get me to touch that towel. Her desire that I serve her in this way makes me punitive and I say: "Why do you balk when they want to do your hair and nails?" She says: "I don't care about my hair and nails one way or another, to stop or help them."

It is possible to say that from my father I learned the sovereignty of the mind and the imagination; from my mother that there is nothing so important as piss and shit and flesh that can rot or be kept from rot. It would be possible, therefore, to say that my father taught me the greater lesson. But there is something so indomitable about my mother's insistence on the body's finality, its determination to exist, that it seems to have a stoic and a tragic grandeur that my father's vision—vague and watery—does not possess. She is older than the rock she has become. My mother has become one of the ancients. She is out of our time, this time, and because she has no memory, out of time as a whole. This gives her a harsh, unloving beauty before which one has the impulse to bend the knee. Simultaneously, the impulse to take one's own life. If this is it, this is life, I want no part of it. My father's vision, less truthful, is far more full of hope.

My friend says to me, "She's not there any more. You have to give her up." I have to give up hope, but her body continues to be there. The hopeless body at the center of the world.

We walk down to the garden. Or, we don't walk, I push her. Making sure not to let her momentum drag us down. We get to the level part, where it is no longer difficult to walk. I point out day lilies, a pair of infant twins, a pigeon pecking at mulberries. I name colors. I insist that she look. I insist that she tells me which of the flowers is her favorite. "I like them all," she says. "No, you have to pick one." "The purple one," she says. "Hibiscus," I tell her.

I say that it's my favorite one too.

"I know that," she says. "That's why I said it."

I would like to believe that she is still capable of liking one color more than another but it's probably too much to ask. Does she still remember that I like purple? Or is she faking again?

I believe that somehow, unfocused, but in a white light she sees all the time, is her love for me. Which may be the only thing that she still knows.

And once again I understand that despite the wreckage of my parent's lives, I have been, I still am, greatly beloved.

She keeps telling me it's too hard for me to push her that far. She keeps telling me the time. It's eleven thirty. Lunch is at noon. She keeps saying we'd better get back, that if we're late to lunch they won't keep anything for her.

I can tell that she wants nothing more than to get back. I have no way of knowing whether it's a good thing to take her to the garden, if she's still capable of being pleased, if she would prefer, above all, not to be bothered, to be left alone. If I am taking her to the garden because I think it is pleasant for her, because I can tell people about it and they will think I'm doing something pleasant for her, think how good I am. Such a good daughter. She takes her mother to the garden. But perhaps my mother would prefer to be left alone.

I leave her in the dining room. She asks when she'll see me again. I tell her in a week. "What are you doing with yourself between now and then?" she asks, with a hint of her old bite.

"Gallivanting," I say.

"Just as I thought," she says, opening the cellophane that holds her plastic fork, a knife, and spoon.

I leave the dining room and, standing a little to one side of the doorway, watch my mother as she eats. She doesn't talk to her neighbors at the table. Her face shows no enjoyment in her food. She stares ahead of her, her glance vacant as a blind woman's, chewing as if it were a mildly difficult task she knows she must perform. She is staring ahead at an infinite present which holds no savor for her. I don't know what it holds.

I can imagine a life for my father. I can think thoughts that I believe might be his. In death, he is more vibrant for me than she is in what is called her life. A life which I cannot understand or recognize. She will go on and on. I will have to see her as she is and not as I have made her. I cannot make her any different. This, of course, is the problem.

My mother is speaking in the desert.
"I think I'm very lucky, not to be in pain."
"I don't remember anything."
"If you knew how much I love you."
"These flowers are yellow. These are purple. Those are blue."
"I don't think of dying, but I'm not afraid to die."

SIGRID NUNEZ IS THE AUTHOR OF THREE WORKS of ficton: *A Feather on the Breath of God, Naked Sleeper,* and *Mitz: The Marmoset of Bloomsbury.* She was born and raised in New York City, where she lives now. She has been the recipient of several literary awards, including a Whiting Writer's Award. *A Feather on the Breath of God,* from which the following piece was taken, was a finalist for the PEN/Hemingway Award for First Fiction.

CHRISTA

I am told that my first word was *Coca-Cola,* and there exists a snapshot of me at eighteen months, running in a park, hugging a full bottle. It seems I snatched this Coke from some neighboring picnickers. I used to believe that I could remember this moment—the cold bottle against my stomach, my teetering, stomping trot, feelings of slyness and joy and excitement fizzing in me—but now I think I imagined all this at a later age, after having looked long and often at the picture.

Here is something I do remember. Coming home from grade school for the lunch hour: It may have happened only once or it may have happened every day. Part of the way home took me through empty streets. I was alone and afraid. The noon whistle sounded, and as at a signal I started to run. The drumming of my feet and my own huffing breath became someone or something behind me. And I remember thinking that if I could just get home to my mother and her blue, blue eyes, everything would be all right.

Here are some lines from Virginia Woolf: "... there is nothing to take the place of childhood. A leaf of mint brings it back: or a cup with a blue ring."

Sometimes—now—I might find myself in a strange town. I might be walking down a quiet street at midday. A factory whistle blows, and I feel a current in my blood, as if a damp sponge had been stroked down my back.

Woolf was thinking of a happy childhood, but does it matter? Another writer, members of whose family were killed in concentration camps, recalls how years later, looking through a book, he was touched by photographs of Hitler, because they reminded him of his childhood.

My mother's eyes were enhanced by shapely brows that made me think of angels' wings. Their arch gave her face an expression of skeptical wonder. When she was displeased her brows went awry; the arch fell; the world came tumbling down on me.

I remember a pear-shaped bottle of shampoo that sat on the edge of our bathtub. "With lemon juice. For blondes only." As the years passed and her hair grew darker, she started to use bleach. On the smooth white drawing paper of kindergarten I too made her blonder, choosing the bright yellow crayon, the yellow of spring flowers: daffodils, forsythia.

Other features: A wide mouth. Good, clear skin. A strong nose. Too big, her daughters said. ("What do you mean? A fine nose. Aristocratic. Same nose as Queen Elizabeth. I don't want a little button on my face.")

And her walk, which was graceful and not graceful. A slight hitch in her gait, like a dancer with an injury.

And her hands: long-fingered, with soft palms and squarish nails. Deft, competent hands, good at making things.

This is the way I see her at first, not as a whole but as parts: a pair of hands, a pair of eyes. Two colors: yellow and blue.

The housing project where we lived. The wooden benches that

stood in front of each building, where the women gathered when the weather was fair. The women: mothers all, still in their twenties but already somewhat worn away. The broad spread of their bottoms. The stony hardness of their feet, thrust into flip-flops. (The slatternly sound of those flip-flops as they walked.) The hard lives of house-wives without money. Exhaustion pooled under their eyes and in their veiny ankles. One or two appearing regularly in sunglasses to hide a black eye.

Talking, smoking, filing their nails.

Time passes. The shadow of the building lengthens. The first stars come out; the mosquitoes. The children edge closer, keeping mum so as not to be chased away, not to miss a riddle. "He married his mother." "I'm late this month." "She lost the baby." "She found a lump." "She had a boy in the bed with her."

Finally a husband throws open a window. "Youse girls gonna yak out there the whole damn night?"

Part of my way of seeing my mother is in contrast to these women. It was part of the way she saw herself. "I'm not like these American women." Her boast that she spoke a better English than they was true. "*Dese* and *dose, youse, ain't.* How can you treat your own language like that!" Her own grammar was good, her spelling perfect, her handwriting precise, beautiful. But she made mistakes too. She said *spedacular* and *expecially* and *holier-than-thoo.* She spoke of a *bone of contentment* between two people. Accused someone of being a *ne'er-too-well.* And: "They stood in a motel for a week." No matter how many times you corrected her, she could not get that verb right. She flapped her hands. "You know what I mean!" And her accent never changed. There were times when she had to repeat herself to a puzzled waitress or salesman.

But she would never say *youse.* She would never say *ain't.*

Parent-Teachers' Day. My mother comes home with a face set in disgust. "Your teacher said, 'She does *good* in history.'"

My mother liked English. "A good language—same family as

German." She was capable of savoring a fine Anglo-Saxon word: *murky, smite.* She read *Beowulf* and *The Canterbury Tales.* She knew words like *thane* and *rood* and *sith.*

Southern drawls, heartland twangs, black English, all sounded horrid to her.

One or two Briticisms had found their way (how?) into her speech. "It was a proper mess, I tell you." And somewhere she had learned to swear. She had her own rules. Only the lowest sort of person would say *fuck.* But *bastard* was permissible. And *shit*—she said *shit* a lot. But she always sounded ridiculous, swearing. She called her daughters *sons of bitches.* I was never so aware that English was not her native tongue as when she was swearing at me.

She did not have many opportunities to speak German. We had a few relations, in upstate New York and in Pennsylvania, and there was a woman named Aga, from Munich, who had been my mother's first friend here in the States and who now lived in Yonkers. But visits with these people were rare, and perhaps that is why I first thought of German as a festive language, a language for special occasions. The harshness that grates on so many non-German ears—I never heard that. When several people were speaking together, it sounded to me like a kind of music—music that was not melodious, but full of jangles and toots and rasps, like a wind-up toy band.

From time to time we took the bus across town to a delicatessen owned by a man originally from Bremen. My mother ordered in German, and while the man was weighing and wrapping the Leberkäse and Blutwurst and ham, he and she would talk. But I was usually outside playing with the dachshund.

Sometimes, reading German poetry, she would start to say the lines under her breath. Then it no longer sounded like music, but like a dream-language: seething, urgent, a little scary.

She did not want to teach her children German. "It's not your language, you don't need it, learn your own language first."

Now and then, on television, in a war movie, say, an American actor would deliver some German lines, and my mother would hoot. If subtitles were used, she said they were wrong. When my elder sister took German in high school, my mother skimmed her textbook and threw it down. "Ach, so many things wrong!"

A very hard thing it seemed, getting German right.

In one of my own schoolbooks was a discussion of different people and the contributions each had made to American society. The Germans, who gave us Wernher von Braun, were described as being, among other things, obedient to authority, with a tendency to follow orders without questioning them. That gave me pause. I could not imagine my mother taking orders from anyone.

I remember being teased in school for the way I said certain words. *Stoomach*. And: "I stood outside all day." ("Musta got awful tired!") I called the sideways colon the Germans put on top of certain vowels an *omelette*. Later, after I'd left home, I had only to hear a snatch of German, or to see some Gothic script, to have my childhood come surging back to me.

My mother said, "English is a fine language, it gets you to most places that you want to go. But German is—deeper, I think. A better language for poetry. A more romantic language, better for describing—yearning."

Her favorite poet was Heine.

She said, "There are a lot of German words for which you have no English. And it's funny—so often it's an important word, one that means such a lot. *Weltschmerz*. How can you translate that? And even if you study German, you can't ever really learn a word like that, you never grasp what it means."

But I did learn it, and I think I know what *Weltschmerz* means.

My first book was a translation from the German: fairy tales of the Brothers Grimm. My mother read these stories aloud to me, before I had learned to read myself. What appealed to me was not so much the adventures, not the morals, but the details: a golden key, an emerald box, boots of buffalo leather. The strangeness and beauty of names like Gretel and Rapunzel, especially the way my mother said them. The notion of enchantment was a tangled one. You couldn't always believe what you saw. The twelve pigeons pecking on the lawn might be twelve princes under a spell. Perhaps all that was lacking in one's own household was the right magic. At the right word, one of those birds might fly to your hand bearing in his beak a golden key, and that key might open a door leading to who knew what treasure. My mother shared this with all her neighbors: the conviction that we did not belong in the housing project. Out on the benches, much of the talk was about getting out. It was all a mistake. We were all under a spell—the spell of poverty. What is a home? We project children drew pictures of houses with peaked roofs and chimneys, and yards with trees. My mother said, "Every decent family is getting out," as one by one our neighbors moved away. "We'll never get out, we'll be the last ones left," meaning: the last white family.

Metamorphosis. First the fairy tales, then the Greek myths—for years my imagination fed on that most magical possibility: a person could be changed into a creature, a tree. In time this led to trouble.

I can still see her, Mrs. Wynn, a twig of a woman with a long chin and hollow eyes: my teacher. The way my mother mimicked her, Mrs. Wynn became a witch from one of the stories. "Your daughter says, In my first life I was a rabbit, in my second life, I was a tree. I think she is too old to be telling stories like that." And then my mother, mimicking herself, all wide-blue-eyed innocence: "How do you know she wasn't a rabbit?"

Oh, how I loved her.

Because my mother gave it to me I read a book of German sagas, but I didn't like them. Heroism on the fierce Nordic scale was not for me. To Siegfried I preferred the heroes of the *Hausmärchen*: simple Hanses, farmers and tailors and their faithful horses and dogs. (In a few more years I'd prefer to read only about horses and dogs.) I did not share her taste for the legends of chivalry or the romances of the Middle Ages. The epic was her form. She liked stories—legendary or historic—about heroic striving, conquest and empire, royal houses and courts. Lives of Alexander and Napoleon were some of her favorite reading. (This was a mother who for Halloween dressed up her youngest not as a gypsy or a drum majorette but as Great Caesar's Ghost—pillowcase toga, philodendron wreath—stumping all the kids and not a few of the teachers.) She read piles of paperback romances too—what she called her "everyday" reading.

One day I came home to find her with a copy of *Lolita*. The woman who lived downstairs had heard it was a good dirty book and had gone out and bought it. Disappointed, she passed it on to my mother. ("So, is it dirty?" "No, just a very silly book by a very clever man.")

The "good" books, the ones to be kept, were placed in no particular order in a small pine bookcase whose top shelf was reserved for plants. To get at certain ones you had to part vines. Dear to my mother's heart was the legend of Faust. Goethe's version was years beyond me, but what I gathered of the story was not promising. I liked stories about the Devil all right, but Faust's ambition struck no chord in me. I was a child of limited curiosity. I wanted to hear the cat speak but I didn't care how it was done. Knowledge equals power was an empty formula to me. I was never good at science.

Shakespeare in one volume. Plutarch's *Lives*, abridged. In the introduction to the plays, I read that Shakespeare had used Plutarch as a source. At first I thought I had misunderstood. Then I felt a pang: The world was smaller than I had thought it was. For some reason, this gave me pain.

I remember a book given to me by my fourth-grade teacher. A thick, dark green, grainy cover, pleasant to touch. A story about immigrants. One man speaking to another of a young woman just arrived from the Old Country. The phrase stayed with me, along with the memory of the feelings it inspired. I was both moved and repelled. "She has still her mother's milk upon her lips."

My mother never called it the Old Country. She said *my country*, or *Germany*, or *home*. Usually *home*. When she spoke of home, I gave her my full attention. I could hear over and over (I did hear over and over) stories about her life *before*—before she was a wife, before she was mother, when she was just Christa.

She was a good storyteller. To begin with, she spoke English with the same vigor and precision with which German is spoken. And she used everything—eyes, hands, all the muscles of her face. She was a good mimic, it was spooky how she became the person mimicked, and if that person was you, you got a taste of hell.

She talked all the time. She was always ready to reminisce—though that is a mild word for the purposive thing she did. The evocation of the past seemed more like a calling with her. The present was the projects, illiterate neighbors, a family more *incurred* than chosen, for there had been no choice. The past was where she lived and had her being. It was youth, and home. It was also full of horror. I cannot remember a time when she thought I was too young to hear those stories of war and death. But we both had been brought up on fairy tales—and what were her stories but more of the same, full of beauty and horror.

She had been a girl, like me—but how different her girlhood from mine. And I never doubted that what she was, what she had been and where she came from, were superior to me and my world. ("What you Americans call an education!" "What you Americans call an ice coffee!")

In memory I see myself always trying to get her to talk. Silence was a bad sign with her. When she was really angry she would not speak to you, not even to answer if you spoke to her. Once, she did not speak to my eldest sister for weeks.

Toward the close of a long dull day. I have lost the thread of the book I am reading. As so often on a Saturday at this hour, I don't know what to do with myself. Outside, it is getting dark. Nothing but sports on TV. My mother sits across the room, knitting. She sits on the sofa with one foot tucked under her. She is wearing her navy-blue sweater with the silver buttons, which she made herself, and which I will one day take with me, to have something of hers when I go away. (I have it still.) The soft, rhythmic click of the needles. At her feet the ball of yarn dances, wanders this way and that, looking for a kitten to play with. On her brow and upper lip, the pleats of concentration. Will it annoy her if I interrupt? (She is so easily annoyed!) I let the book close in my lap and say, "Tell me again about the time they came to take Grandpa to Dachau."

OVER THE LAST 25 YEARS, ANNA QUINDLEN'S work has appeared in some of America's most influential newspapers, many of its best-known magazines, and on both fiction and non-fiction bestseller lists.

A columnist for the *New York Times* from 1981 to 1994, she won the 1992 Pulitzer Prize for commentary. A collection of her Op-Ed page columns, *Thinking Out Loud* (1993), is just one of her bestselling books. Among her other books are the novels *Object Lessons* (1991), *One True Thing* (1994), and *Black and Blue* (1998). She is also the author of a collection of essays, *Living Out Loud* (1988) and two children's books, *The Tree that Came to Stay* (1992), and *Happily Ever After* (1997).

With her husband and three children she lives in Hoboken, New Jersey.

MOTHERS

The two women are sitting at a corner table in the restaurant, their shopping bags wedged between their chairs and the wall: Lord & Taylor, Bloomingdale's, something from Ann Taylor for the younger one. She is wearing a bright silk shirt, some good gold jewelry; her hair is on the long side, her makeup faint. The older woman is wearing a suit, a string of pearls, a diamond solitaire, and a narrow band. They lean across the table, I imagine the conversation: Will the new blazer go with the old skirt? Is the dress really right for an afternoon wedding? How is Daddy? How is his ulcer? Won't he slow down just a little bit?

It seems that I see mothers and daughters everywhere, gliding through what I think of as the adult rituals of parent and child. My mother died when I was nineteen. For a long time, it was all you needed to know about me, a kind of vest-pocket description of my emotional complexion: "Meet you in the lobby in ten minutes—I have long brown hair, am on the short side, have on a red coat, and my mother died when I was nineteen."

That's not true anymore. When I see a mother and a daughter having lunch in a restaurant, shopping at Saks, talking together on the crosstown bus, I no longer want to murder them. I just stare a little more than is polite, hoping that I can combine my observations with a half-remembered conversation, some anecdotes, a few old dresses, a photograph or two, and recreate, like an archaeologist of the soul, a relationship that will never exist. Of course, the question is whether it would have ever existed at all. One day at lunch I told two of my closest friends that what I minded most about not having a mother was the absence of that grown-up woman-to-woman relationship that was impossible as a child or adolescent, and that my friends were having with their mothers now. They both looked at me a though my teeth had turned purple. I didn't need to ask why; I've heard so many times about the futility of such relationships, about women with business suits and briefcases reduced to whining children by their mothers' offhand comment about a man, or a dress, or a homemade dinner.

I accept the fact that mothers and daughters probably always see each other across a chasm of rivalries. But I forget all those things when one of my friends is down with the flu and her mother arrives with an overnight bag to manage her household and feed her soup.

So now at the center of my heart there is a fantasy, and a mystery. The fantasy is small, and silly: a shopping trip, perhaps a pair of shoes, a walk, a talk, lunch in a good restaurant, which my mother assumes is the kind of place I eat at all the time. I pick up the check. We take a cab to the train. She reminds me of somebody's birthday. I invite her and my father to dinner. The mystery is whether the fantasy has within it a nugget of fact. Would I really have wanted her to take care of the wedding arrangements, or come and stay for a week after the children were born? Would we have talked on the telephone about this and that? Would she have saved my clippings in a scrapbook? Or would she have meddled in my affairs, volunteering opinions I didn't want to hear about things that were none of her business, criticizing my clothes and my children? Worse still, would we have been strangers with nothing to say to each other? Is all the good I remember about us simply wishful thinking? Is all the bad self-protection? Perhaps it is at best difficult, at worst impossible for children and parents to be adults together. But I would love to be able to know that.

Sometimes I feel like one of those people searching, searching for the mother who gave them up for adoption. I have some small questions for her and I want the answers: How did she get her children to sleep through the night? What was her first labor like? Was there olive oil in her tomato sauce? Was she happy? If she had it to do over again, would she? When we pulled her wedding dress out of the box the other day to see if my sister might wear it, we were shocked to find how tiny it was. "My God," I said, "did you starve yourself to get into this thing?" But there was no one there. And if she had been there, perhaps I would not have asked in the first place. I suspect that we would have been friends, but I don't really know. I was simply a little too young at nineteen to understand the woman inside the mother.

I occasionally pass by one of those restaurant tables and I hear the bickering about nothing: You did so, I did not, don't tell me what you did or didn't do, oh leave me alone. And I think that my fantasies are better than any reality could be. Then again, maybe not.

CATHLEEN SCHINE IS THE AUTHOR OF FOUR NOVELS, including *Rameau's Niece*, which was named one of the best books of 1993 by both the *New York Times* and the *Voice Literary Supplement*, and was a finalist for the 1992-1993 *Los Angeles Times* Book Prize. In 1997, it was made into a feature film called *The Midadventures of Margaret*. Ms. Schine lives in New York City with her husband and two children.

In Schine's novel *The Love Letter*, published in 1995, Helen MacFarquhar, a bookshop owner and the mother of twelve-year-old Emily, discovers her well-ordered world coming apart after receiving an anonymous love letter. Coinciding with the arrival of this mysterious letter is Helen's developing relationship with Johnny, a twenty-year-old university student, who is helping out in the bookstore during his summer vacation. Nineteen-year-old Jennifer—also hired by Helen during the busy summer season—shares Johnny's admiration for their boss. Although Helen is well aware of Jennifer's devotion, her youth and shaved head cause Helen to struggle with bouts of jealousy. In the following excerpt, Helen tries to cope with the ludicrous complications of this romance during a visit from her mother Lilian and her grandmother Eleanor.

THIRD-GENERATION BITCH

Lilian and Eleanor arrived in a bottle-green Jaguar. It was an old Jaguar, but like a new Jaguar it broke down regularly. Eleanor refused to sell it. She also refused to drive it, and Lilian was at the wheel.

Grandma Eleanor stepped from the car. "I'm here!" she said, holding her arms out, a cormorant on a post, a chorus girl taking a bow, a butterfly, a crucifix, Helen thought. A cross to bear.

"Grandma!" she said. "Mom!" she added, as her mother, a cigarette dangling from her lips, her dark glasses pushed up on her head, climbed from behind the wheel.

"Your grandmother is here," Lilian said. "As she has noted. She's here and she's all yours. What you choose to do with her is your business. But may I suggest strangulation as a most satisfying option." She slammed the car door and stormed, on her little feet in their little high-heeled mules (it was a diminutive but fierce storm), into the house.

"She dislikes having an aged parent," Eleanor said in a bland, even voice. "Imagine how I feel. With an aged daughter."

No wonder I'm such a bitch, Helen thought. Third-generation bitch. Nature and nurture, a conspiracy, a confederacy. Was little Emily also destined to this fate? Secretly Helen hoped so—she was proud of her grandmother, her mother, herself. But my poor Emily. Perhaps just this once, just this one generation could stay benign and sincere, perhaps she could stay at Camp Rolling Ridge, rolling over ridges until it was safe to come home. Until she became an adult and home wasn't home.

Helen hugged her grandmother. She could feel her white hair against her cheek, smell her cold cream. Her make-up, the sweet waxy smell of lipstick, as Grandma Eleanor kissed her, leaving, as she had since Helen was a child, two garish pink streaks on her face. She experienced the familiar sensation of hugging her grandmother after a long absence, and yet the moment pulled away from her, shyly, like a dog from a stranger. Johnny, Helen thought. Where are you now? Staring out the window, your jaw slack, your eyes glazed? Rubbing Jennifer's head for luck, your smile affectionate, contemptuous? Or are you selling one of my customers a book, looking up suddenly from the cash register with a flash of blue eyes?

Johnny, she thought, hugging her grandmother, then noticed over Grandma Eleanor's shoulder a moving van pull into the driveway.

"A moving van is pulling into my driveway," Helen said.

"I thought I might stay awhile," Grandma Eleanor said.

"Here?"

"For a while."

"A while?"

Lilian stuck her head out the door. "You're insane," she said to Grandma Eleanor.

"It's genetic," Grandma Eleanor said.

Helen took a deep breath. It's not my house, she reminded herself. I like my mother. I like my grandmother. I haven't seen them in a year. It's not my house. She watched the screen door swing forcefully shut behind her mother. She smiled, happy at the familiarity of the sight.

Lilian was severe and short-tempered with a throaty voice. She smoked in the bath. When Helen was growing up, her mother treated her like an adult who, for reasons no one cared to go into, was too small to reach the light switches. Helen trailed around after her mother in a soft haze of half understanding. Adult conversations, thrilling and somehow important, surrounded her, as indecipherable and compelling as new art. Lilian, propped against the pillows, would gossip mercilessly and good-humoredly into the telephone. Lolling on the bed, at the foot like a lapdog, Helen listened contentedly to her mother's side of the conversation.

Helen admired her mother, who either never stayed still or stayed absolutely still. As a youngish widow, she took up a desultory study of archaeology, which consisted mostly of visiting museums in European cities and going on digs in points farther east. She still traveled, having left a friend in every port. She had never thought in terms of a career. She didn't need the money and didn't seem to need the assurance of an academic post, or even an academic degree. She was a committed, energetic amateur. When she wasn't globe-trotting, she lay in bed manning the phone, dispensing advice, which she could, and did, give out on nearly any subject and if she turned out to be right, so much the better.

It impressed Helen that Lilian had maintained so many close friendships from her childhood, from college, from every stage of her life. Women who wouldn't dream of speaking to each other all talked intimately to Lilian. The secret, Helen knew, was a combination of intelligence and interest. She, Helen, had inherited the intelligence.

My mother is interested in people; I am merely curious about them, Helen sometimes thought. Lilian regarded others as recipients of her energy, her counsel. She was imperious and generous. They were projects, her projects, and she worked hard at them. Helen saw this, saw the devotion it inspired in people, but she herself wanted only to let live and to live. She had escaped her mother's attention, for which she was grateful. Lilian, busy with bossing her friends about, had simply accepted Helen as a kind of silent accomplice, a junior member of the board, nonvoting.

Lilian never stayed anywhere very long anyway, Helen reminded herself. Neither did Grandma Eleanor. But unlike Lilian, who traveled obsessively, visiting ape preserves in Kenya and digging up shards in Turkey, Eleanor did not travel—she moved. She had moved so many times that she was now quite expert at it. She knew her moving man. She called Atlas Van Lines every few years and asked for him by name, Joe Clancy. And Joe Clancy would drive up in his giant moving van and load the boxes. Eleanor kept empty boxes, labeled and waiting, in the attic or the basement, depending on the house she was in at that moment. Sometimes she moved because her present abode was getting too big for an old woman like her. Sometimes she moved because it was getting too small. Sometimes the north was too cold. Sometimes the south was too hot. The east too wet, the west too dry.

"I want to spend some time with my family," she said now. "I'm getting older." She lied about her age, shaving off five years. "Almost eighty-five, after all."

"Mrs. Lasch!" It was the moving man, removing his baseball cap. He had a spider web tattoo on each elbow. "Welcome."

"Did you have a good trip, Mr. Clancy? Next time I'll travel with you. In the cab."

"You'd be safe with me, Mrs. Lasch."

"But would you be safe with me?" Grandma Eleanor shook her silver-handled cane at him.

"Maybe I should get a tattoo," she said to Helen as they walked in the door of the house.

"Like my friend Lucy."

"Like Cher."

Lilian was short and boyish, as insouciant about clothes as her own mother. Grandma Eleanor, was—was what? Souciant, Helen decided. Lilian threw her clothes on, threw them off, tossed her sweater here, kicked her shoes there. There was always the suggestion of vigorous movement in her attire. Her clothes were good, expensive clothes, and they didn't seem to mind her treatment of them. Like slumming debutantes, they were adventurous, reckless. Like Lilian herself. She and her Armani jackets appeared to have an understanding, not unlike an open marriage, a French *arrangement*.

"Coffee?" her mother said. She'd already found it, made it. She poured Helen a cup, and they stood at the sink, as if they were in a hurry, and Helen wondered again why her mother's coffee, made with Helen's beans and Helen's machine, always tasted so much better than Helen's coffee.

"You make the best coffee, Mom."

Lilian smiled. Helen noticed a ring, a sapphire, round and unfaceted, a ring she'd never seen before on her mother's left hand, on the finger with her wedding band.

"I never saw that. It's beautiful. It's really beautiful. When did you get that? I never saw that."

Her mother shrugged. "It was made for me. Last year. You like it?"

"I want it."

Lilian laughed. She put down her mug and embraced Helen. "My Helen," she said softly. "My dearest."

Helen felt her mother's hug from a vast distance, from childhood. She closed her eyes, pressed her face against her mother's hair, resisted the temptation to say Mommy.

Oh, Mommy, she thought.

"I love this house," Lilian was saying. "You've really fixed it up beautifully. Where is your poor old dog? Jasper!"

Lilian released her, and Helen whistled for the dog, who painfully emerged from beneath the chair he favored. The sun poured in through the big windows and he stood in a yellow rectangular patch of light, his tongue hanging, his tail lurching awkwardly back and forth. He barked.

"Here," Lilian said suddenly. She pulled off the ring and thrust it at Helen. "Take it."

Helen took it and put it back on her mother's finger.

"You're crazy, Mother," she said.

"It's genetic," Lilian said, raising her arm dramatically and pointing a mighty finger at the figure silhouetted in the doorway, an elegant figure in a hat, flourishing her cane.

"I'm not conceited," Helen's grandmother often said. "I'm quoting."

And it was true. She took her new towns, neighborhoods, cities, states, by storm. Helen thought that the local Pequot inhabitants, possessing a blend of sophistication and provincialism that occurs only in those both very comfortable and very geographically isolated, would be charmed by Eleanor. Whether Eleanor would be charmed by Pequot was something altogether different. Having fled a small town to live in New York at an early age, having thrived there, turning herself from a poor seamstress into a well-known hat designer and then, with evident relief and pride, an idle Upper East Side matron, Eleanor might find Pequot as dull and limited as it in some ways was. Or she might see it as fallow ground, just waiting for Eleanor Lasch.

Eleanor always wore a hat. Not a petite perched lady's hat. Not a sensible canvas tennis hat, not a bright baseball cap. Not any of the kinds of hats people wore in Pequot. Eleanor wore her own hats, svelte, dashing fedoras. With her silver-tipped cane. she was the picture of elderly elegance. What Helen marveled at was not so much her perfect taste. It was her energy in exercising it. She tuned her look with gentle, meticulous expertise, a mechanic tinkering with his Daimler.

Lilian carried her one small duffel bag into the house. *"I'm* very considerate when intruding on my daughter, aren't I, cookie?"

"Very," Helen said.

"Am I intruding?" Grandma Eleanor asked, directing Mr. Clancy to put her Adirondack chairs in the front hall, as there was no room for them on the porch.

"Well, there's so much of you," Helen said.

"But so little time," said Grandma Eleanor.

So little time, Helen thought, and she pictured Johnny. Her grandmother patted her on the arm and smiled, and Helen smiled back.

"Yes," Helen said. "So little time."

"Oh, please," Lilian said.

Later that night Helen watched Grandma Eleanor unpack some of her clothes. It was Eleanor's gift somehow not to look eccentric, ever, no matter how polished and self-conscious her outfit. She was eccentric, of course. And the engine that drove her so smoothly through life was sheer vanity. Vanity inspired her, vanity sustained her, vanity

rewarded her. Helen thanked the Fates that Eleanor was her grandmother and not her mother. A generation's distance muted Grandma
Eleanor's effect, like the artful lighting of a photograph.

She would move into the big house in a big way, all those carefully marked boxes, all her furniture, nearly a century of it, hoisted by
Joe Clancy and his twin spider webs. Eleanor moved often, but she
never moved light.

"I have to think of more than myself," she would explain. "There's
Lila, you know." Looming in the background of all family decisions
was Lila, Eleanor's baby sister. Lila, a youthful seventy-nine, had lived
in Florida for decades. She didn't move like Eleanor. She barely left
her house in Palm Beach. For at least twenty years the two sisters had
been promising each to join the other, each to welcome the other
with open arms, neither of which did either of them ever actually do.
But it meant that they both felt it necessary to maintain a household
large enough for two (considerably larger, in fact—what if they
needed live-in nurses?), just in case.

Helen lay in her bed without Johnny. Her house was full of
women and boxes. She imagined Johnny in his messy room, asleep on
his back, one arm flung across the bed, the other across his eyes. She
had barely been able to speak to him today—a quick, awkward phone
call, her mother around every corner, her grandmother shuffling from
room to room.

"I love you," Johnny said. He had found a sweater of hers at the
store and buried his face in the familiar scent, intoxicated, but he
didn't tell her. "Send them away," he said instead. "You're mine."

Helen had listened with a shiver of pleasure. Was she his? He
seemed awfully confident. From the moment she brought him home
to her bed, he had become sure of himself. The awkward teenage
lover seemed to have propelled himself into a new, reckless manhood.
Young and afraid before, he now appeared too young to be afraid.

Helen remembered being too young for fear. Vaguely.

Johnny said, "Stay at my house. Who'll give a shit?" Johnny said, "I love you, I love you, and I love you." He said, "Why don't we do it in the road?" Helen said nothing. Those are just lines from a song, she thought. An old song. Like me. I'm old enough to know not to do it in the road. That's where car accidents happen, in the road. Live and learn, Johnny. Learn and live.

She listened to the night noises rising with the warm air toward her bedroom window. The cicadas were out in full force. The sweetness of the newly mown grass made her rise and look out. The moon was not quite full, and she looked down at her garden, the pine trees, the sparkle of the water beyond. A mosquito buzzed by her ear. She realized she was waiting for Johnny. She stayed at the window, her cheek against the screen with its slight metallic smell, the mosquito invisibly circling her head, until the moon passed behind a cloud and the scene before her disappeared into muffled darkness.

Her mother filled the house with cigarette smoke and coffee cups. Grandma Eleanor, too, found the place comfortable, arriving expectantly at the table for breakfast, which Helen made for her and Lilian.

"Those birds! What a racket!" Lilian said. "The damp! Don't you feel hemmed in sometimes, with all these trees?"

Eleanor asked Helen if she would mind lending her the station wagon, as she absolutely refused to drive the Jaguar. "It's so unreliable."

Helen loved her car, a wagon she'd bought secondhand. When the door was opened and the ignition key turned, the car spoke. In a confident, Hal-like computer voice, it said: "A door is ajar!" Helen found the regularity of this communication reassuring. She liked to have a routine. "A door is not a jar," she would answer, each and every day, several times a day.

But today Helen silently drove off in the bottle green Jaguar and parked beside Johnny's deep blue Lincoln Continental, and rushed, gasping for privacy, into the bookstore.

Johnny looked up from a packing list. He held a pencil in his mouth, like a dog with a bone. He had changed his earring, she noticed, replacing the diamond stud with a small gold hoop.

Don't change, Helen thought. I turn my back for twenty-four hours and look what happens. She saw his lips part, watched the yellow pencil cling to them for a second, a fraction of a second. From the corner of her eye, Helen saw Lucy drinking a mug of coffee, watching. Johnny, she thought desperately. Johnny, you're too far away. Too many hours have passed. "Save me!" she said instead. "They're here for good. The women. They love me!"

For the next few days, Johnny waited for her every morning at the store in a torment of pleasure and resentment, a blur of need. He noticed the older couple, whom he and the girls called the You Sees. "You see!" the wife said, nudging her husband, when Johnny said good morning. He noticed Theresa thumbing through a glossy art book. "Too rich," she said. "I very, very rich," by which he knew she meant the book was too expensive for her. He noticed one of the twins handing him a wet zwieback. He noticed himself thanking the child, taking the gummy cookie from its sticky hand. He noticed that without Helen there the store seemed hollow. He tried to fill it with his own movement, with his own voice, but still he saw the absence of Helen throwing an arm over a customer's shoulder, or heard the absence of her voice murmuring a seductive, triumphant hello.

Where was she? Of course her mother and grandmother wanted to spend time with her. It had been a year, Helen said, and they needed her to referee, as well, for they couldn't stand each other. Still, Helen was a grown woman, the head of her own household. Adults could do as they liked, and wasn't spending every possible moment with him doing as she liked?

Where are you? he thought over and over every morning, until she pushed open the door, a burst of Helen. He knew she was on her way to him, each time. But then, of course, she would stop.

At night, Helen sat at dinner and planned how she would tell her mother. She knew she should just say, "I'm going out to see a friend." But then her mother would say, "Really? Which friend is that?" She knew she should just tell her mother which friend, but she also knew she couldn't. And if Helen lied, she would be caught, as she had always been caught as a teenager. She remembered sneaking out of the house, then sneaking back in hours later only to find her mother reading or listening to Mahler, but really waiting to pounce on her, pulling Helen's sunglasses off to check for dilated pupils. "You stink of marijuana," Lilian would say. She was not a strict parent, but she thought taking drugs was stupid, and it annoyed her to have a stupid daughter. She never told Helen's father, who might have really worried, and for that Helen was grateful, and to show her gratitude became more discreet, swigging Binaca before sneaking back in. But how could she be discreet now? Binaca would not help her.

Perhaps I won't see him, she thought. It is not written in the "Having a Secret Affair Manual" that you have to see each other every night. Tomorrow is another day. I'm an adult. I am a woman of a certain age, a certain stature, a great deal of self-control. I can stay home.

She told herself this as she plotted to see Johnny, for she had to see Johnny. The desire to see Johnny was what put her to bed at night and what woke her up in the morning. Seeing Johnny was the aim of all endeavor.

She said she was doing inventory at the store. The next night, she said the car needed gas. Then, she needed Tampax at the all-night drugstore. "And I took a drive. Such a beautiful night." Then she put on her running clothes and told her mother she was training for the marathon.

"Bad for your knees," said Grandma Eleanor.

"Don't get hit by a car," said Lilian.

Helen ran through the twilight to Johnny's, where, damp and gasping for breath, she faced him and, looking into his eyes, absorbing the violent intensity of his stare, she reached for him and thought, in a confused, ecstatic anger, that he was young and gentle, delicate as the petals of a flower, and she wanted to crush him, velvety and fragrant, in her hand.

Afterward, he looked at her with an expression somewhere between smug satisfaction and terror, and she herself wondered how this had happened—how sex, always a pleasant recreational activity, had grown serious.

For one week, Lilian complained about Pequot constantly. But she showed no inclination to leave. Why had she not brought a moving van as well? Helen wondered.

Her mother often pumped Helen for information about the natives and their habits, as if she herself had never lived in the town. "I like to know the lay of the land, that's all, dear. Any new people?"

"I don't know. I guess so. Hundreds. Oh, and one new old person. Miss Skattergoods, you know that old Pequot family, Skattergoods— she's come back from wherever she was. She took over the library."

"Did she?"

"She used to ride her bicycle. Very picturesque. Now she drives a Porsche—"

"Does she?"

"—like a maniac. Oh, and the ophthalmologist's wife, Janie McMillan, remember her? The shy housewife with her fussy Halloween cookies and Girl Scout troops? She's started a little advertising agency. . . ."

But Helen saw that her mother's attention had already wandered. How alike we are, she thought.

"When do I get to meet them?" Johnny said.

"Are you going to ask for my hand?"

"Maybe."

"Are you chewing gum?"

"Maybe." He blew a large bubble, popped it with his finger, and she remembered the tired taste of bubble gum and wanted to kiss him nevertheless. How, she wondered for the hundredth time, did this happen? Did I flirt with him? Not any more than with anybody else. Did I pay him? Bribe him? Threaten to turn him in to the immigration authorities? The likelihood of this big, gum-chewing boy falling in love with her was statistically nonexistent. Yet here he was.

"I'm too old for you," she said.

He grinned, stood close to her, pushed her hair back, leaned his lips to her ear, and whispered, "I know."

Jennifer came in soon after, carrying an assortment of coffees.

"One has steamed milk and regular coffee, one has steamed milk and espresso, one has regular milk and regular coffee. I don't know which is which, I don't know which is called what, and I don't remember anymore which I wanted."

"I want the biggest. And the hottest. I want the best one," Helen said.

"There's your car," Johnny said.

Helen saw her mother driving up, pulling into a parking space, walking toward the door.

"Yes," she said. She dreaded having Lilian meet Johnny. Or was it Johnny meeting Lilian she dreaded? "That's my mother." Her mother strode. That was the only word for the way she walked, a walk so full of purpose it was almost comical. Of course, I have inherited this walk, Helen thought. This comical walk.

Lilian quickly surveyed the place, saw that not much had changed since her last visit, asked Johnny where he went to college, told

Jennifer her head had a lovely slope in the back, "which unfortunately you yourself can't see, but how nice for the rest of us," dashed upstairs to see Lucy, dashed down again, took several Nabokov novels without paying, and left, roaring off in Helen's car.

"My mother has a thudding ephemeral quality, if you know what I mean."

"I think she's cool," Jennifer said.

Was Jennifer's loyalty flagging? Helen wondered. Would Lilian become her new hero? Would Jennifer now smoke and call complete strangers "cookie"?

"She calls complete strangers cookie," Helen said, as a warning. "I've seen it."

"I think she looks like you," Johnny said.

Helen stared at him. She longed to look like her mother.

"No one ever says that," she said. "They say I look like my father. If they knew my father."

"You move the same way."

"I know."

"The way you walk," Johnny said softly. "The way you turn your head, so suddenly. Your hands...."

Helen noticed Jennifer, remembered she was there, saw how closely she was watching them.

"Thank you," Helen said abruptly. "Now who's going to phone in the order? Jennifer? Would you do that for me? Come on." She put her arm around Jennifer's waist and led her toward the phone. "If you do, I'll call you cookie in public...."

Jennifer giggled gratefully as Helen had known she would.

One morning, when the womenfolk, as she had begun to call them, had been with her for two weeks, Helen got up early, before they were awake, and simply left. I have a business to run, she told herself. My business is not making breakfast for two perfectly capable women as they read the paper and argue about multiculturalism. She got to the store an hour before Lucy or Johnny or the girls and opened up with what was almost excitement. She swept the sidewalk, put out the mat. She vacuumed inside. She loved her store. It made very little money, but it belonged to her, she had made it, she made it run.

The next morning she escaped again before breakfast, and when she arrived at the store found a note from Johnny, who had closed up the night before.

Dear Helen,

Do you want to redo the mass-market table? It's been awhile. Too long. What a long time it's been. I think the mass-market table is calling out to be redone. Redo me! I did the trade paperback table myself. It wasn't the same without you. But desperate times call for desperate measures. As I applied myself to the task, it occurred to me that while our feelings rise against any arbitrary, individual compulsion of fate, such as is presupposed in Grillparzer's *Die Abnfrau*, etc. the Greek legend, on the other hand, seizes on a compulsion which everyone recognizes because he feels its existence within himself. Each member of the audience was once, in germ and in phantasy, just such an Oedipus, and each one recoils in horror from the dream fulfillment here transplanted into reality, with the whole quota of repression which separates his infantile state from his present one. Don't you agree?

Fondly,
Johnny

On the trade paperback table, atop each pile of books, Johnny had put a copy of *The Freud Reader.* One had a bookmark in it. Helen opened it and saw the letter to Fliess. Johnny had quoted from it in his note; he'd quoted the letter announcing Freud's discovery of the Oedipus complex. She laughed. Twelve black-and-white photos of Dr. Freud looked inquisitively up at her.

"Oh, fuck you," she said happily.

[Johnny's summer vacation ends and he returns to his college town across the country. A couple of days later Helen receives his letter in which he announces his transfer to a university nearby and asks her to continue the relationship.]

That night, arriving home from the store, Helen did not go straight into the house. She went around the back and walked through the garden, past the fruit trees, to the cliff and the sea below. It was windy, warm, not quite dark, and a round moon, deep yellow, hovered on the horizon. A bat flew by. She heard a sandpiper. The sea smell, so brisk yet so summery, made autumn seem far off, impossible, irrelevant, but the leaves were already beginning to fade. She had come to the cliffs to be melancholy. She stood for a moment, then got bored, melancholia being too still a pursuit for her, and she strode back to the house.

She could see Emily's window, lit up, Emily at her desk doing her homework, the portable telephone squeezed between her ear and her shoulder, its antenna sparkling in the lamplight. In the nighttime quiet, she heard Emily laugh. Inside, her grandmother was packing boxes. She was moving to Florida to be near her sister, having taken a large house on the same street as her sister's large house.

"I thought Aunt Lila's house was supposed to be big enough for both of you," Lilian said. "I thought that was the point."

"I need room for you to visit, for Helen, for Emily. You will visit, won't you? And what if I require a nurse? I must have room for my nurse."

Lilian shook her head and picked an LP from the pile she had brought with her.

"I'm glad you still have a turntable, Helen."

"Mm-hmm," Helen said. She sat down on the couch and thought about Johnny. She could see him in the shower, his arms lifted to rub shampoo into his hair. Between the muscles in his shoulders, in the slight hollow that formed there, suds gathered, then slid down his chest. From the other end of the tub she watched as he turned toward the water, his eyes closed, his hair streaming behind him.

"Listen," her mother said. And Helen heard the crackling of an old recording, then strings.

"Brahms," said Lilian. "Sextet. Casals."

Helen closed her eyes, the way her mother always did when listening to music. The piece sounded familiar, one of Lilian's favorites, perhaps. No wonder her mother liked this kind of music. Helen felt the sweetness of losing one's way, of being utterly, magnificently lost. No one ever loved me the way Johnny did, she thought. No one ever looked at me like that, up and down, my hands, my face, into my eyes. What rich, weightless, whole music. What will I do without Johnny to look at me like that? Without Johnny to look at? Without Johnny?

"Now listen to the second movement," Lilian said.

"It's so loud," said Eleanor. "I'm going upstairs."

"Louis Malle used this music in *The Lovers*. Do you remember, Helen? I took you to see it. You were about Emily's age. Your first foreign film. God knows what you made of it."

Helen remembered. Jeanne Moreau was in it. Jeanne Moreau picked up a man whose car had broken down. Took him home to her wealthy husband and big country house. Made love to him in the pond. In the dark. Kissed him with her Jeanne Moreau lips.

The music now sounded almost like a march—a solemn, ceremonial march of passion and urgency. When do we call passion love? When it's desperate, exquisite, enormous? When it's delicate and ephemeral? When it's sacred? The music claimed that passion was sacred. The music demanded it. Helen began to cry.

Lilian, wiping tears from her own eyes, stood up to turn it off.

"The rest of the sextet is not very interesting," she said. "But that second movement."

In the Malle movie, Jeanne Moreau leaves with the stranger the next morning; leaves her husband and her whole life behind. Only the French can do that, Helen thought. In their disconnected movies. Why can't I do that? Do I want to do that? Do I want to leave my life? My family, my child? Why do I have to do that? Because I feel passion? Because it's time to call passion love?

"Helen, let's talk for a minute," her mother said, sitting beside her on the couch. "About Grandma leaving. About me. About you, too, cookie."

Helen put her head on her mother's shoulder. She was still crying a little. Her mother put her arms around her and Helen began to sob.

"It's been wonderful to spend all this time with you, darling," her mother said softly, smoothing her hair, kissing her forehead.

"Don't go," Helen said. "Everyone is going."

"Well, that's what we have to talk about. Look, Helen, I know we don't always confide in each other. But I think—"

"Yes. I do, too. Look, Mom—" Helen determined to tell her, right then. She had to. However shocking it would be. She could no longer live like this, secretive, stupefied by passion and by its denial.

"Mommy—"

But her mother continued talking.

"Life does not always take the turn we expect," Lilian was saying.

"No, and—"

"And love hardly ever does, Helen. You can't choose who you fall in love with, you know. I was very lucky with your father, it was all very conventional, but we also truly loved each other. But sometimes, well, conventions get kicked over, knocked over, do you see what I mean? They fall away because...."

Because. Because it's preposterous for a middle-aged woman to fall in love with a boy unless you are that middle-aged woman and you have fallen in love with the boy. Then the thing you scorn as unnatural in someone else seems as normal as the sun coming up each morning, and as miraculous.

"Because," Lilian was saying, "because the conventions have to fall away."

Why is she telling me this? Helen wondered. Does she know? Is she trying to make it easy for me to tell *her*? Or is it all theoretical in some way, inspired by the music? The memory of the movie?

"Mom, I'm glad you understand, I'm glad you think that way because I do, too, recently, anyway, and now...."

"Helen, I'm moving out next week."

"Oh, Mommy, I know you hate Pequot, but I wish you'd stay longer. I never thought I'd say such a thing. I really have gotten used to you and right now especially I need...."

"I'm not leaving Pequot. It is one of the ironies of my otherwise straightforward life that I have fallen in love twice, and each time with someone who insists on living in this town.

"You're—"

"Moving in with Constance."

"Who?"

"Miss Skattergoods, to you. We were together in New York. Well we never lived together, but, you know."

No, I don't know, Helen thought.

"But then she ran off to Pequot. I still don't understand, why. To finish her book, partly."

Book? Miss Skattergoods was finishing a book? Miss Skattergoods's name was Constance? Miss Skattergoods was living with Helen's mother? But not in New York?

"I suppose it was my fault. I'm not very good about these things settling down, commitment. But when she left, well, I can't actually live without her, you know. So there you are. Mommy's a dyke, Helen."

"Ah."

"She gave me this ring, the one you like so much."

"I don't like it *that* much," Helen said.

"No? I do. Well! That's finished! What was it you wanted to tell me, honey? I can listen to you now. I had to tell the truth finally, though, didn't I?"

"Not really," Helen said. She wondered if her mother and Constance Skattergoods would have one of those embarrassing gay weddings. They could both wear gowns, veils designed by Grandma Eleanor, who could also make an extra-thick, extra-opaque veil for Helen to hide behind.

"Helen?"

"Oh, it was nothing." Nothing compared to this, certainly. All this time she had worried about shocking the world with her affair with a young man while her mother was sleeping with an old woman. Helen was mortified. Her secret was so, so second-rate.

"Oh," Lilian said, kissing her forehead. "I thought you might want to talk about Johnny. I suppose you must miss him, now he's off at college again." She smiled. "Very French, Helen, your affair with him. Constance says he's absolutely besotted. Lovely. I don't suppose anyone else knows about it, do they? But we couldn't really help figuring it out. Will he be back for Thanksgiving? Though I do find it difficult to think that I am the mother of a woman of a certain age. I mean, what does that make me?"

BORN IN NEW YORK CITY, CYNDI STIVERS graduated from Barnard College in 1978. While still an undergraduate, she worked full-time at the *New York Post*. Since then, she has worked as a reporter, writer, and editor at several other newspapers and at such magazines as *Life, Vanity Fair, Condé Nast Traveler,* and *Premiere*. She has been editor-in-chief of *Time Out New York* since its founding in 1995, and was named president of the company in 1997. She is on the board of the American Society of Magazine Editors, and of the Associate Alumnae of Barnard College.

CORONARY CARE

I*t was a seemingly menial task that finally brought my mother and me together. After more than twenty years of unpredictability, our relationship has settled at last into more or less unconditional love—and all it took was for me to ask her to get my mail.*

I was moving to Europe for a few years, and I needed someone to be my postal lifeline. In truth, it wasn't a small favor to ask, because I get mountains of magazines and avalanches of catalogs. And I was asking her to sift through the bundles, deposit the checks, and send off the monthlies, weeklies, letters, and bills. To my surprise, she readily agreed. This was in 1989, and at the time I couldn't help but take a mental inventory of other occasions I'd asked for something and been rebuffed. But I held my tongue. I'd been waiting for détente *all my adult life.*

When I set out to write about my mother for this book, I realized I still had many more questions than insights. I was ready to ask and, luckily, she was ready to tell.

My mother, now known as Marguerite Temple Martin, was born in New Jersey in 1932, in the midst of the Depression. She was the youngest of the three children born to her parents. Her brother, Bill, is now an orthopedic surgeon in California; her elder brother, Harold, died of a burst appendix before she was born. She met my father, a budding adman, when she was a student nurse at Columbia-Presbyterian Hospital in New York City. He had hurt his back in a car accident, and Mom was one of his nurses. When they married, he was twenty-one; she was twenty-three. I was born eleven months later in the hospital where they'd met. My sister, Karey, came twenty-two months after that. Before Karey was born, Mom and Dad built a beautiful Frank Lloyd Wright–style redwood and glass house in Wilton, Connecticut, just up the hill from my beloved Stivers grandparents. In 1963, we converted our garage into an apartment for Grandma Temple, Mom's mother, so the gang was all there.

It all felt very fairy-tale until 1966. One day that spring, after their first—and, to my knowledge, only—high-volume argument in twelve years of marriage, Mom told Dad that if he wasn't happy, he ought to leave. The day the three of us got home from summer camp—Mom was working as the camp nurse—he decided to follow her advice. At the time, divorce was rare enough to be the subject of a maudlin public service announcement on TV featuring a sobbing brother and sister. That's what I thought of when Dad told us of the breakup. I didn't have enough drama of our own to replay.

It took years for the adults in my family to admit this had actually happened. No one would discuss it. Although we moved two states away in the middle of a school term, and both Mom and Dad remarried within a year (Mom to a hard-drinking Wall Street stockbroker; Dad to a gorgeous young flight attendant), everyone maintained a veneer of normalcy and deflected all queries. If you had bugged our house, you might have thought nothing extraordinary had happened. Even my grandmothers—on both sides—lacked details.

I now realize that my mother was merely applying one of her pet aphorisms:

If you don't have something nice to say, don't say anything. She was furious at my father. Because I'm a lot like him—and despite the fact that I am also very much like her—I got the sense that she didn't much like having me around, either. The common stupidities of adolescence seemed to register as plots against her. And whenever I notched some small triumph (making honor roll, getting elected to the student council, editing the school paper), the thrill was momentary. She would wave it away and regale me with tales of her own charmed youth, of which she had ample proof: a scrapbook full of clippings and the testimonial of live witnesses. She really had been beautiful and smart and popular. She still was—except it was hard to be that popular when you were living in the suburbs, working at a county hospital, and trying to support two kids on your own. So Karey and I really were part of the problem.

But only part. For many years, I watched my mother grieve for the vanished life she thought she was destined to lead. Why had she stopped being a golden girl? Where had she gone wrong? I kept a wary distance, trying to avoid her verbal paper cuts, and learned to take care of myself. She, meanwhile, slogged away for twenty-five underpaid years at the hospital, teaching coronary care classes on her own time and doing what she could to help the patients and educate the staff. Her work ethic isn't Protestant; it's positively Spartan—and I'm proud to say I inherited it from her.

Her career at the hospital ended badly, when she blew the whistle on several shirking coworkers. For a while she had suffered in angry silence. But her sense of right and wrong is so deeply rooted that her body finally rebelled: Her blood pressure shot up, her asthma grew worse, and it became physically difficult for her to stay on the job. In 1992, for perhaps the first time in her life, she took the easy way out: She opted for early retirement and moved to Cape Cod.

Mom's blossoming, at the edge of a cranberry bog in Yarmouthport, has been wonderful to watch. She bought a house (where the following conversation took place) and fixed it up just the way she wanted, and she now spends her days gardening, working on one of her myriad crafts projects, and trying to keep the red squirrels out of the bird feeder. No longer a slave to hospital shifts, she clocks the *seasons of her life by the growth cycle of the berries out her back window. She is reveling in her leisure, which is a joy to see—especially since the toil that bought it was so often bleak and unrelenting. She'll even allow herself the occasional splurge, figuring she's earned it. She certainly has.*

Of course, she still has her quirks, such as weighing out nutritionally adequate portions of her food before freezing it. But I suppose that's just a Depression baby conserving her resources. Her own mother, after all, lived to be ninety-four.

Cyndi: I thought we could start with your relationship with your mother.

Marguerite: My relationship with my mother—I guess it ran a course, like the average kind of relationship does. I don't have a lot of memories as a young girl of specific things that went on, so I assume she did a good job, because I was happy. And I was safe and well-fed and nurtured. There were not a whole lot of demonstrative kinds of things.

Cyndi: I remember you telling me that.

Marguerite: There was not a lot. I know she loved me, but we didn't go around saying "I love you," and there weren't a lot of hugs and things like that. Yes, we did when we were going away from each other and stuff, but there wasn't, as I was going to bed, a lot of hugging or things like that. Then, as I got older, there was a period when I was busy with getting myself—my life—in order, and growing up and experiencing things, and I didn't, frankly, think a whole lot about my mother. She was very independent and able to take care of herself. She was working, she was healthy, and I didn't think a whole lot about her. She didn't bother me a whole lot—or get in touch with me a tremendous amount that I can remember. So there wasn't a lot of that.

I think our family always felt no news is good news. You know, some people have to talk all the time, but we were secure enough in our relationship and our loyalty for each other. "Leave 'em alone and they'll come home when they need us," you know? So I think that's the way it was. I was busy doing other things in my life. I think when

I really began to feel really close and concerned was as she got older. You realize that they're not going to be around. [*Her voice breaks.*] And I loved her, a lot. I was close to her.

Cyndi: One of the things you told me—I guess it was more than twenty years ago, when I was doing a paper for school—was something I found really amazing, about the orphanage.

Marguerite (*casually*): Oh.

Cyndi: When was that, and how old were you?

Marguerite: I think I was in third grade, which would make me eight, and Uncle Bill was ten. It was just a thing that happened. Mother didn't share that a lot with me in her life, but I guess my dad was out of work. And was he out of work because he was drinking? Or was he drinking because he was out of work? That *was* in his life, which I wasn't aware of. And he wasn't the type that would come home and drink at home. I guess he'd come home late at night, and when I was a little one he'd pick me up when he came home, and he'd take me into the potty and then put me back to bed and say goodnight to me. I just assumed that he was working. Maybe he did work evening shifts—I have no idea. And I don't know why he was out of work.

I do know that Mother had to go back to work [as a nurse] and that debts were building up. And they couldn't keep up the house with her working. Meanwhile, he was looking for work. So they put Bill and me into this home—not an orphanage. I have no idea how many places like that were around, and I don't know what you'd call it. But it was in Newark [New Jersey], and I'm sure they planned that carefully. She would come and see me on weekends. Maybe it wasn't even every weekend, because she probably had to work some weekends. She had gone back to work at St. Barnabus [a nearby hospital] and was, I think, a night supervisor. She probably got the most money that way. I don't know.

Anyway, that time was never discussed—ever, ever. Except that she knew that I didn't like the place. My highlight of the time was when they would come to visit us, and they'd take us usually to East Orange, where we had lived. The neighbors down the street were Bob Spear and his maiden aunts; they lived on the corner, a couple of doors away from us. And we would go and visit. Not overnight—we would just go for the day and have a meal.

Cyndi: So was Grandma living at St. Barnabus?

Marguerite: She was living there, and Dad had a room somewhere. She had trained and worked at St. Barnabus before going to Cuba, where she worked as an OR nurse for United Fruit Company. Cuba is where she met Dad, who was there with National Cash Register Company. He was a salesman. That's where they met and had their romance, and then they came back to the States and got married.

Anyway, I looked forward to seeing them, and I looked forward to playing with a couple of my wonderful dolls: Madame Alexander dolls, Princess Nancy—the really nice dolls I didn't have at the home. We called it "the home." I had my own cubicle there, with my things in it. I don't remember a whole lot about it, and I don't know if I don't remember it because it was an unhappy time and I blocked it out, or if it's just, I don't know, you're just going along, going to school, doing what you have to do, and I saw my mother on the weekends, and played with my favorite dolls on the weekend, and I liked that.

Cyndi: I remember when you told me about that. It really blew me away, because I had never heard about it before. I think you mentioned something about Christmastime. Both of them came and gave you presents, and when they left the people who ran the home took all but one.

Marguerite: I don't remember that. No, I don't remember that specifically. I think that they would take me someplace, like Bob Spear's or something. Where we were, the closest was to go from Newark to East Orange. Other relatives probably came to visit us—I don't know. I don't remember anything about that. I just remember certain routines that we had: filing down to the dining room, and you had to eat all the food whether you liked it or not. I remember vomiting zucchini squash, or whatever it was I didn't like, and liver. Had to eat it anyway.

Bill's supervisor at the home was a little, short, fat thing, and very stern. It was almost Dickensian to me, in my memory, because it was so horrible. He was abused, I think, by her. She was cruel. I can remember them filing by, and sometimes he was in tears. And he was *not* a bad boy. That used to just make me feel horrible. I think I was a little more independent, a little stronger.

Cyndi: You mentioned your dad. He died when you were, what, twelve?

Marguerite: Yes.

Cyndi: You always had a kind of romanticized memory of him.

Marguerite: Mm-hmm.

Cyndi: I think you once told me you were a daddy's girl.

Marguerite: Yeah, I think I was his little girl, although my mother says that he never got over the death of Harold. And I don't think he was aloof from us. Near as I can remember, he was very sweet and tender to me, but maybe a little harder on Bill, because he was the boy.

Cyndi: And because he wasn't Harold.

Marguerite: And because he wasn't Harold. That could be. I don't know if Bill has memories of that. Seems to me he did not say really great things about our dad: "Oh, he was a boozer. Boozer, loser." But I just thought he was wonderful. He was bright; he was talented. [*Tears up.*] Why I cry with all this, I don't know. Sentimental, I guess. But he had a beautiful singing voice, and he drew beautifully. Bill has those pictures—pencil pictures that he did. Bill puts them away in files and drawers; I'd have them framed and on the wall.

Cyndi: That does suggest perhaps that it wasn't entirely uncomplicated for Bill.

Marguerite: Yeah. Dad would sing, and he joked with me. As I say, beautiful singing voice, and he played the piano by ear. He never took lessons. He read voraciously; he did the *Times* crossword puzzle. He died of—he had very, very bad asthma, and back in those days...

He was a pretty big man for his generation; I think he was six feet tall. When he died he was heavy—not obese, but he had a potbelly and his face was a little full. That was probably from inactivity. He enjoyed eating, and he smoked, and there was the asthma. I don't know if it got to the point of emphysema, but it was bad. He died at Thanksgiving time. I didn't see him when he died; he was in the hospital. Mother was in the hospital.

Cyndi: And he was young, right?

Marguerite: He had just turned forty-eight.

Cyndi: And Grandma lived to be...

Marguerite: Ninety-four. You know, I think she had a lot of disappointments with him, but she also had a lot of happy memories. She never chose to marry again, and once in a while she'd say...well, when he was drinking, he wasn't all that nice to her. He probably was obnoxious, but I never saw any abuse or anything like that. In later years he did get a job, and we moved to Ridgewood [New Jersey] and rented a house. He got a job during the war for Wright Aeronautical Corporation, on the night shift, doing precision work. He would be looking at millimicrons of things, pieces that had to be tested. And he would reject things because they were slightly off. He would refuse adamantly to let something go through; it had gone through other people, but not through him. He was just being very careful that what he did was the way it was supposed to be done. So he had high principles.

And he was sort of sentimental, a free spirit—or would like to have been. He didn't have the opportunity to be. He loved fishing and he loved hunting, but he didn't have very much opportunity. Dad just didn't have the time or the money or the leisure to do a lot of that. You would have enjoyed him. So that's Dad.

Cyndi: Among the other things I've noticed little pieces of over the years are the effects of your growing up in the Depression. I remember one time, when I was in junior high school, a friend of mine asked, "Why do you always buy bruised apples?" We didn't have a lot of money.

Marguerite (*slightly annoyed*): I was not aware that we bought bruised apples. See, you have a lot of memories even Karey doesn't have. You do have a very artistic mind, a very creative mind, and Karey and I truly feel that some of these things your mind has embellished.

Cyndi: Like what?

Marguerite: Let's see... I think we'd have to have Karey here to discuss that. Some of the things you've told me, some of them when she *is* here—well, we don't remember the same thing. Karey afterward would say, "That didn't happen." And so I can't... because my short-term memory is not good. But you do embellish things, and they become exaggerated in your mind.

Cyndi: But I wouldn't have made that up. It wouldn't have occurred to me if somebody hadn't come into the house and commented on it.

Marguerite: Well, I don't know why. But I certainly don't think anyone *sold* bruised apples. I bought a bag of apples, and if some of them were bruised—I mean, it sounds silly to me. That kind of a memory, no...

Cyndi: To me, it was just emblematic of having to be frugal.

Marguerite: Buying bruised apples wouldn't be. If you get a bag of apples, you get a bag of apples. We got our stuff up at Tice's Farm a lot of times, and they didn't have bruised apples that were cheaper or anything like that. I often would buy things on sale; I still do that. And there's nothing wrong with it, I don't think. My being very careful with money was because I had to be. Was that because of the Depression—or was it just due to the fact that we grew up in a time when there just wasn't a lot of money?

My mother's kind of occupation... well, there wasn't a lot that was handed down to them, so we didn't have a whole lot. No one went to college before my generation, and we lived a comfortable middle-class existence. Not excessive. We lived very carefully, because we had to. Mother was not one for going into debt; she paid the bills and had to have the ends meet, which is exactly what I always did. There weren't any excesses. If we'd go shopping, I'd say, "I'd kinda like that—no, that's too expensive." Or, "I can go ten dollars, but I can't go twelve dollars."

When you were growing up, it was the same thing, because I was trying to live on my income. I'd know what I could spend and what I couldn't, so it was shop the sales—and you had better energy for that than poor Karey did. I'd say, "Okay, we looked at those things there, and we have to go to another store," and we'd see what the values were. Between them all, we'd get skirts and tops and whatnot, and a lot of stuff was sale things, but I think you dressed fine. It was harder to do it that way. To this day, I shop sales. It's rare that I'll go out and buy a thing full-price; it's become so ingrained in me not to do that. Still, I loved doing what I did with this house, because I spent the money that I had to.

Cyndi: That's one of the main reasons I wanted to talk about all this, because it's been fascinating watching you here, watching you make this house the way you wanted it. It seems as though you're finally getting to enjoy your life, which is great to see. But also there are times when I wonder: Did you delay your gratification on purpose? Could you have indulged yourself or rewarded yourself a little more, once we were out of the house and you weren't having to support us?

Marguerite: I don't think so, because I still didn't have a lot of money coming in. It wasn't until my last five or seven years of work that I could save.

Cyndi: At what age were you happiest so far?

Marguerite: I was very happy in high school. I had an absolute ball at Ridgewood High. I had a lot of friends and received a lot of honors.

Cyndi: That was going to be my guess, because you've always talked about it. It seemed like a charmed life. You were on top of it all.

Marguerite: Yes. I was number one in school and all that stuff. But I'm very happy now, I truly am. You're a very smiley person, and I'm basically a very smiley person. I think we have sunny dispositions. You cross us, and watch out! But for the most part I think we have happy dispositions, and that's what I basically am.

These tears come out because of emotion, but it's not sad emotion. I really am very happy now; I was in high school, and as a little kid. I can remember loving my mom and my dad and my brother. I was not abused. Even if there's a shortage of money or something like that, it doesn't mean you're not happy. I don't know about the money things. I had the toys that I wanted; I had my dollies that I loved. I don't remember being particularly the way kids today are, so hung up on clothes and different outfits. I don't remember that. I loved being pretty, dressing up. I loved to have on my good shoes and my pretty dresses. I did love that. As far as I was concerned, I had it. I didn't have excess, but what did I know?

Cyndi: After your marriage to Dad broke up, there was a sense of "How did I get into this situation?" Your life had run on such a marvelous path, and then, out of nowhere...boom!

Marguerite: I know.

Cyndi: It seemed to me that a lot of the time you were mourning that: "What happened to my charmed life?" Because you hadn't done anything wrong. From my perspective, and from what I pieced together from the grandparents, it was remarkable how little everybody knew at the time about why you two split up. I guess it was a lack of communication over a long period of time.

Marguerite: Yes, I think so. In the beginning of a relationship, when love is new, you listen openly to the other person. But your father became, I guess, disenchanted, or so wrapped up in his own work, and there were money problems, and I was saddled with that. He was in his own dream world. I had to pay the bills and everything, and I couldn't pay them all. I'd give a little bit here and there, and yet he'd still go out and buy his Paul Stuart shirts and his expensive suits and wanted to go on vacations. The only kind of vacation we could afford was camping, and I was not a camping kind of person. So who does it fall on, then?

You've not only got to take care of the kids, but you've got to take care of them under adverse conditions. And I never really was a camper.

Anyway, it got worse and worse. And he stayed away more and more. He "found himself." Again, a dreamer. He was looking for his own . . . can't have it here, so talk to some beautiful young thing who will listen to him and all his problems. At home, he just decided, "That life is past," and he shut that door. It doesn't matter if lives are being hurt in the process. He wanted to be happy, and the heck with everyone else, so he did what he had to do to be happy, and he's done it several times since.

Cyndi: He's started to realize that he really ran roughshod over a lot of lives.

Marguerite: Does he realize that? I think it should be pointed out to him if he doesn't.

Cyndi: Yeah, he does. Anyway, you were a little older when the two of you got married. Regardless, though, you were more mature.

Marguerite: Steady. Straight-through, steady. Maybe a dull person or whatever. . . .

Cyndi: You were about to finish college; you had a career chosen. He was much less focused in that realm than you were. You were also aware of what it meant to get married and have kids, and you faced that.

Marguerite: I loved it. I never regretted it. But supposing I had: There are some mothers who I guess are not nurturing. I didn't demonstrate a lot of love, but I loved you both and I was so proud of you. [*Begins crying.*] Still am.

Cyndi: When we were little, I certainly felt loved by both of you. But I also felt as if Dad favored me, and that was embarrassing.

Marguerite: I felt that, too. And I protected Karey a little more.

Cyndi: I remember sensing when you went out of your way to make her feel good; I knew what you were doing. I totally understood that. I didn't feel as though you were rejecting me.

Marguerite: Because I wasn't. I was proud of you.

Cyndi: I remember your saying once, "Cyndi and Dad are the smart ones." That bugged me, because you're a smart one, too.

Marguerite: I just felt that Karey didn't pick up on things quite so fast, and your father was impatient. You picked up on things yourself, just on your own ability, and I think he felt she should have done that, too.

Cyndi: I think he felt that I was supposed to be a boy.

Marguerite: That was never, ever, *ever* discussed. Well, you were the first child, the oldest child, so there's something special about that.

Cyndi: Well, I also felt, after the divorce, that for some reason I reminded you of Dad, even though I feel I have so much of you in me, too. In fact, he used to say, "Ugh, you're just like your mother." He said that to me all the time—and never to Karey.

Marguerite: I never knew that.

Cyndi: So I suddenly had this ten-year period where I reminded you of Dad and him of you.

Marguerite: You didn't remind me of him....

Cyndi: But during that period, I definitely felt more distant from you.

Marguerite: Of course, if he said it, he would have meant it in a negative way. I don't think he'd think that today, though. And I think it's been good, your having those traits. Most of them that you have of mine are good.

Cyndi: You're right—he got over that a long time ago. I was just trying to identify why it was that I felt we really grew apart at that stage.

Marguerite: We did, I think, when you were in high school. I was aware of it.

Cyndi: Before that—junior high. I felt it once Terry [the stockbroker] entered the picture.

Marguerite: I don't know what stage it was. Maybe Terry was a problem, because you didn't really want that.

Cyndi: Well, I didn't know why you were doing that to yourself.

I understood in raw terms that he had money, so that was good. And I also understood that he needed you.

Marguerite: He didn't need me; I felt *I* needed *him.* I thought he was attractive. And I got a few vacations, which I'd never had before. Unfortunately, the drinking thing—I didn't see that. I knew he had a little too much to drink at times, but I did not realize that it was going to be a problem. When it *was* a problem [*claps*]: "Out you go! Let the police pick you up." I don't put up with that stuff. I'm not the long-suffering, beat-me-up-every-night-I-deserve-it kind of person.

It was a mistake. I can remember that, just a little before Terry and I got married, I talked to your dad on the phone, for whatever reason, and I told him I was getting married again. I said, "I don't know if it's the right thing, but I'm going to do it because I think I love him."

Cyndi: You and Dad both remarried within a year. Did you know that?

Marguerite: Oh, your dad wanted to get a divorce right away. He remarried because he was already going out with someone. As soon as he left the house, he took up very heavily with Nancy. He wasn't really traveling then, so I don't know if he met her in a bar or where he met her. I tried letters and all kinds of stuff to get him to come back, but he was already off. He was into his next life, with her.

There was nothing to get from him. Nothing to get. There were no savings. The house—he'll say I got everything. I did not. The house had to be sold to pay our debts. To somebody, I guess it was Karey, he said: "Your mother got everything. I wasn't left with a thing." I let him take some of his things that he wanted, some things I'd given him. Wedding presents and things like that—well, there weren't that many things, and I had to keep a whole household up. Anyhow, it's not like we had the wedding of the century, where there was a lot of stuff, you know? At one point I said: "We'll sell the house and clear the debts. We'll go rent a place for a while. What's so hard about that?" And if you're really a loving family that wants to stay together, that's what should have happened. But he could not face that failure.

Cyndi: Imagine if you hadn't had your nursing degree.

Marguerite: Well, of course, my mother had problems with her husband, so she said, "You've got to have a career; you've got to be able to take care of yourself."

Cyndi: So that came from her? I didn't know that.

Marguerite: Sure: "You get a career. You never know what's going to happen. You cannot rely on anyone else but yourself. If you have a career, it's something you can always do." She fell back on hers, and it's a good thing I had mine.

But getting back to your feeling that I resented you. I think what happened then was that I was able to get a little place in Waldwick [New Jersey]. My salary was still small. So in order to get the house, I had to work full-time—which I didn't want to do in the beginning, because I figured the two of you had only me. Once in a while I'd get some alimony from your dad, but that stopped, so I went full-time in order to have a big enough salary to be able to get the house. That was hard on me: Between the house and working full-time, it took me about a year to adjust. I was exhausted all the time—and I'm a pretty high-energy person. It was probably emotional as well, worry stuff. I think my nose was mostly to the grindstone, and I probably came across as stern, which I . . . well, I was afraid. I had to raise the two of you alone!

Still, I loved having children. There was not a minute I resented it. But I thought: You guys are depending on me, and I want you to do well in school, and I want you to do well for yourselves, and I want you to go to college. I probably hounded you a little bit. I don't think I *had* to, because I think you both had strong work ethics, but I didn't want to see that ethic not be there. I wanted honesty; I wanted you to be able to face yourself and feel good about yourself.

You and I both have a tendency to be headstrong and think, I know I'm right. I've found that I'm wrong sometimes, but I basically have a very strong sense of what's right and wrong, and I'm pretty much right on a lot of stuff. And I'm stubborn that way. I don't remember a whole lot of discipline from my mother. I mean, I did have to clean my room; I had to do all this stuff. But I don't remember giving her a lot of lip or anything like that. Nor did you give me much, though you did have a rebellious phase, and it might have been the way I handled you, because we both have that strong personality. You look very much like Grandma, by the way.

Cyndi: Which grandma?

Marguerite: Stivers. You have a lot of her—the skin, the dimples. I think you have a lot of her looks. I guess you have a lot of mine, too, but there's a lot of her in you. And your frame is large. You've got a big bone structure.

You were big into junk food and stuff like that, and you did put on some weight. I thought, Uh-oh, I don't want her to get fat. Again, for your own good. And then: She's going to be stuck in this fatness, and it's too late then. It's hard to get it off. I was trying to make you aware, to look at yourself, to be able to look at that scale and say, "I weigh 100-whatever." You don't want to weigh 130 or whatever and say, "I'm about 120. The scale must be wrong." I didn't want you to get in that head-in-the-clouds, "I'm okay" frame of mind. That's how the weight goes on, on, on, on, on. And I think because you were stubborn, you took it that I was always nagging at you. All I was trying to do was say, "Look at yourself and be honest about yourself, and realize you do have some faults." We all have some faults. But in your mind I was constantly nagging you, and I know I wasn't.

Cyndi: That's not what I was about to bring up.

Marguerite: All right, but let me just finish this. They say teenage years for a lot of people are tumultuous years: "The hormones are fighting against each other, and it's a rough time, and kids are rebellious." I never felt that. I was happiest, as I say, in high school. I don't think I was rebellious. I was so busy doing my thing. Yes, I had to clean my room Saturday mornings—"Darn!"—and before I could go out to the game Saturday afternoon, I had to do certain things around the house. I didn't really like it, but I had to do it, and that was good.

With you, when it came to certain things, I'd say, "That's the way it is." And you would not really give me any lip, but sometimes you'd look at me, and you had such...you couldn't say anything back to me, because I wanted respect. But you looked at me with such an "I hate your guts" look in your eyes. Which is okay. I even understood that as a rebellious thing. You didn't say it, but I knew you were feeling it, and I also know it was a stage that would pass. But that's as far as I saw the rebellion in you. And it was more you than Karey. Karey was more "Okay, Mommy." She was more willing to give in. Today, she's a little tiger. I think she's gotten really—she can really handle herself very well against anyone.

Cyndi: I was going to say that the thing I found most dismaying—and it was part of the reason I went toward my friends—

Marguerite: Toward friends is fine.

Cyndi: Well, I was testing the limits of what I could get away with—but just out of boredom, really.

Marguerite: You didn't do much. One time, you skipped school. Again, I didn't have a husband there to help guide me through this. I had to do my own thing, and my own thing tends to be kind of harsh. I can't soft-pedal. I'd never have made a politician or anything like that. Some parents might have said, "Okay, I'll let her get through this, and then talk to her afterward and say, 'Don't you do that again.'" But I said: "Hey, you know what? You made your bed; go lie in it," you know? And to the school: "No, I can't give her an excuse. She wasn't sick." That might have been a little harsh. Maybe I would have done it differently if I had a husband to talk to. I'm not really good at talking at that level. Didn't know how to do it.

Cyndi: It didn't matter. You know what it was about? To see what would get your attention. This probably happened during the time you were feeling completely exhausted. Now, as I look back on it, some of the turmoil probably was due to that exhaustion and your trying to make money to feed all three of us. But I also got a sense from you of "How did this happen to me?"

Marguerite: No, because if that was the feeling I had, I would have been resentful, and I would have resented what I was doing. And I was not resentful.

Cyndi: It did feel that way at times.

Marguerite: I am very much nose-to-the-grindstone. And if this is what I have to do—well, I took the whole thing very seriously. I wasn't light and laughing at life particularly, at that point. I think that's probably true. I wasn't *un*happy. I just was very serious about what I was doing.

Cyndi: Well, you seemed unhappy. And it was *much* later when you said, "I'm proud of you." You never said it then, and that struck me. Maybe it *was* a symptom of your being businesslike. But it just seemed as though I could never make you happy or proud of me. It was always: "Oh, yeah, I was in that club, too. I was on student council, too; I was an officer."

Marguerite: Maybe so.

Cyndi: Maybe you didn't mean it that way. But I'd look at your scrapbooks and say: "Wow, she's beautiful, she's popular, she's all these things. I'll never be that good." That was the message I got *all* those years. I got over it! But I felt like it was a competition.

Marguerite: I don't think I consciously tried to be competitive. My times were a whole generation earlier. They didn't have the Girls Club; they didn't have all the same kinds of stuff. I don't know if they had National Honor Society back in my day—I'm not sure I would have been in it. But I was so proud of you. I don't know what I could have done. I went to the services and went to your plays and all that, and hugged you and said, "You did a good job." Maybe you needed to hear the word "proud" or "You make me proud." I don't know. I don't remember.

Cyndi: I can recall giving you my report cards, and your reaction: "Well, yeah. That's what you always get."

Marguerite: No, I think you're making it harsher. You have to remember: There's only one place to go from A, and that's down. So it was a challenge to you to keep it up there. I was always proud of those, and I thought I let you know it, but I guess you needed to hear it better.

Cyndi: Okay: my high-school graduation. You invited family that I'd never met before, so it didn't feel intimate to me. In fact, it felt really weird to me.

Marguerite: I don't know why we did that.

Cyndi: It seemed like a way to keep us from communicating.

Marguerite: Hmm. What do you do for a high-school gradua-tion? I suppose I didn't know. I'd never done that before. And your dad—it was awkward, because he wasn't around. I truly would have loved to share that stuff, for you to share it with your mother *and* father. It was hard.

Cyndi: And then, for my college graduation, *nobody* showed up.

Marguerite: Yeah, afterwards, I felt bad.

Cyndi: That was it. For me, that said it all.

Marguerite: You told me, "Ah, it's going to be in the gym." You didn't sound like . . . you were not giving true signals.

Cyndi: I know! Because I had learned the hard way that from my perspective, all my growing-up years—from ten to eighteen, or even into my early twenties—whenever I tried to reach out, my timing was bad.

Marguerite: I think so. That can happen.

Cyndi: Either you would be distracted—you wouldn't hear it for what it was—or you'd have your own problems. So I felt that when I did make myself vulnerable and did reach out, I was either not heard or rejected.

Marguerite (*genuinely empathetic*): Oh. . . .That's too bad.

Cyndi: Also, I got the distinct feeling that you felt I was working against you in some way.

Marguerite: Well, I think there was a time when you really did reject me. I also felt: The Stivers are a big family, and I loved that family, really, and all of a sudden I'm not in it anymore. I always felt that the things the Stivers did were much more important to you than what my little family did.

Cyndi: No, there were just more of them. And, of course, Grandma Stivers and I had a particularly great relationship. She was the only person in the family that I felt—and I still feel it to this day, really—loved me unconditionally. Grandma Temple loved me, but not really unconditionally. As you say, your mother had her own needs and her own way of doing everything, and nobody ever really got around that.

Marguerite: It was just her reserve, which I have, too. That's all it was. You and Karey were the first grandchildren she had. You were very important to her. It was just that reserved, cool, aloof gene, which I have. You have it, too.

Cyndi: Yeah, I do.

Marguerite: After your graduation, I thought, I really would have liked to go. But you almost made it sound, well, like: "We can only have two people if it's in the gym. Because it's raining, it's going to be in the gym." And I can't remember now if your dad was there, and that was going to be a problem. I thought you felt: "Ah, no big deal. If it's going to be in the gym, why bother?" So there again, it was a mis-reading.

Cyndi: I think I was trying to make the best of it.

Marguerite: Where was your dad?

Cyndi: That same morning, the phone rang: "Well, the weather's kind of bad. I don't know." Both calls came in: "Well, it'll be inside anyway, so it won't really be that festive. So I guess I won't come."

Marguerite: I don't remember saying that.

Cyndi: Anyway, it was just one of those things. That was why I felt I had to be resourceful. I remember the little rebellion period, but it was not particularly directed at you. It was to see what I could get away with: at school, with my parents—you know?

Marguerite: I don't think you ever did anything at school other than skipping that one time. Your teachers all adored you.

Cyndi: And I *loved* school. I wasn't really trying to subvert any-thing major. I knew I was lucky to have a roof over my head.

Marguerite: So, misreadings.

Cyndi: For the longest time, I just felt that I'd better make my own way and not look to you for approval, because that would mean dis-appointment: I looked for it, I didn't get it, then I felt bad. And then, the next time you reached out, I was probably still wounded.

Marguerite: Yes. I also thought you were probably feeling more loyalty to your father at that point, which maybe you were.

Cyndi: Actually, he thought the reverse. That's the thing: I was in a Catch-22 all those years. He thought I was more loyal to you, and you thought I was more loyal to him.

Marguerite: Well, in a way, he shouldn't feel so bad about your being more loyal to me, because usually a daughter is to a mother, and he had all those other kids [from his two subsequent marriages].

There was one other thing I wanted to mention: The first year you went to college, I turned over my—whatever it was—$1,000 tax refund. I used it to help you for school. One time. But you know what happened to me? I never got out of debt that year. Usually, I would use the refund to pay up the bills. Then I'd get behind again, of course, and so I'd have to pay them again. The next year, I really needed to have that money to catch up. And you were furious with that. You once said, "You owe it to me."

Cyndi: I don't remember that.

Marguerite: I do remember. You see, we remember things that we want to remember a lot of times, you and I. But there was one time when I just had to take that money.

Cyndi: It would make sense that this was right around my sopho-more year in college, when I thought I'd never be able to finish school.

Marguerite: Well, maybe that's the one year that I gave you the $1,000.

Cyndi: No, that was the problem. For my freshman year, I had a

$500 one-time gift from Dad; I thought it was more like $500 from you. There was another $500 from the state of New Jersey, and one gift from you. Plus my life savings. That's how I had paid for freshman year, and I just didn't know how I was going to continue.

Marguerite: Well, life savings—nobody has much of that.

Cyndi: It was all my high-school babysitting money. That's what my life savings were.

Marguerite: That's what it's for. I saved money to put myself through school.

Cyndi: Well, I don't regret any of this, as you know.

Marguerite: Did you have a college loan at all?

Cyndi: No, there wasn't much to get. So if I freaked out and said something like "You owe it to me," I'm sure that's why. Because you had said, "Count on this money," and then I couldn't count on the money. I wouldn't have thought that otherwise. I *didn't* think that.

Marguerite: I couldn't believe it. I couldn't believe that I heard that. I didn't really owe you anything.

Cyndi: I know I didn't feel that way, or I'd remember it. I must have felt that you had said it was coming.

Marguerite: Or you thought it. You have a wonderful memory, but anyone—there's a natural. . . just like I don't remember a lot of stuff.

Cyndi: If it really was something I felt I was owed, I'd be bitter and resentful about it.

Marguerite: Oh, I get you.

Cyndi: That's my point: It was a stupid thing to say, and I shouldn't have said it. But I obviously didn't feel deeply that way, or I would have remembered it. It was a momentary thing. The money was never really the issue. It was only the fact that I felt that neither of you was participating. I had a sense of being in the middle of the two of you all the time.

Marguerite: But then, I was not involved with your father at *all* after a certain point.

Cyndi: Still, I ended up in a no-person's land.

Marguerite: I think with you and me it was timing. And you misreading me, and me misreading you. I think that's what it was.

Cyndi: I've been trying to figure out why I felt there was a real breakthrough at Karey's college graduation, in 1980. You finally relaxed with me.

Marguerite: Well, I was probably stiff because I thought you were resenting me, which is a normal process. As I told you in the beginning of this, I went through that stage with my mother. I didn't resent her. It was just: "Okay, she's here. I love her, and she's fine." And I was absorbed in myself and my life. It's perfectly okay to be that way, I think. I'm not the mama who says: "Write me every day. I want to talk to you every day." That's not my personality. It wasn't my mother's, and it's not really yours, either.

Anyway, that was a process that I thought was going on. I said to myself, "I did the same thing," and so it didn't bother me. Yes, there was still a bit of a . . . there was a thing of timing and misconception—a bit of that, I think. Maybe it was a time when I was feeling alone and wondering: Am I doing things right? Am I going to be able to make it? [*Her voice breaks.*]

You needed to have more, and I couldn't give it. Or whatever. I don't know. I don't really know.

Cyndi: Back when we were not communicating well, I would sometimes ask something of you, and it didn't always necessarily mean money. Sometimes it was time: "Would you do such-and-such with me?" And sometimes the answer was no. Since I didn't ask very often, that "no" would hurt me, and then I wouldn't ask for a while.

But I feel as though things between us have been absolutely fine since John [my husband] and I went to Brussels. I asked you to do this incredibly boring, nasty task: getting our mail while we were in Belgium for two years. And not only did you do it, but you seemed to do it joyfully.

Marguerite: Yes, I enjoyed it.

Cyndi: Howard [her companion of more than twenty years] said to me: "But don't you understand? You asked her to do something for you." And I just thought, Gee, as far as I'm aware I've asked her to do a lot of things for me. This is one of the stranger requests, but okay! I feel that, ever since then, everything's been fine.

Marguerite (*teasing*): Just don't ask me to do it again! Well, I enjoyed that. I think a lot our difficulty was timing and misinterpretations. You needed when I couldn't give, and I needed when you couldn't give. Or something. I don't know.

Cyndi: So what are you most proud of, and what do you most regret? And what are your goals for the rest of your life?

Marguerite: That's kind of tough, because, you know, right off the top of my head I think what I'm most proud of is my two kids. Is that what I should say? Is that really what I feel? [*Chokes up.*] I think so. You know, having the two of you and doing the best I could. I'm proud of what I did. I know I did some wrong things, but for the most part I think I got you where I could.

Cyndi: I don't think you did wrong things. I think omissions were the main problems on all sides of our family. Not commissions, mostly.

Marguerite: I would agree. Okay, so…can I say anything more than that? I mean, you have things down the list, but you kids are number one. I've been pretty much pleased with myself. I've been pleased with the way a lot of things have gone.

And then what—goals? Very simply, to be happy and healthy and enjoy life, sort of the way I'm doing it. There's a part of me that says—because I did volunteer stuff all my life, from the time I was in junior high, I guess, and then work and everything—there's a part of me that says, "I'm not doing anything really constructive." I'm not hurting society, but I'm not doing anything constructive, and there's a part of me that feels guilty about that.

When I first came up here and started a few things, I said: "I'm getting inundated with this. Enough, already." I'm a homebody. I don't need to get out a lot and do things. I should probably, more than I do. But I am very peaceful here.

MARGUERITE TEMPLE

Cyndi: It's been really gratifying to watch.

Marguerite: I hope to continue on that way. And when it's too much for me, I hope I'll know it. And I'll have to rely on you, like my mother said to me, the last couple years, maybe the last three years. Even while she was still up and around, she said: "You know, the roles have reversed. You're the mommy, and I'm the child." That's gradually happening between you and me—you taking on more of that kind of a role with me. I think it'll happen more and more, and I probably will rely on you and have less confidence in myself. I just hope I have enough sense to listen to you when you say, "Mom, you really shouldn't drive anymore."

Right now, I think I could hear it and say, "Okay." Those kinds of things are hard. But I have to rely on you to help me. You're the older one, and Karey's busy raising two of her own. I'll probably be your baby at some point, but I don't want to be a burden. I just want to be able to have the money set in such a way that it will take care of me and not be a burden to you, and still leave a little something for you guys.

NATALIE ANGIER, A PULITZER-PRIZE WINNING SCIENCE
WRITER for the *New York Times*, is the author of *Natural
Obsessions*, *The Beauty of the Beastly*, and a forth-coming
book about women's bodies. Her essays and articles have
appeared in many print and on-line publications, includ-
ing the *Atlantic*, *Time*, *Discover*, *Parade*, *Natural History*,
UnderWire, and *Orion*. She lives in Takoma Park,
Maryland, with her husband and daughter.

MAMA TOLD ME HOW TO COME

The second best thing my mother ever did for me was to be a bad
mother. No, she didn't beat me, abuse me, neglect me, ridicule
me in front of friends, or otherwise attempt a personal take on Joan
Crawford. I was the third of four children, and she loved us all,
fiercely and absolutely and without making a holy fuss about it. But
my mother did what few mothers did in the 1960s: she worked full-
time. When the other students in my class went home at the end of
the school day to their mothers, I accompanied a girlfriend to her
home, where her mother looked after me until one of my parents
picked me up in the evening.

I'll get to the best thing my mother ever did for me a bit later.

My mother worked because we needed the money—oh, yes, we
needed the money, we could not have gotten by on my father's modest income alone. Yet I sensed that she also worked because she
wanted to work, and that she wouldn't have stayed at home even if

given the option. She didn't convey the sentiment, so popular in these neo-post-feminist days, that she would love to devote herself body and brain to her children if only, sigh, our father's salary were enough. She didn't exalt us or place us at the geographical center of the known galaxy or make us out to be more captivating than we were. And we weren't captivating; we were kids. We liked kiddie stuff, we read kiddie books, we read comics and *Mad* magazine, for crying out loud. We didn't live to entertain our mother, and she, with all due courtesy, returned the favor.

It's not that my mother enjoyed working because she had a great career, chosen from the Hollywood hit list of glamorous careers. She wasn't a paleontologist or a television reporter or the owner of a Soho gallery. She had a job, or rather a series of jobs, which she regarded as jobs rather than as callings. She didn't romanticize her jobs any more than she did her children, and she had no monomaniacal drive to scale professional heights or put in more than an eight-hour day. She worked in a meat packing plant for awhile and then as a substitute teacher in inner-city schools. For a few years she was a cooking teacher in a Bronx junior high school, where the most complicated dishes she taught the girls to make were chocolate chip cookies and pigs-in-a-blanket.

Sometimes my mother hated her jobs, but she always liked the independence and self-respect that a job, and its paycheck, brought her. She liked getting out of the apartment and into the world. She liked being around other adults. She liked feeling, in every way, that she was the equal of any man, including, or perhaps especially, my father. My mother worked with the presumptuous attitude that of course she would earn a living: she was healthy, wasn't she? And there was always some way to patch together child care, wasn't there?

In sum, she was, by the standards of her era, a bad mother. Which is why I salute her with a raise of an empty fork, in honor of all the apple pies I'm glad she never stayed at home to bake.

As a girl, I absorbed her sense of entitlement. It seemed to me natural that a woman should work, so I took offense at my Dick and Jane schoolbooks. I couldn't stand that stock suburban family and its stay-at-home Mom, with her white apron and her butterscotch hair and her ceaseless efforts to keep Dick and Jane and Spot and Puff in line. In her iconic position as the First Lady of literacy, every child's intro-duction to the power of the Word, Dick and Jane's mother seemed to me to be offered up as the ideal mother, or at least the normative mother—and this mother had nothing in common with my own.

Pretty soon I was finding fault with all my schoolbooks. I remem-ber flipping through the reader in third grade and noting that all but one of the stories in it were about boys: boys rafting down rivers, boys confronting ethical dilemmas, boys getting in trouble and making grand amends. The one story about a girl was the story of a quiet, contemplative girl who learned a quiet, contemplative lesson from an older, contemplative poet. I wanted to stomp up to my teacher and complain. I wanted to ask her, Where are the girls? Why aren't there more stories about girls? Are they all at home being quiet, good girls? Even then, in 1967, I was a pissed-off radical feminist, although I was too shy—too much the quiet, good girl, I must admit—to confront the teacher with my observations and complaints.

Having adopted a querulous form of egalitarianism practically from the moment of sentience, I was excited when my mother joined the fledgling women's liberation movement. She started going to meetings of a chapter called OWL, for "older women's liberation," older in those demographic times meaning any woman over thirty. My mother's newfound activism didn't help my parents' marriage, which was already starting to disintegrate from the weight of time, adulterous dabblings, my father's explosive temper, my mother's deri-sive handling of that temper, and other noxious ingredients. Now, with feminism, my mother was able to give the personal predicament a political cast. My father subscribed to *Playboy*, for example, a mag-azine that arrived each month flamboyantly fat and glossy, its smut so coy and pert as to be G-rated. (In fact, I loved flipping through

Playboy; I liked the Little Annie Fannie comic strip, the mountains of creamy flesh, and the girlishly handwritten autobiographies of the centerfolds). For my mother, though, *Playboy* was no innocent. Before feminism, she had regarded it merely as a low-brow picture book with middle-brow pretensions; now she began to see it as a rank parser and objectifier of the female body. My father's patronage of it struck her as a gratuitously hostile act. "You wouldn't even associate with the sort of man who normally reads *Playboy*," she said to him. "You would find him utterly beneath you." And while he didn't deny the accusation, her opposition to *Playboy* only made the job of its subscription renewal department that much easier.

For his part, my father, a former member of the Communist youth party and a man to the left of red, nonetheless saw my mother's feminism as a psychospiritual act of war. He trotted out the insults that eventually would become anti-feminist cliches, calling her a "castrating bitch" or a "bull-dyke." He'd come up with elaborate arguments for why women were designed to cater to men's needs: genetic arguments, physiological arguments, historical arguments, Zen Buddhist arguments. Time and again, she ground his reasoning down with acrid dismissiveness. I didn't always take my mother's side in the increasingly brutal Angier conflicts, but on this issue, of the role of women in this world, she was my hero and my voice, while my father, quite frankly, was full of shit.

I appreciated growing up with feminism, rather than having to discover it on my own during, say, college, because I thus grew up without any doubts or soul-searching about the rights and capabilities of women. I never thought that women and girls should behave in a particular way, or that there was any such thing as a male or female profession. True, I made the not necessarily intelligent decision at a young age to become a writer, and writing has long been accepted as a lady's pursuit, but in girlhood I toyed as well with other careers, like medicine, law, architecture—never once believing that my sex could be a rate-limiting step in my success. I also loved my precocial exposure to the women's movement because, in the late sixties and early seventies, it was suffused with larger political possibilities, which now may sound quaint but at the time were thrilling: of demolishing capitalism and the patriarchy, of upending our concepts of the family, the tribe, and the nation. I loved the giddiness and the fury of revelatory feminism, the razzing and tazzing and outrage. I loved reading Shulamith Firestone argue in *The Dialectic of Sex* that we must turn pregnancy and childbirth over to machines if women are ever to be set free, Mary Daly in *Gyn/Ecology* reclaiming once-hated terms like "spinster" and "crone," Germaine Greer extolling in *The Female Eunuch* the joys of prancing around without panties. And I read all these books when they came out because my mother brought them home and read them first.

As I entered adolescence, my scratchy feminism influenced my relationship toward boys. For one thing, I didn't like the rules of dating. I didn't like waiting for boys to make the first move. Who voted for that one? I wondered. So, sometimes I'd do the asking myself. And sometimes the boys reacted very badly: first confused, then surprised, then nastily rejecting. But in other cases they were delighted, as was the boy I invited to the senior prom. Through it all, my mother cheered me on, though it disturbed her to see me get hurt on occasion. She still remembers vividly and angrily the time I called up a guy whom I had dated once to ask him out for dinner, and he practically shouted, "Why are you calling me? I told you I'd call you when I was ready!"

I also disliked the rules of sex that prevailed in the small midwestern town where I spent my adolescence. I rejected the tired but enduring double standard that allowed the boys I knew to fuck around as much as they pleased with no judgment slung around their neck, while the girls were ideally supposed to guard their virginity until marriage, or, barring that, to restrict their activity to a single boyfriend lest they be branded a floozy or a tramp. I knew from my immersion in feminism that women were entitled to a lusty, rollicking sexuality, and that to deny a woman her libido is to stifle the pith of being: to Eros is human! Even better, it's mammal! Besides, I was a teenager, and I was ravenous. If it took the declaration of radical principles to satisfy that appetite, I'd use whatever utensil was at hand. My mother regarded my teenage sexuality with wary pragmatism. She didn't try to stop me, she didn't encourage me, she simply did a very sensible thing, and took me to get birth control. She knew I was smart, and her preemptive move made me smarter. I never got pregnant, as some of the more prim girls in my high school did. When I dated a boy who tried to convince me to have sex without birth control, I told him he was an idiot and made that date our last.

Ah, but my mother not only helped me secure a diaphragm. Which brings me to the best thing she ever did for me. I was in college, and by conventional measures I'd lost my virginity several years earlier. Yet by a standard that I considered essential, I'd never had sex at all: specifically, I had never had an orgasm. Goddess knows I'd tried—with boys, by my own hand, with the stream of water running out of the bathtub faucet, but so far, feh! Nothing had happened, and I knew it. The books all say you know it when you climax, and no matter how many angles I tried to squint at it and say, well, maybe that time I. . . . I knew I hadn't. I had started a serious relationship with a fellow student, we'd had sex once, I'd failed yet again to have an orgasm, and I was afroth with frustration. I didn't know what to do or who to turn to. And then I thought of my mother. I knew my mother enjoyed sex. I knew she sought it out. She had separated from my father when I was twelve, and she had a robust relationship with another man. So I said to her (with a certain amount of shame, admitting as I was to frigidity), "Mom, I've never had an orgasm. What am I supposed to do?"

She paused, and then asked me if I'd ever tried smoking grass before sex. I was surprised by the suggestion, not for its implication that my mother smoked marijuana, because I knew she did; but for its ordinariness. Pot? I'd smoked pot a number of times during high

ADELE ANGIER, 1967

school; I'd also had sex a number of times. Surely the two must have corresponded at some point? "I don't know," I said to her. "I *think* I have...."

She told me she thought that she might never have had an orgasm herself before smoking pot. This was even more shocking to me, and slightly depressing. I knew that she and my father had been married for years before they first discovered grass—or turned on, as the still-lovely phrase has it. So all those years, including during her childbearing years, she'd been having sex without climaxing. She'd conceived me, and my three siblings, through one-sided comes. Oh well.

The next time I saw my boyfriend, I raised my mother's suggestion with him, and he, being a college sophomore, swiftly acquired the putative aphrodisiac. We smoked, got to work, and, whoa, it was like the most overheated, bodice-ripping description of an orgasm ever written—the swelling waves, the bells, the fireworks, the entire choir of heavenly angels, all singing just for me. It was a gorgeous, magical orgasm that seemed to last for hours. I'd done it. Grass had done it. It had connected my central and peripheral nervous systems into a flawless glittering matrix of pure pleasure.

Not being much of a pot smoker, I didn't use it very often afterwards, but I didn't need to. I'd learned to have an orgasm and, like riding a bicycle, you never forget. There's an element of cosmic justice here. Sex, at its basal level, is about continuity, regeneration, the compact that the living make with both the past and the future. Sex is also about present pleasure, the declaration of the individual that it is here, thunderously here, and not to be ignored. Sexual pleasure, in my book, is orgasmic pleasure. So it is fitting that I can thank for my knowledge of the body's greatest gift the woman who gave me life.

AWARD-WINNING JOURNALIST AND AUTHOR **MARIA HINOJOSA** is a New York-based correspondent for CNN. She is also the host of NPRs *Latino USA*, a nationally broadcast program about news and culture in the Latino community. A frequent guest on local and national television news analysis programs, Hinojosa focuses upon urban affairs, youth issues, multiculturalism, labor, politics, and Latinos. In 1995, *Hispanic Business* magazine named her one of the 100 most influential Latinos in the United States. She is the author of *Crew Gang Members Talk with Maria Hinojosa* and is currently working on a motherhood memoir about raising a Latino child in a multicultural society. Born in Mexico City and raised in Chicago, Hinojosa now lives in New York City together with her husband and their son.

MAMI'S INNER VOICE

"Pant, pant, pant...."

"*Mami?*"

"Pant, pant. *Si?*"

"*Mami? Que haces?* What are you doing?"

"*Ay m'ija! Como estas?* I'm doing my Jane Fonda abs of steel! Can I call you back?

"No! *Mami!* Do you have any idea what you have done? What exactly did you say to Bob Dole?

"Nothing! What are you talking about? I didn't do anything."

"Mom, you're gonna be all over the papers tomorrow! They say you stood up to Bob Dole! They say you finally put him on the spot. All my reporter friends are calling me to tell me how incredibly strong you were! What exactly did you say to him?"

"*Ay, mi vida,* I just told him the truth. I just told him he was wrong. I just said what my heart knew was right.... That's all!"

That's all! What her heart knew was right! Sure, but my mother said these things to Bob Dole while a small crowd of the most influential reporters watched and listened. My mother had no idea what that could mean, for her and more importantly for candidate Dole. All she knew was that someone had said something unjust and she was not going to let the statement go uncorrected no matter who said it!

As I turns out, my mother had been invited to speak to Bob Dole as part of a small roundtable discussion about domestic violence. My mother is one of the top organizers and counselors for Latinas who are victims of domestic abuse. After an uneventful meeting, Dole had opened up the floor to questions from the reporters who were in the room for the session. And then Bob Dole made the mistake of saying that welfare had a lot to do with domestic violence. (I guess he had forgotten about the O.J. Simpson case...) My mother couldn't contain herself and so there, in front of everyone, she stood up to correct Bob Dole, telling the presidential candidate that he was wrong. She told Bob Dole that abuse against women had nothing to do with welfare. She said that domestic abuse does not discriminate, the only color abuse knows is the color purple, the color of the bruises on the women she sees. Whether they are women who wear Chanel No. 5 or women who work in a factory.

The next day the papers ran with the story. One important newspaper had a headline "Dole Scolded by Angry Social Worker." Another said the event was one of the most awkward moments in the Dole campaign.

I thought about my mother's words. "I just did what my heart knew was right." So simple, stand up to Bob Dole, become a feminist in her fifties, counsel Latina victims on domestic abuse, answer back to the husbands who don't think twice about slapping their wives across the rooms, learn how to drive after forty years, and learn how to scuba in her sixties. And do abs of steel three days a week.

My mother has always followed her inner voice, what I now know is also her pure intuition. These days so many parents obsess over what they do in front of their kids, over the example they are going to set, over what kind of a message they want to send to their children as they are growing up. But as far as I know my mother didn't read a lot of the parenting books to learn how to be a mother. She was in training from the time she was twelve years old and her older sisters started to have babies and she was around to take care of them.

I think when you start developing your mothering skills when you are just twelve years old you start to trust your maternal intuition at a much earlier age than maybe those of us who start our mothering much later in life. And then we are bombarded with parenting how-to books which give you a million different philosophies and which so often contradict each other that you are left not knowing what is right or what is wrong. Learning to trust your maternal inner voice is key. And I turn to my mother as my example.

I have always said that my mother's innocence was one of the traits I admired most in her. That same innocence that never let her imagine that correcting Bob Dole would land her all over the headlines. She did what she did because in her mind and in her heart, her inner voice just told her what was right. And she knows how to follow that voice.

I think back about the time when I was eight years old growing up in Chicago and Cesar Chavez was going to be at a rally at our local supermarket to urge people to boycott grapes. My mother kept me out of school that day to take me to the protest. It wasn't like my mother was a full-time political activist back then. She had just heard about migrant workers who were working in horrible conditions She had heard Cesar Chavez was a wonderful speaker. Who knows why she decided to take me to that demonstration. I'm sure it was because something inside told her this was the right thing to do. But going to that demonstration changed my life.

The struggle for justice became central in my life and watching my mother, I learned to help others who were less fortunate to get justice for themselves.

There was also the time when we were in Mexico, all six of us, making our annual pilgrimage via station wagon from Chicago to Mexico. We stopped in a desert town in northern Mexico to sleep for the night and we went to the hotel restaurant for dinner. It so happens that a Hollywood crew was there filming a western. We kids were all excited because we recognized one of the actors when the crew came in to eat their dinner. But my mom spotted something else. The Americans sitting at their table got cloth napkins. The rest of us in the restaurant, all Mexicans, had paper napkins. Feeling embarrassed by what my mother was about to do, we pleaded with her to keep quiet, not to say anything, not to make a scene. She did. We all got cloth napkins. And I learned to never keep my mouth shut, to never be afraid to ask for what you deserve.

Many years later, when I was in college taking Women's Studies classes in my first semester and beginning to appreciate what being a feminist was, I remember calling my mom on the phone. "*Mami*, you know you are such a *feminista* I am so proud of you," I told her.

"*M'ija*, I am not a feminist. Please don't call me that. I haven't burned any of my brassieres," she said, saying the word in Spanish.

"Ma, for me a feminist is any woman, or person, who is helping women empower themselves. Every time you counsel one of the women who are getting beat up by their husbands and you help them see the power they have for themselves to do what they want to do with their own lives, you are being a *feminista*." I was speaking from the heart, listening to my own inner voice. In my class nobody had ever defined feminism in that way, but my gut told me I was right.

BERTA HINOJOSA

Fifteen years later, my mom calls herself a *feminista* more than I do. Years ago, her life was dedicated to her children, raising us by the book of her heart, by the book of her maternal inner voice. Now her days are dedicated to Latinas who in the face of spousal abuse are reaching out for help in finding their own inner voice, their own inner *fuerza*—strength. And as I embark on this new stage of my life, learning to be a mother, I call on my own inner voice. The voice I learned was there by watching my mother. But when my intuition is drowned out by my doubts, I call on my mom and listen closely to what she has to say. Even when it means waiting for her panting to stop in the middle of one her "Abs of Steel" workouts. Because an inner voice is no good unless you have a strong *corazon*.

EDWIDGE DANTICAT WAS BORN IN HAITI in 1969. She came to the United States when she was twelve years old and published her first writings in English two years later. She holds a degree in French literature from Barnard College and an MFA from Brown University. Her short stories have appeared in twenty-five periodicals. She won the 1995 Pushcart Short Story Prize as well as fiction awards from *The Caribbean Writer, Seventeen,* and *Essence* magazines. Her first novel, *Breath, Eyes, Memory,* won wide acclaim. *Krik? Krak!,* from which the following piece was taken, was a National Book Award finalist in 1995.

NEW YORK DAY WOMEN

Today, walking down the street, I see my mother. She is strolling with a happy gait, her body thrust toward the DON'T WALK sign and the yellow taxicabs that make forty-five-degree turns on the corner of Madison and Fifty-seventh Street.

I have never seen her in this kind of neighborhood, peering into Chanel and Tiffany's and gawking at the jewels glowing in the Bulgari windows. My mother never shops outside of Brooklyn. She has never seen the advertising office where I work. She is afraid to take the subway, where you may meet those young militant street preachers who curse black women for straightening their hair.

Yet, here she is, my mother, who I left at home that morning in her bathrobe, with pieces of newspapers twisted like rollers in her hair. My mother, who accuses me of random offenses as I dash out of the house.

Would you get up and give an old lady like me your subway seat? In this state of mind, I bet you don't even give up your seat to a pregnant lady.

My mother, who is often right about that. Sometimes I get up and give my seat. Other times, I don't. It all depends on how pregnant the woman is and whether or not she is with her boyfriend or husband and whether or not *he* is sitting down.

As my mother stands in front of Carnegie Hall, one taxi driver yells to another, "What do you think this is, a dance floor?"

My mother waits patiently for this dispute to be settled before crossing the street.

In Haiti when you get hit by a car, the owner of the car gets out and kicks you for getting blood on his bumper.

My mother who laughs when she says this and shows a large gap in her mouth where she lost three more molars to the dentist last week. My mother, who, at fifty-nine, says dentures are okay.

You can take them out when they bother you. I'll like them. I'll like them fine.

Will it feel empty when Papa kisses you?

Oh no, he doesn't kiss me that way anymore.

My mother, who watches the lottery drawing every night on channel 11 without ever having played the numbers.

A third of that money is all I would need. We would pay the mortgage, and your father could stop driving that taxicab all over Brooklyn.

I follow my mother, mesmerized by the many possibilities of her journey. Even in a flowered dress, she is lost in a sea of pinstripes and gray suits, high heels and elegant short skirts, Reebok sneakers, dashing from building to building.

My mother, who won't go out to dinner with anyone.

If they want to eat with me, let them come to my house, even if I boil water and give it to them.

My mother, who talks to herself when she peels the skin off poultry.

Fat, you know, and cholesterol. Fat and cholesterol killed your aunt Hermine.

My mother, who makes jam with dried grapefruit peel and then puts in cinnamon bark that I always think is cockroaches in the jam. My mother, whom I have always bought household appliances for, on her birthday. A nice rice cooker, a blender.

I trail the red orchids in her dress and the heavy faux leather bag on her shoulders. Realizing the ferocious pace of my pursuit, I stop against a wall to rest. My mother keeps on walking as though she owns the sidewalk under her feet.

As she heads toward the Plaza Hotel, a bicycle messenger swings so close to her that I want to dash forward and rescue her, but she stands dead in her tracks and lets him ride around her and then goes on.

My mother stops at a corner hot-dog stand and asks for something. The vendor hands her a can of soda that she slips into her bag. She stops by another vendor selling sundresses for seven dollars each. I can tell that she is looking at an African print dress, contemplating my size. I think to myself, Please Ma, don't buy it. It would be just another thing that I would bury in the garage or give to Goodwill.

Why should we give to Goodwill when there are so many people back home who need clothes? We save our clothes for the relatives in Haiti.

Twenty years we have been saving all kinds of things for the relatives in Haiti. I need the place in the garage for an exercise bike.

You are pretty enough to be a stewardess. Only dogs like bones.

This mother of mine, she stops at another hot-dog vendor's and buys a frankfurter that she eats on the street. I never knew that she ate frankfurters. With her blood pressure, she shouldn't eat anything with that much sodium. She has to be careful with her heart, this day woman.

I cannot just swallow salt. Salt is heavier than a hundred bags of shame.

She is slowing her pace, and now I am too close. If she turns around, she might see me. I let her walk into the park before I start to follow again.

My mother walks toward the sandbox in the middle of the park. There a woman is waiting with a child. The woman is wearing a leotard with biker's shorts and has small weights in her hands. The woman kisses the child good-bye and surrenders him to my mother; then she bolts off, running on the cemented stretches in the park.

The child given to my mother has frizzy blond hair. His hand slips into hers easily, like he's known her for a long time. When he raises his face to look at my mother, it is as though he is looking at the sky.

My mother gives this child the soda that she bought from the vendor at the street corner. The child's face lights up as she puts in a straw in the in the can for him. This seems to be a conspiracy just between the two of them.

My mother and the child sit and watch the other children play in the sandbox. The child pulls out a comic book from a knapsack with Big Bird on the back. My mother peers into his comic book. My mother, who taught herself to read as a little girl in Haiti from the books that her brothers brought home from school.

My mother, who has now lost six of her seven sisters in Ville Rose and has never had the strength to return for their funerals.

Many graves to kiss when I go back. Many graves to kiss.

She throws away the empty soda can when the child is done with it. I wait and watch from a corner until the woman in the leotard and biker's shorts returns, sweaty and breathless, an hour later. My mother gives the woman back her child and strolls farther into the park.

I turn around and start to walk out of the park before my mother can see me. My lunch is long since gone. I have to hurry back to work. I walk through a cluster of joggers, the race to a Sweden Tours bus. I stand behind the bus and take a peek at my mother in the park. She is standing in a circle, chatting with a group of women who are taking other people's children on an afternoon outing. They look like a Third World Parent-Teacher Association meeting.

I quickly jump into a cab heading back to the office. Would Ma have said hello had she been the one to see me first?

As the cab races away from the park, it occurs to me that perhaps one day I would chase an old woman down a street by mistake and that old woman would be somebody else's mother, who I would have mistaken for mine.

Day women come out when nobody expects them.

Tonight on the subway, I will get up and give my seat to a pregnant woman or a lady about Ma's age.

My mother, who stuffs thimbles in her mouth and then blows up her cheeks like Dizzy Gillespie while sewing yet another Raggedy Ann doll that she names Suzette after me.

I will have all these little Suzettes in case you never have any babies, which looks more and more like it is going to happen.

My mother who had me when she was thirty-three—*l'âge du Christ*—at the age that Christ died on the cross.

That's a blessing, believe you me, even if American doctors say by that time you can make retarded babies.

My mother, who sews lace collars on my company softball T-shirts when she does my laundry.

Why, you can't look like a lady playing softball?

My mother, who never went to any of my Parent-Teacher Association meetings when I was in school.

You're so good anyway. What are they going to tell me? I don't want to make you ashamed of this day woman. Shame is heavier than a hundred bags of salt.

YOUNG VOICES

She's a Tomboy

Prim and proper, neat and clean, that was the way little girls were expected to be in the 1950s, when my mother was a child. "This was before the hippies," she reminds me, "when women had to wear gloves, and always be ladylike in public." My mother was not at all like this, and that made her a misfit during her childhood. My mom always felt as if there was something wrong with her in a classroom full of perfect little girls who whispered and giggled at her wrinkled blouse and messy hair. But her untidy appearance was not her fault. While the other girls had mothers who made sure that they washed their faces and had clean clothes, my mother was neglected. My mother and her sisters had to take care of themselves.

With the absence of an authoritative mother figure, the oldest child, Tricia, assumed this role. Tricia was more mature and took better care of her appearance. However, she was also very critical of my mother and lost no opportunity to point out her faults, and make her feel inferior. "No one ever believes me when I tell them that you're my sister," Tricia would casually remark.

What made it even worse is that my mother was also a tomboy. During recess she played with the boys because they didn't mind if she got dirty. My mother often got her revenge on Tricia by digging up worms and giving them to boys to chase her with, but Tricia just used this to further ostracize my mother.

My mother was put in the slowest class in school. Her teachers were not very sympathetic to her. "Monica Riley, come up to the front and face the class," the teacher would say. She hated this humiliating punishment, because up in front of the entire class, all her flaws seemed magnified tenfold. She would look down shamefaced at her sagging socks and shoes with holes in them, as she felt the burning stares of her classmates.

What *was* wrong with my mother? Years later she finally realized that she was not stupid. My mother has a learning disability called dyslexia, but at the time she was growing up it was not recognized. Her failing performance in school was also a result of her being neglected. No one ever helped her do her homework, and since she had so much trouble with school, she just tried to escape those pressures.

One good thing did come from that need to escape though. My mother was able to find sanctuary at the library. The first time my mother went into the library she could not believe that they would let her take books home. She was so excited that she took home about fifteen books. So began my mother's love of reading and her self-education. She went to the library almost every day and read not only fiction but also books about science and technology. The system failed her, so she had to learn on her own. It is amazing that someone who did so poorly in school is one of the most intelligent and educated people I know.

My mother not only overcame her learning disability; she also overcame having been neglected by her parents. Instead of repeating the pattern, she was determined to do everything for her children that had not been done for her. This is why I think that my mother is one of the most admirable people I know

> Lisa Ponomarev
> Bronx High School of Science
> Bronx, N.Y.

Description of a Mother

She's a rather tall woman. She stands about five-ten without heels. She has medium brown hair cut short just above her shoulders. Her hair is lightly streaked with fine grey hairs, but it doesn't bother her. She says they give her character and that she's "earned them." She's in her mid-forties and likes listening to the oldies station. I occasionally might find her bopping away to some old favorite while doing the "mashed potato." She wears reading glasses that are a bit too large for her face. She likes them that way. The small wrinkles around her mouth crinkle when she smiles. She wears partial dentures, but you wouldn't know it if you looked. She's not a big fan of wearing make-up and is most content in a pair of jeans and a comfortable cotton t-shirt. She keeps slender but complains that she's getting fat. Her friends ease her fears by flattering her. She goes through this whole routine because she enjoys the flattery. She has a long slender neck that I can tell she is quite fond of. She loves wearing necklaces and V-neck blouses that complement it. I don't blame her—it's quite exquisite. She enjoys having late-night talks with her daughter and baking chocolate chip cookies that come in a tube.

She may not seem to be spectacular by any means, and she just might be the most ordinary kind of person you could ever meet. She doesn't really stand out in a crowd, and you might just miss her if you're not looking. I'm pretty sure that you've met her on more than one occasion. But don't get me wrong, she's unmistakable. She's patient and caring even when it seems that the rest of the world is not. She is a loving and nurturing mother. She's a strong woman, not always certain of the future, but makes the best of her present situation. She's a single mother raising her children the best way she knows how. She is the woman I admire. She is the foundation for the future.

Clara Torres
Midwood High School
Brooklyn, N.Y.

The Gift of Life

The air was full of anxiety and tension, my teeth could not stop grinding and my knees could not stop knocking. At this point I had feelings of doubt, excitement, and anticipation. When I turned to my right to look at my mother, she seemed calm, confident, and assured. I stared at her for a moment, and the nervous twitch in her eyes let me see that she was feeling the same emotions I was, which made me realize that I was not going crazy.

Just at that moment the door to the waiting room creaked open and a tall, sturdy, serious man of about forty-five called my mother and me into his office. As we walked in we looked at each other hoping for the best. It was then that my mother squeezed my hand and told me that everything would be fine.

The doctor then said, "The lab results are here, and I'm happy to inform you that you are an excellent candidate to donate a kidney to your daughter."

At the moment I was ecstatic, because it meant no more dialysis and a chance to have a more normal, stable life. The doctor continued to remind my mother of the seriousness of this decision and urged her to take her time before coming to a decision.

Before the doctor finished making his statements my mother said, "Yes, I'm positively sure I want to do this. I have no doubt in my mind."

Hot flashes of doubt and guilt swept through my body. My mother always puts me before anything else in her life. She brought me into this world and guided me through rough times. Through all the years of my illness she has been my backbone of courage. She taught me that fighting the enemy and thinking positive was the only way I can heal myself. She was ready to give up yet another part of herself for me. I felt I was taking advantage, being selfish. The idea that my mother didn't have a doubt in her mind and it was not an issue to do such a remarkable task was amazing.

My mother turned to me and stated, "Isn't it wonderful? I'm so happy I can do this." This time the twitch in her eye was of relief and joy. (I guess the type a mother feels toward a child.) The doctor scheduled another appointment so we can meet the other nephrologists, renal surgeons, and speak more in depth about the procedures we would both have to go through.

As we both walked out of the office, I faced my mother and commented, "Ma, I don't want you to feel obligated to do this. You're making a very critical decision."

Her response was, "I'd give my life for you. This is not an obligation, this is what I want to do. I only want the best for you. If this is what it takes to see you happy and most of all healthier, then there's no question."

"Aren't you afraid?" I said. "Sure," she said, "I'm frightened, but it's nothing compared to the hurt I feel when I see you suffer and all I can do is hope, pray, and be strong."

At this point, I had knots in my throat and I was holding back the tears. She said, "I love you and I'll always want the best for you. Someday you'll understand when you have your own children."

Right then and there, I realized that all the sacrifices she made and is still making for me is her belief of what a good mother is all about. To her this decision was something she happily wanted to do. This whole theory is what makes her so extraordinary.

Six months later we went through the kidney transplant. My mom was out in six days and I was out in fourteen. I felt stronger than I had felt in a long time. The first part of the battle was over, there still was another one waiting. I know I can get through anything because my mother is at my side and had made me everything that I am today. She truly is my heroine. She gave me the gift of life twice. If this isn't someone to admire, who is?

Jennifer Hobot
Grover Cleveland High School
Queens, N.Y.

Foreign Tongues

After four years of hell, she arrived in American, the land of hope, opportunity, and freedom. She had only one thought in her mind—to go home to Taiwan. She hadn't wanted to come to the United States, but her father forced her, just like he had forced her to go to college in Japan. With only a limited beginner's course in Japanese and the real world experience of a child, she was sent to Japan to attend college to learn complex ideas in an incomprehensible foreign language. It was a laborious struggle for someone so young and naive to learn how to survive on her own in a foreign land. She loathed being unwillingly transplanted once again. To her, the United States was worse than Japan because she had a different face and everyone knew she was a foreigner. Being conscious of this, she would become nervous and tongue-tied.

She had always asked me if what she said was grammatically correct and to correct her if ever she made even the simplest mistake. I didn't see the importance of her request so I never bothered to help her, even though I knew the way she spoke was somewhat faulty. When my brother or I had friends over, I was sometimes embarrassed by her old-fashioned jokes, her slight accent, and moments of broken English. At times, her minor language difficulties seemed to be magnified by the presence of my English-speaking friends. One day I asked her not to be so "friendly." With mouth and eyes wide open she demanded to know the meaning of my abrupt request. I tried to clarify my meaning, but we ended up having an argument. Behind a closed door, I felt shame creep up into my eyes until I could no longer hold back the swelling tears. I knew I had hurt her, had not shown respect for her feelings, and I felt overpowering guilt overcome me.

One day I happened to be tidying up the house as I awaited guests when I found a small notebook covered with a brightly colored flower pattern. I opened it, and found the pages were still clean except for a dozen pieces of scrap paper with words, phrases, and Chinese translations next to them. I recognized her neat and tiny handwriting and I suddenly understood. She could have been like one of the many immigrant women who stayed only with others like themselves and spoke their native tongue, oblivious and indifferent to the world around them. Instead she had ventured out into a foreign land; she had found a job instead of hiding in seclusion; she had asked me, a child, to correct her grammar. I remembered the difficulty I had experienced in learning French in school, the sometimes cursory homework I dashed off when I found the assignment hard. Yet, alone, without instruction, she was determined to learn, to improve herself. This is why "the woman I most admire" is my mother.

> Melody Ou
> Bronx High School of Science
> Bronx, N.Y.

There's No Cooler Mom

The alarm clock goes off at 7:00 A.M. My mom gets up and tries to get my lazy, hardheaded brother out of bed. She wrestles him out of the sheets and tosses him in the bathroom. "Come on, Todd! Let's go!" she shouts through the door. My brother gives a sleepy, whiny reply. Then she whirls around the apartment picking up misplaced objects and washing dishes from the night before. My brother is still in the bathroom. She gets fed up and drags him out.

"Get dressed!" she says. "Hurry up or you'll be late!" My brother couldn't care less. I like watching my mom drag my brother around. It's actually very funny. Finally he's ready and she shoves him out the door.

"Go to the bus stop and hurry up!" she calls. Then she has to get ready herself. She turns on the TV for the morning news.

"Did you hear that, Donna?" my grandmother asks.

"Yeah!" my mom calls back. "Well Ma, I guess the president has got his work cut out for him." She talks, does her hair, puts on make-up, and gets dressed at the same time. She gets ready to leave.

"Donna, do you have your key?" my grandmother asks. My mom nods. "Did you drink your orange juice?" My mom rolls her eyes as she pulls on her coat.

"Yes," she says sweetly. My grandmother goes on and so does my mom. Then she's out the door. I go to school and sit around waiting to go home. I get home and watch TV.

"Y'all so lazy," my grandmother mutters to my brother and me. At 7:00 p.m. my mom knocks on the front door. She puts her stuff down and takes a deep breath.

"We need eggs and milk," my grandmother says.

"And brownies," my brother adds. My mom gets ready to go out again. I decide to go to the store with her. We walk around the super-market and pick up everything we need, as well as things we really don't need, like brownies. We wind up buying too much, as usual, and the bags look heavy. I go to lift one and nearly break my young back. My mom lifts it from me with one hand while she carried two bags in the other.

"I can take it," I say, trying to be useful. She shakes her head.

"Don't worry. I've got it," she says. I feel silly. Here I am, supposed to be young and strong and my mom is carrying all the groceries! I often wonder how she got to be so strong. I've seen her move the fur-niture around just so she could vacuum in all those hard-to-reach places. The fact that she even bothers to vacuum is amazing to me. I hate that loud, sucking machine. We get home and I put the groceries away. I could at least do that. My mom takes a long bath because it's one of the few times she gets to relax. When she gets out she eats and then goes to do the laundry.

"You and Todd have more laundry every day than anybody!" she says. I laugh out loud. She's being sarcastically funny. She sits down and turns on *Roseanne* to see what she's up to but she has to pull my brother away from the TV set to get him to do his homework.

Roseanne Connor says something and my mother starts to laugh. I even start to laugh just because I heard her. Later on she watches the news with my grandmother. It's like a nightly ritual. They must watch the news. It starts quietly but then they get into really loud, political discussions.

"Now, if I were him . . ." she starts, about a murder case. Her eyes get wide and expressive and she talks strongly. I bet she would have made an awesome lawyer. It's late now and my brother and I go to bed. He should've been in bed, but he had to watch *Beavis and Butthead*. Before he goes to sleep, my brother tells my mother all about it. She curls her lips and rolls her eyes.

"Beavis and Butthead are hideous!" she cries. My brother and I laugh. My brother keeps talking. My mother waves her arms.

"SHUSH! Shush and go to sleep!" she shouts. She leaves the room singing a song by Whitney Houston.

"You can't sing," I say. She pokes her head back into the room.

"Shut up!" she growls, trying to be mean. I laugh. Maybe I'll be like her when I have my own family. If not, I at least have to learn that trick where she talks, does her hair, puts on make-up, and gets dressed at the same time.

Joy Buchanan
Midwood High School
Brooklyn, N.Y.

The Guiding Light of My Life

My family came to America in 1985. No one spoke a word of English. In school, I was in an ESL class with other foreign-born students. My class was so overcrowded that it was impossible for the teacher to teach English properly. I dreaded going to school each morning because of the fear of not understanding what people were saying and the fear of being laughed at.

At that time, my mother, Tai-Chih, worked part-time in a Chinese restaurant from late afternoon until late in the night. It was her unfamiliarity with the English language that forced her to work in a Chinese-speaking environment. Although her job exhausted her, my mother still woke up early in the morning to cook breakfast for my brother and me. Like a hen guarding her chicks, she never neglected us because of her fatigue.

So it was not surprising that very soon my mother noticed something was troubling me. When I said nothing was wrong, my mother answered, "You are my daughter. When something is bothering you, I feel it too." The pain and care I saw in her moon-shaped eyes made me burst into the tears I had held back for so long. I explained to her the fear I had of going to school. "Learning English is not impossible," my mother said. She cheerfully suggested that the two of us work together to learn the language at home with books. The confidence and determination my mother had were admirable because English was as new to her as it was to me.

That afternoon I saw my mother in a different light as she waited for me by the school fence. Although she was the shortest of all the mothers there, her face with her welcoming smile and big, black eyes was the most promising. The afternoon sun shone brightly on her long, black hair creating an aura that distinguished her from others.

My mother and I immediately began the process of reading together and memorizing five new words a day. My mother with her encouraging attitude made the routine fun and interesting. The fact that my mother was sacrificing her resting time before going to work so that I could learn English made me see the strength my mother possessed. It made me admire my mother even more.

Very soon I began to comprehend what everyone was saying and people could understand me. The person solely responsible for my accomplishment and happiness was my mother. The gratitude I owe her can never be fulfilled. The reading also helped my mother learn English so that she was able to pass the Postal Entrance Exam.

It has been seven years now since that reading experience with my mother. She is now forty-three and is in her second year at college. Watching my mother enjoying her studying is an inspiration for my brother and me. My brother and I have a strong sense of who we are because of the strong values my mother has established for herself and for her children. My admiration and gratitude for my mother are end-less. That is why my mother is truly the guiding light of my life.

Yu-Lan (Mary) Ying
Bronx High School of Science
Bronx, N.Y.

Marie Carmelle Borgella

The woman I most admire is my mother, who makes the word *woman* glow with grace and elegance. She is a woman of courage and dignity.

My mother, Marie Carmelle Borgella, grew up in a world of hatred, violence, and disloyalty, in Haiti, under the regime of Papa Doc. She lived through the terror of those years. She saw her older brother murdered in front of her. Why was he killed? My mother's brother—the uncle I never knew—was killed for the following "crime": While playing soccer with friends, he kicked the ball and accidentally hit the daughter of a captain of the Tontons Macoutes, Papa Doc's secret police.

My mother watched her older brother being beaten to death. She saw him fall down in the middle of the street. No one would help. They were too afraid of what might happen to them. She cried for help, but everybody—all the people she thought were her friends—stood there, looking at her.

She ran home for help. When she returned with her mother, he was dead. Flies covered him. Still nobody would help. My mother looked into her mother's eyes and saw a never-ending pain. My grandmother sat in the middle of the dusty street, holding her dead son. My mother promised she's never go through an ordeal like that again.

After my uncle's death, my grandmother went into shock. She could not work anymore. My mother, determined to keep the family together, left school and went to work to support herself, her mother, and her three remaining brothers. My mother, only seventeen, would go to work, and when she came home, she had to cook, do laundry and other household tasks. She didn't trust anybody anymore. She felt betrayed, without friends. When she went to bed, she worried about her other brothers and what might happen to them.

After a few years, she found a doctor who helped my grandmother deal with her son's death and make her realize life goes on. Life, for my mother, was no picnic. When she found a better job as a phone operator, it was the phone company owned by the same government who caused her brother's death. She worked for the Tontons Macoutes even though she hated them. She knew one of them murdered her brother. That awful memory would never go away. Still, she worked her way to the top. They were so pleased with her work they made her an assistant operator. Later she became head of the international department and was given her own office and secretary.

My mother, Marie Carmelle, is the most courageous woman I know. She sent me to New York to have a better life than she had—or will have. It hurt her to see me go, but no matter how great the pain, she knew she was going to do the right thing for me.

In my heart my mother will always be the greatest heroine of all time.

Trezia Jean Charles
Springfield Gardens High School
Queens, N.Y.

Mama's Dark World

It's ten o'clock; time to wake up Mama. Frustration washes over me because I'm sitting on my bed, covered with books. One by one, I push them aside.

I open my bedroom door into a wall of darkness. I look back into my lighted room with regret. I turn around and creep into the living room. All the lights are off and the shades are drawn. My sister Sally must have gone to bed, and I don't know where my sister Chandra is or when she'll be home.

On the couch, covered with blankets, because Mama is always cold, she lays. Her hair is standing on all ends, as it has a tendency to do, and her face is a perfect mask of peace. I give her shoulder a shake, telling her that it's ten o'clock. Instantly her eyes pop open and she starts to get up.

I turn to leave and go back to my bright room when she asks me to make her a cup of coffee. I swivel around and a spark of anger flicks through my eyes. The guilt quickly replaces it. How can I be angry? Every day she gets up and goes to work on barely four or five, sometimes only two, hours of sleep. She even works overtime every chance she gets. I tell her not to push herself, but she says we need the money. And all she's asking me for is a cup of coffee.

So I go to the kitchen. I leave the lights off, as if light would be an intrusion on Mama's dark world. I pour a cup of coffee, and add milk and sugar just the way Mama likes it. Then I put the cup in the microwave oven we got Mama for Christmas last year. When it's done, I take it back to her. She's already dressed and sitting up on the couch.

I hand her the cup of coffee and she thanks me. I tell her Dad called and said he wasn't coming to do work on the porch on Saturday. She simply nods her head as she drinks her coffee. Then she walks into the kitchen placing her empty cup by the sink, reminding herself that she has to do the dishes.

All too quickly, she has to leave. I follow her to the door. She hands me my $3.60 for school the next day and kisses me on the cheek. As always, she tells me she loves me. Then she walks out the door and drives off to her job.

I watch from the door in wonder. How does she do it? How does she always remember to give me $3.60 for school? How does she always remember to tell me that she loves me? How does she work all night and do errands all day? How does she raise me and my sisters on her own? She never gives up or says, "I can't go today." She never, ever, doesn't get up, no matter how little sleep she's gotten.

I shut and lock the door. I walk silently through Mama's dark world and go back to my bright room. I replace the books on my lap. Before I begin again, I turn my eyes towards God and silently thank the Lord for Mama.

Amelia Chamberlain
Townsend Harris High School
Queens, N.Y.

A Remarkable Woman

The phone rings every afternoon at around 5:00 p.m., and I am always greeted by the comforting voice on the other side of the line. "Do you want me to bring anything home?" she asks. I clumsily reach over the phone cord and open the refrigerator to check. "I don't think so. Should I take something out for dinner?" I reply. "No, that's fine, honey. I'll decide what to cook on my way home." Click goes the phone. At this point, I know that I will not hear her voice again until she walks through the front door forty-five minutes later.

"How was your day, Mom?" I ask. I watch her walk up the steps, pocketbook on her shoulder and bag in hand, having to practically drag herself up the stairs. She immediately lays her bags down and plops herself on the couch. Her feet, she tells me, are throbbing and feel like they're on fire. As I gaze at her, I can only feel helplessness in my heart. I hate seeing her as this tired, working woman. Sometimes I do not realize that she is human too. In my mind, I think of her as a type of "bionic woman" who has the ability to take care of ten things simultaneously. My worst fear is that one day she will just collapse and break down, just as a robot would. She uses her time so efficiently that when I observe her from a distance I sometimes wonder if she has her work timed down to the second.

My mother is the woman I most admire. I need not be modest when I say that she must be one of the most compassionate, patient, and wise people I have come in contact with in my sixteen years of life. I don't think I could muster up the courage she did when she decided to leave her stable life in Korea in 1975 to move here to start a new life, a life guaranteed to be filled with uncertainty and doubt. Knowing few words of English, she and my father began their own grocery store and so began her long struggle to become a part of American society.

"I hated the discrimination," she always tells me. The discrimination took such forms as rude phone calls in the middle of the night to remarks from customers at the store. She was determined to learn the English language thoroughly so that one day she could become fluent. I cannot say that I know how she felt, that feeling of not knowing what people were saying to you. I give her great credit for not giving up and staying here in the United States despite the hardships and struggles. I know that I would not be living this life today if she had given up. I am proud to say that now she is probably more "American" than I am, surprising me all the time with new vocabulary and phrases.

As one of the strongest people I know, my mother has always been there for me, in both struggles and celebrations. This is the reason I admire her most of all. I sometimes wonder how she has the remarkable ability to put her feelings aside and help me with my problems. I can only hope that I have been blessed with that same ability. As I watch my mother every night, I know people cherish and appreciate that heart of gold that is tucked underneath that yellow apron.

Chaeri Kim
Tottenville High School
Staten Island, N.Y.

One Hundred Eighty Degrees

Above her chafed arms, her forearms are as alabaster, smooth and very pale. She has that Asian gift of fair skin with pores so tight that water dances off her wet arms. Her small hands exude warmth.

Her eyes are doe-like, not the narrow almond type. There's a shininess in her eyes even if she has been standing all day. Although she spends most of her day in the kitchen, although she is hidden from customers, and although it is the florid young waitresses whom the people see, it is the short and weary woman who opened and owns the restaurant.

Most of her customers who have a fancy for her cooking are young city inhabitants. Their favorite, they tell me, is the broiled pot chicken. Even if their unaccustomed tongues cannot tolerate the generous helping of red pepper, their grimace is interpreted as delight. It is amusing that many people take such an interest in what is to us Korean house cooking.

When she opened the restaurant she took a chance. That was nearly three years ago. It has been three years of hugging her as I detect traces of food absorbed by her hair; it has also been three years of not seeing her for several days at a time; and it has been three years of eating out or alone. It is hard because she is the main chef and the owner, so I see her less often as the restaurant gets busier. There are three others who can help her with the increased work, but she insists on handling the matters personally. "How could they manage?" she questions. Although they have worked together for three years, they do still need her. As I see the restaurant growing, I realize the wisdom of her decisions.

I don't know where we would be had she not opened the restaurant. We had experienced a drought not only of money but of hope. I know it hurt her and scared her the most—but she didn't show it. In Korea, she had married well; she didn't expect to come to America to be a working Korean lady. All her assets resided in being a mother, preparing mounds of dumplings for her querulous children. She came to America knowing nothing other than her name in English. She acquired various jobs to support us as children. She began by studying styles of cooking and improving her own. Then she made the premeditated decision to open her own restaurant. She overcame her fears and gambled with the little security she had to fulfill her decision. She rejected the role of woman that had been taught to her. She was able to change, and she achieved success through hard work. She taught this to me, her daughter.

And down in the Lower East Side, as the streetlights flick on, and the restaurant opens, people crowd into the restaurant. I too join them with the comforting thought of my mother, the source of all I am and hope to become, working diligently in the kitchen.

Jae Jong (Jane) Kwak
Bronx High School of Science
Bronx, N.Y.

Body Language

My mother and I have a serious communication problem: we don't speak the same language. I know that practically every teenager says that, but in my case it's more literal. My parents, my three older brothers, and I immigrated to America from Korea when I was in the second grade. Over the years, English has become more fluent for me while my parents have not been able to grasp the new language. At home, we mainly send messages across through gestures. It is frustrating at times and I am often angry when they ask me to translate something.

The only good thing about my parents not being able to speak English is that they can't understand when I'm cursing. However, after eight years of living in New York City, even my mom learned the "f" word fairly soon. It became very trying when she started to accuse me of cursing every time I spoke any word that started with that inauspicious letter.

Several years ago when one of my older brothers and I were arguing over some trifling matter, my mother abruptly stopped in the sidewalk and started yelling at me not to curse my brother. For such a petite woman, my mother could scream like a foghorn during the rare times she lost her temper. The fact that I was unjustly condemned and that we were on a public street in broad daylight created a fervor in me to either pull out the roots of every gray curl on her head or to hide in a hole.

I inhaled deeply to yell back at her when the sun suddenly struck her face. The harsh glare highlighted every one of its lines and grooves, declaring all of its fifty-seven years. The large eyes that caused her to be nicknamed Frog Eyes had slowly sunk into the sockets, half-buried beneath the drooping lids, weighed down by the years. The long black hair that I once saw in a faded photograph was now severely cut and unfashionably permed. She used to pay me and my friends one cent for every gray hair that we plucked out. Now, there is not enough money.

I stared at the murky eyes that seemed to be permanently tinted with pink; the result of working more than twelve hours for six days a week. The sky became cloudy again and I exhaled. I explained to her that I was not cursing. Mom warned me quietly not to say them in the future. An uncomfortable silence followed as we continued our walk. Suddenly I tripped over a crack in the sidewalk. Before I could fall, a calloused but warm hand gripped mine, steadying me. I started to laugh and my mom joined in.

Mi Hui Pak
Townsend Harris High School
Queen, N.Y.

A Tall Woman

It was 1982 and a thin, young woman was moving nervously along the Bronx streets holding her daughter's hand tightly. She was searching for the nearest hotel, trying not to think about what her husband was going to do when he discovered that she hadn't returned home with their daughter.

The woman was twenty-two years old, with medium length brown hair. There was an ugly bruise on her cheek. At 5'7", she had often been teased about her height, and just now she felt as conspicuous as a totem pole: she wished she were invisible. Her name was Nereida Rosado and she had just left her husband.

As Nereida walked she carried on a conversation with herself in Spanish about how she was going to survive on the little money she had. "Great! Little one, we have found a hotel. I hope they don't charge too much." She entered under a garish neon sign and walked to the front desk. "How much does it cost to stay here for a night?" my mother asked. The man said, "Fifteen dollars." "Good, then I'll stay here for—she counted again—two nights," she said.

Nereida knew that she couldn't stay longer because she would run out of money; worse, she felt instinctively that somehow her husband was going to find her if she stayed in one place. Her next check was due in one week so she had to weigh money and safety. We went to our small, overheated hotel room and Mommy plopped herself on the well-used bed. Tired of walking and worrying, my mother lay down and went to sleep, and I was glad to nestle close to her. I don't think we even took our shoes off.

For a year her husband continued following her every move and she was sick at heart. "If he tries to scare me out of my new apartment, I think I'll kill him. I'm tired of playing this cat-and-mouse chase. I'm starting to grow a great hatred against this man," my mother said in her poetic way. Moments when we forgot my father and breathed easy were rare treats.

On one such evening we were watching television when suddenly he was banging on the door very hard and shouting. We panicked and ran to the fire escape. We climbed up the ladder to the second floor and started rapping on a family friend's window. Our neighbor, Mrs. Gonzales, opened the window and let us in. My mother was so nervous she could not speak. She managed to tell her friend to call the cops and tell them that her husband tried to break in. By the time the police came my father had left. The next week my mother hired a lawyer and won a restraining order. "I hope that this restraining order will protect us from your father. He's getting more vicious all the time. There's no way to know when he'll try to hurt us again." I later found out that our neighbors and my aunt all contributed to paying the lawyer's fee.

Soon after my eighth birthday—it was 1986—Nereida placed her hands on my shoulders and said, "This is our fourth year on welfare. If we don't do something we'll spend the rest of our lives this way. I need you to be a big girl for your aunt during the evenings so I can go to school." We had grown so close, and it was just like my Mom to be considerate and think to prepare her daughter for any changes that might be upsetting.

In 1987 a moment of great excitement arrived one Saturday morning. Nereida checked the mail and quickly opened the envelope. She scored fifty points above the passing score of the GED. She started to run up the stairs and into our apartment, jumping up and down. Her friend Monica was an accountant at Henri Bendel, and as soon as Mommy's diploma arrived, she started there as a bookkeeper.

Over the years, Nereida Rosado took to wearing business suits to work, and matching shoes with high heels. When I first noticed, I said, "Mommy, you look so tall—and so good." She turned from checking herself in the mirror to look me straight in the eyes and said, "What makes me tall is being your Mommy, Ivellisse."

Ivellisse Rodriguez
Harry Van Arsdale High School
Brooklyn, N.Y.

Barbara Rosen

It was a little over fifteen years ago. I was two and my brother was four. My father was gone. My father didn't want to be away from his children or his wife. He was being held hostage for 444 days. My mother had the almost impossible responsibility of holding our family together and, at the same time, struggling to free my dad.

On November 4, 1979, Ayatollah Khomeini, the religious leader in Iran, ordered his followers to capture my father and fifty-one other Americans working in the American embassy. This takeover became an important political crisis but it almost became a family tragedy.

While this was an unimaginable ordeal for my father, my mother was being torn apart. My mother had to remain strong for us, but in reality she was terrified that she would never see my father again. Only now has my mother started to confide in me. She said she would never cry in front of us, but let out all her emotions by endlessly crying in the bedroom.

Eventually my mother took over her life. She became a founding member of FLAG, the Family Liaison Action Group, an organization representing the families of hostages. My mother was a teacher before she took a leave of absence to take care of us. Often she called press conferences to comment on events and criticized the media for their simplistic coverage. What was also amazing was her trip to Europe to convince America's allies to boycott Iran. I look at old albums and I see her with the Premier of France, the Chancellor of Germany, and the Pope. That's my mom; she's some lady.

Her most courageous moment came when she met President Jimmy Carter. My mom was just finishing a conversation with the president. She got up the courage to tell him that while American dignity was important, it was also important that we see our father one day. President Carter understood her pain.

Though I was very small I remember the moment when my dad came home. We were waiting at an airport. Then a man came toward us holding something in his arms. The man, the stranger, gave me the doll and gave my brother a toy police car. He started to hold my mother and kiss her a lot and wouldn't let her go. Yes, it was my father, and he was home.

He couldn't know that the lady he left for more than a year, the quiet but determined woman, became a dynamo. She may not have been the person who freed my dad but she was the person who made a real difference in my life and in the lives of others. She was a symbol of determination but, most of all, a symbol of the power of love.

Ariana Rosen
Bayard Rustin High School
for the Humanities
New York City, N.Y.

The Woman I Plan Someday to Be

I walk towards the door, shoulders bowed under the weight of a day that is now, in the darkness, present only in memory. I can see her through the open window, her presence as inviting as the warm light that spills out towards me, filled with the full smells of her cooking. She looks tired. Her hair, which is curly and turning gray, is growing long again, beginning to escape its close-cropped neatness. I knock on the screen, forsaking the loudness of the bell, and she turns.

Her face is marked by her life, its wrinkles serving to pull her mouth down into a frown. Still she pushes against the years, winning long enough to make a funny face at me. I smile and make a face at her, our strange ritual of greeting as she opens the white wooden door.

She asks how my day was, and as usual I don't have much to say. I can't remember most of my day because I left it behind at the door, with the darkness, and that is as it should be. I become a different person around her; older and younger, rebellious, acquiescent. Sometimes I just sit back and watch her, listen to her. Her voice, its hard insistent accent which grates on my nerves when she is discontent, is always beautiful when she sings. It is the first voice I ever heard croon at me, high and impossibly sweet, a wonderful vibrato that may not have any musical value but still makes me sigh as I bask in it.

Hers are the first hands I knew; I can compare a person's worth to her hands. Her fingernails are short, cracked because of their weakness, which I have inherited. Her hands are calloused and rough, better testimony than any piece of paper that she has worked hard all her life. The whole of her is like that. Well-worn but strong. I would not be as proud of her had she manicured nails and unmarred skin.

I can see myself becoming like her in some ways; I am her reflection in a clouded mirror. It used to scare me, but that was before I knew her, understood who she was. Before, when I thought her life began with mine, that she had lived only as long as I had been there to see her, I had no idea that I had come to her after she had lived a fuller life than most I know. Now, knowing a little of who she used to be, I wish for her strength, her willfulness, her wisdom, in having lived so much. It seems she has lived three or four lives in the space of one.

Sometimes, sitting together in the living room, watching television while we eat dinner on the coffee table, she will bring out a small bit of her life as it was before I knew it. I marvel at her, the things she's done, the things she's lived through. She'll throw out a memory nonchalantly; I wonder if she knows that I covet them like jewels. I save them up as reminders of who she really is, not the mother, but the woman. The woman I plan someday to be.

Carla Aparecida Ng
Midwood High School
Brooklyn, N.Y.

Preserving Our Heritage

One day, as I was rummaging through a cabinet in the basement, I came across a note, yellowed with age, and stopped to scan the first few lines. Suddenly I had the feeling I was reading something not meant to be read—something that had been misplaced and forgotten—but the old letter caught my attention and I looked it over more carefully.

The note was coupled with a picture of my mother from elementary school and I recognized the penmanship to be hers. However, it was the content of the letter that interested me. It began with "Dear God," and proceeded to ask Him for help in escaping home. The words were simple, but expressive, with a desperate tone. It was not the ordinary letter of a kid who had been angry at the moment, stating that she was running away from home. It ended with the words, "Because I just can't take it anymore."

The letter had been written years ago by my mother. I already knew she'd had a difficult childhood from the rare occasions during which we talked about her parents, but the letter suddenly made everything so real. For once, I was able to understand the pain my mother felt when she was young.

My grandparents (my mother's parents) have always retained the old Chinese belief that boys are better than girls. My mother, their first child, was disliked and mistreated by them because she was a girl. I believe this added to her determination to make my sisters and me believe that women and men are equals. She tells us to fight for what we believe in and to never let a man stand in our way. Once in while, she'll even mention that women are better than men, especially when she is annoyed with my father.

I remember visiting my grandparents' house and seeing a row of portraits of their grandsons decorating a bookcase. I used to wonder, "What about me? What about my sisters? Where are we?" After all, we are their oldest grandchildren. My mother would then take us aside and whisper, "Don't worry, they don't know any better," in an attempt to reassure us. Then she'd add, "My girls are prettier anyway." I used to think this was a little funny, but I eventually realized she was very serious. In our house, my mother proudly decorates the walls, tables, and bookcases with pictures of all her daughters.

My mom is a nurse who works twelve-hour shifts three days a week. She purposely entered this profession to allow herself more time with the family. My mom is always available for a talk, and almost always willing to hear how my day went. She forces me to think about my future, encourages me to pursue my interests, and always worries about my safety.

One thing I admire most about my mother is her strength. Despite the insults and abuse she endured as a child, she has always been a loving and supporting mother to me. Sometimes I wish I could turn back time and give her a better childhood with happier memories, but that wouldn't have necessarily made her a better person. What makes her a great person is her ability to overcome negative situations, and turn out to be the winner.

Veronica Lee
Townsend Harris High School
Queens, N.Y.

Dear Mom

You've always understood me. You have known or tried to know my feelings and problems as well as someone else could. Sometimes your powers of perception startle me. How many times have you been there for me when I should have been there for you? How many times have you known exactly what the problem was and helped me fix it? Perhaps you can do this because somewhere inside of me I carry a small piece of you, perhaps you see a little of yourself when you look at me—I know I see a little of myself in you.

About one or two years ago I went through a period where I didn't quite understand what our relationship meant. I tried to separate myself as much as possible from the family, afraid to express my feelings because I was afraid of dependence. I met some people who didn't have what I took for granted—no home, no family and no love—I wished I was like them with no one hurting when I wanted to be alone, no one to ask when I wanted to leave, no one who loved me enough to care.

Not until recently did I really realize that I was destroying our relationship. Soon enough I would be on my own, but what would happen then—would I all of a sudden just be an independent person who had no need of support or guidance? I understand now that you would never *not be* a part of my life, no matter where or who I am.

I've always loved you but I've just recently realized how much I respect you. I respect you because you have always believed in yourself as a person. You have never in your heart believed what others told you or thought of you. Always you have kept your purpose and your intuition in front of you and have never let anything deter you from following them. You have taught me a strong lesson about my own self-worth. You have helped me deal with the problems of insecurity around looks and weight as well as the issue of sexism. Because of you, I am unafraid to be who I am no matter what others might say.

I respect you because you have single-handedly raised me and my brother to be upstanding, intelligent, and independent. You are always helping us develop our own opinions and ideas and to grow as people. Constantly listening and aware, you have always kept our family together in the face of overwhelming problems and situations—destitution, moving, custody problems—there are so many. Some have affected our lives in small ways and some have stayed with us for a long time. The point is, no matter what, you could always find the courage inside yourself to handle them.

But mostly, you have been a shoulder to lean on, a listener, and a guide. You have been a friend, a teacher, and a disciplinarian; you have been a mother.

> Chlöe Garcia-Roberts
> Urban Academy
> New York City, N.Y.

Women, Infants, and Children

The throng of impatient Chinese mothers congested the cramped WIC department of Governeur Hospital. Ear-splitting cries issuing continuously from irate babies, faintly resembling the rhythmic wailing of police sirens, completed the picture of total chaos. This was "Women, Infants, and Children," a welfare program that distributed food stamps to impoverished parents having difficulty purchasing milk for their children.

As a volunteer, my duty was to translate for the clerk the impassioned pleas of those applicants whose heritage I shared. What appeared at first to be a dismaying task turned out to be an immensely rewarding experience. Every day I came in and was faced with an array of Chinese mothers. I saw the same things mirrored in the face of every woman. She was either searching anxiously for a dear one or glancing occasionally at the sleeping child nestled in her shoulder. Tired, baggy eyes, glossed over from hours of waiting, told of endless miseries and unshed tears.

She is the immigrant who left everything behind, eyes overflowing with hope, in order to have a chance to attain the American dream. She boarded the plane, five, two, or perhaps one year ago, with a daughter strapped to her back and a querulous son led by the hand. She had to make the fearful trip alone, for her husband had already come to the United States. He would be there to greet her at the airport, but how would she be able to manage until then? How could she make the attendant understand that her son only ate rice or that her daughter might get plane sick?

Upon arriving in her new home, she had to quickly find a job and assist her husband in supporting the family. She was ushered into the only profession that was available to a non-English-speaking, female immigrant, a seamstress at a garment factory. The tedious care she put into learning how to sew might have made her vision a bit blurry, but she had to do what was essential to survive. The pay was barely enough to buy food, but maybe after a couple of years they could afford to move into their own apartment. As months turned into agonizing years, her once plump and youthful face showed signs of lines. Smiles were rare and only given to comfort her children. Her sunken cheeks and gaunt figure denoted the tremendous stress she was subject to daily. Her children's cries for nice clothes, books, and toys echoed continuously within her head as she worked feverishly at the hem of a dress. One gust of wind, it seemed, would have been enough to uproot her beanpole legs and send her gliding above the crumbling apartments.

"That's my mother, not my grandmother!" her children would cry indignantly. She seemed to be forever coughing as more and more dust from the clothes settled in her lungs. An examination from the doctor revealed that her heart was beating irregularly, as if to protest the heavy burden being laid upon it. "Just a few more years," she would console herself. Once her children were older and could provide for themselves, she would finally be able to rest.

"Don't knock yourself out trying to answer their questions. Once they see someone Chinese, they ask questions nonstop and drive you crazy. They ask the same things a dozen times even though they know the answers already," the clerk informed me.

"It's all right. I don't mind," I answered. The mother across from me smiled and I continued explaining. These are women who sacrifice their lives, leaving friends and culture behind in order to improve the future of their children. Their pathetic situation is vivid, yet pale compared to their incredible endurance and ability to subsist. I have realized many things since my first day here and have developed a great admiration for my fellow women. No wind is ever going to blow down a willow that is stronger than iron.

Sally Chu
Bronx High School of Science
Bronx, N.Y.

Barnard College is a selective, independent liberal arts college for women affiliated with Columbia University and located in New York City. Founded in 1889, it was among the pioneers in the crusade to make higher education available to young women. Over the years, its alumnae have become leaders in the fields of public affairs, the arts, literature, and science. Barnard's enduring mission is to provide an environment conducive to inquiry, learning, and expression, while also fostering women's abilities, interests, and concerns.